BY
AMY ANDREWS

THE BOSS AND
NURSE ALBRIGHT

BY
LYNNE MARSHALL

...ings
...d lo...
about to...

FIND A FAMILY!

A MOTHER FOR MATILDA
by Amy Andrews
Diary of Matilda Lawson, Aged 8:
*Dear Diary, Today Victoria came over again
after I got back from school. She's so lovely
and easy to talk to—I wish she could be my mum!
How can I get her and Daddy together…?*

THE BOSS AND NURSE ALBRIGHT
by Lynne Marshall
What I did at nursery by Gina Albright, Aged 2½:
*I drew a picture of me and Mummy.
And then I added Dr Rogers because he makes Mummy
smile. If they got married I would have a real family…
and I could be bridesmaid!*

A MOTHER
FOR MATILDA

BY
AMY ANDREWS

MILLS & BOON®

*I dedicate this book to one of the most talented writers I know,
and the woman who knows me better than any other—
my amazing sister, Roslyn. I carry her heart in my heart. As she does mine.*

First published in Great Britain 2010
Harlequin Mills & Boon Limited,
Eton House, 18-24 Paradise Road, Richmond, Surrey TW9 1SR

© Amy Andrews 2010

ISBN: 978 0 263 87683 3

Harlequin Mills & Boon policy is to use papers that are natural,
renewable and recyclable products and made from wood grown in
sustainable forests. The logging and manufacturing process conform
to the legal environmental regulations of the country of origin.

Printed and bound in Spain
by Litografía Rosés, S.A., Barcelona

Dear Reader

After eighteen books this is my first 'friends become lovers' story. I'm not sure why I've never tackled this one before, because as far as storylines go I'm a bona fide fan! The angst and the yearning in these plots are so tangible you can feel them seething around you as you read.

Poor Lawson and Victoria are no different. Not only have they known each other for twenty years, having formed a dynamic and vital paramedic partnership on their small island community that neither want to jeopardise, Vic is counting down the days until she leaves the island for foreign shores. And then there's Matilda—Lawson's eight-year-old daughter. Victoria has spent the last seventeen years raising her twin brothers after their mother's tragic death—she yearns for a freedom that she's never known. She certainly has no plans to be a mother—ever.

But sometimes fate has other things in store, and Victoria and Lawson are about to discover that some things just can't be denied. It's a bumpy ride, but one that will be well worth the bruises.

I hope you enjoy.

Love

Amy

Amy Andrews has always loved writing, and still can't quite believe that she gets to do it for a living. Creating wonderful heroines and gorgeous heroes and telling their stories is an amazing way to pass the day. Sometimes they don't always act as she'd like them to—but then neither do her kids, so she's kind of used to it. Amy lives in the very beautiful Samford Valley, with her husband and aforementioned children, along with six brown chooks and two black dogs. She loves to hear from her readers. Drop her a line at www.amyandrews.com.au

Recent titles by the same author:

A DOCTOR, A NURSE, A CHRISTMAS BABY
GREEK DOCTOR, CINDERELLA BRIDE
THE SINGLE DAD'S NEW-YEAR BRIDE*
DR ROMANO'S CHRISTMAS BABY*

Brisbane General Hospital

CHAPTER ONE

AN EARLY morning sea breeze caught the sleeve of Lawson Dunlop's paramedic overalls as he sat on the wooden picnic table devouring a bacon and egg roll from the nearby twenty-four-hour café. His booted feet were evenly spread and braced on the seat. His elbows propped on his powerful quads. His lean torso angled forward.

The first rays of sunlight reached across the ocean to illuminate the island and in the half-light the water in the passage was a deep velvety blue. The surface was still, millpond still, yet to be fractured by the activities of the day.

Already a steady stream of workers in their cars trundled over the bridge heading to the mainland and Brisbane, one hour's commute away. A few eager fishermen, their lines hanging over the side, paid no heed to the daily island exodus as the cars rumbled past them.

A gull wheeled and cried overhead as Lawson's gaze tracked the path of a nearby pelican waddling up the narrow strip of sand ceded by the tide. The breeze blew a faint tang of salt towards him and he inhaled deeply, enjoying the serenity of island life and the respite from a long and busy night duty.

A rustle beside him disturbed the peace and he turned to look down at his partner of five years sitting next to him in much the same fashion, their thighs almost touching. She was also making short work of her breakfast, which at least meant he could enjoy the scenery in silence. Eating was about the only time Victoria Dunleavy was ever quiet.

Vic inhaled, also admiring the view. 'Don't guess I'm going to get this in London,' she said around a mouthful of burger.

Lawson shook his head. 'Nope.'

'Did I mention it's ninety days?'

'Yep.' *Once or twice.*

'Nine. Zero. Then I'm out of here. Gone-ski. Vamoosed.' She ignored the way her gut clenched at the thought of being so far away from her beloved Brindabella Island. It was way past time for her to fly the nest.

'Uh-huh.'

Lawson took another bite. He'd miss his partner. In a strictly professional way, of course. Good partnerships were rare and, in their line of work, vital. He wasn't looking forward to having to build a rapport with someone else. He'd miss the synergy that flowed effortlessly between the two of them.

'I'll miss the twins. And Dad, of course.' The thought of leaving her family struck like an ice pick to her heart as she sat and absorbed the scenery already embedded in her DNA. *She was twenty-six, for crying out loud. It was time!*

Lawson could hear the wistfulness in her tone and

immediately felt selfish for thinking of himself and the impact her leaving would have on his workload. Victoria deserved this. She'd sacrificed a lot for her family and now the twins were grown she was free to get out and explore the world. As he'd done.

'The twins will be at uni when you leave and probably too busy chasing girls to notice,' he hastened to assure her. 'Bob will be fine. Go and see the world. Sow your wild oats.'

Lawson was surprised at the catch in his chest as the old-fashioned saying pinged a nerve ending or two—the thought of her with the opposite sex not sitting well.

Vic nodded. He was right. Of course he was. Still, every now and then, the decision to leave her family, leave the island and everything she'd ever known and loved, had the power to stop her in her tracks.

It *was* the right decision, the *only* decision, she just hadn't realised how hard it was going to be. A year ago when she'd booked the ticket it had been a long way off but with ninety days to go it was suddenly looming. And it was disheartening to think her departure might barely be noticed.

They finished their breakfast in companionable silence. Lawson checked his watch as he screwed up his paper bag. Six-thirty. Another hour and a half before they knocked off. He should just make it home in time to see Matilda before she left for the day.

Victoria was quiet beside him, unusual to say the least but he knew it wouldn't last long. He'd known her since she was a skinny six-year-old and he'd been for-tunate enough to be partnered with her father as a rookie paramedic. She'd been a chatty kid and nothing much had changed over the years.

'I'll be missed too, right?'

He glanced at her pensive face as she stared out over the water, attuned to the slight trace of doubt he heard in her voice. 'Of course.'

Very few people got to see this side of his partner. To the outside world she was capable Victoria Dunleavy— dedicated daughter, big sister/surrogate mother and ultra-professional paramedic. But having known her for ever and having sat in a vehicle with her four out of seven days a week for the last five years, he'd been privy to the other Victoria Dunleavy. The one nobody got to see. The one who'd had way too much responsibility thrust on her long before she should have and wasn't always certain of herself.

'Ryan and Josh and your dad will miss you desperately,' he assured her. 'And everyone at the station. I know for a fact that Matilda will miss you like crazy.'

Vic chewed her last mouthful very carefully. So, her brothers would miss her, her father would miss her, her colleagues would miss her, even his eight-year-old daughter would miss her. But what about him? Would he miss her?

The fact that he hadn't included himself was a little depressing. Vic had had a crush on her partner for as long as she could remember. Given that he'd known her for ever and there was a twelve-year age difference, she'd never expected it to be reciprocated. After all, it was just a harmless crush on an older man who'd been a family friend for ever and her mentor for the last five years.

Things like that happened all the time. It wasn't as if she was in love with the guy. But surely, *surely*, he'd miss her too? She scrunched up her packet and turned to him. 'What about you, Lawson? Will you miss me?'

Lawson gave her a startled look. Her steady whiskey gaze held him captive and he was struck again by that look he sometimes saw in it. He wasn't sure what it was but it was frank and seemed to reach right inside him.

He nodded and looked back out to sea. 'Of course. I've spent five years training you to do things my way. Your father will probably stick me with a newbie straight out of the academy.' Bob Dunleavy, his old mentor and her father, was Officer-In-Charge of Brindabella Station. 'Now I'll have to start all over again with someone else.'

Vic realised she was holding her breath and she let it ease out slowly. *Of course.* He would miss her as a colleague. Her skills, their teamwork, their synergy. Why had she expected anything else? He'd never been anything other than one hundred per cent professional with her.

Which only proved further how badly she needed to get away from the island. She needed to broaden her horizons, both personal and professional. She needed to experience a variety of working environments, be exposed to different ideas, meet new people. Including men.

Every boyfriend she'd dated had suffered in comparison to Lawson. It wasn't that she meant to compare or even realised she was doing it half the time. It just happened. Somehow, they'd all been a little lacking. Perhaps if he was out of her life, the silly crush would be forgotten and another man might just stand a chance.

Quite why she felt the way she did was a mystery. It

wasn't as if Lawson had ever given her any encouragement. Or ever treated her as anything other than Bob's daughter. Just another paramedic at the station.

It wasn't even as if he were the best-looking man she'd ever known. On the contrary—she'd been out with some exceedingly good-looking men. Lance Coulter in particular had been so sexy she'd been the envy of the entire island. Everyone from teenagers to grannies had swooned over the locum island doctor.

But there was something about Lawson Dunlop that was compelling. He certainly wasn't classically good-looking. In fact the features of his face taken individually could best be described as interesting. A freakishly square jaw line, crooked nose and deep furrows lining his brow and around his eyes and mouth.

His eyes were grey. Nothing special. Except they could look warm like the soft folds of a cashmere jumper when he was calming a frightened patient or ominous like a storm-ravaged sea when stupidity caused needless carnage. His hair was dark brown and worn severely curtailed in a closely cropped fashion—not stylish or fussy. Just functional. No nonsense.

And then there was his scar. The one he never talked about. A thin white blemish that slashed from just beneath his nose down through both lips and ploughed a furrow in the stubble covering his chin.

She'd heard mountains being described as craggy and it was the best adjective she could come up with that suited his face. His height also leant to this appearance. He was well over six feet, his broad shoulders seeming to occupy all the space around him.

He certainly loomed above her, making her feel strangely fragile. Which was utterly ridiculous. She might have been petite but she was no dainty flower. She was strong, a requirement of her job, and most definitely robust.

An insistent beeping noise interrupted her thoughts, for which she was most thankful. They simultaneously reached for their pagers. Lawson pulled his off his belt first.

'Forty-four-year-old female. Chest pain. Borilla Avenue.'

Vic nodded, her brain already switching from her personal life to work mode. 'Let's go.' She vaulted off the table, landing cat-like on her feet, eager to banish the doubt demons and throw herself into what would hopefully be their last job before they clocked off. She headed for the nearby ambulance, not bothering to look back.

Lawson followed her, his gaze drawn to the bob of her auburn ponytail and the way her neat little frame fitted snugly into her navy paramedic overalls. He'd been doing that more and more lately. Noticing how her uniform clung to the contours of her bottom and how the functional government-issued belt she wore at her waist cinched her in, emphasising her curves.

Curves? Up until about a year ago he hadn't even noticed she owned curves.

What the hell was the matter with him? He'd known her since she was a six-year-old in pigtails. He had no business noticing how much of a woman she'd become. How her wide-set eyes were balanced by the fullness of her lips. Or how those cute cherubic cheeks and dimples she'd had as a kid were just plain sexy twenty years later. It was just…wrong.

He banished them from his head and put his mind firmly to the job.

A few hours later Vic was in the depths of a sleep so deep that it took several insistent bangs on her bedroom door to drag her back into consciousness. She surfaced from the pillow she had jammed over her head and yelled, 'What?' in the general direction of the door.

Her brothers were in their senior year at high school and were currently in their exam block, which meant unless they had a test they didn't have to be at school. This afternoon they had a biology paper and were supposed to be using the morning to cram for it.

'Ryan's cut his finger.'

Vic's heavy lids battled to stay open. She'd worked her tail off last night and she was dog-tired. 'Stick a Band-Aid on it,' she grouched, placing the pillow back over her head.

'I think it needs more than that.'

Vic sighed and threw the pillow away as the hesitation in Josh's voice nagged at her gut. It had to be reasonably bad—both brothers knew a fate worse than death awaited them for trivial interruptions to her post-night-duty coma.

She looked at the clock. She'd been asleep for two hours. No wonder she felt like hell—those first few hours were always the deepest.

She opened the door and a blast of heat pushed into her air-conditioned bedroom. She looked up at her brother towering over her. She was barely five one; everyone towered over her. He was as blond as she was olive, the twins taking after their mother, whereas she had inherited the darker Dunleavy colouring.

'There'd better be blood.'

Josh swallowed. 'Oh, there is.'

Vic followed feeling weary to her bones but not overly concerned. She knew non-medical people often misjudged blood loss and that a small amount of the red stuff could often look like a massacre.

Her eyes felt gritty as she entered the kitchen unprepared for the sight that greeted her. For a brief moment she wondered if Ryan had been shot. Blood was splattered on the bench and congealed on the floor tiles. Her brother was standing at the sink, his wrapped hand hovering above the stainless steel.

'Bloody hell, Ryan.' Vic, suddenly very awake, flew across the kitchen. A metallic aroma wafted around her as she disturbed the warm air currents and she half slipped in a patch of smeared blood. 'What on earth did you do?'

'I told you not to wake her,' Ryan said, turning accusing eyes on his brother. 'I said to get some Steri-Strips.'

Vic unwrapped the wound carefully. The blood-soaked tea towel dripped into the sink. She somehow didn't think Steri-Strips were going to do the job. 'What happened?' she asked, her heart slamming in her chest as her suddenly razor-sharp thought processes calculated his estimated blood loss.

Ryan didn't look at her and a moment passed before Josh spoke. 'The knife slipped when he was cutting through his shoe.'

Vic glared at Ryan, always the more daring of the twins. 'Your shoe?' she demanded.

He shrugged and winced as her unwrapping became a little rough. 'They were an old pair.' When Vic glared at him he hastily added, 'The ad said you could do it with those knives.'

Vic shook her head, not sure how Ryan had ever made it to almost eighteen alive. This had to go down as the winner in the annals of dumb Dunleavy males. 'I bet it also said not to try it at home.'

She finally uncovered the wound. Ryan's middle finger appeared deeply lacerated, holding on by not much more than a thread. 'A Steri-Strip?' she said incredulously. Ryan shrugged. 'How long ago did this happen?' she asked.

'About twenty minutes ago,' Josh answered, his voice small.

Twenty minutes ago? No wonder it looked as if a massacre had taken place in the kitchen. Vic valiantly tried to recall her anatomy lessons and picture the blood supply to the hand.

What the hell they thought they were going to accomplish with a thin, weak, sticky strip she had no idea. Were they going to lasso the finger back in place and go back to watching television while Ryan slowly exsanguinated? Would she have woken to find him near death?

She shuddered at the thought. Losing her mother at the tender age of eight had been devastating. Losing one of the twins would be a blow neither she nor her father would ever recover from.

'It's practically severed. It's going to need more than a bloody Steri-Strip. It's going to need surgery.'

She shook her head at her brother. 'Joshua,' she said urgently, twisting Ryan's bloodied hand upright, encircling his wrist with her thumb and forefinger to form a tourniquet. 'Get me some clean tea towels and bring me the phone.'

Josh delved in the nearby drawer, pulling out the requested cloths and shoving them at his sister. He stalked from the kitchen and returned shortly after with the phone. Vic was re-covering the wound. He thrust it at her.

She rolled her eyes as she deftly wound the makeshift bandage in place. 'Ring the station for me.'

Josh paled as he punched in the numbers. 'You want me to tell Dad?'

'No. I'll tell him.' She finished with the wound and tied a clean dishcloth firmly around Ryan's wrist to stem the flow of blood to the wound.

Josh held out the phone to her. 'Dad's not there. It's Lawson.'

Vic frowned. What the hell was Lawson still doing at the station? They'd knocked off over three hours ago. Vic reached for the phone. 'Hold on a sec,' she said into the receiver.

She directed Ryan to a nearby chair and pushed him into it. 'You,' she said to Josh. 'Hold his arm up above his head like this.' She supported her brother's arm in the air and Josh took over.

'Lawson?'

'Victoria.'

Apart from her mother, Lawson was the only person who'd ever called her by her full name and, as much as she grouched about it, secretly she adored it. As a six-year-old it had made her feel very grown up and today, with her brother's blood drying on her hands, it gave her an added dash of courage.

'Why are you still there? Where's Dad?' she said, staying close to her brothers.

'He had some meeting in Brisbane to attend. I'm covering for him until he gets back. What's wrong?'

'Ryan's practically severed his left middle digit. I could drive him to the hospital myself but I really think he needs a medical professional with him while I drive. Is there an ambulance free?'

Lawson, well used to Ryan's litany of injuries, didn't even bat an eyelid. 'How'd he do that?'

Vic sighed. 'Trust me, you don't want to know.'

Lawson grinned. 'Is it haemorrhaging much?'

'It has been. I've controlled the bleeding now though.'

'Nine sixty's available. I'll call it in to Coms and be at your place in a few minutes.'

Vic hung up the phone. 'Lawson will be here in three.'

'I'm sorry, Vic, I—'

She slashed her hand through the air, bringing Ryan's apology to an abrupt halt. 'Don't talk to me. Just be quiet.'

'But—'

'Don't,' she snapped.

Now the emergency was under control and she was away from sickening amounts of her brother's blood other feelings flowed. Disbelief, anger, relief. She allowed herself to be a sister for a moment.

'I can't believe I raised you. How bloody stupid,' she said to Ryan. 'How am I supposed to go off to the other side of the world when you two are still acting like children? Hell, even little kids know not to play with knives. You're nearly eighteen, for crying out loud. You're supposed to be mature. Responsible. You're supposed to be studying for your biology exam.'

'Vic—'

'I said don't talk,' she snapped again. Ryan was looking pale and she guessed from his blood loss he was a little shocked. The what-ifs were starting to circle.

'I've worked all night, for Pete's sake. All you had to do was let me sleep and be uninjured until I woke up. Is that too much to ask?'

Ryan and Josh looked at their feet and shook their heads. 'Dad's gonna have a fit,' she continued. 'Do you think his blood pressure can take this?' Their father was borderline overweight and on medication for his hypertension. They both shook their heads again. 'I swear you two are going to be the death of him.'

Moments passed in silence while she took stock. Ryan's face was twisted into a permanent wince and she felt a momentary streak of sympathy. 'Does it hurt?'

'Yeah.' Ryan grimaced.

The streak fizzled as quickly as it had arrived. 'Good.'

She pushed some hair off her face and realised her hand was shaking. The sound of a distant siren reached them and Vic had never heard a sweeter noise. Not that she thought Ryan was about to expire from blood loss, but he had lost a good amount of the red stuff and would definitely be anaemic. She wouldn't be surprised if he required a transfusion.

And had Lawson been much longer she might well have succumbed to the urge to do something drastic to prevent him from doing anything else so overwhelmingly stupid again.

She put her hand under Ryan's elbow and urged him up. 'Come on. Walk. We'll meet Lawson out the front. Keep your arm above your head.'

'Jeez, Vic, is your bedside manner always this good?' Ryan grouched as he stumbled beside her.

'No. I reserve this treatment for too-stupid-to-live teenagers.'

Lawson pulled up at the Dunleavy residence, a place he'd been to hundreds of times since he'd taken up residence on the island. He killed the siren at the same time the trio reached the driveway and jumped down from the cab. Striding around the back, he opened the doors as Victoria and her brothers appeared at the rear.

He took one look at a worried Joshua, an obviously chastised Ryan and a thunder-faced Victoria and made an executive decision. 'Why don't I look after Ryan in the back and you go and get cleaned up, put on your uniform and drive us in?'

Vic was about to argue when she noticed Lawson's eyes taking in her attire. Amidst the crisis she'd forgotten that she was in her pyjamas. Not that there was anything indecent about them—they certainly covered more than a lot of clothes did these days.

Brief silky boxers with high scooped-up side seams and a shoestring-strapped grey singlet that didn't quite meet the waistband of her shorts. But it was perhaps the blood that was most off putting.

She gave Ryan one last big-sister glare. 'Fine. I'll be ten minutes.'

Lawson tried really hard not to look as she walked away. She was his partner, for crying out loud. He'd seen her out of uniform hundreds of times. Hell—he'd seen her in a bikini! But he'd already noticed the way her bed-rumpled hair hung loosely around her face and the slight chest bounce as her unfettered breasts had jiggled against the taut fabric of her shirt. The desire to look a bit more was strangely compelling.

So he failed miserably at the not looking and allowed himself a second or two to indulge in her unselfconscious swagger. The words *bite me* printed across the backside of her boxers swayed hypnotically in front of his eyes and for a second he imagined just that.

'Er, hello, Lawson? Bleeding here.'

Lawson startled and dragged his gaze away, horrified at where his mind had been. *This was crazy.* It was the abstinence. It had to be. Being a sole parent and a shift worker to boot wasn't exactly conducive to dating.

He forced himself to focus on the Dunleavy twins, noting the beginnings of red seepage on Ryan's outer dressing. He helped Ryan into the back of the ambulance and laid him on the gurney using two pillows across the teenager's chest to elevate the injured hand above heart level.

He pulled the BP cuff from its receptacle on the wall and wrapped it around Ryan's uninjured arm. Eighty on fifty. A little on the lowish side. 'I might pop a drip in while we wait for Victoria.'

Ryan lifted his head off the pillow and screwed up his face. 'What? No way. I hate needles.'

Lawson chuckled. How many times over the years

had he tended to Victoria's brother in the back of an ambulance? 'Ryan, you just almost hacked off your finger. Do you think one little tiny needle can compare to that?'

Ryan held his head up for a few more seconds, then let it drop back in surrender. 'I guess not.'

Lawson grinned. He reached into the nearby IV drawer and pulled out the things he was going to need. He glanced at Josh sitting in the back passenger seat looking pale, his knee bouncing, his fingers drumming against his thigh. 'It's okay, mate. He'll be all right. Really.'

Josh looked at Lawson intently and then nodded, his shoulders sagging, and the fidgeting stopped.

'So, do I want to know how you managed to nearly amputate your finger?' he asked as he swabbed the crook of Ryan's elbow with alcohol. There was silence from both the boys and Lawson pressed his lips together to suppress the smile. 'Hmm,' he said, uncapping the needle and lining it up with the bulging vein staring at him. 'That stupid, huh?'

'Ow!'

Lawson ignored Ryan's protest as he slid the cannula straight into the vein and got an instant flashback. He taped it, flushed it and set up a drip to replace some of the volume Ryan had lost.

'Vic's pretty ticked,' Ryan muttered.

Lawson looked up at anxious Josh, then back at the more robust Ryan. 'You probably scared the hell out of her.'

'Will it really need surgery?' Josh asked.

'I haven't seen it but if it's as bad as Victoria says, and she does know her severed body parts, then yes.'

As if she could hear her name, Vic appeared at the back doors. 'Righto. Are we ready?'

Lawson, pleased to see her in something neck to toe, her hair pulled back in its regulation ponytail, nodded. 'You going to be okay to drive?'

'Sure.' She flicked a glance at Josh. 'Buckle up,' she said as she slammed first one door then the other.

Lawson whistled. 'She is really ticked.' And smiled as both boys squirmed in their seats.

Vic didn't bother with the siren. She knew Ryan's blood loss was controlled and being replaced and that, under Lawson's care, Ryan was in the best of hands. She trusted her partner implicitly. Hell, the man was an Intensive Care Paramedic; she'd trust Lawson with her life. So there was no point driving like a crazy thing, endangering all their lives for something that wasn't life-threatening.

The trip took fifteen minutes and Ryan was seen immediately. Two hours later he was on a ward, prepped and ready to go to Theatre, when Bob strode into the room.

'Ryan Dunleavy,' he boomed. 'What the hell were you thinking?'

Vic, her hand entwined with her brother's and her head on the bed, catching some shut eye, was immediately alert. Ryan, slightly woozy from morphine and looking like little-boy-lost in his white hospital gown, opened heavy lids. 'Sorry, Dad.'

His voice cracked and Vic felt it reach right inside her gut and twist. She squeezed his hand. It obviously had the same effect on her father, who strode across the short distance separating them and enveloped his son in a huge bear hug.

'Bloody silly kid,' he said, his gruff voice not fooling anyone.

Bob reached out for Josh and put his arm around his other son's shoulders. After a few moments he straightened and cleared his throat, placing a hand on her shoulder. Vic knew that her mother dying from a pulmonary embolism a few days after the twins had been born, in this very hospital, had for ever altered her father. As it had her.

Her father's heavy hand, his comforting squeeze, said it all. Neither needed words to express how confronting it was to have another member of their family lying pale and silent in a bed in this hospital.

Bob placed a kiss on the top of his daughter's head. 'Lawson, take her home,' he instructed.

Vic looked behind her, surprised to see Lawson was still there. 'It's okay, Dad,' she protested, looking up at her father. 'I'll stay.'

'No.' Bob shook his head. 'You're done in, Vic. You both are. I'm here now and HQ is sending a replacement to the island to cover me for the next few days. You've just come off three nights—you both need to sleep.'

'Come on, Victoria.' Lawson stood. 'The boss has spoken.'

Vic, weary beyond what she would have thought even possible, knew her father was right. She stood and dropped a light kiss on Ryan's brow. 'See you in a few hours,' she murmured. He didn't stir.

She gave Josh a hug. 'He'll be fine,' she assured him, knowing that Josh was probably the most worried of them all. She gave her father's cheek a kiss. 'I'll be back later. Ring me if…for anything,' she quickly amended and then departed with Lawson, too emotional to look back.

They'd nearly reached the lifts when a female voice pulled them up. 'Lawson? Oh, Lawson?'

Vic turned to see the nurse who'd been looking after Ryan. She was young. Younger than her by a few years. Tall and well endowed too. Vic suddenly felt like a dwarf next to the blonde, oh-so-curvy woman who was fluttering her eyelashes at her partner. She couldn't help but look down at her own rather lacking chest, petite as the rest of her, and sighed.

The nurse had been flirting with Lawson from the minute Ryan had been admitted. Vic had thought it in rather poor taste, but then she'd been tired and cranky and worried about her brother. Night duty generally brought out her prickly side.

'Hi. Brianna, isn't it?'

Vic watched as the poor woman almost nodded her head right off her shoulders, obviously reading way too much into Lawson remembering her name. Lawson re-membered names—it was an occupational necessity.

'You were telling me about that great traumatic am-putation website,' Brianna said. 'Here's my email address.' She handed Lawson a piece of paper. 'Could you email me the link?'

Vic, pushing the lift-call button several times, just stopped from rolling her eyes.

'Oh, I can write it down for you,' Lawson offered.

Vic watched as the nurse's confidence faltered slightly. 'Oh, no, it's okay. You're off now. Just email me.'

The lift dinged but not before Vic was privy to the look of frank sexual interest infusing the nurse's smile.

'Sure.' Lawson smiled, slipping the paper into his breast pocket before following Victoria into the lift.

They rode down in silence. Lawson could feel the tension radiating off Victoria, filling the confines of the lift. He watched her surreptitiously as it descended. He knew she was worried about her brother. She had, after all, helped raise the twins from babies. Biologically she might be their sister, but in every other way she'd been their mother.

'He *is* going to be fine,' Lawson said as the lift touched down and the doors opened.

Vic, still annoyed at the nurse, frowned. 'I know that,' she grouched.

She strode out of the lift tired and cranky. At the whole world. What the hell was wrong with her? Females had been making goggle eyes at Lawson the entire time they'd been partnered—why was it bothering her so much now?

Why?

CHAPTER TWO

Vɪᴄ steamed ahead. She needed to sleep. She wanted her bed. In fact she was already on sandman autopilot just putting one foot in front of the other, counting down the minutes until her head could hit the pillow. The day had been emotionally draining and right now she felt as if she could sleep for a week.

It took a few moments for her brain to register the fact that the couple a few paces in front of her had stopped to have a passionate kiss. She was almost upon them before the signals from her eyes penetrated her foggy brain.

'Oh, God, I'm terribly sorry,' she apologised as she pulled herself up just short of careening into them.

The couple broke off and the woman gave her a dreamy smile. 'That's okay.'

Vic was about to launch into a whole explanation when she realised the man was familiar. A prickle straightened her spine and cleared the fog. 'Lance?'

She hadn't seen her ex since he'd been caught with his pants down and they'd split four years before. Thankfully he'd moved to a hospital on the Gold Coast shortly after their break-up. He was still dazzlingly good-looking and yet somehow he just didn't do it for her.

God! She must be tired!

Lance stared at Vic but recovered quickly. 'Vic. How lovely to see you again.' He gave her a decidedly uncomfortable half-smile. 'Darling, this is Vic Dunleavy.'

Vic appraised the other woman, a young willowy blonde with an impressively perky chest.

Good grief—they were everywhere she looked today.

'Pleased to meet you,' she said politely. Even though she couldn't have cared less. In truth, she was too tired to care about much of anything.

Lawson joined them and she immediately felt his hand at her elbow. The comfort of his touch, his superior height and bulk were the perfect emotional anchor and she leaned into him a little. 'You remember Lawson?' she offered.

Lance nodded stiffly. 'Of course. Lawson.'

Lawson nodded back not giving a damn whether the jerk remembered him or not. He'd always found Lance a little too pretty for his own good and he guessed it was inevitable that a young, naive Victoria would fall for him. But he hadn't been surprised when it had ended in Lance's infidelity.

There was a moment of awkward silence finally broken by the woman. 'Hi.' She held out her hand. 'I'm Kathy.'

'Oh, sorry,' Lance apologised. 'This is Kathy. My…'

Another pregnant pause and then Kathy added, 'Fiancé. I just called in to bring him lunch. Doctors work such awful hours, don't they?'

Vic shook Kathy's hand automatically, noticing the big fat solitaire sparkling in the sun filtering through the atrium skylight. The smile on Kathy's face was a mile wide and Vic suddenly felt very lonely.

Every relationship she'd been in had suffered because of her family commitments and she'd learnt early that her situation wasn't conducive to falling in love. She just didn't have the time. And then there'd been the inevitable comparisons to Lawson. Maybe in London she'd finally be free to connect with someone…

'Mmm,' Lawson muttered.

They made polite conversation for a few more moments and then Lawson intimated they were late for a job, for which Vic could have kissed him. By the expression on Lance's face, he could have too. No doubt he didn't want an ex-girlfriend blowing the whistle on his inability to keep his pants on.

'You okay?' Lawson asked as they headed for the ambulance bay.

'Fine.'

It wasn't until they passed a vending machine that Vic realised she wasn't feeling at all fine. She was light-headed and a little nauseous. 'You got some change?' she asked Lawson.

Lawson fished in his pocket and handed it over without comment. He'd known women long enough to know that some situations required a shoulder, others a hefty dose of alcohol, and the really bad ones chocolate wrapped in some pretty foil packaging.

Vic retrieved the bar from the machine and a few minutes later they were buckled in the van and leaving the hospital. She opened the wrapper and devoured the chocolate bar in a minute.

'Better?'

'Marginally.'

'You want to talk about it?'

'What?'

'Lance. Or Ryan.'

'Thanks, but no.' She turned away and looked out of the window.

Lawson took the hint and let it be, even though it irritated him to think four years down the track her jerk ex still had the power to upset her. Why it irritated him so much, he wasn't quite sure.

Vic watched the world whizz by for a few moments, her thoughts tumbling around in her head. Lance the Unfaithful was settling down. 'I can't believe he's getting married,' she said after a while.

Lawson looked at her sharply. 'I thought you were over him?'

Vic snorted. 'I am.'

'Really?'

She turned to him and rolled her eyes. 'It was years ago. The man is an adulterous lech.'

'Yeah. I remember.' She'd cried on his shoulder for three months. 'So—' he shrugged '—who cares that he's getting married?'

Vic watched as the lines on his forehead and around his eyes converged into a frown. How could he possibly understand? Lawson, who had travelled the world without a care until Matilda had come along. It seemed everybody else's life had begun while she'd been treading water. Hell, even Ryan and Josh were heading off into the world, going to uni in Canberra in a few months' time.

Seeing Lance today had been unexpected. Add to that lack of sleep and the emotional upheaval of the morning and she was coiled so tight she was ready to burst. It was totally irrational. Ninety days couldn't come soon enough as far as she was concerned.

'I don't.' Vic faltered. She really, really didn't. So why the hell was she feeling so churned up? 'I'm just… tired, I guess.'

Lawson nodded, not overly convinced. But he could most definitely relate. He had to be pretty damn tired himself for this to be bothering him. 'Why don't you put your head back and catch some Z's.'

Vic shut her eyes gratefully. They felt as if they were sticking out of her head on stalks and the relief was instantaneous. She let her head loll back against the padded rest and almost sighed out loud.

When she opened them again fifteen minutes later, Lawson was pulling into her driveway.

'This is your stop.'

Vic unbuckled. 'Thanks.'

Lawson nodded. 'Will you be okay? Want me to stay for a while?' He thought about her boxer-short pyjama bottoms and prayed like hell she'd reject his chivalrous offer.

'Nah. You need your sleep too. I'll be fine. I'll see you later.'

Lawson nodded. 'Sleep tight.'

Vic alighted the vehicle and waved her partner off. She walked through the front door that none of them had thought to shut never mind lock as they'd left. It was at times like these she appreciated living in a small community where theft or crime of any nature was practically non-existent.

It took her half an hour to clean up the kitchen, take a shower and ring the hospital to check on Ryan, who wasn't back from Theatre yet. By the time she was done it was early afternoon and Vic would have crawled on broken glass to get to her bed. Her head hit the pillow and the feel of Lawson's hand at her elbow guided her into the comforting embrace of sleep.

Lawson was contemplating hitting the sack again at nine that night when there was a rap on his door. He'd been lying on his couch in front of the television pretending interest in some B-grade movie.

He frowned, rising from the lounge and making his way through the darkened house. He didn't bother with switching lights on, not wanting to wake Matilda, who was a notoriously light sleeper.

He wondered who it was, hoping it wasn't a neighbour requiring medical assistance who'd decided it was quicker to knock on his door than call an ambulance. Unfortunately in their small community it was a reasonably common occurrence.

Lawson was surprised to find his partner standing there when he opened the door. She was wearing jeans and a red top—a top Lawson couldn't stop himself from noticing clung temptingly to her petite frame. Her hair was loose around her face, and her lips shimmering with gloss. 'Shouldn't you be tucked up in bed asleep?' he asked.

Vic smiled. Even in the subdued lighting she could see the man filled out blue jeans and a T-shirt better than any guy she'd ever known. 'Probably.' She shrugged. 'I don't know why I'm here.' The words tumbled out before she'd given them adequate consideration. But it was true—she'd been in the car coming back from the hospital and suddenly she was here. 'I've just come from seeing Ryan and guess I'm too restless to go home yet.'

Lawson, used to having Victoria in his house, stepped back. 'You don't need a reason, Victoria. Come in.'

His partner liked to talk when something was troubling her and, as it was usually about a case they'd done, he was generally the first port of call. At least he didn't have to stand on any ceremony with Victoria. She was a familiar fixture around the house, being a regular babysitter for Matilda over the years and totally blind to any sloppy housekeeping. Thankfully living with two teenage boys had inoculated her against mess.

'Is everything okay with Ryan?'

Vic nodded as she made her way into the lounge room. 'Yep. All good. The operation went well. The surgeon's happy. His haemoglobin was low though and they transfused two bags of blood.'

Lawson nodded as he flicked on a couple of lamps that threw a warm glow around the room. 'Hang on a sec.' He tiptoed into the hallway and quietly shut Matilda's door. 'He looked good a couple of hours ago,' he said, rejoining her. 'Tilly and I dropped by for a while.'

Vic sat on Lawson's very comfortable, saggy old leather lounge and felt instantly at home. 'Dad said you called in.'

Lawson shrugged. 'Tilly was fretting. Would you like something to drink?'

'Sure.' Vic sighed and snuggled into the cushiony folds of the three-seater to the muffled sounds of Lawson in the kitchen. The television was down low and the flicker of light emanating from the screen was hypnotic to weary eyes.

'Here you go.' Lawson handed her a glass and placed a bottle of red wine on the coffee table. He sat at the opposite end of the sofa to her and turned three quarters so they were facing.

Vic took a sip of the rich Shiraz and shut her eyes as the heavy bouquet filled her senses. Her eyes fluttered open as Lawson took a swig out of a long-necked beer. 'Real men only like to drink beer, huh?'

Lawson smiled. She had her glass snuggled against her chest, her legs tucked up and her feet bare. If she knew what he was thinking now about real men and what they liked she'd be shocked.

Despite himself his gaze was drawn to her wide mouth and the way the glow from the lamps glistened in her lip gloss. Watching her mouth was dangerous, but then looking at any part of her tonight was dangerous. Her clingy red top touched all the right places, destroying his concentration.

This sudden awareness of Victoria, of his partner, of Bob's daughter, was getting out of hand. He wisely chose to change the subject instead. 'So, what gives?'

Vic shrugged. 'I don't know.' All she knew was she didn't want to go home. She didn't want to have to play any roles tonight. To be the dutiful daughter, the caring sister. The 'parent'. Reassuring her father and Josh, building them up, being there for them. Maybe tonight she just wanted someone to take care of her for a change.

Lawson nodded. 'Okay.' It was obvious something was eating her and he knew if he waited she'd tell him.

She dropped her head on the side and inspected him through lashes at halfmast. Just hearing his voice was enough at the moment. It was deep and calming and oozed a confidence that was soothing to the sudden well of conflict that had risen, unbidden and unwanted, inside.

'I should have known Ryan would do anything to get out of his biology exam.'

Ah. Here it was. The recriminations. 'Victoria.'

She ignored the gentle reprimand in his voice, staring into the ruby depths of her glass. 'I should have stayed up until they'd gone off to school. Like I did when they were kids.'

'Victoria. They're not little boys any more. They're seventeen. You'd just come off three nights. You're allowed to sleep.'

She looked at him and nodded. 'What the hell was Ryan thinking? He should have known better than that. I don't know how often I told those boys not to play with knives.'

'Of course you did, Victoria. You raised Josh and Ryan with textbook perfection. The twins knew right from wrong from very early. But they're not little any more and they're responsible for their own actions. They're going to be flying the nest in a few months. Maybe its time to let go a bit, huh?'

She looked back into her wine. With the bloodied kitchen floor still playing in her head and the worst-case scenario taunting the edges of her consciousness his praise over her mothering skills was just what she needed right now. As was his unsolicited advice to cut the apron strings.

She was going overseas in ninety more sleeps, for crying out loud. They were all going to have to get along without her. And as much as the thought of leaving them and this place snagged at a place deep inside her like a jagged nail, they were all going to have to get used to it.

She dragged her gaze away from the glass. 'Tell me about working in London again. I'm sure you have some stories you haven't told me yet.'

Lawson regarded her for a second. Was she just changing the subject because he'd hit a little too close to home or did she need some kind of assurance that she was doing the right thing? He wasn't sure what it was about—he'd never seen her quite this melancholy before—but he obliged anyway.

Having kicked around the world for most of his twenties, he always had another story. He'd studied to become a paramedic straight from school but the minute he'd qualified he'd taken off for foreign lands, working and playing wherever the whim took him. Until the bombshell that had been Matilda, anyway.

She had well and truly forced him to reassess his life when her mother, a fling on a brief sojourn home, had literally left him holding the baby. So he understood Victoria's itchy feet and her desire to do something with her life. To live it.

And if he could help her along by enticing her with his adventures, then he was more than willing. Even if the prospect of losing her to the wild blue yonder was disturbing on levels he didn't want to admit.

A couple of hours later Vic was nearing the end of her second glass of wine and a lovely buzz had settled in her veins. She felt just brave enough to pry. 'So have you emailed Brianna yet?'

Lawson, who had finished his beer a long time ago, frowned. 'Brianna?'

Vic laughed and rolled her eyes. 'From today. At the hospital? *Lawson, oh, Lawson,*' she mimicked.

Lawson chuckled. 'Not yet. I'll have to do that tomorrow.'

'You know she doesn't give two hoots about the website, right?'

Lawson looked affronted. 'What are you suggesting?'

Vic slapped her forehead. 'Good Lord, for an intelligent man you're thick sometimes.'

Lawson stilled. 'You think she was flirting with me?'

'Lawson, she was coming on so heavy I thought Ryan would asphyxiate from an overdose of oestrogen before they got him to Theatre.'

It'd been so long since he'd been in the game Lawson was pretty much ignorant to the subtleties of flirting. His priority had been Matilda and, Lord knew, life as a single father was a constant enough juggle without throwing a relationship into the mix. He shrugged. 'I didn't really notice.'

Vic tisked. Sometimes she thought her crush would evaporate if Lawson weren't so damn available. 'All work and no play makes Lawson a dull boy.'

'I play,' he protested.

'Lawson, you haven't been on a date in I don't know how long. Well over a year. What happened to the love-them-and-leave-them Lawson I knew when I was growing up? What's the matter with you?'

'I became a father.'

Vic rolled her eyes. 'Yeah, sure, but you didn't die, Lawson. There was a great-looking woman making eyes at you and you were completely oblivious.'

'I'm out of practice.'

She shook her head.

'I'm…busy.' God, he sounded pathetic. 'I have Matilda to think about, after all.'

Vic rolled her eyes. 'Oh, please! Your kid is dying to be a flower girl again. You could marry the archetypal wicked stepmother and she couldn't care less as long as she got to throw rose petals at her feet.'

Lawson laughed. Matilda had been rather transparent in her attempts to marry him off since his sister got married a few months back.

He shrugged. 'You know how hard it is with kids to form relationships. It takes a really understanding person. Someone selfless. And that's hardly a fair ask.'

Vic nodded. She did know. None of her boyfriends had understood her commitment to her family. They said they did, paid lip service to it, but when push came to shove, and she had to cancel yet another date because the twins were sick or her father had been called out, they never stuck around.

Hell, Lance had even gone one step further and looked elsewhere when she wasn't around to service his needs.

So she could certainly sympathise with Lawson. At least he could get some comfort from the fact that he'd had a life first. That was something she couldn't claim.

She glanced at him. They were closer now than they'd been earlier. He looked all brooding and intense and so all she wanted to do was lay her head on his shoulder and go to sleep. To forget about her responsibilities for a night and have someone look after her for once.

Obviously the wine had gone to her head.

She yawned and sat her empty glass down on the coffee table. She hiccupped and then laughed. 'Wow, I think I'm a little tipsy.'

Lawson raised an eyebrow. She'd had two glasses of wine in a couple of hours—hardly excessive. 'I didn't realise you were such a cheap date.'

Vic nodded, shutting her eyes. 'I'll probably have an almighty headache in the morning.'

Lawson's gaze was drawn to the way her lashes grazed her cheeks. 'I'll call you a cab to take you home.'

Her eyes fluttered open. Home? No, she wasn't ready for that. She didn't want to leave. Not yet. Here with Lawson she could just be herself. She wasn't ready to go back to reality. 'Do you think it would it be okay to crash here?'

Lawson hesitated. He wasn't sure why—it just didn't feel…appropriate. Which was ridiculous. It wasn't the first time she'd bunked down here. Most times she watched Matilda for him she usually slept the night on his couch. Lawson wavered. He knew it should be cut and dried but for some reason it wasn't. He became aware of their closeness and consciously sat up straighter.

Vic frowned at her partner's continuing silence, searching for another reason to stay. 'Please, Lawson. The last thing Dad needs on top of a son who nearly bled to death in the kitchen today is an inebriated daughter.'

'You're hardly inebriated, Victoria.'

She dismissed his observation with a wave of her hand. 'I have two teenage brothers, remember? I have to set a good example for them.'

If anyone knew the extent of Victoria's sacrifices for her brothers it was Lawson. But even so they occasionally slapped him in the face. Victoria hadn't had a normal childhood or teenage years. She hadn't had a chance to rebel or experiment like a lot of teenagers, as he had.

Which was probably why two glasses of wine on top of three night shifts had gone straight to her head.

She'd had her hands full helping her dad bring up two babies and run the house. Even when she'd done her paramedic training in Brisbane she'd commuted every day for three years. No wonder she was counting the days down until her life could begin.

Vic watched as Lawson hesitated. A funny thought drifted through her head and with the alcohol blunting her inhibitions she spoke it without further analysis. 'I promise not to try and seduce you.'

Lawson almost choked on his tongue, which developed into a coughing fit. He leapt to his feet. 'Not funny, Victoria,' he rasped when he'd regained his breath.

Vic laughed. She supposed not. Although the idea was seriously tempting here in the half-light after two glasses of wine. What would happen if she took her crush one step further?

'You are my partner,' Lawson continued. 'I have known your father for twenty years. I have a child. You are leaving in ninety days.'

Vic laughed. 'Yeah, yeah. Relax, Lawson, I'm only joking.'

Lawson rolled his eyes as his heart rate settled. 'Bloody hell,' he muttered, heading for his bedroom. 'Take my bed. I'll have the couch.'

'Oh, no, no, no,' she protested, following him. 'It's okay. I'm smaller. I always sleep on the couch. The couch is fine.'

Lawson stopped just inside his door and turned, not expecting her to be so close. He took a step back, narrowly avoiding a collision. 'My room has black-out blinds. I have a feeling you may need them in the morning. Plus Tilly will be up at the crack of dawn and I doubt that's something you want to experience with a thumping head.'

Vic couldn't fault his thinking. 'Okay then. You've sold me.'

They stood for a moment looking at each other. 'Well,' Lawson said, stepping to the left. Victoria moved at the same time in the same direction. She gave a half-laugh and stepped to the right as Lawson also dodged right. He laughed this time and grabbed her by the shoulders, holding her in place as he stepped around her.

'Goodnight,' he said on his way out of the door.

Vic turned. 'Lawson?'

He swung around. 'Yes?'

'I don't suppose you have something I can take to cut the headache off at the pass?'

Lawson chuckled. 'Sure. I'll get it.'

Vic watched him leave, slipped out of her jeans and then lifted her top over her head. She pulled his bed covers back and gratefully crawled beneath. Lawson's bed felt like a feather duvet floating on a cloud. But then anything that allowed her to recline would have felt as soft—even a bed of nails. The alcohol and a mere four hours' sleep enveloped her and she shut her eyes surrendering to the bliss of being horizontal.

Not even her weird-o-meter, which was blaring loudly, was enough to rouse her. The vague feeling that being in Lawson's bed was blurring their professional and friendship boundaries nagged at the peripheries of her rapidly dwindling consciousness, just out of her grasp. Hell, she'd never even been in his bedroom before. It was…intimate. Not something friends, colleagues, did. Certainly not something they did.

Lawson entered the darkened room a few minutes later with a glass of water and two headache pills. Some ambient light from the street outside filtered through his curtains and he looked down at her, the covers pulled up to her chin, her hair loose on his pillows.

'Victoria?'

She stirred as his voice floated towards her. 'Mmm?'

He sat on the side of the bed. 'Here.'

Vic prised open an eye and saw the white tablets on the palm of his hand. Sleep clawed at her bones, making them heavy and resistant, but she pushed through it, sitting up. She drew her knees to her chest and downed the pills gratefully along with the entire glass of water.

'Thanks, Lawson.' She handed him back the glass.

'For everything. For coming to my rescue with Ryan. And the company tonight. And the bed. And the tablets.'

Lawson watched as the sheet slipped a little to reveal a red bra strap before she hiked it back up again. He looked away quickly. 'What are partners for?'

Vic smiled and stroked her cheek against the sheet covering her knees. 'I like the smell of your sheets,' she murmured.

He grimaced. 'Sorry, I should change them.'

'No, they're fine,' she dismissed. The bed was all she needed—sheets were a luxury. 'They smell like you.'

Lawson's breath caught in his chest. 'Oh? And how do I smell?'

Vic sighed, closing her eyes, inhaling his essence again. 'Like Matilda's strawberry-shortcake soap I buy her every Christmas and that great aftershave you wear.'

Lawson's belly clenched. *She noticed his aftershave?*

'And freshly cut grass.'

Lawson laughed as the tension inside him uncoiled a little. 'Grass?'

'Yeah, you know. Earthy. Male.'

'Well, thank you. I think.' And he laughed again.

Vic lifted her head off her knees. She liked hearing him laugh. He didn't do it often enough. The light coming in through the window illuminated his face, emphasising his masculinity and highlighting his scar. Curiosity and no doubt the effects of alcohol had her crossing a line she'd never crossed before.

She lifted a hand and touched her finger to it, tracing it from just under his nose across his lips and down his chin. Lawson stopped laughing and pulled away from her as if she'd trekked a burning match across his face.

'I'm sorry,' she murmured, dropping her hand. 'I was just curious. You never talk about it and Dad's warned me it's a touchy subject but...I don't know... blame the Shiraz...'

Lawson made a conscious effort to relax his jaw. 'No. It's okay. It happened a long time ago when I was in a different place in my life that I don't like to dwell on.'

Vic nodded. 'Of course.' But she was curiously hurt by his reluctance to share it with her. They were partners and yet sometimes she felt as if she didn't know him at all. God knew, he knew everything there was to know about her.

Lawson felt a spike of guilt lance him at her downcast face. 'I was in an accident. When I was sixteen. My home life was...unhappy. We moved around a lot and my father liked to drink. One night some mates were going on a late-night high-speed joyride with some older guy they knew who had this souped-up car and I thought, Why not? The car crashed. The driver died. Everyone was seriously injured. I had facial and chest injuries and had to be cut out of the vehicle. I spent nearly three months in hospital.'

Vic gasped. 'I'm so sorry.'

Lawson shrugged. 'I was trapped for two hours. This paramedic stayed with me the entire time. I've never forgotten it.'

'Is that why you became one?'

Lawson nodded. 'If it hadn't been for that crash, I don't know where I would have ended up.' He'd certainly been heading for a dead-end job and a chip on his shoulder.

Vic felt a rush of incredible tenderness for the man and heartache for the teenager he'd been. She'd always known her partner was a complex human being with a rough childhood, but this put him in a whole new light. She couldn't bear that he'd been through so much pain.

She touched his scar again and this time, though he flinched, he allowed it. Then, she wasn't sure why, maybe it was the alcohol, maybe it was the whole emotional upheaval of the day, she leaned forward and pressed her mouth to it, the desire to kiss it better too powerful to resist. 'Poor Lawson,' she whispered.

Lawson sat very still, her lips at his chin. He shut his eyes as the fleeting press of her lips stirred desires he'd long ago forgotten existed. She was so close. Her warm breath wrapped his gut in seductive tendrils.

He only had to shift slightly and he could claim her mouth. He didn't move as the battle raged within him. He wanted to kiss her so badly he was salivating. Like a starving man being led into a bakery. But she'd been drinking. And she was his partner. His much younger partner whom he'd known since she was in pigtails. And she was leaving.

Vic liked the spikiness of his stubble against her lips and this close to him she got to smell all those aromas she'd told him about but with the added mix of his warm male skin. The room was utterly silent except for their breath and even in her tipsy state she was hyperaware of a very weird vibe settling around them.

Lawson dragged in a breath. This was so screwed up and he wasn't going to add to it by doing something totally unforgivable. With a mammoth effort he sat back from her.

'Go to sleep, Victoria. It's been a long day.' He stood and reached over to pull the blind down. 'When you wake up it'll only be eighty-nine more sleeps.'

Vic smiled at the thought as she slid down into the bed and snuggled into the sheets, sighing as her eyes drifted shut. 'Night, Lawson. Sweet dreams.'

Lawson watched her for a few seconds before turning on his heel. *Sweet dreams*? Was she kidding? Something had shifted between them tonight, the boundaries had moved, and with the imprint of her lips still scorching his chin he'd be lucky if he ever slept again.

CHAPTER THREE

LAWSON woke to a finger lifting his eyelid. 'Daddy, why are you sleeping on the couch?'

Considering he'd not long closed it, Lawson almost groaned out loud. 'Morning, Tilly.' It took a superhuman effort but he managed to force the other one open. He glanced at the clock. Three minutes to six. This time he did groan.

Why couldn't his daughter have been one of those kids that he'd heard mothers talking about at school? The ones that required a crowbar to lever them from their beds?

'Did you fall asleep watching TV?'

Lawson sat up. His chest was bare and he'd undone the top two buttons of his fly. He rubbed his hands across his face. 'No, Victoria is sleeping in my bed.'

Matilda's face lit up like Guy Fawkes Night. 'Vic's here?' She jumped up and down clapping, making little happy noises at the back of her throat.

He winced as her excited reaction bordered on a squeal. 'Shh.' He placed his fingers on Matilda's lips. 'She's…not well.'

'Can I go wake her up, Daddy?'

'No, you may not.' He ruffled his daughter's blonde curls, the only thing she'd inherited from her mother. The rest was all him. 'She had a big day yesterday with Ryan. She needs her sleep.'

Matilda's enthusiasm waned. 'Will she be awake before I leave for school?'

Lawson prised himself out of the lounge and stretched his back out as he rose. 'I doubt it.' If she was anywhere near as tired as he'd been last night, as he was right now, she'd probably be in his bed all week. His thoughts drifted to her innocent sort-of kiss last night before he could put it firmly from his mind.

'Phooey.' Matilda pouted. 'I wanted to ask her how many more sleeps it is.'

'Eighty-nine.' The answer fell from his lips automatically. He'd been privy to the countdown for the past twelve months. It was as if the numbers had been engraved on his soul.

Matilda put her skinny arms around her father's waist. 'I'm going to miss her, Daddy.'

Lawson smiled down at his daughter. 'We all will, Tilly.' He hugged her for a moment, his mind drifting to *that* kiss again. That non-kiss kiss. Or whatever the hell it was. 'Come on, let's get breakfast.'

For the next couple of hours he and Matilda went about their usual morning routine. Not that there was anything usual about it with Victoria sleeping soundly in his bed the entire time. He'd tried to keep Tilly's noise to a minimum but sometimes that was like trying to keep a wave on the sand. Especially when his daughter's motives weren't exactly pure. Despite Tilly's best efforts, Victoria kept sleeping.

When it came time to take Matilda to school he picked up his shirt where he'd discarded it last night, right next to Victoria's shoes, and threw it back on. It was creased but it wasn't as if he had to get out of the car and it beat the alternative—tiptoeing into his room to retrieve a fresh one.

Tilly chatted non-stop on the drive to school about her teacher and her spelling and the excursion coming up in a few weeks' time. She reminded him of Victoria, who also seemed to think silences were there to be filled.

'Have you got the tuck-shop bags I did up for you?' he asked.

Matilda nodded. 'And the excursion forms. Don't forget to ask Vic's dad for some time off next week to come and see me play my recorder at assembly.'

Lawson nodded. He handed her the library book that had been due back yesterday and he'd turned the house upside down looking for after they'd got back from the hospital, finally locating it in the hammock outside.

'Can Maddy come over this afternoon? We're doing our pirate project together and she doesn't have any Internet at her house.'

Lawson groaned inwardly. He was so tired he could sleep for a week. The last thing he wanted was the presence of giggling Maddy. 'Sure. I'll check with her mum before pick-up this afternoon. I think her number's on the phone tree on the fridge.'

He pulled into the set-down zone in front of the school and Tilly kissed his cheek. 'You're the best.'

Lawson chuckled. 'Yeah, yeah. Get out of here.'

He watched as she met up with Maddy and they skipped into the grounds without a care in the world.

He couldn't believe how eight years had flown by as if they'd been mere seconds. He remembered the first time he'd laid eyes on his daughter. She'd been wrapped in a little pink bundle. Everything about her had been pink, from her booties to the tiny pink bow in her hair. She'd been two weeks old when Deb had handed her over and said *I can't do this*.

He remembered looking at Deb, whom he'd slept with on only a handful of occasions several months prior, as if she'd gone mad as she'd thrust the pink package at him, trying to compute what she was saying. That their liaison had yielded a child. That her baby was his baby. That he was a father. And it was up to him.

But it had only taken an instant for Matilda to totally capture his heart. One glimpse at her little bow mouth and tiny pink nose and he'd been a complete goner. In one glance Matilda had become his everything. And he wouldn't have traded the steep learning curve, the single-father juggling act, the sleepless nights or giggling Maddy for anything.

Matilda turned before she disappeared from sight completely and gave her father another wave. He smiled, returning it, her cheeky grin pulling at his heart-strings. A short toot of a horn behind him reminded him he'd lingered too long in the drop-and-go zone and he pulled out.

He smiled to himself as he rejoined the traffic, proud and relieved that his little girl was a happy, carefree child. Heading home now to Victoria, he was very conscious of the fact that at eight years old, the same age as Matilda, Victoria had lost her mother and had become default mother to her newborn twin brothers.

He and Bob had been partners when it had happened and he still remembered with chilling clarity the devastation of that time for both Bob and Victoria. Tilly might never have known her mother, and he had no doubt that she might go through a stage where that affected her more deeply than it did now, but being motherless was all she'd ever known.

He would do anything, whatever it took, to protect his daughter from the kind of devastation Victoria had faced. Which was one of the reasons he'd chosen to eschew any involvements in the last eight years. He'd never risk Tilly's heart—which was huge and generous and tender—on something that might not work out.

Victoria's tear-stained face at her mother's funeral was too potent a reminder. While he could still draw breath, he would inoculate his daughter against life's rocky road. Because he loved his little girl more than he'd ever thought possible to love another human being.

And because that was what fathers did. The good ones, anyway.

Lawson pulled into the driveway ten minutes later. Victoria's car was still parked on the street. The house was stuffy, already warm from the early heat of the day. There was silence. No evidence that Victoria had risen while he'd been gone. His door was still closed; there was no extra coffee mug in the sink.

He yawned, still dog-tired from his sleepless night

trying not to think about the kiss and Victoria all-but-naked in his bed. Telling himself it was wrong to think about his partner like that unfortunately hadn't helped and it hadn't been until exhaustion had finally overcome him at dawn that he'd slept.

He'd like nothing more than to go back to bed for a few hours in his dark, cool room. Maybe even sleep until it was time to pick Tilly up from school. But, as that wasn't possible and he hung over the edge of Matilda's bed, the couch was his only option.

Lucky he was too tired to care about the light and the air-conditioner would take care of the heat. He pulled his shirt off again and dropped it on the floor near Victoria's shoes. He undid his top couple of fly buttons, flicked the air-con on with the remote and collapsed onto the lounge. Blissfully, sleep pulled him under immediately.

Vic woke slowly, momentarily disorientated by the gloom. Then she remembered. She was in Lawson's bed. She gave a half-laugh. How many times had she fantasised about that over the years?

She turned her head—nope, he wasn't there beside her. Her gaze fell instead on the red digital numbers of his bedside clock. Ten-thirty.

'Crap.' Vic vaulted upright. Ryan. She should have been at the hospital by now. Why the hell had Lawson let her sleep so late?

She stumbled out of bed and reached for the blind, inching it up a little so she could see what she was doing. She found her clothes and threw them on. She had to go home, ring her father, have a shower, change into fresh clothes and get to the hospital.

Vic bolted out the door wondering where her bag and shoes were and desperately needing coffee but knowing she didn't have time to linger. Her head swivelled from side to side—where had she left her things?

She headed for the lounge room, rounded the couch and pulled up short. A bare-chested Lawson lay passed out on the three-seater. She froze for a moment, hoping she hadn't woken him. And then, with the very distracting sight of all that skin goading her, she let her breath out slowly and allowed her gaze to wander over all his maleness.

He truly was a magnificent specimen of man. Tall and broad-shouldered. Well-formed pectorals segueing into the bony ridges of his ribcage, rising and falling with each deep, measured breath. Further down the hard muscularity of perfect abdominals were very easy on the eye. His thighs, hugged by denim, were bulky, strong, his hips lean, his legs long.

One hand rested on a muscular thigh, the other arm flung above his head was bent at the elbow, his forearm covering his eyes and half his face. She noticed the soft hair under his arm was the same that surrounded his flat male nipples, dusted his stomach and narrowed towards his waistband.

His half-open fly caught her attention and, involuntarily, she rose up on her tiptoes and angled her head to see if she could ascertain whether he was commando beneath the denim. Unfortunately there wasn't enough revealed to tell and she lowered her heels back to the floor extraordinarily disappointed.

Still, as she took him all in once again a surge of feminine appreciation rippled from somewhere in the vicinity of her womb and flushed through her system like a shot of vodka on an empty stomach. Her nipples were painfully hard and she actually felt her pelvic floor contract.

There was something almost primal about the way he affected her. His body, even relaxed in sleep, oozed virility. It said, *I'm strong, tough, capable. I am man.* And tens of thousands of years of evolution and a hundred years of feminism were wiped out in the blink of an eye.

He turned his head slightly and she froze again. His face was now angled towards her, his lips nuzzling the fat pillow of bicep covering his eyes.

Frantic signals from her brain flashed multicoloured warnings. *Stop ogling shamelessly and get out of here!*

Finally sense made it through to her muscles and she dragged her gaze away from him to search the floor for her shoes. They were beside the sofa and she crouched to retrieve them.

But that just brought her closer to him and when she turned her head his face was right there. Even covered with his arm it was obviously a man's face. Craggy and interesting—lived in. His scar-ravaged lips were a testimony to this.

A shard of a memory pierced her consciousness and the scene from last night, kissing his scar, came crashing back in full Technicolor detail. She pressed her finger to her mouth as the memory of his stubble grazing her lips tingled as if it had just happened.

She shut her eyes. *Stupid, stupid, stupid.* What must he have thought?

But even in the cold light of day, his lips within reaching distance, the temptation to do it again was a living, breathing animal inside her. She opened her eyes. His lips were slack, slightly parted, and for a fleeting second her hand actually crept towards him.

Then she caught herself. In eighty-nine days she was out of here. She'd kept her crush secret for five years— she could certainly go the next few months without blowing it.

Steadfastly ignoring Lawson and his mouth, she scooped up her shoes and got the hell out of the house.

A few days later, on their first day shift back from nights, Lawson and Vic were sitting at the station when their pagers activated. They'd not long returned from transporting a dislocated finger from a rather vigorous game of lawn bowls to the mainland and Vic had taken her first sip of coffee.

'"Near drowning at Wattle Beach,"' Lawson read. '"Twenty-year-old male."'

Vic looked at her coffee longingly, took another sip and stood. 'We'd better take the four-wheel drive.'

The island had three ambulances. Two were standard vans and were the transport of choice on a daily basis. The other was a heavy-duty vehicle expressly used for beach jobs because it allowed them to drive on sand directly to the patient. It stayed at the station ready to go if needed.

Vic opened the driver's seat door. It was her turn

today to be Patient Care Officer, which would normally mean he would drive, but on cases like this, with Lawson's intensive care stripes, she happily yielded to his superior experience.

She didn't need to consult with him. It was natural, unspoken between them. The patient might need intubating, a procedure she wasn't yet qualified to perform, so Lawson was the best paramedic for the job.

In a precisely executed manoeuvre she swung up into the cab. Her short legs made the seat a long way up and she often felt as if she were doing some sort of modified pole-vault routine. She reached under the seat for the lever and hauled it forward. With the twist of her wrist the engine started with a roar, chugging diesel fumes into the ambulance bay, and she inched the vehicle out.

Lawson pushed the responding button on the vehicle computer system to alert the coms centre to their departure and they were off.

'Do you suppose it's a tourist?' Vic asked as she flipped on the siren.

She'd grown up in this small island community and the downside of being a paramedic here was that, too often, she knew the people she was sent to help. Which was one thing she was looking forward to about her upcoming move to London—in eighty-five sleeps—total anonymity.

Lawson shrugged non-committally, only half listening. This was her process. He preferred quiet on the way to a Code One, to gather himself, plan for different contingencies. Victoria liked to fill up the silence with nervous chatter. He let her go. He knew by the time they pulled up she'd be in the zone.

And it certainly beat the alternative. Talking about what had happened a few days ago. So far they'd managed to avoid it completely. But it was there between them—he sensed it.

'It's not so sheltered around the other side and the wind's up,' she mused. 'Most locals know rips can form in this kind of weather.'

'Uh-huh.'

'We have a perfectly good patrolled beach, for crying out loud,' she said, flicking her eyes briefly from the road to look at him. 'Why the hell can't they just swim there?'

Unlike the island's most popular beaches, Wattle wasn't patrolled by surf lifesavers. Those that were had access to a high level of first aid should it be needed. But unpatrolled areas were a wild card and already Vic's brain was turning to what they might be faced with in a few minutes. Would any first aid have been rendered to the unfortunate victim of Wattle's rocky shoreline?

'Uh-huh.'

'I mean, it's one o'clock on a Monday for Pete's sake. It's not like Banksia Beach's crowded this time of the day. Why don't they just go there?'

'Mmm.'

'But oh, no, they have to go where it's a little more edgy. A little more of a challenge. Dad'll go nuts when he finds out.'

Lawson couldn't agree more. Bob took every drowning on the island to heart. Luckily the station OIC had decided to take the rest of the week off to be home with a recovering Ryan. But Lawson knew the latest near-drowning news would be around the small island community within a few hours and, even though he was away for the weekend camping with the twins, Bob was still on the island and so would be one of the first to know. 'Yep.'

The one-sided conversation continued for the next two minutes as the ambulance raced through the sleepy streets, lights and siren blazing.

As they approached the beach a teenager was waving at them wildly from the car park and pointing down the beach to a huddle of people. Vic used the nearby boat ramp to access the beach and drove the vehicle straight to where the action seemed to be going down.

The wind had whipped the waves up into choppy peaks and they were crashing against the shore. In the distance she could see the rocky headland where she'd spent many a summer holiday as a child exploring the caves that riddled the area.

Vic hadn't quite pulled up when Lawson exited. He was at the back doors, opening them and grabbing equipment as Vic turned off the engine. He retrieved the life pack containing the portable monitor, defibrillator and oxygen.

'Grab some blankets,' he threw over his shoulder as he slapped his cap on his head and headed for the small group of people nearby.

Vic, pulling her ponytail through her own cap, strode to the back of the ambulance and grabbed two blankets. She didn't bother to shut the doors, following her partner as fast as she could with significantly shorter legs.

When she reached the patient, Lawson was kneeling in the wet sand, hooking up an oxygen mask while five girls all in wet bikinis and various stages of hysteria spoke to him at once.

'Excuse me.' Vic raised her voice to cut through the emotion. The group parted and she knelt beside her partner. The patient was lying supine in his boardies, wet and cold and gasping like a fish out of water. And about as grey as one. His mouth was ringed with sand, his lips tinged a dusky purple.

But he was conscious, if a little stunned. And he was breathing, although it seemed somewhat laboured. Lawson had already placed a collar on his neck.

'Just popping some oxygen on, Michael,' Lawson said as he applied the mask.

Vic threw the blanket over the patient using the cotton weave to dry the teenager's chest to ensure the electrodes she was applying would stick. A green squiggly line spiked to life on the monitor. His heart rate was a little on the slow side. She placed a peg-like device on Michael's finger and watched as his oxygen saturations registered in the high eighties—far from satisfactory.

Vic got a cobbled history from Jacinta, who identified herself as Michael's sister. 'He just got dumped by this massive wave. He didn't come up again,' she wailed. Vic marked everything down on the large patient care sheet, including the observations and his personal details.

Lawson watched as his patient's lips pinked up and the oxygen saturations climbed steadily. Michael moaned and then coughed, which changed quickly to spasmodic retching as it continued. Lawson removed the mask, quickly helping the teenager roll on his side as his patient spewed up a bellyful of sea water onto the sand. He flicked on the portable suction.

'It's okay, mate,' he murmured, resisting Michael's feeble attempts to push the Yankeur sucker away as he cleared his airway. 'Better out than in.'

Michael stopped retching and Lawson pulled the mask back over his patient's nose and mouth. He placed a stethoscope in his ears and listened to the shallow breath sounds.

'Let's scoop him and go,' Lawson murmured.

Ten minutes later Michael was in the back of the ambulance with Lawson and Vic had radioed Coms of their twenty-minute ETA at hospital. Jacinta rode in the front seat with Vic, a blanket draped around her shoulders.

An hour later Vic put her signature to the completed paperwork she'd finished up in the privacy of the accident and emergency staff room. She handed it over to the nurse in charge and headed back to the ambulance bay and their vehicle.

Lawson was lounging against a wall near the exit, the five girls from the beach, still in their tiny bikini tops and brief boardies, gathered round him. They were obviously now sufficiently recovered from their shock and ever so grateful to the big, strong paramedic.

Vic grinned as she heard them asking him about how many people he'd saved with the kiss of life. She pulled up behind them and winked at him. His loose stance was deceptive. His jaw muscle was clenched as he shot her a get-me-out-of-here look. 'Ready?'

Lawson, grateful for the interruption, crushed his empty polystyrene coffee cup in his hands and pushed away from the wall. 'Remember,' he said, tossing the cup in the nearby bin, 'next time swim on patrolled beaches, between the flags.'

'Oh, we will, Lawson,' Jacinta said. 'And thank you again so much for saving my brother's life.' She touched his sleeve. 'I'm never going to forget you or what you did for Michael.'

Vic rolled her eyes. Had Jacinta deliberately dropped the blanket a little lower? And hello? What was she? Chopped liver? Lawson hadn't exactly been Robinson Crusoe down on the beach. 'Coms had a patient transport job for us,' she lied.

'Right.' Lawson extricated himself from the circle. 'Bye.'

'Bye,' they said in unison.

Vic looked back over her shoulder to see them all twinkling their fingers at his back and looking at him as if they wouldn't mind giving him a little mouth-to-mouth of their own.

Oh, please!

Strangely it irritated her. Her lips tingled again with the memory of her kiss. Although they'd studiously avoided talking about it, it was always there, in the back of her mind, and she was beginning to think of it as the elephant in the room. She'd kill to know what he was thinking.

Had he put it down to her being a little tipsy or excused it as one of those strangely intimate moments between people who had known each other for ever that was almost inevitable after an emotional event? Or was he just not thinking about it at all? Was that why he hadn't mentioned it?

Somehow that was an even more disturbing thought...

She waited till they climbed back in the cab before she commented. 'Ooh, Lawson, you're so-o-o brave,' she cooed, and turned to him to bat her eyelashes in an exaggerated fashion. She kept it light but couldn't deny there was a degree of the green-eyed monster involved.

Lawson frowned. 'Cut it out.'

Vic laughed. 'Oh, but, Lawson,' she said breathily, touching his sleeve, 'I'm never going to forget you.'

He jammed his seat belt buckle into its clasp, shaking her hand aside. 'Yeah, yeah.'

She pulled out into traffic with a smile on her face, comfortable now with their familiar patter. She knew where she stood with the banter that was the hallmark of their relationship. The grizzled veteran and the rookie. She didn't know where she stood after the kiss. She didn't know how to talk to him about that.

'You won some hearts there.'

'Please. I'm old enough to be their father. Speaking of which.' He looked at his watch. 'Looks like we'll make *Kids Quiz* today.'

Vic nodded enthusiastically. She enjoyed the day-shift ritual almost as much as Lawson. And at least with Matilda's endless prattle she didn't have time to think about her error of judgement. 'One dose of PG TV coming up.' She grinned.

'Daddy!'

'Tilly!' Lawson grinned, holding his arms out to his

daughter, who'd run out of the front door the minute the ambulance had pulled into the driveway.

Matilda hurled herself into her father's arms and squealed, clutching his big shoulders as he spun her around and around, her blonde curls flying behind.

'What'd you learn at school today?' he asked as he gave in to her *'stop Daddy'* giggles.

'Miss Simpson taught us the eight times tables.'

'Oh, yeah? What's eight times zero?'

Matilda giggled again. 'Daddy, that's the easy one.'

Vic, who was lounging against the side of the van, shook her head as she watched father and daughter with a big grin. Lawson's kid was great. And an absolute credit to him. Deb had literally left him holding the baby and he hadn't blinked. Just totally changed his lifestyle and committed every cell he owned to the raising of his daughter.

Vic smiled as Lawson tickled his daughter, feeling a strange affiliation with the little girl. Matilda too was growing up without a mother and it clutched at Vic's heart, resonating deeply. Sure, Matilda hadn't known any different, but it didn't make it any less sad that she would never know that special bond. The type of bond Vic had had with her mother.

It was a credit to Lawson that, despite Deb's desertion, Matilda was a happy, secure child. 'Eight times nine,' she said, entering the game.

Matilda's face, noticing her father's partner for the first time, lit up. 'Vic,' she cried, running around Lawson to launch herself at Victoria. 'Vic, Vic, Vic.'

Matilda locked her arms around Vic's waist and

jumped up and down. Vic laughed and hugged the dear
little thing tight. She was going to miss Matilda's zest
for life and her unconditional love. The twins had been
like that and sometimes she could still feel their skinny
arms giving her a double-trouble hug.

'*Kids Quiz* is starting.'

Vic looked up to see Dorothy, Matilda's part-time
nanny, a marshmallow-centred ex-schoolmarm,
standing at the front door.

'Yippee! Come on, Vic. Come on, Daddy.' Matilda
pulled at both their hands. 'Miss Simpson says this is
her favourite show.' Matilda looked meaningfully at her
father. 'She's really pretty.'

Lawson rolled his eyes at Victoria as his daughter
dragged him into the house. 'Yes, I have met Miss
Simpson, remember?'

For the next half an hour the time passed as it always
did on the days their jobs and the pager allowed them
to drop in and visit with Matilda in the afternoon. On a
day shift Lawson wasn't home until after his daughter
was in bed so if he could get these precious moments
with her, he grabbed them with both hands.

They all huddled on the lounge over coffee and some
home-made goodies Dorothy had whipped up, shouting
at the television, competing with each other. Vic loved
these times. Matilda held her hand and seemed to hang
off her every word. It reminded her of the foggy
memories she had of sitting on the couch watching television with her own mother and the overwhelming
feeling of being loved.

Lawson was lucky to have a job where he could

spend this precious time with his daughter—and he knew it. She guessed it was one of the many advantages of working in a small community. Something else she'd miss in giant, anonymous London.

Not that she'd miss anything about this life too much, she told herself. After eighteen years of helping raise her twin brothers, shackled through grief and love and an innate sense of responsibility, she was well and truly set to fly the nest.

This was her time and she was going to live it. Crush or no crush. Kiss or no kiss.

Their pagers remained silent for the duration of *Kids Quiz,* for which they were both thankful. Afterwards Matilda rushed off to get ready for her piano lesson and Vic and Lawson got back on the road.

As they drove away Vic said, 'I know I say this every time but, jeez, you've got a good kid there.'

Lawson turned to look at her. Victoria and Matilda got on famously. He'd go as far as to say that his daughter worshipped the ground Victoria walked on. Why then, he wondered, was it that Matilda, who had tried to set him up with every available female under ninety on the island the last six months, hadn't ever tried to set him up with his partner?

Probably because Victoria had just always been around. More like a big sister than a mother prospect. Or maybe Matilda also thought it utterly preposterous.

Vic could feel his eyes on her as she drove. 'What?' she demanded, looking at him briefly before returning her eyes to the road.

'You're good with her.'

Vic snorted. 'I raised my brothers from babies. I have two X chromosomes. I know kids.' She shrugged. 'Big deal.'

'You'd make a good mother.'

'Oh, no.' She shook her head vigorously. 'No way. Never ever. I've raised my babies.'

It was a familiar denial he'd heard fall from her lips numerous times. Not that he could blame her. He just thought it was a shame to discount it for all time. 'Fair enough.'

Vic shook her head as she tried to keep up with his ever-changing view of her. Today he could see her as a mother. Other days he saw her as his work partner, as a babysitter for his child, as Ryan and Josh's sister, as Bob Dunleavy's daughter. But mostly she was convinced he still saw her as the six-year-old he'd first met.

Why couldn't he see her as an adult? Maybe a reminder that she was fully grown and ready to fly the nest would force him to see her in a different light. As a woman.

'Hey, have I mentioned today that it's only eighty-five more days?'

Lawson turned away from her and looked out of his window. 'Once or twice,' he said dryly.

Or maybe not.

CHAPTER FOUR

THE ominous grey breakers rolled onto the beach, slapping against the sand with relentless savagery as the tide clawed its way steadily back. The wind howled around them as they lounged against one of the wooden crossbeams of the fence that formed the perimeter of the Wattle Beach car park.

It ripped strands of Vic's hair from her ponytail and she flicked her head as another chunk was whipped across her face. She took a sip of her take-away coffee and hunched further into her overalls as the inclement weather goosed her bare forearms.

'I'm going to miss the ocean.' She raised her voice to be heard over the roar of wind and water.

Lawson warmed his hands on his disposable mug. 'What? Even on days like today?'

Vic nodded. True, it was one of those miserable days, with scattered misty rain and a churning sea. But there was nothing like the unbridled power of the ocean to make you know you were alive. There was something elemental about it and Vic felt an utterly biological connection. 'Especially on days like this.'

Lawson shook his head. It had been Victoria's idea to grab their afternoon coffee and come down to Wattle. The beach was deserted. They were the only two fools stupid enough to brave the weather on this utterly miserable Saturday.

Personally he'd rather be at the station than freezing his butt off in the great outdoors. But with seventy more sleeps to go he'd noticed the closer her countdown got to zero the more she insisted on getting out and about for their breaks and he figured she was just trying to commit things to memory.

As much as she wanted out, he knew she was going to miss the island terribly. At the moment she was focused only on missing people. But despite what she thought, she'd always been a homebody hopelessly in love with the island lifestyle. From the poem she'd had published in the local paper when she'd been ten, entitled 'My Island', to her position on the Island Progress Committee.

Brindabella was in her blood and Lawson didn't think for a moment it was going to be as easy as she thought to turn her back on it.

Lawson looked at his watch. 'Seen enough now?'

Vic drained the dregs of her cappuccino, her fingers cold despite the warmth of the mug. 'Yeah, yeah. Grouch, grouch. Where's your sense of adventure?'

'It died from hypothermia about ten minutes ago.'

Lawson was approaching the four-wheel drive when the first faint cry for help carried to them on the wind.

'Did you hear that?' Vic asked.

With his hand on the door handle Lawson turned

towards the sound. It came again from the track to his right and he headed in that direction. The track wasn't used any more but both of them knew it led to the distant headland.

A child appeared, running full pelt. She looked no older than Matilda and Lawson felt his stomach plummet.

'Help. You have to…help.' The wide-eyed child clutched her side as she fought for breath.

Lawson knelt beside her. 'What's happened?' he asked.

'It's Bella. She fell…down a hole…in the cliff.' The child pointed towards the headline. 'She's in some sort of…cave. She's just laying there. I think she's… hurt.'

Vic felt her pulse spike as a shot of adrenaline charged her system. She looked at the angry waves and the approaching tide and knew that caves on the headland filled with water very quickly as the tide came in.

Lawson grabbed the child's arm. 'How old is Bella?'

'Four,' the child croaked.

He looked at Victoria and didn't have to have a conversation with her to know that the situation was extremely alarming. He stood. 'Right. Come with us,' he said, turning back towards the vehicle knowing time was of the essence. 'What's your name?'

'Annie.' Her lip wobbled. 'Pete reckons Dad's going to kill us. He told us not to go on the headland without adult supervision.'

'Pete?' Vic asked.

'He's my brother. He stayed behind to talk to Bella 'cos I'm a faster runner than him.'

The thought of another child on the headland in this filthy weather sent a prickle up her spine and Vic hoped they didn't have two children to rescue when they got there.

Lawson gunned the engine. Luckily their last job had involved a suspected spinal injury at Brigalow Beach so they still had the four-wheel drive. He picked up the radio to alert Coms.

'Coms this is truck three zero five on Brindabella. Four-year-old girl reportedly fallen into a rocky cave on Wattle Beach headland with incoming tide. Going to investigate now. ETA three minutes. Can you alert local authorities and nearest police rescue crew.'

Vic squeezed Annie's hand. The girl was starting to shiver and she threw her ambulance coat around Annie's skinny shoulders. 'You did the right thing. You came and got help. You're very brave, Annie.' She looked at Lawson, his face grim. 'We'll get Bella out. I promise.'

Lawson glanced at her sharply. Making promises, especially before they'd assessed the situation, was rash. And stupid. But then he looked at Annie's pale face and trembling body and didn't have the heart to reprimand his partner. The poor child needed some reassurance.

The vehicle bumped along the deteriorated track on a steady incline. When they reached the top they swung into the headland car park and alighted the vehicle.

'Bella got through the fence somehow,' Annie said as she led them over the sturdy chain mail that had been specifically constructed years before to prevent such excursions onto the notoriously potholed headland.

When she'd been a kid and when the twins had been little, it had all been open to the public, but a couple of rock fishing accidents had led the council to take evasive action and now the headland could only be viewed from a special lookout area.

'There he is.' Lawson saw Pete first and made his way sure-footed across the rocks.

The headland for the most part was a gradual descent rather than a sharp drop. Towards the sea line it became a much steeper gradient, but thankfully where Pete was lying the slope was still very manageable.

'Hi, Pete,' Lawson said as he approached.

Pete raised a tear-stained face from the hole in the rock. 'Hurry, you have to hurry. I think she broked her leg. The water's getting higher.'

Lawson felt dread punch him in the stomach both at the little boy's wretchedness and the plight of his sister. 'It's okay, mate. She'll be all right now,' he said, sending a quick prayer out to the universe that it actually would be all right. 'Do you think I could have a look?'

Vic and Annie arrived as Lawson was lowering himself to the ground. Pete went straight to his sister and hugged her and Vic's heart melted as she pulled the siblings in close.

Lawson was on his stomach peering through a hole not much bigger than a Frisbee trying to fathom how a child could even fit through when he heard the low whine. He angled his head and could just make out a furry body about three metres below.

Bella was a dog?

A surge of relief swept through Lawson as he momentarily laid his forehead against the rock. It was cool against his face and he couldn't believe the furnace running through his veins when ten minutes ago he'd been freezing cold.

He pushed himself upright and grinned at the questioning look on his partner's face. He looked at the children, huddled together in the confines of Victoria's arm. 'Is Bella a dog?'

Annie and Pete nodded at him with sad, solemn eyes as if he should have known it all along. He noticed Victoria's shoulders sag.

'Bella's a dog?' She looked down at the children, who looked up at her and nodded again.

'She's my dog,' Annie confirmed. 'I got her for my birthday when I was three.'

Vic grinned back at Lawson. 'A dog.'

Annie, obviously shrewder than her brother with her advanced years, looked from one to the other. She pulled out of Victoria's grasp. 'You're still going to get her out, right? Just because she's an animal doesn't mean you can let her drown.'

Pete's eyes grew round in his head. 'You're going to leave her there?' he squeaked, staring at Lawson.

The wind whipped the sound of a siren towards them and Lawson knew pretty soon half the emergency services on the island would be on the headland.

'No,' Vic denied, placing her hand on Pete's shoulder. 'We're not going to leave her there. We'll get her out, don't worry.'

But maybe they could call off the chopper that Coms had told them was on their way in case an amphibious rescue had been their only option. And call in the Animal Rescue people.

'What have we got, Lawson?'

Vic turned to see two of the island's volunteer fire-fighters picking their way towards them and, further behind, two policemen climbing the fence.

'It's okay.' Lawson put up his hands. 'It's not a child. It's a dog.'

The men stopped in their tracks and within seconds were laughing and slapping each other on the back.

'It's not funny.'

Annie's little voice cut through their cheer. She was standing, her hand on her hip, glaring at them. Pete edged closer to his sister and she put her arm around his shoulders.

'Annie? Pete?'

They all looked back towards the car park as a very worried-looking man and a woman also scrambled over the fence.

'Oh-oh,' Pete whispered.

Vic crouched beside them. 'Are they your parents?'

'Yup.' Pete's look of impending doom said it all.

'Okay.' She nodded. 'Let me handle this.'

The couple approached and the mother was the first to let fly. 'Oh, my God,' she said to the guilty parties, grabbing them and giving them each a fierce hug. 'We've been looking everywhere for you. You scared the living daylights out of us.'

Vic jumped in to soothe the waters a bit and five minutes later, after a round of introductions to the Bradley family, all had been forgiven. They tried to usher the children back to safety but they refused to budge.

Annie moved out of her mother's tight embrace and

turned imploring eyes on Vic and Lawson. 'What about Bella. You have to get Bella.'

This time she burst into tears and Vic crouched beside her again. 'I promise we'll try as hard as we can to get Bella out.' Vic had checked out Bella's position and thought she could help. 'Don't tell my dad but I used to play in these caves when I was a kid.'

Annie gave her a watery smile and Vic's heart squeezed painfully in her chest. The girl had been so mature and she knew she'd do her damnedest to save Bella from drowning from the incoming tide. 'I reckon I know a way we could get to her. But you have to go back behind the fence and let us do our work. Okay?'

Annie scrubbed at the tears trekking down her face. 'You promise you'll try?'

Vic crossed her heart and held out her crooked little finger. 'Pinky swear.'

Lawson watched as Annie linked her little finger with Victoria's. How many times had he seen Victoria Pinky swear with Matilda? He felt a surge of emotion in his chest and had to look away.

'Right,' she said as the Bradleys made their way back to the lookout area to wait. The police rescue unit was half an hour away. They were it. 'I think I know a way in to where Bella is. Follow me.'

Lawson, the two fire-fighters, two police officers and a community first responder—all men—followed Vic down the sloping headland.

Vic talked as she picked her way over the wet rocks. 'It's been a few years but I think the cave that Bella's fallen into is the main cavern. And there're many different entrances, like a rabbits' warren. Some are too small but there's one I reckon we could get in through.'

She led the men to the opening she'd used often as a child. The sea churned not far below their feet so she knew that Bella's time was running out. The rock where she was lying would soon be submerged and if, as they suspected, she'd broken her leg, she'd have no hope of making it.

The vertical fissure was about five feet high and easily breeched as a skinny kid. As an adult, not so much. They all looked at the narrow aperture in dismay. Vic peered through the opening and could just make out Bella's rump in the distance and fading light. She could also see the ocean encroaching on the bank of rock onto which the dog had fallen.

'It's okay, Bella,' she called. 'We're coming, baby.' The answering whine was heartening.

She looked at the assembled men. Lawson was the fittest but the tallest and too broad to fit through the opening. The others were of similar stature, the shortest one being too broad around the middle to even be considered.

'I guess it's me, then?' Vic calculated she could squeeze through, go in, grab Bella, pass her out and be back out again in just a few minutes. She outlined her strategy to the men.

Lawson, growing more and more horrified by her plan, was suddenly cold again. Chilled. 'No.' He shook his head. 'Absolutely not.'

Vic blinked. 'I'm sorry?'

'It's too dangerous. What if you slip? What if you can't get back out again?'

Vic felt the first bubble of anger churn in her stomach. Did he think she wasn't up to this? 'I won't slip. I can get back out again. I know these caves, Lawson.'

'No.' His voice brooked no argument. 'We wait for the experts.'

Vic watched as Lawson's gaze became as cold and grey as the sea and opened her mouth to protest. 'Bella doesn't have time. The cave is going to be submerged by the time they get here.'

'We can put her in a harness, rope her off,' Stan, one of the fire-fighters, suggested.

'No.'

Vic, incensed at Lawson's propriety, ignored him completely. 'Good idea, Stan. Can you go get it from your truck? And ring Doug while you're up there. Tell him we're going to need a vet. Pronto.'

Lawson turned frigid eyes on his partner as they watched Stan depart. She'd always been gung-ho and up until recently he'd been supportive of that, admiring her courage and exuberance. Even recognising a younger version of himself. But this was too... 'Victoria, I said no.'

Vic stuck her hands on her hips and her chin right out. 'I can go in with a rope, or without one. But I'm going in.'

A muscle jumped in Lawson's jaw. 'I can't let you risk your neck for an animal that sustained a fall that's probably going to leave it with severe internal injuries that may not be compatible with life. It's too risky.'

Vic pushed. 'I have a risky job.'

He watched his warning have precious little effect. 'Your father will have my guts for garters.'

Vic felt a completely irrational surge of frustration well inside. Not caring about the interested onlookers, she levelled her partner with a dangerous look.

'If you could fit through that hole, would you do it?'

Lawson shrugged. 'Of course.'

Vic nodded. She'd known his answer. She'd known Lawson to knock down a wall when Matilda's cat somehow managed to give birth to kittens in the wall space of their house. 'Exactly. Stop treating me like I'm a still a child, Lawson. I'm a paramedic. This is what I do.'

'No. This is not your job. It's Rescue's job.'

Vic glared at him. She got why he thought it was dangerous. She knew from her childhood adventures the rocks would be slippery and therefore potentially fatal. But when was he going to see her as a grown-up? 'Today, right now, with Rescue miles away, it is.'

Lawson felt ill. A hundred worst-case scenarios raced through his mind. 'As your superior officer, I forbid you to do this.' He felt about as low as he could get.

Vic couldn't believe what she was hearing. Heat rose in her face as the men around her shifted uncomfortably and looked at their feet. She looked at his impenetrable face and threw out one last-ditch appeal.

'Lawson, I made a promise to Annie. If this was Matilda's dog, if I made a promise to Tilly, wouldn't you want me to keep it? Let me do this, Lawson. I'm a big girl. I can do it.'

Lawson knew she was right. And if it were anybody else—male, female or alien—as long as they fitted through the hole, he would have tied the rope himself.

But the thought of her getting hurt was too much to bear. He was supposed to look out for her, not let her take unnecessary risks.

'Lawson.' She placed her hand on his sleeve. 'Please have some faith in me.'

Lawson could see his perceived lack of faith hurt her and the plea in her voice travelled straight to his core, like a burning arrow tip singeing his flesh as it went. It meant so much to her. Could he deny her this?

Stan arrived back with a harness and a helmet and everyone looked at Lawson expectantly. 'All right. But one slip and you're out of there.'

Had she not been standing on a narrow rocky shelf with the roiling ocean not far from her feet, Vic might well have hugged him. But there was no time for that anyway so she climbed into the harness and helmet Stan had delivered instead and waited impatiently while Lawson took for ever to fuss with the ropes.

'Lawson,' she chided. 'Enough already. The tide is coming in.'

Lawson gave the ropes one last yank, checked her helmet was securely fastened, shoved a torch in her belt and sent her on her way. 'Make sure you can come back out again before you step in there proper,' he instructed, taking up first position on the rope just outside the opening of the crevice.

The others fell in behind him, each grasping a section of rope. Lawson sent one of the policemen up to the top where Bella had fallen in so he could have another pair of eyes on Victoria.

Victoria slipped through the narrow space. It was a

bit of a squeeze but she managed it okay both ways. 'I'm going in.'

'Be careful,' he warned.

She nodded and turned away. His gaze had lit with a startling fierceness and she didn't need that as she attempted the potentially treacherous trek. She'd rather focus on her anger at him for coddling her, for treating her with kid gloves. It would keep her determined.

The air inside the cave was dank and salty. Light filtered in through the many small holes in the walls eroded away over the years but it was still significantly darker. 'Hey, Bella,' she called, inching slowly forward on the narrow ledge she found herself on, concentrating on each footfall. 'I'm coming, girl. I'll be there soon.'

The answering whine was comforting and gave her a focus in the ever-encroaching dark. She stopped and fumbled for the torch, flicking it on. The sucking noise of the sea creeping up the ledge seemed less ominous in the torchlight.

Lawson's pulse thundered through his head as he watched her slow creep forward, ready to snap hard on the rope should she stumble. He couldn't hear a thing over his heart rate and the noise of the surf as he concentrated on her progress.

He finally lost sight of her as she veered to the left, and felt his pulse accelerate. Then her shadow sprang to life on the opposite wall of the cavern and he breathed a sigh of relief. She must have flicked on her torch. 'How much further?' he called.

Vic could see Bella fully now and smiled at the shivering mutt. 'A few metres,' she said, turning her head back towards the opening so she could be heard above the surf that echoed loudly all around the cave.

She turned back in time to see the cocker spaniel trying to get up and then yelping as the pain stopped her progress. 'Stay still, Bella,' she crooned, putting out her hand frantically to still the dog's efforts.

In desperately trying to comfort the injured Bella, Vic's concentration lapsed for a second. One fatal second. A quick unchecked step towards Bella and she was slipping, teetering, falling. The torch fell out of her hand as she grabbed the rope. She called out but it was too late, her body falling hard against the rocky surface, winding her as she was sucked under the water.

Lawson felt the tug on the rope and reacted within a split second, yanking hard on the rope. 'Victoria!' he roared. He turned to the men behind him. 'She's down. Pull! Pull, damn it!'

The men, also reacting within seconds of Lawson, heaved and hauled while Lawson called out. 'Victoria! Victoria.'

Vic felt the tightening around her waist as she grappled with the rock surface, trying to get a hold beneath the water. She felt herself being dragged up and broke the surface quickly, gasping for breath. Tears stung her eyes as pain slid like a stiletto between her ribs with each inhalation.

The tension on the rope continued to pull her higher, scraping her cheek and her hands against the rough rock as she regained ground. She could hear Lawson yelling her name, hear the note of absolute panic.

She took a breath to call out to him, but it hurt too much to breathe. To move. To think. Her heart hammered in her chest and that hurt too.

'Victoria!' Lawson pressed his face to the crevice but he still couldn't see her. 'Heave,' he shouted again.

Victoria lay like a drowned rat clinging to the rock surface. Slowly the winded sensation eased and she could breathe easier. She pulled herself into a sitting position.

'Lawson,' she called. It was pretty feeble so she tried again. 'Lawson!'

'Victoria?' Lawson angled his head to try and see her. 'Are you okay?'

His voice sounded marvellous and she wished he were here beside her. 'Just a bit...winded,' she panted.

'Hang on, we'll haul you back.'

Victoria looked up at Bella, who whined and watched her with wise eyes. The noise strummed at her heartstrings. She felt the tension on the rope again and she was yanked a foot back the way she'd come on her backside.

It jarred through her sore ribs and she grabbed the rope. 'Stop,' she shouted, wincing at the effort. The rope slackened immediately.

'What's wrong?'

'Nothing.' She grabbed the cave wall and pulled herself up, pain shooting a hot arrow up her side. 'I'm not coming out without this damn dog.'

'Yes, you are,' he shouted. 'Even if I have to drag you out on your backside all the way.'

'Don't think I won't cut this rope loose, Lawson,' she threatened.

Lawson swore under his breath. He believed her. He took a deep breath, his heart rate still not returned to normal from the scare she'd just given him. 'Hurry.'

This time she didn't take her eyes off the rocks. Luckily for her the torch had landed on the ledge further along, illuminating her path.

She reached Bella within a minute and the dog seemed to know what a tight spot they were in, licking Vic's hand as she reached out to pat the frightened animal. 'It's okay, Bella. I've got you now. Annie's waiting for you.'

Vic could see blood on her hind legs and the left one looked badly broken. 'I'm sorry, girl,' she crooned. 'This is going to hurt a little. For both of us.'

Vic lifted the animal, the pain in her side intensifying. Bella yelped. 'Shh, Bella. I know. You're hurt. We both are. Let's get out of here.'

Vic tucked the dog's body into hers, grateful for the warmth. She was totally soaked and shivering from the shock and the dank coolness of the cavern. 'I've got her,' she called. 'I'm coming out.'

And just in time too. The water was lapping the ledge as Vic inched her way back to the crevice. Bella was whimpering quietly and Vic didn't mind admitting she was petrified she would slip again. When Lawson came into sight she almost wept.

'I can see you. You're doing well,' he called. 'Just a little farther. Don't rush.'

Vic nodded. She was so cold, her teeth were chattering now. She reached the opening and Lawson was just on the other side and it was only Bella in her arms that stopped her from reaching through and grabbing him. He'd never looked better.

Lawson couldn't see her that well in the darkened cavern. All he knew was that she'd made it back and he wanted her out of there ASAP. 'Pass her through to me,' he instructed.

Vic's wince as she manoeuvred Bella into a good transfer position was covered by the dog's yelp. 'Her leg's bad,' Vic said. 'Be careful.'

Lawson eased the dog gently through the opening and passed her on. Doug was waiting further up in a safer spot to receive his patient.

'Now you.' Lawson's heart thundered again. He knew it wouldn't return to normal until she was safely out of the cave.

Vic nodded, turning on her side to squeeze through the crevice. She put her arm out first to anchor herself to the outside and shimmied through. The tight squeeze seemed tighter in her wet overalls and abraded her injured side so that she was gasping when she finally emerged into the daylight straight into Lawson's arms.

Lawson held her tight, his relief overwhelming. She looked awful. Pale and wet, her lips practically blue, her teeth chattering. She had scratches on her face and her hands were bleeding. She winced and he stepped back. 'What's wrong?' Lawson demanded.

'Fell hard on my ribs,' she dismissed.

Lawson's hands tightened around her arms. He could see from the dullness in her whiskey eyes she was hurting. If they hadn't been on a rocky outcrop, the sea pounding not far below them, foaming against the rocks, he would have swept her up into his arms and carried her back up the headland.

'Come on.' He placed a blanket Stan had passed him around her shoulders. 'Let's get you to a hospital.'

CHAPTER FIVE

THE next couple of hours passed in some weird kind of
vortex. Lawson reacted automatically; his years of
practice and experience as a paramedic came to the fore
as he did the things that needed to be done. He shut out
who his patient was altogether. It wasn't Victoria—he
just didn't allow it to register.

He sat her in the back of the ambulance, slapped on
some chest dots, put the saturations peg on her finger.
When it was obvious pain made it difficult to remove her
overalls so he could inspect where she'd impacted the
rocks he simply took out his shears and cut them away,
ignoring her protests and attempts to cover her modesty.

He forced the nausea down as the livid bruise,
already a deep purple-black, came into view. It marred
her entire side from the top of her ribs to her waist and
he tuned out her wince as he methodically but gently
palpated around it.

Satisfied she hadn't done any obvious internal
damage—her sats were good, her lung fields clear and
her pulse and blood pressure were normal—he wrapped
her in several blankets and requested Stan drive them

in to the hospital. He stayed in the back and watched her as he would any patient, refusing to let his mind wander to the what-ifs.

They didn't talk. She drifted to sleep, he watched the monitor, tapping his foot as each mile seemed like one hundred. When they finally reached the hospital he handed her over to the medical staff as if she were any of his patients with a precise, methodical summary.

He didn't protest when they swarmed around her, pushing him to the back. No siree. She was in safe hands now and he had other things to do before he could stop and think about the events of the day.

He went back to the island and returned the ambulance and organised cover for the remainder of the shift and their day shift tomorrow. He also dropped into the Dunleavy residence. He marched straight to her bedroom, opened her wardrobe and searched through her drawers, looking for something suitable for her to wear. It wasn't exactly an appropriate thing to be doing but Bob and the twins were camping for the weekend a couple of hours' drive away and she'd refused to let him ring them.

So she needed a change of clothes, which left it up to him. And anyway, this wasn't about Victoria the woman. This was one partner doing the other a favour. She would have done the same for him.

In her second drawer he found some loose-knit tracksuit pants and a stretchy-looking T-shirt. He contemplated opening the top drawer, where he could already see interesting hints of lace and flashes of colour through the partial opening. But he couldn't do it. She was just going to have to go commando.

He strode out of the house, got in his car and headed back to the hospital. He steadfastly refused to think about her pale face, her bloodless lips, her bedraggled hair as he drove. And every time his mind wandered to the afternoon's incident he consciously dragged it away, forcing himself to concentrate on the peak-hour traffic and getting to the hospital safely with her change of clothes.

It wasn't until he arrived at the hospital and the doctor informed him that her tests were fine that Lawson allowed himself to feel anything. His insides were trembling and there was a roaring in his ears so loud he could barely hear the doctor talking about her X-ray and abdo ultrasound being clear. And how satisfied they were with her observations and how lucky she'd been.

'I think it's wise she stay overnight though,' the doctor concluded. 'Just for observation.'

Vic, who'd been dozing on and off, had tuned into the low rumble of the voices beside her trolley a few minutes ago. Her eyes fluttered open. 'No,' she croaked.

She hated hospitals. The smell and the tragedies found inside their walls. Her mother had died in this hospital. Ryan had not long been an inpatient here. It was bad enough she spent most of her working life in and out of this place without being an overnight guest.

The noise inside his head snapped off as if a switch had been flicked. She looked like hell. Better, but still awful. The graze on her left cheek was more pronounced now she had some colour back in her face. He gave his partner a stern look. 'Doctor's orders.'

'I suppose you could go home if there was someone there with you.'

Lawson shook his head. 'It's just her. Her father and brothers are away this weekend.'

'I can stay at Lawson's,' Vic told the doctor. She turned pleading eyes in his direction. 'Can't I?'

Lawson blinked. Another night under his roof? He wasn't sure he could do that and not end up throttling her for scaring the living daylights out of him. Or after what happened last time. 'You're better off here.'

'I'm fine,' Vic insisted. 'You heard the doctor. It's just a precaution.'

Lawson gave her an exasperated look. Was she being deliberately argumentative today? If she'd just listened to him on the headland she wouldn't be in this predicament. He folded his arms across his chest. 'Maybe one that should be heeded.'

Vic frowned. Was the prospect of spending the night with her that awful? 'Please, Lawson.'

Lawson expelled a breath succumbing to the inevitable. 'Okay.'

'Good.' The doctor nodded. His pager beeped and he pulled it off his belt and read the message. 'I'm sorry I can't stay. A multi-trauma's two minutes out but you're free to go when you're dressed and ready. Just see the receptionist before you leave and sign your papers.'

Vic and Lawson watched the harried young doctor slip out of the curtains. 'Right,' Vic said, kicking off her sheet and swinging her legs over the side of the trolley. 'Did you bring me some clothes?'

Lawson placed the eco-friendly shopping bag on the trolley beside her as he held out his hand to help her down. She landed on her feet, her shapeless hospital gown swimming on her, and swayed slightly. 'Easy,' he said, supporting her around the waist.

Vic shut her eyes and clutched his hand as her vision temporarily darkened around the edges.

'Right. That does it,' he growled. 'You're staying.'

Vic opened her eyes, the dizziness gone. 'Don't be silly. I've been lying flat for hours—it's just a bit of postural hypotension. I'm fine.' Lawson raised his eyebrow at her. 'Really. Now wait outside while I get dressed.'

'I'll get a nurse to help you.'

Vic huffed out an exasperated breath. 'Oh, I'm sure that's just what they want in the middle of a multi-trauma—some princess who needs a hand to get her pants on.'

Lawson stood his ground. 'You're too unsteady on your feet to be in here by yourself.'

'Fine, then, you stay. Just turn around already so we can get out of here.'

Oh, for Pete's sake. 'I don't think this is very appropriate, Victoria.' *Wasn't it enough that he'd gone through her drawers for her?*

'Yeah. Yeah,' she muttered, grabbing his shoulder and exerting pressure until he turned around. Once his back was to her she searched through the meagre bag contents for some underwear. There was none.

She was just about to demand to know where her knickers were when the thought of him riffling through her underwear drawer heated her face. Had he? Or hadn't he? She felt it wise not to speculate when he was close enough to reach out and touch. She climbed awkwardly into her loose-fitting tracksuit pants and T-shirt without further comment.

But still she felt very exposed in front of him when she tapped him on the shoulder and he turned. No bra. No knickers. Knowing that he knew she was totally naked under her clothes was suddenly like an intimate little secret between the two of them and despite the throb of her injuries she felt a lurch of awareness as he looked at her.

Lawson studiously avoided looking at anything other than her face. 'Okay, then. Let's get going.'

Vic followed him out and was eternally grateful to him when he took charge of the discharge stuff and then made her sit at the front entrance until he brought the car around.

She was utterly exhausted, the thought of walking another step too much to bear, and she'd never been more pleased to see Lawson's sturdy four-wheel drive. It was a real man's car. Big and solid, like him. The wheels and sides were splattered in mud, every panel displaying wear and tear. Also like him.

He helped her up into the cab and within a minute they were on their way back to the island. She waited for him to say something. The reprimand she knew was coming. She knew she'd frightened the hell out of him and that things could have ended very differently than they had.

They were halfway to the island and she couldn't bear it any longer. Lawson's knuckles were so white around the steering wheel they practically glowed in the dark. 'Just say it, Lawson.'

Lawson clenched his jaw. 'You should have stayed in hospital.'

'You know I hate hospitals. And that wasn't what I meant and you know it.'

He turned to look at her. 'I know. But we're not going to talk about that. Not now.' Lawson couldn't even bear to relive that moment again.

'It was safe,' she said stubbornly. 'I just took my eyes off my feet for a second. We couldn't just stand there and let that little girl's dog drown.'

Lawson took a couple of deep breaths. 'Victoria, I'm not going to talk about it now. It's a work-related matter. We'll deal with it at work.'

Vic looked at the obstinate set to his chin and gave up. If she was honest, there was a sense of relief. She was too tired and she had the feeling that he was never going to see it her way anyway. The rock and sway of the car were wonderfully hypnotic and with Lawson being all brooding and silent it was easy for her to shut her eyes and let herself drift off.

They were pulling into the Dunleavy driveway when Vic woke. She frowned. Weren't they going to his house? Was he that annoyed with her he'd decided to ignore medical advice and leave her to her own devices?

Fine by her. She didn't need any of Lawson's passive-aggressive nursemaiding. And after the huge scare she'd had she wasn't entirely sure being alone with him was a good idea. The last time they were alone in a house she'd kissed him and she felt a hundred times more vulnerable tonight having just faced her own mortality.

She unbuckled. 'Thanks for the lift, Lawson. I'll talk to you tomorrow.'

Lawson gave her a grim smile. 'Oh, no, you don't. I'll be staying the night on your couch.'

Perversely, part of her rejoiced at his imperious command. Perversely, despite her misgivings, she didn't want to be alone tonight. 'But…what about Matilda?'

'She's at a birthday-party sleepover at one of her friend's houses.'

'Oh.' Vic shrugged. She knew she should push harder. Insist she'd be fine. She was a strong, independent woman who'd been looking after herself, and others, for a very long time. She didn't need him hovering. Particularly when he inspired such twisted feelings in her gut.

But deep down she was relieved he cared. And frankly, she was way too tired to argue. If he wanted to sleep hanging from her rafters like a bat, she wouldn't get an argument from her. 'Fine.'

He exited the vehicle and crossed to her door, helping her out, keeping his hand at her elbow as they made their way into the house. She moved out of his hold immediately she was inside, the heat from his palm radiating to places that hadn't felt this sort of heat in a while.

She turned away from him, suddenly regretting letting him have his way. The quietness of the house throbbed around her and she was acutely aware that Lawson's big strong body was very near. Her hands trembled and she couldn't decide whether she was about to burst into tears or reach for him.

She felt a surge of jumbled emotions well in her chest and she was suddenly overwhelmingly weary. Physically and emotionally.

She yawned loudly and Lawson said, 'Go to bed. I'll be on the couch if you need me.'

She opened her mouth to protest his bossiness, but his mouth was set in that stubborn line she'd seen so many times before and another surge of weariness battered her defiance. Sleep. Yes. Relief for her body. And her mind.

Vic headed straight for her room not bothering to acknowledge him. She was so weary she didn't even shower and change, just crawled onto her unmade bed and collapsed on top of her sheets. And even though it was only seven-thirty and the temptation of Lawson was mere metres away, she slept like a baby.

Lawson, on the other hand, couldn't sleep at all. Instead he was hunkered down on Bob's couch pretending interest in crap late-night television, occasionally checking on Victoria, who hadn't moved from the foetal position in the centre of her bed all night.

Now the emergency was over and Victoria was out of hospital with no serious injuries, reaction had set in. The moment when she slipped replayed over and over in his mind, as did those awful seconds that had felt like hours, when she hadn't responded to him.

And the way she'd looked as she'd emerged from the crevice. All grazed and banged up. Loose bits of her hair hanging in wet strips down her forehead, her face pale, her lips blue from the cold. His hand shook as the images flashed on his inward eye.

What if she'd broken her neck when she slipped? What if she'd got herself caught on some rocky protuberance beneath the water line? What if she'd broken a leg and hadn't been able to move? Or the blow to her ribs had been more serious and she'd fractured them, puncturing her lung?

Lawson tried to imagine what he would have said to her father had any of those things happened to her and she'd perished in that cave. Bob, who adored his daughter and had already been through the heartbreaking loss of one woman in his life. He didn't have the words for that.

And what about him? They'd been partners for five years. Hell, he'd known her for a lot longer than that— twenty years. And he couldn't imagine a world without Victoria Dunleavy in it. Yes, she was leaving in seventy days and he didn't know if he'd ever see her again, but that was different. At least he'd know she was out there in the world living her life.

Just after three the what-ifs were driving him crazy. They were exceptionally loud in the silence of the house so he got his butt off the couch and riffled around in the pantry. He could hear Victoria coughing as he located some microwave popcorn. He got it started and went to check on her.

She'd moved and was now lying spreadeagled on her back. She seemed settled, her chest movement deep and even. But the relief he felt just to see her breathing warred with less honourable thoughts, like her lack of underwear, and he got out of her room pronto.

He took the popcorn back to the couch and channel-surfed for a while. He finally found some infomercial with women wearing very little selling a natural breast augmentation product, and figured the absurd advertisement was as good a distraction as any from the horror of the pictures in his head.

Victoria continued to cough intermittently and nothing could divert him from wondering if they'd missed something at the hospital. He was about to go and check on her again when she appeared in the doorway.

'Hi.'

Lawson almost inhaled a kernel of corn. He coughed and spluttered to clear his airway. 'Jeez, you scared me,' he said after he'd recovered.

'I seem to be doing that a lot today,' she murmured as she sat on the end of the sofa next to him and dipped her hand into the popcorn. 'I'm starving.'

'How are you feeling?' He watched as she stuffed a handful of popcorn in her mouth. 'Apart from starving.'

With some sleep under her belt she felt a hundred per cent better than she had earlier. Invigorated and much more emotionally stable. 'Sore,' she said around her mouthful of food. 'I just took some painkillers.'

'You've got a nasty bruise there. It'll be sore for a few days.' He grabbed her closest hand and inspected the grazes on her palm, tracing the nearest one lightly with his forefinger. 'They must sting too.'

Vic looked down at his long finger against her injured palm. It grew warm and started to tingle. She wasn't sure if it was because of the graze or just the way he affected her. She pulled her hand away. 'It'll be worse tomorrow.'

She burrowed her fingers in the bowl and stuffed another handful of popcorn into her mouth. The flicker of the television caught her eye and her gaze was drawn to the colourful images of several well-endowed bikini-clad women. 'Lawson Dunlop,' she mused. 'What on earth are you watching?'

Lawson turned his attention to the television and cringed inwardly for a second. 'Oh, just some ridiculous infomercial,' he said, reaching for the remote and flicking it off.

'Oh, no,' Vic said, snatching it off him, wincing a little as her palms protested. 'I've gotta see this.' She flicked it back on and turned the volume up.

Lawson rolled his eyes, uncomfortable to be caught watching something that was so far removed from his normal viewing it was laughable. 'It was just on as background noise.'

'Sure, sure.' Vic grinned.

He squirmed in his seat as the over-the-top extended advert extolled the virtues of its product. Women with obviously surgically enhanced assets paraded around in skimpy clothes demonstrating how the cream worked.

Vic was laughing so hard she had to hold her side. 'Didn't realise you were a breast man, Lawson.'

Lawson frowned. 'I'm not.'

Vic raised an eyebrow. 'Really?'

Lawson had had enough. He reached for the remote, but she snatched it away. 'This is not a very appropriate conversation for two work colleagues to be having.'

Vic sobered. Was that truly the way he saw her? Always? 'But we're not. Not tonight. We're just two old friends who've known each other for donkey's years.'

'Exactly. I'm not talking about this with someone who I used to babysit.'

There it was again. He kept doing that and it was

driving her mad. Making her feel like a kid and he was the adult. That might have been so twenty years ago, but it wasn't now.

She felt sufficiently goaded to push a little. 'So…they don't do it for you?'

'Victoria.'

'Oh, come on.' She nudged him in the ribs. 'I could have died today. Cut me some slack. I'm curious.'

Lawson shook his head. 'I don't believe you just played the near-death card.'

Vic grinned. 'Shameless, aren't I?' She watched his face, intense in the half-light, the play of light from the flickering television dancing over the forbidding planes. She raised an eyebrow. 'Well?'

He sighed. 'Of course I like *breasts*.' He looked away, not quite able to meet her in the eye as he'd hoped. 'I'm a man, aren't I?'

'What about bums and legs?'

'Yes, Victoria. Them too.'

'Do you have a preference?'

Lawson squirmed in his seat. 'No. I love all of a woman's body. Equally. Any man who has a preference is getting laid too much for his own good.' He turned back to face her. 'There. Satisfied?'

Vic blinked. She didn't think she'd ever heard Lawson say the word *laid* to her—ever. Not that she thought he was a saint. He no doubt used more colourful language around his male co-workers, but he'd always been totally circumspect with his language in her presence. It was kind of dirty and the temperature raised a degree or two.

She looked away, her eyes seeking the television, unable to hold the intensity of his gaze.

Satisfied? Absolutely not.

She glanced at the television, suddenly a little depressed. She looked at her own small assets, even less impressive without the uplifting support of a bra. Maybe this was why Lawson had never looked at her in any other than a strictly professional way. Maybe it was why he never saw her as a woman.

'Maybe I could use some miracle cream myself,' she said forlornly. She turned to him and puffed her chest out. 'What do you think?'

Lawson dared not look, stuffing popcorn into his mouth instead. 'They're fine.'

Vic let them deflate. 'They're only B cups,' she lamented.

'They're fine,' he repeated, staring at a point on the wall.

Really? Lance obviously hadn't thought they were fine. Why else had he looked elsewhere? To the Kathys of the world. Maybe that was why she hadn't been a raging success at relationships—maybe she just wasn't desirable enough? She hung out with guys at work; she was surrounded by males at home; she wore overalls four out of seven days, for crying out loud.

Maybe she just wasn't feminine enough. Maybe if she had a bigger chest more men would notice she wasn't just one of the guys? Maybe Lawson would.

Vic rolled her head towards him. He wasn't even interested enough to look at her. 'You're not even looking,' she muttered.

He was just humouring her, as he used to when she

was little. And after her scare this afternoon she wasn't in any mood to be humoured. She wasn't a girl any more. Surely he could see that? A well of emotion rose in her chest and lodged in her throat. It stung her eyes and snatched at her breath.

Lawson clenched his jaw. If he didn't get away from her now he was going to do more than look. He pushed himself off the couch and stuffed his hands in his pockets. 'Victoria, I think you should go back to bed.'

Tears blurred in her eyes as pure frustration drove her to her feet. She ignored the pain that tore at her side. The one building in her chest was far greater. 'Why do you do that?' she demanded huskily.

Lawson eyed her warily. Her whiskey gaze was glassy and he had an awful feeling she was about to cry. *And how the hell could he resist that*? 'Do what?'

A tear escaped and she dashed it away. 'Treat me like I'm still a child. Like I don't have the right to have a perfectly adult conversation with a man.'

He took a step towards her. 'Victoria, please don't cry.'

She screwed up her face and shook her head, determined to hold back the flood of tears although her chest was a dam wall at bursting point. 'Just answer the question, damn it.'

The question? *What was the bloody question?* He backtracked for a moment. 'I don't,' he dismissed. 'Treat you like you're a child.' God knew, he'd been having a really difficult time this last year remembering she'd ever been a child.

Vic opened her eyes and let the build-up of emotion ease out a little. She snorted. 'You're doing it again.'

Tears trickled down both sides of her face and she didn't care. 'Talking at me like I'm some little kid you can just dismiss out of hand.'

He felt totally helpless watching her tears. He was torn between pulling her close and getting the hell out of the house. He raked a hand through his spiky hair and took a step back. 'You don't know what you're talking about.'

Vic choked out a sob. 'Try me.'

Lawson shut his eyes briefly, wishing he were anywhere but here. 'I'm not just any random man you can have a conversation about breasts with. I'm your partner.'

His partner. There it was again. 'Oh, God,' she wailed. 'I'm a woman, damn it. Can't you see that? A grown, adult woman. I know to you I'm just…Bob's daughter, Ryan and Josh's sister…another paramedic at the station, your *colleague,* but…' She scrubbed at her face, brushing away the tears. 'I. Am. A. Woman.' She poked herself in the chest to emphasise each word.

Vic felt half crazy. Her heart ached so much it burned like a molten chunk of metal in her chest. She wiped at her eyes with the heels of her palms. Goodness knew, she must look a right state.

Lawson was staring at her as if she'd grown a second head. 'You've never seen me as a woman. I'm just Vic. Good old Vic. Someone to babysit and get the gurney for you. Not beautiful or desirable. Not female. Just one of the boys.'

'No.' The admission was torn from him. He knew he shouldn't have given it voice, but he couldn't bear to witness her pain. What the hell was she talking about? Not desirable? Not beautiful? Standing here in the flickering light of the television, fragile and vulnerable before him, he wanted her so much it scared him.

He took a step closer and grasped her by the shoulders. 'Do you know the first thing I thought today when you slipped on the rocks? When you screamed and the rope went taut?' Lawson shut his eyes briefly as the horrifying memory revisited.

Vic was conscious of the rasp to his voice and their closeness. His hands on her skin, their bodies separated by a whisper of air. She watched as his lids fluttered open again, her heart pistoning in her chest as she waited for him to continue. If anything, waiting for his words was more terrifying than being cold, frightened and disorientated for those horrifying few seconds underwater.

'All I could think was that I hadn't ever got the chance to kiss you. To…touch you.' The air felt like soup as Lawson dragged in a breath.

Vic's heart danced a wild flutter in her chest at his startling admission. He'd thought about kissing her…touching her? 'You've kissed me plenty,' she murmured absently, trying to compute what he'd just said. Impersonal pecks on the cheek as hellos and thankyous and happy birthdays. Friend kisses. Buddy kisses.

Lawson heard the huskiness in her voice. 'Not like this, I haven't.' And on a muffled curse, not giving himself time to think better of it, he yanked her closer and mashed his lips onto hers.

It was no gentle, tentative, feeling-the-waters, first-kiss type of kiss. It was hot and heavy in a flash, as if they'd been a powder keg just waiting for a match.

Lawson led and Victoria followed. He demanded entry into the heat of her mouth and groaned as her hands snaked around his neck and her tongue invited him inside.

He rode it, letting the sensation wash through him, succumbing to its power for a few magical moments suspended in time before common sense returned and he wrenched his mouth away with a level of self-control he hadn't even known he possessed. His hands grasped her upper arms, holding her at a distance.

Their breath was harsh in his ears. 'You are a beautiful, desirable woman. Don't think for a moment that I'm not aware of it.' He dropped his arms and took a deliberate step back, stuffing his hands back into his pockets.

Vic felt the impact of his words deep down low as if he'd licked her belly. He might have moved away, but he was looking at her mouth with a gaze that was stormy with lust and struggle. He did desire her; she could see that. Even if he didn't want to.

A crazy plan reared its head and she swallowed, wondering if she had the courage to put it into action. Certainly her awful fright this afternoon made her feel bolder than she ever had and Lawson's kiss had definitely set a tantalising precedent.

But Lawson was so strong. Already she could see his stormy gaze being pulled under control as he mentally withdrew from her, from his actions. Could she bear it if her seduction fell flat? If he rejected her out of his strong sense of honour and propriety?

But his chest still rose with breaths that sounded as if they were being dragged from him and he was looking at her mouth again as if he wanted to devour it. She licked her lips, savouring the taste of him. There was butter and salt and man. And she wanted more.

She took a deep breath and stepped into his space. 'So why stop?'

'Because it's crazy, that's why.' He was captivated by the way her tongue travelled across her already moist lips. It didn't help his breathing settle or calm the roaring pulse beat in his head. 'Jeez. I went to your mother's funeral. You were eight.'

She ran her fingers down his forearm and tentatively lifted his hand. She prepared herself for resistance but when none came she grew more daring, placing his palm over her breast. It couldn't compete with the women still cavorting on the television screen, but it was aching for his touch.

'I'm not eight any more. I haven't been for a long time.'

Lawson swallowed. *Hard.* Her breast was soft beneath his hand, the nipple pressing into the centre of his palm obviously aroused. 'Victoria,' he groaned.

'Lawson,' she whispered, stepping closer again, desperate to persuade him, not strong enough to handle him withdrawing from her now. 'I get that you do everything with measured caution and that this is a little out of the ordinary.'

She moved closer still so his hand was hard against her softness, her nipple unbearably tight. 'But can you just, for once, just today, be thankful that we're both here and just go with what you really want to do?'

Lawson felt the graze of her nipple as she rubbed against his palm and he squeezed the flesh involuntarily. 'No. This is wrong.' He stared at his hand covering her flesh, at her mouth. 'I don't want this,' he denied in a voice that was so husky with desire he was for sure about to be struck down by a lightning bolt for his obvious lie.

Her fear of rejection melted in an instant at his denial. She could hear how much he wanted her, wanted this, in the way his voice trembled. In the way he looked at her mouth.

'It's okay. I want it enough for both of us.' And she raised herself up, confident for the first time since she'd started just how much he actually desired her. She twined her hands around his neck and kissed him again.

Her lips teased his, her tongue stroking along the seam of his closed mouth, begging for access, and his resistance lasted about ten seconds before he opened to her on a groan that must have come all the way from his toes. The kiss was deep and wet as he unleashed a torrent of passion that left them both clinging to each other. He grasped her face in his hands and plunged his tongue into her mouth as she met him with equal ardour.

Beyond her conscious control her hands strayed to his back, clawing at his shirt, and before she knew it it was off and his chest was warm and bare beneath her touch. Even her injured palms were totally forgotten in the sensual exploration. She broke off to press her mouth to the hard ridge of his collarbone and the soft thrill of his carotid.

With her lips elsewhere Lawson felt the fog clear and sense returned. How the hell had his shirt got on the floor? 'Whoa. I think we're taking this a little too fast.'

Vic smiled. 'I'm not a teenager, Lawson, and I'm not

a virgin. I don't want to court. Or go steady. I'm leaving in seventy days and tonight, I want this.' She lowered her head and kissed one perfectly formed pectoral.

Lawson shut his eyes as the huskiness of her voice combined with the tiny, almost innocent gesture travelled straight to his groin. Without further thought he snagged the hem of her shirt and dragged it over her head. He looked down at her nakedness, her perfectly shaped breasts with nipples the colour of her lips, brushing his chest.

Vic blushed at the intensity of his gaze; it was as if he was working out the best way to devour them. 'Not quite Boobylicious, huh?'

'They're perfect,' he murmured, brushing a finger along one dusky tip, feeling its instant pucker. He dropped his mouth to hers, determined to show her just what an effect her body, her breasts, had on him.

The kiss escalated and for Vic it just wasn't enough. She wanted to press herself along the length of him, feel the breadth of him, she wanted to melt into him, absorb him. She wanted all of him, at once.

His hands ran down her back and her skin was so responsive it felt as if he'd stroked an icecube down her spine and then trailed a burning coal back up again. When they wandered again it felt as if his hands were made of feathers dusting ever closer to the sensitive swell of her breasts at her sides.

Her head was spinning. His hands forged havoc. His lips, ecstasy. Her pulse thundered, her breath barely kept up with the demands of his open-mouth kisses as their heads twisted and fought for the deepest angle.

Emotions churned and mixed inside and popped behind her eyes like fireworks and Ferris wheels.

So the pain, when it came totally ripped her out of the moment. She broke off, gasping and clutching at her side where Lawson's hand had strayed seconds before. She doubled over as the pain paralysed her breath.

'Oh, God!' Lawson removed his hand as if it had touched an electric fence. 'I'm so sorry,' he panted. 'I just…forgot. Are you okay? I'm so sorry.'

'It's okay,' she whispered, shutting her eyes, riding out the pain that sucked at her breath. They'd both been out of control, not thinking.

He sat on the lounge staring at her. Her nakedness didn't register—just the livid bruise. He could hear the pain he had caused catching in her breath. *Talk about the proverbial cold bucket of water!* What the hell had he been thinking? She was injured and he was pawing at her like a marauding teenager.

The pain easing, Vic straightened and took a step towards him and enfolded his head in her arms, urging it against her good side. He resisted for a second and then let her cradle him. 'It's okay, Lawson.' She stroked his hair. 'We were both a little…carried away.'

'I'm so sorry,' he whispered against her belly. Her skin was warm and smelled amazing, but he could see the bruise even more pronounced in the flicker of light from the television and he felt sick.

Vic nodded. 'I know. It's okay. We just have to be a little imaginative tonight, that's all.'

Lawson shut his eyes. *No, no, no.* This was insane. There were so many reasons why this was wrong, not least of all her injury. She needed him to look after her, pamper her, not take advantage of her on her father's couch.

It had been wrong of him to start it. But she'd sounded so hurt, had looked so bereft. Her anguish and tears had been too hard to take. After nearly losing her today, he had found her vulnerability unbearable.

But. Oh, God—what had they nearly done…?

She was his partner. Had he really been going to throw that to the wind for a night in her arms? Was a few hours of bliss going to be worth the fall-out? If they did this, then what next? Where was this heading? She had said it was just about tonight but would that ever be enough for them if they crossed that line? Would they want more?

He sure as hell would.

And how was that going to work? He being a single father with no room in his life for any relationship, never mind the type of relationship, that Victoria deserved. And what would that mean for her? She was about to embark on a great adventure. He didn't want to hold her back from that. She'd been counting down for the last year. He couldn't let her get distracted from her goal because of him.

Thank God the brakes had been applied and they could still salvage something out of the disaster. He moved out of her embrace and stood, finding their shirts. He handed hers to her and threw his back over his head.

She shook her head. 'Lawson? No.' He wouldn't leave her like this, would he? Aching for his touch? Taunted by the memory of how good his kiss had been, how his hands had felt like fire and ice on her skin?

'I think we need to look upon this as a good thing.'

'You're stopping?' She could hear the squeak in her voice and she knew later she'd regret not acting more sophisticatedly.

'Please, Victoria. Put your shirt on. Don't make this harder.' Her bruise was making him feel ill—how could he have forgotten about that? Forgotten, too, that they were partners and had to work together. Forgotten about Matilda being his number one priority. Forgotten that she was leaving.

Vic felt the bite of tears at the back of her eyes but refused to let them any further as she threw her shirt back on. She would not compound her humiliation by crying.

'This shouldn't have happened.'

Vic couldn't listen to whatever excuses he was going to drag out. She didn't want to hear him try to treat her like a child again when for the first time he had actually touched her and looked at her as a woman. She just wanted to run away and hide. Be left alone to lick her wounds.

'Damn right about that.' She injected as much disgust into her voice as she could muster—which happened to be a lot at this precise moment in time.

And then she walked out of the room and didn't stop until she'd reached the safety of hers. She shut the door and then locked it.

And as far as she was concerned, seventy days couldn't come fast enough.

CHAPTER SIX

IT HAD been five days since she'd seen Lawson when Vic arrived at the station for her first shift back at work since the incident in the cave. Her father had been furious and insisted she take a few sick days until her side was fully recovered. Which, given what had happened with Lawson, had suited her just fine.

She wasn't generally a coward, but that night in all its embarrassing glory had played in her head a thousand times and she didn't know if she could look Lawson in the eye.

He'd rung several times while she'd been away—not that she'd bothered to return his calls. She had to face him with as much nonchalance as she could muster and for that she'd needed a little distance. But with the bruise now a light yellowy-green and diminishing rapidly she couldn't put off the inevitable any longer.

She heard voices in the ambulance bay to her right as she entered the station for her night shift. She picked up her pager and wandered there first, her backpack slung over her shoulder, her heart tapping a frantic tattoo in her chest.

Lawson was checking the equipment in the van while chatting with Carl, one of the day-shift paramedics. Carl spotted her first. 'Hey, here she is,' he said. 'Our hero.'

Carl grinned at her and held up a copy of the local paper, the *Brindabella Gazette*. There, on the front page, was a huge splashy headline.

Local Paramedic Saves Family Pet From Flooding Cave.

On the front a picture of Vic with Annie, Pete and a plastered Bella.

Vic, avoiding Lawson's intense gaze, grinned back at Carl. The story had been big locally and the island paper had been right on it. In a place where the front headline usually involved the ant threat to the grass at the lawn bowls club or the rates hike at the caravan park, a local hero was breaking news.

She shrugged. 'All in a day's work.'

Carl nudged Lawson. 'Better watch she doesn't get a swollen head with all this publicity.'

Vic risked a quick glance in Lawson's direction and saw him give Carl a tight smile. 'Oh, I'll be watching her.'

Lawson's ominous tone sent a shiver right up her spine. *What exactly did he mean by that?*

'Anyways, I best be off,' Carl said, and bade them both a good night.

Which left the two of them facing each other with a wall of growing silence and the memory of the other night between them.

Lawson let his gaze roam over her face. His heart banged against his ribs and for the hundredth time he castigated himself for screwing everything up so resoundingly. He knew with utter certainty their relationship had irrevocably changed. And there was no going back.

'I've been trying to ring you.'

Vic looked at her boots. 'I know.'

'We need to talk.'

Vic nodded and raised her whiskey gaze to his turbulent grey one. She wanted to talk about as much as she wanted to drill a hole in her head. She didn't want to revisit the humiliation of the other night. Once had been bad enough. But he was right—they had to work together and they at least needed to clear the air.

She shrugged, reaching for the nonchalance she'd been practising all day. 'Okay, so let's talk.'

Lawson opened his mouth, but was interrupted by two pagers beeping into the cavernous space of the garage. He cursed under his breath and pulled the pager off his belt. 'D.I.B. Four-year-old. Query croup,' he read.

Vic nodded. It was that time of year. The seasons were changing and croup was more prevalent, particularly at night.

She threw her backpack on the garage floor near the wall. 'Let's go, then.' When a child had difficulty in breathing, parents understandably panicked. There was no time to hang around.

They were in the van and Lawson was driving them to their destination, lights flashing and sirens blaring, within thirty seconds. It was quiet inside the cab and Lawson glanced at his partner's profile. It was never quiet when she was around.

'Victoria.'

She turned to face him and shook her head. 'Not now, Lawson. We're two minutes out. After.'

The last thing she wanted to do was have this conversation all night in dribs and drabs, picking up the threads in between jobs. When they talked about it, she didn't want any interruptions. She wanted it over and done with in one fell swoop.

'Fine. But don't think you can put this off all night,' he warned.

Vic bristled. He sounded like a father talking to a petulant teenager, as if he were talking to Matilda. Hadn't she already well and truly proved she was an adult? A woman?

'Well, I guess that depends on the pager, doesn't it?' If he was going to treat her like a child she sure as hell could act like one.

They pulled up a couple of minutes later and could hear seal-like barking interrupting the cries of an obviously fractious child as they alighted the vehicle and made their way to the front door. A haggard-looking man, who introduced himself as Warren, ushered them inside down a long central hallway.

'He woke up with this terrible cough,' Warren said. 'He's been unwell for a couple of days now with a runny nose and a bit of a cough, but this is much worse.'

Lawson nodded. Without his having even laid eyes on their patient, the distinctive bark, the hallmark of what was medically known as laryngotracheobronchitis, had confirmed the diagnosis of croup. The history was also typical. A mild viral infection, more often than not the common cold, developing into an inflamed and irritated airway exacerbated by the cooler night air.

The hallway opened into a large lounge area. A young woman who looked to be barely in her twenties turned a tear-stained face to Vic.

'Hurry, please, he can't breathe. He can't breathe.'

Vic flicked a quick glance at Lawson. The little boy was most definitely breathing. He was coughing and crying fit to wake the entire neighbourhood. Unfortunately his cries were contributing to his airway irritation and making his mother more frantic, which, in turn, was making the child more upset. At the moment they were stuck in a vicious escalating cycle.

She moved forward. 'Hi. I'm Vic,' she said. 'And what's this little fella's name?' She placed her hand on the child's back and gave it a gentle rub.

'Jayden,' the mother said on a sob.

'Hi, Jayden,' Vic crooned, continuing the back rub. 'Jayden's doing fine,' she assured above the noise of the still-bawling, coughing little boy. 'I think he has a touch of croup and it sounds very scary but that's something called stridor, which is all part and parcel of croup. I know he's upset but he's very alert and pink—he's doing well.'

'Really?'

'Absolutely.' Vic nodded. 'What's your name?'

'Cindy.'

'Okay, Cindy. The most important thing we can do right now is try to get Jayden to stop crying and be calm. The more he cries, the more stress he puts on his airway. I think he senses that you're upset. Do you think he might come to me?'

Cindy's arms tightened around her son. 'I don't know.' She sniffed. 'He's usually happy to go to anybody but when he's sick…'

'Of course.' Vic nodded. 'Only Mum will do when you're feeling rotten.'

Cindy gave a watery smile. 'Something like that.'

'How about we try it? Pass him over and then Lawson and I can check him out.' She reached for the child and eased him out of Cindy's arms, hoping Jayden wouldn't protest further but ready to put him straight back if the move made him any more distressed. There was no point exacerbating his airway any more than it already was.

Jayden was still crying, but no more than he had been. For the moment. 'Maybe you can get him a nice cold drink of water,' Vic suggested. The water would help to soothe Jayden's inflamed throat and give Cindy a chance to collect herself. 'Has he had some paracetamol lately?'

Lawson pulled some equipment out of the pack he brought in, watching Victoria as she did her thing. She was Patient Care Officer tonight and doing a brilliant job. She really did have the touch with kids. But then, as she frequently pointed out, she would, wouldn't she?

It seemed such a shame that she'd vowed never ever to have children of her own. Sure, he understood why, but he couldn't help but feel she was cutting herself off from one of life's greatest adventures. Matilda had brought untold joy into his world and he knew he was a better man for her presence in his life.

Victoria rocked from foot to foot while flashing her

pen-light at Jayden a few times and waving it around to attract his attention. The little boy's cries fell to a grizzle as he reached for the torch. She gave it to him, talking calmly and gently, constantly rocking.

She nodded at Lawson and he moved closer with the hand-held sats monitor and stethoscope. He stood in front of her, the child between them, as he surreptitiously tried to place the probe on the child's toe. The immediate foot wiggle made application difficult and Lawson fixed it quickly while Victoria distracted the child.

She shifted her hands from his back next so one was cradling his bottom, the other his head, giving Lawson full access to listen to Jayden's chest. He placed the earpieces in his ears and lightly laid the bell against the child's singlet-clad back.

He shut his eyes and tuned into the air rushing in and out of the lungs rather than the transmitted noise from the patient's upper airway. He moved it around instinctively, quickly assessing all the lung fields, deeming them clear.

He opened his eyes again to find Victoria looking at him with her whiskey gaze. She had her chin on top of Jayden's head, the child's wispy hair feathering against her face, still rocking. Their gazes locked. It reminded him of the times she'd held Matilda like this when she'd been littler. His daughter's chest snuggled into hers as Victoria swayed and hummed.

An odd thought whammied him from nowhere. What would a child of hers look like? Of theirs look like? What kind of a child would they have together? Would it have her auburn hair and olive colouring or his darker genes? Would it look like Matilda or the twins?

'How does he sound?'

Lawson blinked. He could see her lips moving but it took a second or two for the words to reach through his stunned thought processes. 'All clear.'

The beeping of the sats monitor caught her attention and Vic dragged her gaze from his. For a second his stare had been so intense it had transported her right back to the other night.

'Ninety-two per cent,' she murmured. Not awful. Not great. But at least, with Jayden having settled they were finally able to get a good trace and an accurate reading.

Cindy returned with some water and a syringe containing some clear liquid. Vic smiled at her. She'd obviously washed her face and was looking much more in control.

'He sounds a lot better, thank you.' Cindy smiled. 'I was so worried. His breathing was so loud.'

Vic nodded. Jayden's airway noise had settled but he was still sporting a decent inspiratory stridor, which was a bit of a worry now he was calm and at rest, especially as his sats were on the lower end of normal.

'How about I sit down here, little buddy, and Mummy can give you some medicine?' Vic parked herself on the lounge chair behind.

Lawson watched as Jayden clung to Victoria's front on the way down like a baby monkey and then sat on her lap, one hand still firmly attached to the torch, the other bunching up the material of her overalls.

He'd managed to pull the fabric aside slightly, flashing Lawson an enticing glimpse of cleavage. Lawson was mesmerised for a second before pulling himself back into line. He turned away disgusted at himself. *He was at work, damn it. She was his colleague—his partner.*

Wasn't it enough that he'd spent the last five days fluctuating between self-loathing and arousal thinking about her and her damn cleavage? That his dreams had been laced with the memory of her mouth, her smell, the taste of her skin?

He'd been afraid this was going to happen because the truth was they'd overstepped a mark and there was no going back.

Jayden barked again like a seal and Lawson pulled himself together. Their patient's airway, already small enough owing to his age, was inflamed, and that was what he should be concentrating on. Not Victoria. Not how close he'd come to dragging her down on the couch with him and succumbing to crazy.

He forced himself to kneel in front of the chair where Victoria was sitting with Jayden. Ignoring her and the proximity of her still-half-exposed cleavage, he smiled at the little boy, inspecting his face closely, noticing the slight nasal flaring.

'Whatcha got there, matey?' Jayden flashed the torch at him. 'Ooh, you got the spotlight? You're the man.' He gently lifted Jayden's singlet and looked to see if the little boy was using any of his accessory muscles to help him breathe. There didn't appear to be any recession of his intercostal spaces or any retraction of his sternum.

He turned to Warren and Cindy. 'I think, just to be sure, we should transport Jayden to hospital where they can monitor him for the night. He still has quite an obvious stridor. I'd like to give him a special nebuliser for that on the way to hospital. It helps to reduce the swelling in his airway and should improve that noise we can hear when he breathes in.'

As an intensive care paramedic Lawson was licensed to administer an adrenaline neb, which should have an immediate impact on Jayden's stridor. Given in an inhaled dose, adrenaline acted locally on the irritated tissues of the larynx and airway to decrease the inflammation.

Cindy clutched her husband's hand. 'I thought he was better.'

Lawson heard the edge of panic return to her voice and nodded calmly. 'He's sounding better now he's settled, but his airway is still inflamed and it can be a long night. I'd feel happier if he was seen by a doctor. I think he may need some special medicine called a steroid, which will also help with the stridor, that they can give him there.'

Warren squeezed his wife's hand. 'It's okay, darl. Better safe then sorry, huh?'

Tears filled Cindy's eyes. 'Can I go with him?'

'Of course,' Vic hurried to assure the fragile, young mother. 'We put you on the trolley and him on your lap and strap you both in.'

Cindy sniffed. 'Okay, then. I'll just go and throw a few things in a bag.'

Five minutes later, with Cindy and Jayden secured on the stretcher in the back of the ambulance, Vic started up the ambulance. Lawson, who'd taken over as Patient Care Officer to administer the adrenaline, applied the paediatric nebuliser mask to his little patient's face as Vic pulled into the street.

Vic heard the little boy's protests at the confines of the mask and the noise made by the flow of oxygen. She could hear Lawson's low murmurings as he distracted and cajoled Jayden into keeping the mask on, and she adjusted her rear-view mirror so she could surreptitiously watch him in action.

For a guy who was an enigma most of the time he could certainly be animated when he wanted to be. She'd seen that in his interactions with Matilda and now with Jayden. He was rarely that way with her and she'd known him for ever. She watched as he handed over his pen to the little boy and the notebook he kept in his breast pocket. A grin split his face as Jayden obviously took to the offering with gusto.

Lawson really was a sight to behold when he smiled. The neutrality of his features was totally transformed. The craggy planes softened, the tautness disappeared, the grey of his gaze changed from watchful to warm. He looked relaxed and at ease. And very, very desirable.

Lawson's gaze met hers in the rear-view mirror. The smile he'd been sharing with Cindy died a quick death and a shutter came down as the watchfulness returned. Vic looked away, concentrating on the road, his need to hide himself from her hurting more than his rejection.

Lawson looked away too. He'd managed to forget about their indiscretion for a few minutes as he'd focused on Jayden, but it all came crashing back again. Her mouth, the huskiness of her voice, how her naked breasts had felt against his chest. How could they work together when every time he looked at her all he could think about was the perfection of her body?

He was a professional, for God's sake. So was she. And she deserved to be treated like one. Not as some object of desire. Up until recent months in their working relationship he'd thought of her as a paramedic first and a woman second. Which was as it should be. But he knew he couldn't go back now.

He was always going to see her as a woman first.

It actually ended up being past midnight by the time they got back to the station. A baby post-ictal from a febrile convulsion, an overdose of sleeping tablets and a suspected stroke kept them on the hop transporting all three patients to the mainland hospital.

Lawson made her a cup of coffee and plonked it down in front of her at the staffroom table. He pulled up a chair opposite and sat. 'Before I leave in the morning I'm going to request a new partner.'

Vic was so startled she sloshed her coffee all over the table. 'What?' Whatever she'd been expecting, it hadn't been this.

'I think you heard me the first time.'

'But…why?' she spluttered. Their personal stuff aside, she didn't want to work with anyone else.

Lawson shot her an impatient look. 'I would have thought that was obvious.'

'I think that's a slight overreaction, Lawson.'

'Victoria. We almost slept together.'

Vic felt heat rise in her face. '*Almost* being the operative word.'

Lawson pushed back his chair and stood up. 'Victoria, do you think the degree matters?'

Well, obviously not to him. But it sure as hell mattered to her. Being left high and dry in a highly aroused state mattered a lot. Her body had ached, throbbed, for him ever since. Her dreams had been haunted by their kisses and she'd woken each morning with a fire roaring out of control deep down low. Even looking at him now at his most distant and forbidding she wanted to reach out and touch.

She took a steadying breath. 'I think it does if you're talking about busting up a highly successful team, especially when we've only got sixty-five days remaining until we split anyway.'

'Maybe now's the perfect opportunity for it. I was always going to get a new partner when you left anyway. This will just be moving it forward slightly. Give me an adjustment time.'

'And what the hell do I do for the last couple of months while you're adjusting? It makes no sense for me to be partnered with someone new for such a short period of time and you know it.'

Lawson sighed. He did know it. 'Yes, you're right. But what happened between us changes everything, Victoria. It was wrong. I should never have let it get out of hand. It was a mistake.'

Inexplicably, the barb hurt and she clutched her mug hard while she took a moment to recover from its impact. A moment in which she realised that was what all this was about. Lawson Dunlop didn't make mistakes. Not since he'd been sixteen and a mistake had nearly killed him. All she was going to be from now on was a painful reminder of their indiscretion. Their *mistake*. Day after day.

'Well, guess what? We're grown-ups. And grown-ups just have to live with their *mistakes* and get on with it.'

Lawson shut his eyes and turned away from her. He wandered over to the window that overlooked a large parkland area. 'You don't get it.'

Vic watched the breadth of his shoulders. Admired the way his overalls fitted glove-like around his magnificent physique. Framed against the window, he looked such a lonely figure and she was standing before she knew it, her feet moving towards him before she could question the wisdom of it.

She drew level with him, her hands wrapped around her mug. She looked out over the view for a moment or two, took a sip of her coffee and said, 'So explain it to me.'

'Do you know what I was thinking about tonight at every job we did?'

She glanced at his stern profile, his jaw clenching reflexively. 'I'm guessing it wasn't D,R,A,B,C?'

Lawson gave a half-smile at her attempt to lighten the mood. Then the reality of what he had been thinking about returned. He daredn't look at her as he gathered the courage to be frank.

'I was thinking about your kiss, and your smell and the way you make that moaning noise at the back of your throat when you're turned on and how perfect your breasts are and how much I wished I hadn't been noble and just lay you on the couch and had my way with you.'

Vic felt heat flare from her toes and scorch a path right up to her face. She gripped the mug hard, clamping her lips together as a moan fought to escape. His words stoked the fire that had been smouldering since he'd rejected her the other night.

She swallowed. 'Oh.'

Lawson nodded grimly. 'Yes. Oh.' He turned to face her and put his hands on her shoulders, holding them firmly. 'Even now I want to push you hard against this window and kiss you until you're moaning into my mouth.'

Catching his breath with difficulty, Lawson let go of her shoulders, and turned back to face the view again, firmly crossing his arms across his chest.

Vic reached for the window sill as she swayed forward when he released her. She wanted to kiss him so badly now everything in front of her was a red haze. She was trembling and her pelvic floor responded shamelessly to his blatant description.

'I can't afford to be thinking about this on the job, Victoria. Putting aside the whole other issue of our long association and how it impacts that, it's just not appropriate. Not when I should be thinking about things like danger and the ABCs. It's not safe. I should be focusing on what I'm doing, not on what you look like out of your uniform.'

He was right. She knew he was. But his husky voice was taking her back, trailing verbal fingers over her skin like the silken caress of cobwebs.

With a mammoth effort she pulled her mind away from the contractions of her internal muscles to the most pressing issue coming from his decree. 'How exactly are you going to explain that to my father?'

Lawson sighed. Victoria had put her finger directly on the problem. Bob Dunleavy, his old mentor and dear friend, wasn't going to be fooled by any old explanation.

'Are you going to tell him we made out? On his couch?'

Lawson hadn't quite figured that out yet. He didn't know how to tell Bob, the man who'd shown him how to be a man, that he'd been fooling around with his daughter. The daughter Bob had entrusted him with.

From the minute Victoria had taken an interest in the opposite sex, Bob had wanted all of them dead. And while he might not have been a horny teenager after only one thing, he wasn't sure Bob would see the difference.

And he didn't think he could bear to see the disappointment in the older man's eyes. Bob's faith and trust in him meant a lot to Lawson. Bob Dunleavy had been more of a role model to him than his own father had ever been. He didn't want to lose the man's respect. Losing his own had been bad enough.

'He won't be happy about splitting us up and you know it, Lawson. Unless you're prepared to tell him the truth, he's not likely to even agree. Not with my departure so close.'

Lawson nodded. Unfortunately Victoria was right.

But he didn't see any way out of it. He owed Bob one-hundred-per-cent honesty. 'Then it looks like he gets the truth.'

Vic screwed her face up, not quite believing what she was hearing. 'Are you kidding? He'll have apoplexy,' she spluttered. 'His blood pressure will hit the roof and he'll probably stroke out.'

While Bob was hardly the healthiest specimen of manhood, Lawson did feel that was a slight exaggeration. 'I'm not going to lie to him, Victoria.'

Vic put her hand on his arm. 'I don't want my father knowing my personal business.'

'When we crossed the line, we made it his business.' He turned away from the window and moved back to the table, her hand falling away.

Vic looked out of the window for a moment as a helpless feeling of things spinning out of control enveloped her. She couldn't believe that only five days ago her life had been on track. Now a whole other dazzling world had been opened up to her for a brief moment and then the door had been firmly shut in her face again and things just weren't the same since.

She needed to get back control.

Vic straightened her spine and marched back to the table. 'I don't want to be palmed off to a new partner in my last two months at the station. Let's make a pact.' She stuck her hand out. 'Let's agree to pretend what happened didn't. Let's go back to what we were before. Strictly partners.'

Lawson glanced at her hand, then up into her face. He shook his head. The memory of what happened the other night was going to fuel his dreams till the day he died. 'That's what I've been trying to say. There's a thing between us now. Our relationship has changed irretrievably. We can't go back. What happened the other night…that's all we'll be able to think about while we're out there.'

Vic left her hand out. 'Speak for yourself,' she said calmly. 'I'm a professional. Taught by you. Another professional. I hide lots of things on the job. My distaste for men who assault women. My annoyance with people who ring up for an ambulance who just need a Band-Aid. My dislike of Saturday-night drunks. We can do this. I know we can.'

'Victoria.'

The exasperation in his voice was mildly arousing and she quashed the thought as further proof she could put this stuff between them aside. She pulled up a chair beside him and placed her hand on his forearm. She looked into his eyes even though she felt too exposed.

'Please, Lawson. I don't want to have to spend the next two months with someone I don't respect as much as you or having to explain to all and sundry why we're not partners any more.' *Least of all her father.*

Lawson could feel himself wavering. This close he could smell the same perfume she wore the other night and it triggered another potent memory.

'Come on, Lawson, all we have to do is make a concerted effort. Yes, it'll probably be awkward at first but we've got twenty years of history between us before this.' God knew, she'd kept her crush a secret for all that time. 'All I'm asking is that you put up with me for another two months. Compartmentalise what happened and lock it somewhere at the back of your head. That's what I'm going to do. You're a strong person, Lawson. If anyone can do it, you can.'

He was strong. He knew that and, sure, she was probably right, he could do it. But what if he didn't want to? With a new partner he wouldn't have to compartmentalise anything and when she left for distant shores in a couple of months what was in his head wouldn't matter.

'I've never asked you for any special favours or considerations. Ever. But I am asking for this.'

That was true—she hadn't. She'd taken what he'd thrown at her and never questioned him or shirked her responsibilities on the job. She'd been an excellent paramedic and a perfect partner. 'Okay.' He moved his arm so hers slipped off.

Vic grinned at him on a surge of relief. 'Oh, thank you. Thank you so much.'

'But at the first sign this isn't working, for either of us, I'm pulling the plug.'

Vic nodded wildly. 'It'll work. I promise.'

Lawson wasn't so sure as she leapt from her seat to make them another coffee and his gaze travelled straight to the contours of her butt.

It had only been a few seconds and already he was compartmentalising like crazy.

CHAPTER SEVEN

'HEY, Vic, how many days now?'

Vic smiled at Carl and his partner, who were vacating the lunch table as they sat down. It was the first time she'd seen the other team working the same shift with them. She and Lawson had been called to an incident as soon as they'd come on so there'd been no time to chat with the other crew.

'Thirty.' She grinned. Even though all the excitement had gone for her. It was more about relief now. Only thirty more days to put up with the polite civility that had become her relationship with Lawson.

'Where are you off to?' she asked, her heart sinking that she would be left alone with Lawson. She'd been hoping for a buffer.

'To the nursing home. Ninety-year-old female, suspected fractured neck of femur.'

'You guys going to the pub after work tonight?' she asked hopefully. It was a weekly ritual, one that Vic had quickly embraced. Being the only female at the station, she'd felt the need to integrate. To be one of the boys.

'Sure.' Carl nodded. 'It's Saturday, isn't it? You want to join us?'

She slid a glance Lawson's way. He was munching on a sandwich, reading the paper. 'Why not?'

'Lawson?' Carl asked.

'No, thanks.' Being a single father made it hard to socialise. But his daughter had always come first and as far as Lawson was concerned it was no sacrifice.

Vic felt her mouth tighten as Lawson didn't even bother to look up from the paper. Given that he rarely joined them it was no surprise, but he could have at least acknowledged Carl.

The other crew left and Vic went to the fridge and retrieved her lunch. She sat opposite Lawson, who didn't look up when she joined him. She reached for the latest gazette that was on the table and feigned interest in it.

The last month had been difficult. More difficult than she'd first appreciated. Compartmentalising was easy for her—she'd had five years of practice with her crush. But it obviously hadn't been so simple for Lawson. He'd become distant—emphasising his already famous reserve further—and businesslike, careful not to share any of himself other than what was required from him professionally.

They didn't venture out of the station during their breaks to eat somewhere picturesque and interesting anymore. Eating at the station usually guaranteed someone was around. They didn't hang out with Matilda in the afternoons if the pager allowed. He hadn't asked her to babysit.

In fact anything that put them alone together any more

than necessary he'd avoided like the plague. When she'd ventured a complaint a few weeks back he'd given her a direct look and said it was the way it had to be. He'd sounded so detached she lost the nerve to push him further.

Her father had noticed the difference in Lawson and had asked her if everything was okay. Vic had assured him everything was fine and hoped her father hadn't detected the flush to her cheeks at the blatant lie.

'You're going out with Carl?'

Vic stopped eating mid-chew. It was so rare for him to address her these days other than the minimum required during cases she almost fell off her chair. He hadn't looked up from the paper but he'd still initiated a conversation. A non-work-related one to boot. 'Sure.'

Lawson had been battling with himself to stay quiet. He'd read the same sentence in the paper about fifty times. Who Victoria chose to go out with was none of his business. *But Carl*? 'You do know Carl is an incorrigible flirt? He prefers to play the field.'

Vic gaped at him. *What the hell did he care*? 'So?'

Her dismissal grated. Was that what she wanted? Did she want to make a fool of herself with Casanova Carl in her last weeks on the island? The thought of Victoria letting the other man touch her made him want to break things. In London, she could do what she wanted—he wouldn't have to see it or hear about it. Could he bear to watch it right beneath his nose?

Lawson shrugged with what he hoped was nonchalance as he concentrated on the print in front of him. 'I didn't think you were that kind of girl.'

Vic felt an eruption of suppressed emotions from the

last month explode inside her. She narrowed her eyes and snatched the paper out of his grasp. 'What kind of girl?'

Forced to look up, Lawson was surprised to see the fire in her whiskey gaze. 'To let a bit of flirting go to your head.'

'I'm young and single, Lawson,' she goaded. 'It's supposed to go to my head.'

'Yes, but Carl is only likely to offer you a quick fling.'

'Well, maybe I need a quick fling, Lawson. Personally I think I'm ripe for one.' God knew, she was so frustrated she could scream.

Lawson felt her comment punch him low in the gut. If she was ripe it was because he'd primed her and he was damned if Carl was going to benefit. 'I just think it's a bad idea to get involved with a colleague'

Vic felt an irrational urge to launch herself at him. Whether it would end up with her shaking him senseless or kissing his lips off, she wasn't entirely sure. All she knew was she trembled just below her skin with a suppressed emotion that she didn't want to examine too closely.

'So, let me get this straight,' she said, breathing slow and deep to stop from screeching like an irrational female. 'You don't want me, but you don't want Carl to want me either?'

God. Lawson cringed inside. It sounded totally screwy. But she was right. Carl. Some random guy on a job. The entire male population of the British Isles. He wasn't particularly fussy. *Jeez. What was wrong with him*?

One thing he knew for sure: this conversation had fraught written all over it and he needed to back away.

Should never have let the green-eyed monster goad him into starting it in the first place. 'I think this is a totally inappropriate conversation to be having at work.'

The steam finally found an escape and she leapt to her feet, her chair scraping back and falling to clatter on the ground behind her. 'Damn it, Lawson. Don't do this. Don't retreat on me now. Answer the bloody question.'

Lawson was surprised at her outburst. She'd seemed so calm over the last month, coping much better with their mutually agreed upon amnesia than he had. He knew he'd been a total pain in the butt and his forced reserve had both annoyed and hurt her. But it was the only way he could deal with what had happened between them and continue to work together.

Their pagers beeped and he'd never been more grateful to hear the noise in his life. *Saved by the bell.*

'Damn it!' Vic swore as she wrenched hers off her belt and contemplated throwing it across the room.

'Fifty-six-year-old male. Central chest pain, diaphoretic, S.O.B. Query M.I.'

Vic followed the message with her own gaze as Lawson read it off. She got to the address and map coordinates, the small printing leaping out at her. She looked at him dazedly. 'That's my place.'

Lawson frowned and scrolled down to the address. Yes, it was. He looked at her. 'Let's go.'

Vic, unable to move, stared at the message. Her father? Could her father be having a heart attack?

'Victoria!'

Lawson's voice cracked across the room, yanking her out of her paralysis, and she scurried after him, a host of awful scenarios tumbling through her brain. She climbed in the truck and buckled up as Lawson screeched out of the garage. She pulled her mobile off her belt and her fingers shook as she punched in her home number.

She chewed on her bottom lip as she waited for it to pick up. 'It's not answering.'

'Who's home?'

'Just Josh. Ryan's out with some mates.'

Lawson groaned. Ryan would have been more likely to keep it together than sensitive Josh. 'He probably doesn't want to leave your father to answer the phone,' Lawson assured her.

Vic nodded. 'I guess.' She pushed the end button. A rush of emotion swelled in her chest. Could her father really be having a heart attack? Pictures of patients they'd lost on scene to myocardial infarction flicked through her head.

She turned to Lawson. 'Oh, God, what if…?' She stopped, her voice cracking.

'No.' Lawson shook his head and gave her a hard look before returning his gaze to the road. 'Don't go there, Victoria. I'm going to need you. When we get there, I'm going to need you. If he is having an M.I., I don't need to tell you how critical that makes him or all the things that can go wrong. I'm going to call for back-up but until then it's going to be just you and me and, I'm sorry, you don't get to be a daughter right now. You're going to have to be strong for Josh and I'm going to need you to help me save his life.'

Vic blanched, shying from his demands. She couldn't

do what he was asking of her. She couldn't. Just thinking about what might greet them was causing a massive lump in her throat. She didn't want to see her father grey and in pain. 'But...'

Lawson shook his head again. 'No buts.' He gave her hand a quick squeeze. 'You can do this. You've done it a hundred times. I need you. Your dad needs you.'

Vic swallowed past the painful lump of emotion that was battling to find an outlet. It hurt and her eyes burned. She sucked in a breath and nodded. 'Okay.'

Lawson waited for her affirmation and immediately radioed Coms. 'Coms this is nine six zero. Please note the patient to which we have been sent is Bob Dunleavy, OIC of Brindabella Station. Am responding with Victoria Dunleavy. Please send back-up ASAP.'

Lawson knew the coms centre would be able to read between the lines. One of their own was down and his daughter was having to attend. He knew they'd send every resource available.

Josh, who had obviously heard the siren, was waiting at the door when Lawson pulled into the drive. Victoria didn't even wait for the van to fully stop before jumping from the vehicle and running to her brother.

Josh's face crumpled. 'Vic, he's bad.'

She gave him a fierce hug, wishing she could make it all better for him as she could when he'd been little. 'It's okay, Joshy, we're here now.' She caught his hand and dragged him inside with her.

'Dad?'

He was on the couch and Victoria gasped as she crouched beside him and reached for his hand. It was cool and clammy against the warmth and dryness of hers and her anxiety increased another notch. He looked exactly like every heart-attack patient she'd ever known: grey, perspiration running down his face, rubbing at his chest.

'Lawson,' she called, trying to keep the panic out of her voice as she smiled at her father.

'He's going to be all right? Isn't he, Vic?'

'Of course…going to be…fine,' Bob puffed and sent his son a weak smile.

'Don't talk, Dad,' Vic murmured as Lawson entered laden with equipment.

'Bob,' he said. 'Always wanting to be the centre of attention.'

Bob gave a half-smile. 'Got some GTN?'

Lawson nodded. 'Absolutely.' Giving the drug used to dilate coronary arteries was governed by strict protocols but he wasn't about to question his old mentor's clinical judgement. If anyone knew what having an M.I. looked like it was Bob. And the evidence of his own eyes confirmed the diagnosis. If Bob Dunleavy weren't having a cardiac event, he'd give up his stripes.

'Hook him up,' he said to Victoria as he reached for the medication pack.

Vic felt all fingers and thumbs as she went through the motions she could usually do with her eyes shut. But sticking dots to her father's chest was so much more personal. Watching as the ECG trace revealed massive ST elevation, indicating cardiac ischaemia, was utterly sickening.

Placing an oxygen mask, wrapping a cuff around his arm and taking his blood pressure, putting a sats peg on his finger, witnessing Lawson spray the GTN under his tongue—it was all too close.

She could hear Josh's low whimpering in the background and it tore at her professional veneer. She was the big sister—she fixed things; she'd always fixed things. From homework to a disappointing test result, from a severed finger to a falling out with a friend. But she didn't know if she could fix this.

Lawson viewed the monitor with a sinking feeling. Bob was in trouble. They needed to get him to hospital ASAP. He needed a special drug to help dissolve the blockage that was restricting his coronary blood flow and he'd probably need some kind of surgical intervention.

He gave Bob an aspirin to chew. 'I'll get the trolley, Bob. We need to get you to hospital.'

Bob, too short of breath to talk effusively, just nodded and said, 'Hurry.'

Vic felt her father's plea slam straight into her gut. She squeezed her father's hand and said, 'It's okay, Dad. We got you now. We're not going to let anything happen to you.'

Her father smiled at her, squeezed her hand and then grimaced as a loud moan tore from his throat.

'Dad!' Josh's voice cracked with emotion as Bob clutched at his chest.

Vic's own heart hammered in her chest as she watched the trace on the ECG deteriorate into VF. 'Get Lawson,' she instructed her brother as her father slumped forward. 'Now.'

Josh ran as instinct came over Vic and she pushed her father back, delivering a pre-cordial thump directly to the centre of his chest. The monitor rhythm remained unchanged and for a second she let helplessness engulf her.

'Victoria! Get him on the ground.'

She looked up to see Lawson striding towards her and it was just the slap in the face she needed. She leapt to her feet and grabbed his legs at the same time Lawson reached them and he grabbed Bob's torso and they lowered him to the ground.

Lawson depressed the button on his radio. 'Coms, this is nine six zero, CPR in progress.' He took his finger off. 'Josh, move the coffee table. Give us some room. Victoria, do compressions while I hook him up to the defibrillator.'

Victoria didn't even hesitate, just responded to his commands as she always did on the job. She put her hands in the centre of her father's chest and pushed down rhythmically as she'd done a hundred times before. She tuned out Josh, who was now sobbing, tuned out whose flesh it was beneath the flats of her palms, and counted.

But as she shifted her hands to allow for Lawson to place the defib pads she made the fatal mistake of looking down, seeing her father's still, grey face looking back at her, his mouth slack beneath the mask and pulling into a grimace with every downward pump to his chest.

'Come on, Dad,' she whispered, feeling a pressure behind her eyes that was burning unbearably. 'Come on!' Louder this time, more insistent.

'Stand clear,' Lawson demanded, and again she reacted automatically, removing her hands and putting the required distance between her and the electrical current.

Lawson noted the trace on the monitor was still VF. 'Coms, this is nine six zero, defibrillation in progress,' he said into the radio as he pushed the button to deliver three hundred joules to Bob's heart. He held his breath, but when the trace on the monitor returned it was still VF.

'Go again, Victoria,' he instructed as he recharged the machine.

He noticed the silent tears streaming down her face as she pumped at her father's chest and it was like a knife to his gut. He could hear Josh, who had totally lost it behind him. He wanted to pull both of them into his arms and tell them it was going to be okay. But he didn't know if it was and he couldn't be the person they needed him to be if he succumbed to the emotion of the moment.

Seeing one of his oldest friends in such bad shape was shocking, but he couldn't go there. He had to succeed. He had to keep it together for Victoria and Josh. He would not think about losing Bob, about not being able to revive him. He had to detach himself from the situation. This wasn't Bob his friend and mentor. This was just another patient. Just another resus.

'Damn it, Dad,' Victoria puffed as she pounded on his chest. 'Don't do this to us. We need you.' Her voice cracked and she didn't know how much longer she could hold it together.

Lawson blocked out the emotion fracturing her voice. 'Stand clear again.'

Vic ceased the compressions and sat back on her haunches. She looked up at Josh, who was a blubbering mess, and wanted nothing more than to go to him.

But she couldn't, not now. She didn't know how much longer she'd need to do this for, but she knew it was her father's only chance. And she'd already lost her mother way too early—damned if she was going to lose her dad before his three score years and ten.

Lawson heard a siren in the distance as he flicked the discharge switch again and prayed it was the cavalry. Victoria needed to be the daughter and be with Josh. This time the joules managed to shock the damaged heart back into a sinus tachycardia and Bob stirred immediately.

'Dad!' Vic sobbed his name as she threw herself against his chest. 'Thank God.'

Bob, weak and confused, raised his arm to pat his daughter on the shoulder. 'It's okay,' he whispered.

Vic felt an absurd urge to burst into tears and stay right were she was, safe in her father's arms, as she'd done a hundred times as a girl. But right now her father needed to lean on her and she had to rise to that occasion.

And then another crew entered the house and when she looked up she saw Carl smiling down at her, easing her away, directing her to Josh. She reached for her brother and they both cried together as Lawson and Carl lifted their deathly ill father onto the trolley and then transported him to the ambulance.

'Don't even think I'm not sitting in back with you,' she said as Lawson clicked the gurney in place.

Any other person he would have said no to. But he didn't have the strength to say it to her pale, distraught face. He just nodded and waited for her to strap herself in before he took his position next to Bob. Josh rode up front with Carl and with lights and sirens going they made it to the mainland hospital in twelve minutes.

The next two days passed in a total blur for the Dunleavys. Bob was admitted to the coronary care unit, where he had thrombolytic treatment to dissolve the clot that was causing his tissue ischaemia and underwent an angiogram to ascertain the damage. During this procedure he had placement of three stents in his three partially blocked coronary arteries.

Vic and the twins lived at the hospital, dozing in the relatives' lounge at night curled up on hard chairs. Lawson stayed with them. He'd arranged for time off for them both and for their shifts to be covered from HQ as well as a replacement for Bob. He organised Dorothy to be with Matilda so he could stay by their sides. He was their gofer, bringing them food and drink regularly, and their chauffeur, shuffling them back and forth between the island and the hospital.

Vic was grateful for his presence. In fact, she was in such a daze, going through the motions, putting on a brave face for her brothers and assuring her father she was coping, that she didn't even question it. He was just there, good old Lawson, as he'd always been, and she leant on him unashamedly.

All their recent baggage faded into insignificance. After a month of trying to avoid what had happened between them it finally became a non-issue. The tension between them oozed into nothingness and it was like it used to be. Lawson there, as always, in the background.

* * *

After four days in CCU, Bob was moved to a ward and Vic finally relaxed a little. They spent their first night at home in their own beds and Vic was able to send Lawson home to his daughter. She slept like a rock that night stretched out in her bed after four nights of minimal sleep scrunched in a chair.

After two more days on the ward her father was looking very well and had even lost a few kilos. He was back to his chipper self, joking with the nurses and winning their favour with a bottomless box of chocolates that never found their way past his lips. He was eager to get out, co-operating with the physio and impressing the dietician with his knowledge of good nutrition.

Still, Vic was nervous about him coming home. He was raring to get back to work whereas she'd been hoping he might retire. High blood pressure and being overweight had been the main factors in his heart attack, but stress had also contributed and being an OIC of a station was about as stressful as it got.

And she was going to have to postpone her trip. She wasn't sure what that meant for Lawson and her and, in truth, that was low down on her list of things to worry about. She couldn't leave with her father still in the recovery phase of his heart attack. He needed her. And so did the boys. She'd thought she'd be disappointed but nothing was more important to her than her father's recovery. London would still be there in a few months' time.

Vic came in after the afternoon rest period to visit her father. He was expecting the doctor any minute and she wanted to talk to him about his future. 'Dad, I think we need to talk. About what happens next.'

Bob kissed his daughter's cheek. 'We most certainly do, my lovely.'

Vic frowned. That was easy. She'd expected him to wave aside any attempts to talk to him about his future.

'I think you should retire.'

Bob laughed and gave her hand a squeeze. 'Oh, my dear girl, I do love you, but I'm not retiring. I'll take the full six weeks off, I'll walk every morning, I'll change my diet and I'm going to drop to part-time, but I'm not leaving the job.'

'But what about the stress, Dad? The understaffing and the rosters and the skill mix?'

'Part-time will help reduce that load considerably.'

'I don't know, Dad…'

'Sweetie, I've only ever wanted to be two things. A father and a paramedic. And I'm not ready to give up on either of them. Not yet.'

'Oh.' She didn't know what to say. Her father had obviously been thinking about the future and had most definitely made up his mind. It wasn't what she'd hoped for but at least he was thinking about lifestyle changes and it was a good compromise.

'Now. Let's talk about your future.'

'It's fine, Dad,' she dismissed. 'I've already postponed the air ticket.'

Bob frowned. 'I certainly hope you didn't,' he said. 'You've been looking forward to this trip for a year. Go and get it changed back.' Bob looked at his watch. 'You have a couple of hours before the travel agent closes.'

Vic shook her head. 'No, Dad. I'm not going to take off to the other side of the world when you've just had a heart attack.'

'Vic, you deserve this. You've given up so much of your life to help me with your brothers. And now the boys are grown and it's your time. You have to do this.'

She noticed the worry lines around her father's eyes and mouth and didn't want to upset him. 'London will still be there in a couple of months.'

'Do you know what your mother said to me just before she died? She said, "Help Victoria be the person she wants to be."'

Vic felt that whammy hit her chest and clutched her father's hand. 'And I will. I just want to see you through this time, Dad.'

'I'll be fine,' he said gruffly.

'I think the boys would prefer it if I stayed for a bit longer.'

'Victoria,' Bob said sternly. 'They're not boys any longer, they're men.' Vic raised an eyebrow at him. 'The shoe incident aside,' he clarified. 'They have to stop relying on you to wipe their noses and pack their lunches. They'll be fine.'

'And what if you—?' She stopped. She didn't want to entertain the thought that her father would have another heart attack, but his grey face was indelibly printed on her retinas.

'If I have another M.I.? Well, let's just say that I've had a very big wake-up call and I don't plan to, *but,* Vic, it can happen any time whether you're here or there. It could happen while you're on a night shift or away visiting your aunt at Noosa or at the emergency care convention you go to every year. It could happen in ten years' time.'

Vic blanched. 'Gee, thanks, Dad. I think I can dream up enough scenarios without you giving me any more.'

'My point is there aren't any guarantees in life. You and I both know that already with your mum.' He gave her hand a squeeze. 'You can't hang around indefinitely just in case.'

She sighed. 'Look, I promise I'm just talking until you start back at work and you're coping okay.'

Bob shook his head. 'I'm not happy about this.'

'You think I'll be able to enjoy London if I'm fretting about you?'

Bob conceded the point. He smiled at her. 'We're a fine pair, aren't we?'

'I'll get there, Dad. I promise.'

'You'd better.' He pulled her forward into a bear hug. 'Otherwise I'll just have to sack you.'

Two weeks later, Vic was really happy with how her father was progressing. She'd organised a schedule with the twins so between them all he was never alone in the house. He'd managed to organise a staggered return to work in four weeks and she'd made sure she was rostered on the same days as him to ensure he wasn't overdoing it.

'What you watching, Dad?' she asked as she plonked herself down next to him on the couch. She realised as she did so she hadn't thought about what had nearly happened on it for what seemed like ages. The whole incident with Lawson might have been a million years ago now.

Bob looked down at his daughter. 'A documentary on the life cycle of the silkworm.'

Vic nodded enthusiastically even though the thought of watching another doco was enough to make her scream. But they were her father's favourite and she wanted to spend as much time with him as possible so silkworms it was. 'Sounds great.'

Bob frowned, grabbed the remote and muted the television. 'Victoria Dunleavy, for goodness' sake, get out of this house. It's your day off and you've been hanging around me like a blowfly all day. It's Saturday night. You're young. Go join the crew at the pub. Or meet a friend. I'm fine.'

'Dad, it's okay. I want to spend time with you.'

Bob ignored her and reached into his pocket for his mobile phone. 'What's Brenda's number.'

Vic grabbed the phone. 'I don't need you to make a play date for me.'

'Then go,' he said. 'Quick sticks. Get on your glad rags. Go have some fun. Ryan and Josh are both here.'

Vic wavered. It had been a while since she'd been out for anything other than work and she was starting to get a little cabin fever.

Bob could see her weakening. 'Please, sweetie, I hate seeing you lock yourself away in here. I worry about you.'

Vic started. The last thing she wanted was her father fretting about her. He was supposed to be having a stress-free recovery—the fact that she'd delayed her trip had already caused him undue anxiety; she certainly didn't want to be the cause of any more.

'All right,' she conceded, rolling her eyes and kissing his cheek. 'If it means that much to you.'

Bob grinned. 'Atta girl.'

There were two drinking holes on the island—the upmarket Beach Hut, also known as the club, and the Brindabella Pub. The club boasted cover bands on a Saturday night, a dance floor and expensive cocktails.

The pub, on the other hand, had cheaper drinks but the ambience was slightly less lacking. It was also the place she'd often spend a working Saturday night, treating the victims of bar brawls. Generally it wasn't the place she chose to go to relax.

Vic entered the Beach Hut a little after eight. There were two bars in the club. One near the dance floor, which was rocking at the moment, and the other out the back servicing a large lounge area dominated by floor-to-ceiling windows affording striking views of the beach just across the road.

She approached the quieter one and sat at a stool. She looked around while she waited for the bartender and was surprised to see Lawson sitting at the other end.

Their gazes met and he sent her a mock salute before picking up his beer and moving towards her.

'What's a nice girl like you doing in a place like this?' he said as he sat on the stool beside her.

Vic smiled. It was nice to hear him joke. The stuff with her father seemed to have wiped out all their recent baggage and it was nice to feel back on an even footing with him. Of course, she'd always have that crush, but she was done beating her head against the wall.

'My father ordered me out of the house.'

'Ah.' Lawson nodded. The bartender approached. 'What can I get you?'

Vic thought for a moment. 'A chocolate martini.'

Lawson screwed up his face. 'What the hell is a chocolate martini?'

'Two of my favourite things—vodka and chocolate. It's like dessert you can drink with a straw.'

Lawson raised an eyebrow. 'If you say so.' He ordered the drink and they both watched as the bartender made it in front of them.

'What are you doing here?' she asked.

'It's Saturday night. I joined the guys for drinks. They left to go into a bar in Brisbane. I was just finishing up.'

'I didn't think you went to the club nights.'

Lawson shrugged. 'I don't. Not usually. But Matilda's at a sleepover and I felt at a bit of a loose end.'

Vic nodded. She knew how he felt. The bartender placed the drink in front of her and she dipped her head to take a sip from the straw. 'Hmm.' She shut her eyes and savoured the alcohol-laced chocolate. 'You should try this.' She held it up to him.

Lawson looked at the lipstick-coated straw and felt a little pull in his groin. Drinking from it seemed intimate. And he wasn't about to cross any more lines with her. Especially with alcohol involved. 'Thanks. Think I'll pass.'

Vic shrugged. 'More for me.'

Behind the bartender large porthole-style windows gave glimpses of the beach and they watched the waves roll in as they chatted about Bob and other neutral topics as they sipped at their drinks.

Lawson drained his beer glass. 'You meeting some friends? Going to do some dancing?' Maybe she was meeting a guy?

Vic shrugged. 'I was going to see if I knew anyone. Maybe have a couple of dances. But this band's not very good, is it?'

Lawson smiled. 'I thought it was just me.'

Vic laughed. 'You know what I'd really like to do?'

Lawson looked at her warily. 'What?'

She nodded in the direction of the window. 'I feel like walking on the beach. You wanna come?'

Lawson looked at the sandy vista and felt a tug at his soul. There was a three-quarter moon caressing the beach with milky fingers and it called to his inner rest-lessness. Except it screamed bad idea. His strange jumbled-up attraction had been put on ice the last couple of weeks, but he didn't trust how quickly a tropical moon might melt it away. 'I don't think so.'

Vic nodded. She was disappointed. But it was probably for the best. 'That's fine. Think I will, though.' And she slipped off her chair. 'Thanks for the drink.'

He watched her hips sway in the black dress she wore that seemed to tie in a bow at the back. Her auburn hair swung loose, brushing her shoulders, and she looked small and very feminine as she walked away.

He sighed. He couldn't let her walk on the beach by herself. The island was a pretty safe place and he knew she had no fear about anything bad happening to her. She'd grown up here. She practically knew everyone.

But assaults had been known to happen and he'd hate for anything to befall her.

'Wait up,' he called as he slid off his stool and headed in her direction.

CHAPTER EIGHT

A STIFF breeze caressed her face, blowing her hair back as Vic kicked off her strappy heels. She jumped down onto the soft sand, eager to feel the crunch of it against her soles. Huge rollers broke the surface of the ocean, curling towards the beach and dumping against the shoreline with crashing precision, and Vic felt them reverberate through her cells.

She looked behind her and watched as Lawson kicked his shoes off. Whether it was the incandescence of the moonlight or his greater elevation, his shoulders seemed broader, his legs longer. Her fingers itched to feel the fabric of his shirt beneath them, her dreams haunted by the swell of muscle beneath crisp cotton.

'Come on, slow poke,' she called as she set off without him. The tide was out and she walked towards it, suddenly impatient to get her bare feet in the Pacific Ocean.

Lawson shook his head, wondering why the hell he was here putting temptation firmly in his path. Bob's heart attack had relegated his attraction to the back burner, but with her hips swinging in front of him it brought it all crashing back.

He should leave now. While his sanity was still intact. But something, maybe the moonlight, maybe the fact that he'd missed their old dynamic and it finally seemed normal between them, egged him on.

'Do you have some direction in mind?' Lawson mused as he caught up with her. 'Or are we just going to wander aimlessly?'

Vic grinned. 'I thought we'd paddle along the edge for a while and end up at the rocks.' She pointed to the rocky outcrop a couple of kilometres away.

They walked side by side for a while without talking, letting the water lap around their ankles as it followed its age-old rhythm. Vic yearned to slip her hand into his but was too frightened he'd reject her again and break the ease they were sharing, so she contented herself with the occasional arm brush.

The water felt cool between her toes, the sand squelching and grainy. She inhaled deeply. 'I *am* going to miss this.'

Lawson waited a beat or two. 'They do have oceans in England,' he teased. 'Like us, they're an island.'

Vic shoved him with her shoulder. 'Yes, but they don't have the mighty Pacific lapping their shores, do they?'

Lawson turned to face the force of nature before him. The night was reasonably cloudless and the moon shimmered across the surface. 'No. That's true.'

Vic shook her head. 'Just think. I've never known another ocean. I'm twenty-six and the Pacific's all I've ever known.'

Lawson started to walk again. 'You wait till you see the Mediterranean. It's...I don't know if there are words for it. It's calm…not like this. And the most incredible blue. Like uncut sapphires. And then the sun sparkles on it and it's like the Crown jewels.'

Vic inspected his profile. It'd become quite expressive as he grappled with finding the exact description. It should have inspired in her a lust to see it. To dabble her toes, to witness its glory. But it didn't.

He turned to her. 'Italy is amazing. You have to go there. Venice is a must.' He turned to her. 'Promise me you'll go to Venice.'

She looked up into his face. His eyes were in shadow and hard to read. Wind whipped stray hair across her face. 'I promise,' she whispered. Even though the thought of going there alone had no appeal.

Lawson nodded and moved on, his feet dragging through the shallows, sand gritty and viscous between his toes.

'I'm glad you're still going,' he said after they'd walked some more. *He was, really*. 'Your dad's been worried you'll decide to stay. He wanted me to talk to you about it.'

Vic stopped in his tracks. 'Did he…did he set us up tonight?'

Lawson laughed and continued walking. 'If you're asking me did I know you were going to show up tonight, then the answer's no.' He looked behind him. She was standing with her hands on her hips like a petulant child. He turned so he was facing her, walking backwards. 'Did your father know I was going to be at the club? Yes.'

Vic shook his head. 'That wily old…'

Lawson laughed. 'Yes. I don't think his down time affected his brain any.' And then he turned back so he was facing the way he was walking and trudged on.

Vic caught him up. 'I *am* going, Lawson. But…'

He looked down at her. She was looking at her feet, her face screwed up, her cute cherubic cheeks pronounced. 'But?'

'It's complicated. I can't just leave when he's had a major heart attack. And what if—?'

Lawson waited a beat. 'What if what?'

'What if I'm gone for two months and get a phone call in the middle of the night to say he's had another one? A massive one. One he…'

The ocean beat against the shore as she grappled with the unthinkable. One wave. Two. Three. It was too hard to say. To give voice to. She stopped, her feet sinking as the waves eroded the sand around them. She took a deep breath. 'Couldn't be revived from?'

Lawson stopped too, feeling her pain. Bob Dunleavy was like a father to him. The old man had taught him respect and hard work. He'd shown him the difference between going through the motions and getting invested. He'd turned him from the punk he'd been to the man he was today. 'I'll watch out for him, Victoria.'

She felt tears prick her eyes. 'You have Matilda, Lawson. You have other priorities.'

He grabbed her hands. 'If Matilda and I have to move in with him, I will watch over your father. Like he did for me when I was a rookie. I promise.'

Vic felt a wave of emotion swell in her chest. It built like the breakers crashing against the shore until it clogged her eyes and choked her throat. Before she could stop herself she snaked her arms around his neck, raised herself on her tippy-toes and pressed her mouth to his.

It was a kiss of gratitude. Of thanks. She felt his resistance, his mouth closed. But then, like the push and pull of the tide, his hands travelled up her back and pulled her closer and the kiss took on a life of its own. The waves crashed around them as the kiss deepened and she clung to his shoulders, opening her mouth to him, baring her soul. His tongue stroked against hers and she felt a heat spread from deep inside her to the tips of her toes.

Lawson wrenched his mouth away, his breathing ragged, his head spinning. He looked at her for a long time, his hands gripping her upper arms. 'What was that for?'

'Because you know how to say the right thing at exactly the right moment. And because I'm tired of pretending I'm not attracted to you and we didn't nearly have sex on my couch.'

Lawson's fingers tightened around her arm. The fantasy of throwing her against the sand and having their own *From Here to Eternity* moment warring with his responsibilities. Warring with his innate sense of propriety. 'We should go.'

Vic laughed. She couldn't help herself. Any other man would have flipped her on her back and had her half naked in the sand right now. She linked her arm through his. 'C'mon, I want to show you something.' And she pulled against his resistance, pleased when he gave in and followed her.

Lawson walked beside her, aware of the rub of her

side against his as he'd never been before. Her kiss—their kiss—still burrowed into his groin and sung like a heavy-metal guitar sonnet in his blood. It felt mind-altering like vodka and tasted like chocolate—sweet and addictive. The chocolate martini of kisses.

He could feel the beat of the waves pounding in time with his pulse. It was as if the wildness of the ocean had given him permission to be himself. To be the primal man that lurked beneath the surface, the one he'd tried so hard to suppress.

So he followed her. They didn't speak, their bodies communicating without words. The heat building inside as the friction from their occasional body contact tantalised and seduced.

When they reached the rocks at the end of the beach, Vic used the light from the moon to guide her to a place she hadn't been in years. Lawson followed, her behind bending and shimmying tantalisingly in front of him as she scampered and twisted to navigate the rocks. With the tide out, they were dry but still dangerous in the reduced light.

'Where are we going?' he grouched when she unknowingly shoved her butt close enough for him to lean forward and take a bite.

'Patience, grasshopper.' She grinned as she spotted her destination.

She clambered over the last few rocks and jumped down onto a sheltered area of sand bordered by a crescent-shaped rock formation that had been partially eroded into an overhang. It was like a half-cave with a completely exposed opening, but hidden amidst the rocky outcrop.

'Mum and Dad and I used to come here before the twins were born,' she said, turning to watch him leap down into the sheltered area. 'It was like our special place.'

She looked out at the vista before her, the ocean lapping the sand in the distance as it continued its tidal march away from the island.

'Dad would build a bonfire and we'd toast marshmallows as the sun went down.' She looked at the pile of charred wood, cold and dead now, just inside the entrance to the overhang. Someone else had found the secluded spot.

'We came here a few times when the boys were little but…it just wasn't the same without her and we stopped coming.'

Standing in this special place, it finally hit her. She wasn't just leaving the island and her family and friends and everything she'd ever known, but she was also leaving the place that connected her to her mother.

Lawson watched her closely in the moonlight, her features plaintive. She looked melancholy and utterly lovely. 'She was a wonderful woman, your mother.'

Vic felt his voice draw her out of her reverie. She looked at him, leaning against the rock, his hands in his pockets. The moon blazed behind him, leaving his eyes hooded in shadow. 'I forget sometimes that you knew her too.'

'She used to bake me cakes. Your father would bring them to work with him and tell me it was a sin to refuse such divine cooking.'

Vic smiled. 'Yes. She was a great cook.'

'She'd want you to go.' It was surprising how much

it hurt him to say it, but Lawson knew it to be true. Mary Dunleavy had always wanted a life bigger than the island for her little girl.

'What about you?'

Lawson shifted uncomfortably against the rock. 'Of course.'

The rock formation sheltered them from the wind and muffled the raw power of the ocean, but she could still see and hear the waves crashing down the beach. She listened for a few beats as she sought the right words.

'Is that because you want me to fulfil a lifelong dream or is it because of the guilt you feel over what happened between us? Will it be easier to bear if you don't have to look at your *mistake* every day?'

Lawson shut his eyes. 'Victoria.' He stuffed his hands in his pockets. He could still taste her on his lips. 'I really don't want to talk about this.'

Vic nodded. Of course. His policy of denial had served him well until now; why change? She held up her hands in a gesture of surrender before turning away from him and plonking herself down under the overhang.

The sand was cool but dry beneath her. She raised her knees to her chest, pulling the material of her dress down over them until just her bare toes peeped out. She scooped up a handful of sand and let it drift between her fingers and slide over the sides.

She raised her face to him. He seemed a long way away, leaning against his rock. She patted the sand beside her. 'Come sit next to me.'

Lawson shook his head emphatically. *Did he look insane?* Their kiss still hummed in his blood and a moonlit beach and a melancholy mood were not good deterrents. 'Thanks. I'm good here.'

Vic could see the waves pounding the shore from her vantage point. She could see the moonbeams playing tag with the waves. 'You have your back to the ocean. You're missing the view.'

That was what she thought. The moon was aligned perfectly, capturing her in a milky beam of light. It fell softly against her features, caressing her full cheeks and her cute nose, and glistened in her lip gloss. 'It'll be there tomorrow.'

Vic sighed. There was no way she was going to break him. His will was all-powerful. Even caught up in their kiss he'd been the one to step away. She rested her head on her knees for a while, her gaze watching the push and pull of the tide, her mind as restless.

She stirred from her reverie. 'I never did thank you. For that day. With Dad.'

Lawson shrugged. 'I was just doing my job, Victoria.'

She shook her head. 'No. Without your pep talk on the way there…I would have fallen apart. I would have been useless. Dad owes his life to you. Had it been up to me I don't know if I could have kept it together.'

'He's your father. No one, least of all me, expected you to be able to separate from that.'

Vic nodded. 'Sure. But I forgot it amongst all my anxiety about your feelings.' She stood and brushed sand off her dress as she approached him. 'I know you and my father have a…bond. It can't have been easy for you to have seen him like that either.'

Images of a grey Bob Dunleavy assaulted him. The

lifeless form of his friend as his daughter pumped his chest, silent tears streaming down her face, her heart shattering with each compression. It was a day he never wanted to see ever again. 'I've had better days.'

Vic felt laughter bubble in her chest. Lawson's face was impassive as he delivered the understatement. Why was it so bloody hard to squeeze an emotion out of him? He'd been absolutely professional that day and then super efficient in the days after when she'd leant on him and politely supportive ever since.

For once she'd like to see some extreme of emotion. She knew he was capable. She'd seen how animated he could become around Matilda. How great he'd been with the little croup boy. But stepping back from their kiss just now was a classic example. Even when she'd been half naked in his arms he'd managed to restrain himself. Was it so hard to show her something other than rigid control?

What exactly did she have to do to get him to show himself? The real man? The one who had made a stupid mistake at sixteen, the one who had a two-week-old baby dumped in his arms, the one who had kissed her so passionately for a brief few seconds not even half an hour ago?

A moonbeam on the ocean caught her gaze and her attention returned to the view over his shoulder. The ocean never lied, never hid its moods. She could feel the force of it buffeting her body, stirring her cells, and suddenly she knew why she'd come to the beach tonight.

Her hand twisted behind her as she fumbled for the bow that held the wrap-around dress together. She found the end and pulled it undone.

Lawson frowned for a minute, wondering what the hell she was doing until her cleavage parted slightly and he could see a dark shadow of fabric covering a partially exposed breast. He pushed himself off the rock, holding out his hands, miming her to stop.

'Whoa. What are you doing?'

Vic smiled. Suddenly she had his attention. Suddenly he was looking a lot more spirited. 'I'm going swimming.'

'But—' Whatever he'd been about to say died on his lips as Victoria parted her dress, shrugged her shoulders and the entire thing slithered to the sand in a pool of black temptation. Lawson swallowed as his gaze travelled from her toes up.

Up her ankles to her knees. From her knees to her thighs. From her thighs to the scrap of lace that covered her modesty. Up over the curves of her hip and belly to her ribs and matching lace half-cup bra that lifted her breasts as if in silent offering to the moon. Up over her collarbones and her neck, all the way to her face.

Vic smiled. Finally she had him. Finally he was looking at her like a human being. Not his colleague. His partner. Not someone he'd known for two decades. Not as Matilda's father. But as a man looking at a woman. In all his open-mouthed glory. She should have been embarrassed but she wasn't. He'd seen her in less.

'Coming?' she asked as she passed by him and headed to the ocean.

Lawson pivoted on the sand and tracked her path to the shoreline. The moonlight outlined her figure perfectly. Short and curvy, the cheek of her left buttock more exposed than the other, her hips swaying and her hair blowing behind her as she headed into the breeze. Like a water sprite returning home.

He shut his eyes, trying to deny the tug. But standing on the beach, his body feeling the raw vitality of the ocean as a true primal force, nothing could be denied. When he opened them again she was standing in the shallows. Waiting.

Waiting for him.

Without further dissection Lawson stripped off his shirt, shucked off his trousers and strode down to join her.

Vic didn't have to turn to know he was coming. It was as if her heartbeat were tuned into every fall of foot on sand. When he stopped at the water's edge beside her she didn't even look at him. She just slid her hand into his and they waded out.

The waves buffeted their bodies as the pulse of the ocean enveloped them. She walked until she was waist deep and then dived beneath the surface, Lawson beside her. They swam out past the row of breakers until she could barely stand, the water level with Lawson's chest. And when she reached for him his hands encircled her waist and glided up her ribs, pulling her close, settling her torso against his, her legs automatically locking around his waist.

Lawson could hear her breath, rough with anticipation. Her hair was plastered to her face and water droplets beaded on her cheeks and eyelashes and it was the most natural thing in the world for him to lower his head and capture her mouth.

Her lips were moist and cool and she tasted like salt and chocolate. And after the earlier appetiser he was suddenly ravenous for her. He lifted a hand to cup the back of her neck, urging her mouth closer as he deepened the kiss.

Heat flooded his groin and his erection strained against the confines of his wet underwear. The current swirled around them, dragging her bottom and inner thighs against his hardness, nudging its length, and he groaned into her mouth. Unable to bear the erotic torture, he lowered his other hand, splaying his fingers across the small of her back to anchor her there.

Vic smiled against his mouth and broke away. 'Damn, I was enjoying that,' she teased.

Lawson gave a half-laugh. 'You shock me.'

Vic rolled her eyes. 'Really.'

He grinned. 'Really. You're Bob's daughter, you're… Victoria. You're not supposed to…know about things like that.'

'You might be surprised what I know,' she murmured, and deliberately traced her tongue along his lips. 'Hmm, you taste good.' She unlocked her ankles and let her body slide down his, her arms still firmly entwined around his neck. She pressed against his erection. 'You feel good.'

Lawson closed his eyes. He grabbed her hips, holding her firmly against him, trapping her there. 'Isn't this what you want?' she whispered in his ear. She released one arm from his neck, slid her hand down his belly and burrowed beneath the waistband of his underwear until she was grasping his girth, revelling in the size of him.

Lawson, his eyes still closed, just managed an 'umph' noise.

'It's what I want,' she continued, sucking on his ear lobe as she ran her fingers up and down his length. It felt hot amidst the cool water. And incredibly potent. She parted her legs, guiding him between them, rubbing herself against his length, wishing she didn't have the lacy barrier of her own underwear.

She raised her lips to his and their mouths meshed. His hold on her hip became vice-like and somewhere at the back of her brain she knew she'd have bruises there tomorrow. His tongue invaded her mouth and tangled with hers. His breathing was harsh as their intimate connection continued and she held onto his shoulders for dear life as his deep wet kisses pushed her head back and spun everything like a kaleidoscope inside her head.

Lawson broke off, unable to bear the friction any longer. He didn't want to mimic the sexual act—he wanted to do it. 'Let's go.' He grabbed her hand and pulled her along beside him.

Vic laughed as she struck out beside him. 'Where to?'

'My place. Hurry.'

Vic followed him, sobering a little. Did he mean, *Hurry, I can't wait any longer*? Or, *Hurry before I change my mind*? Given how quickly he'd changed his mind last time, she didn't want to give him twenty minutes to rethink the wisdom of the situation.

By the time their knees scraped sand she knew she couldn't let him out of the ocean. She didn't want his ardour to cool and his strong sense of propriety to take over. When he helped her to her feet she rose in one fluid movement, plastering her body against his. He staggered a little and she used his temporary mis-footing to over-balance him.

He landed on his back in the shallows with an, 'Oomph,' and she followed him down. She didn't give him a chance for evasive action, playing dirty straight off the bat. She pinned his arms above his head and straddled him, rubbing herself against his erection, instantly paralysing any intent he had to move.

Lawson opened his eyes, the earth tilting a little as he did so. He looked up at her, her head blocking out the moon, her face in shadow. 'What was that for?'

'I don't want to go back to your place. I want to stay here.' She lowered her head and kissed his chest, his neck, his mouth. Trailed kisses along the length of his scar.

Lawson let the heat from her kiss wash over him. Deepened it until he was thrusting against her. He dragged his mouth away, her head falling to his chest, her forehead resting against its ragged rise and fall. 'I have condoms at home. And a bed.'

Vic felt his words rumble against her skin. He also had reality back there. Matilda and all his responsibilities, including her, his partner.

She pushed herself up, releasing his hands so she could reach behind her and unclip her bra. It released easily and slid down her arms. She pulled it off and threw it aside uncaring that she'd never see it again as it was swallowed by the eddying current.

She thrust her chest slightly and looked down at him. 'I don't need a bed.'

Lawson was momentarily stunned as the moonlight coated the pale tips of her breasts in alabaster. As he watched they beaded and blushed a darker shade of pink. And then he didn't even think, just curled up, wrapped his arms around her waist and captured a moist wet nipple in his mouth.

Vic cried out as the heat sucked at her belly. She ground against him and jammed her fingers into his hair, holding his head to her, arching into him for more.

In one fluid move Lawson flipped her on her back in the shallows and moved on to the other nipple, paying it equal homage. Water surged and foamed around them, but it didn't register. His cool fingertips, pruned from the water, replaced where his mouth had just been and he felt a surge of lust undulate through his gut as Victoria cried out again, her chest rising off the sand.

Lawson released his mouthful and traced his tongue up her sternum to the pulse fluttering in her neck. 'Let's go,' he murmured.

Vic felt the delirium ease. 'No. Let's stay here.'

Lawson felt her tense. He pulled back. 'What's wrong?'

She turned her face away. 'It's a moonlit beach. It's perfect for this.'

Lawson wasn't buying it. 'Victoria?'

She sighed, turning her face back. 'Because I'm afraid you're going to change your mind if you're given any time to think about it all.'

Lawson looked into her eyes; even with his head blocking out the moonlight, his shadow darkening her face, he could see the anguish in her whiskey gaze. He shook his head, kissed her brow, her nose her mouth. 'I won't change my mind. I know this isn't wise but I don't care. You're going overseas for an indefinite period and I have Matilda to think about. Our lives are at completely different stages. But I've been going crazy thinking about this. There can only be tonight, I can't offer you any more and I'm probably going to hell for it, but I'm not backing out.'

Vic's heart smashed against her ribs. 'Tonight's all I need.'

Lawson had never wanted anything more in his life. He knew he'd pay for it later, in the days and months to come, but that wasn't what he was thinking as he shook the sand off her dress and passed it to her, watching while she wound it around her wet body. Nor when he held her hand as they walked back up the beach. Or when they reached her car and he pushed her against the cold metal of her door and kissed her thoroughly before letting her in.

All he could think about was the culmination of all the dreams that had afflicted him since that night on her couch. That she was going to be soft and warm beneath him. And the noise she'd make when he entered her for the first time. And the way she'd moan his name when she came.

They were at his place in eight minutes and not a single doubt had entered his mind. They were kissing before the door was even open. His shirt was off and her dress falling from her shoulders as they hit his bedroom. Seconds later they were tumbling, still wet and sandy, but utterly naked onto his unmade bed.

And it was as if they'd done it a thousand times before, moving with a symmetry that was breathtaking, an anticipation of each other's needs that had them gasping, slavishly addicted to the next touch, the next caress. And yet the sensations were totally new. Stroking and sighing and trembling as each built on the other.

When he slid inside her it was like he was coming home. She gasped and arced into him, gripping his shoulders, and he put a hand under her back, pulling her closer. Her reaction shook him to the core. He'd been so busy thinking it was impossible he hadn't considered that it could be so right.

A sob tore from her throat and he whispered, 'Easy,' into her neck.

Vic would never have believed a first time with any-one could be this perfect. She wanted to hold him inside for ever. Stretching her. Filling her. Completing her. But the need took over and a rhythm surged through both of their bodies as primal as the waves had been on the beach. It built. It would not be ignored. Their bodies moving to its beat, reaching for its promise.

It itched beneath her skin and hummed in her blood, building all the time like bongo drums in the jungle. Rising to a crescendo. Their cries echoed down through eons and mingled together with all who had come before them in this primitive tangle of limbs.

And it was in the instant that it broke over them, pulling and tumbling them through a whirlpool of pleasure, that she realised she'd lied. To him. To herself.

Tonight's all I need.

That was what she'd told him. But she'd lied. She needed more. She was always going to need more.

She loved him.

Lawson didn't know how long it took to spin back

to earth. He'd collapsed on top of her and they seemed to drift for ever on some astral plane where both their bodies and minds touched. He moved after an age, rolling off her onto his back. *Man, he was in serious trouble.* He didn't speak. He couldn't. He didn't have the words. He just lay there catching his breath.

It was left up to Vic to fill the silence. She waited until her breathing had settled, psyching herself into it. 'I've made up my mind,' she announced into the silence. 'I'm not going to London. I'm staying here. With you.'

CHAPTER NINE

LAWSON'S post-coital glow evaporated in a nanosecond.

Oh, no. No, no, no.

This wasn't the way it was supposed to go. He'd told her he could only give her the night. And he'd been deadly serious.

This was bad. It was exactly what he'd feared would happen. She'd give up on her dream to settle for a second-class relationship. He vaulted upright, groped around the floor for his clothes and stepped into his underwear quickly.

He stood at the end of the bed looking down at her, hands on hips. 'I'm sorry? You're not going? Since when?'

Vic smiled at the forced impassivity of his face betrayed by the stormy turbulence of his gaze. She stayed calm. She'd known it would be a bombshell, which was why she'd chosen not to tell him the true depths of her feelings. That she loved him. That she'd always loved him. She knew it was cowardly and wished she had the courage to tell him the truth. But she couldn't. He needed to get used to the idea of having her around first.

Which was fine. She had all the time in the world. She wasn't going anywhere.

She shrugged. 'Since now. Lawson, I've had a crush on you for ever—'

Lawson groaned, interrupting her. He shut his eyes and pressed the heels of his palms into his eye sockets. 'Oh, God.' His hands dropped to his side. 'Please don't tell me you've had a crush on me since you were six.'

Vic laughed. 'Of course not, but probably from the moment we were partnered together.'

Five years? 'Five years?'

Vic nodded, finding his abject misery mildly amusing. 'Except it wasn't a crush. I know that now. It goes much deeper than that.' It was as honest as she could get now with Lawson looking at her as if she'd just grown a second head.

Lawson stared down at her. *What the hell was she talking about?* He groped around for a response while trying to ignore the fact she was gloriously, shame-lessly naked on his bed. 'Sometimes…it can be easy to get sex…great sex,' he amended, 'confused with… other feelings.'

He picked up the sheet and threw it over her. Certain parts of his anatomy weren't confused at all. They wanted more and didn't particularly care that she'd dropped a bombshell.

'Lawson, I'm an adult.' She rolled onto her side, sup-porting her head with a hand. She'd panicked him. Of course he was going to fight it. She was instantly grateful she'd not blurted out her love for him. It was something he was obviously not ready to hear. 'I know you have a hard time remembering that. But I do know the difference between post-coital gratitude and real feelings.'

Lawson couldn't believe what he was hearing. 'For God's sake, I'm twelve years older than you.'

The corner of Vic's mouth quirked upwards. 'So what, that makes you more grown up than me?' She laughed. 'Let's see…I'm adult enough to apply for my own passport. I'm adult enough to vote in the last two elections. I'm adult enough to babysit your daughter. But not enough to share your bed, your life?'

Lawson clenched his fists by his side. Surely she could see what she was suggesting was totally preposterous. 'I said tonight only. I said I couldn't offer you anything.'

She shrugged, her heart aching for him as he grappled with the enormity of what she'd just thrown at him. 'It doesn't matter—I'm staying anyway.'

Lawson ran fingers through his hair. 'No. You're going to London. To the Mediterranean. To Venice.'

'I'm not going.'

'You have to. Your father wants you to. I want you to. Damn it, Victoria—you want to.'

'Not any more. Not without you.'

'Victoria, this is crazy. I don't have the time to give to you.'

'I know that. I'm not asking for that.'

'But you should. You deserve the best, Victoria. Courting, dating. Candlelight and roses and long weekends away in the mountains. A proper relationship. Matilda takes up a lot of time. She's my priority. Between shift work and her needs I'm too exhausted for anything else. I'm in bed at eight o'clock most nights. I'm…boring. You deserve to be someone's priority.'

'I understand, Lawson. I, of all people, know what it means to have to put a child first. I know it won't be all hearts and flowers.'

He shook his head. 'Maybe when you get back…if you come back…it'll be different. Matilda will be older.'

'So, what, just go and explore the world in the meantime?'

'Yes.'

'See things, expand my horizons?'

'Yes.'

'Live a little.'

'Exactly.'

'Sleep with other men?'

Lawson opened his mouth to agree, but snapped it shut as a rush of pure jealousy charged through his veins. Of course that was what she should do. Part of travelling involved meeting people, indulging in flings. Brief and intense. Totally frivolous. And absolutely exhilarating.

'Lawson?'

He looked away from her. 'Of course.'

Vic's heart swelled as he refused to meet her eyes. He had feelings for her too—she knew it. She just had to get him to open himself to them. She kicked off the sheet and rose from the bed, padding naked to where he stood. He took a step back from her but she wasn't going to pay into his keep-off signals any longer.

She covered the distance between them and pressed herself against him, her ear to his chest. His heart beat like a sonic boom, reverberating through his chest wall. 'I don't believe you,' she murmured.

Lawson, who had resisted touching her, felt his arms come around her of their own volition. Her damp hair smelt salty and he could smell himself on her skin. It filled his senses and fed the primal beast that lurked beneath.

'You should,' he murmured. 'Logically I know you should. I have no rights to insist otherwise.'

Vic pulled away slightly. She looked into his face, past the cragginess and the scar. 'But?'

His arms tightened around her. 'I can't bear the thought of another man touching you.'

Vic felt sunshine burst in her chest and she grinned up at him. That was all she needed to hear. She rose on her tippy-toes and opened her mouth onto his, feasting on him, powered by a surge of pure feminine possession. And when he groaned she felt bullet-proof, her hands snaking around his neck as his slid up to cradle her jaw. She deepened the kiss, wanting more, needing to get closer.

Lawson tore his mouth away. He wanted this. Wanted her. But he didn't want to mislead her. Whether she liked it or not, whether she fancied herself attached to him or not, she had a plan and he was going to make her stick to it. He didn't want to be the reason she hated herself and resented her life in a decade.

'Victoria,' he groaned against her lips.

Their breath fell harshly between them as he feathered tiny kisses against her mouth, her eyes, her cheeks, stroking his thumbs down the sensitive line of her throat.

Vic placed her hands over his and tugged them gently

away. She could hear the anguish in his voice, feel the battle that raged inside him. She knew she had to leave. She didn't want her presence, naked in his bed or the potency of their sex to sway him. When he next opened his arms to her, she wanted to know it was because he'd finally acknowledged his feelings for her. Whatever they were. She could only hope they mirrored hers.

She stepped back. He didn't stop her. He didn't reach for her. Even though part of her wished he would. Just watched her as she found her clothes and got dressed.

She tied the bow on her dress and looked at him. 'This is a lot to take on board. You need some time.' He didn't say anything, just looked at her with wary eyes. 'Goodnight, Lawson. I'll see you at work next week.'

And with the ocean still clinging to her body and the memory of their love-making insinuating itself into her DNA, she brushed past him and let herself out of the house.

Two weeks later Vic had gained no ground with Lawson. His strategy to ignore what was between them and the intimacies they'd shared frustrated her greatly. But amazingly a well of patience had sprung within her and with an instinct born out of her love she knew she'd wait as long as it took for him to realise the truth.

She could see that he desired her. In rare unguarded moments she caught him watching her and she could see lust turn his gaze smoky. But she didn't want that from him. She knew he wanted her—the memory of their incredible night together never far from her thoughts—she needed to know he loved her.

They were crossing the bridge on their way back to the island from a job when Lawson's mobile rang. She listened unashamedly to the one-sided conversation as she drove. Something was up with Matilda.

'That was Dorothy. Matilda's come home from school very upset. Swing by my house, will you?'

'Did she say about what?'

Lawson shook his head. 'Tilly won't tell her.'

Vic nodded. His profile looked forbidding. Tense. Instead of continuing straight ahead to the station, she turned left at the roundabout and headed for Lawson's.

They were pulling up two minutes later. Matilda flew out of the house and was running across the lawn to her father even before Vic had shut the engine off.

Lawson swung her up into his arms. 'Hey, hey,' he crooned softly, his heart thumping in his chest. Someone had obviously hurt his little girl and he was ready to kick down doors and knock heads together. 'It's okay, Daddy's here.'

Vic's heart went out to Matilda as she sobbed into her father's neck as if the world were about to end. She related to Matilda in a way no one else could. She knew what it was like to grow up without a mother and a groundswell of empathy clogged her chest.

Lawson held Matilda tight and Vic didn't think she'd ever seen him more masculine. Her pulse did a funny triple beat.

They went inside and sat around the kitchen table while Dorothy made hot chocolates and Lawson tried to get to the bottom of his daughter's heartbreak. Matilda was being unusually close-mouthed.

'Is it your teacher?'

Matilda sniffled. She loved her teacher. 'Nope.'

'Did you do badly on a test?'

'Nope.'

'Is someone calling you names?'

'Nope.'

'Did you…get kicked off the netball team?'

This time Matilda just shook her head, looking progressively miserable.

Vic had an inkling what might be wrong. 'Is it a boy?' she asked gently.

Lawson's head shot up in alarm. 'Don't be ridiculous,' he dismissed. 'She's eight years old.'

But when Matilda wailed, 'Yes,' and dissolved into another puddle of tears he was forced to reassess.

'Okay.' Vic stood. 'I know exactly what we need.' She went to the freezer and pulled out the tub of ice cream Lawson always had on hand. The perfect salve for man problems. God knew, she'd eaten gallons of the stuff in the last fortnight.

She retrieved two spoons from the drawer and sat down next to Matilda. 'What's his name?' she asked as she peeled the lid off and pushed a spoon towards Matilda.

'Hamish Jones.'

Lawson, his head spinning from the unexpected turn of events, subconsciously cracked his knuckles. He didn't know this Hamish kid, but he disliked him—immensely.

Vic loaded her spoon with ice cream. 'Does he like you?'

Matilda nodded, her mouth full.

'Well, that's good, isn't it?'

'No,' Lawson interrupted, looking at Victoria as if she'd grown another head. 'No. That's not good. She's way too young for boys.'

Vic glared at him and then looked back at Matilda. 'Don't worry about your dad. He thinks all girls are too young for boys. Even me.'

Matilda giggled. And Lawson ignored her. 'She's eight. It's ridiculous to be crying over some silly boy.'

Vic noticed Matilda's smile die and tears filled her eyes again. How typical of him to dismiss his daughter's feelings because he was running scared. She gave Matilda an encouraging smile and kept it plastered to her face as she shot him a withering look. 'Not. Helping.'

He looked at Matilda as she sniffed back more tears. To say he felt out of his depth was an understatement. He sent Victoria a *fix this* look.

Vic dipped in for more ice cream. 'So is he your boyfriend, then?'

Matilda's bottom lip wobbled. 'No.'

'Ah,' Vic said around a mouthful. 'But you want him to be your boyfriend?'

Matilda nodded. 'But he wants me to kiss him and I said I wouldn't 'cos Daddy always says that you should only kiss a boy when you're married to him and now he doesn't want to be my boyfriend.'

Lawson felt sick. *Kiss him*? They were kissing at eight? He was going to school tomorrow to kick little Hamish's butt. How dared he…put the hard word on an eight-year-old girl?

Vic raised an eyebrow at Lawson. 'Married?' she enquired sweetly. 'You're kidding, right?

He shook his head. 'Deadly. Serious.'

Vic rolled her eyes. 'I think we better leave the sex education to me.'

Lawson clenched his jaw at the thought of her in their lives, being able to discuss girl things with his daughter. As she was doing now. As if she were born to be the mother of an eight-year-old girl. 'You're going overseas, remember.'

Vic smiled at him. 'No. I'm not.' She turned back to Matilda. 'Do you think it's okay for a boy, for anyone really, to make you do something that you don't feel right about?'

Matilda thought for a while. 'I guess not.'

'So do you really want a boyfriend who's going to be that selfish?'

Matilda shook her head. 'I guess not.'

Vic grinned. It was obvious Matilda wasn't one hundred per cent convinced. 'There are two types of boys in this world, sweetie. Boys who would never ask a girl to do something they didn't want to do and boys who think only about themselves and what they want.' She looked at Lawson. 'Isn't that right, Lawson?'

He nodded vigorously. 'Absolutely.'

Lawson watched as Victoria dug her spoon in again and she and Matilda sat and savoured the ice cream together for a few minutes. She was handling this beautifully and Matilda was hanging on every word. Unlike his first reaction, which was to lock Matilda in her room and not let her out until she was thirty.

It was at times like these he really felt that Tilly had missed out. He knew he'd been a good parent and he knew he could tackle the inevitable girl questions as his daughter went through puberty, but he doubted he could manage them as well as a woman. As well as a mother.

How much easier would his life be, would Matilda's life be, if she had a mother? A rush of something he didn't want to analyse blossomed in his chest as he watched Victoria with his daughter.

I think we better leave the sex education to me.

That was what she'd just said. As if she were going to be around for it whether he liked it or not. As if she didn't doubt for a moment that she was going to be part of their lives.

She'd handled this perfectly and had always been great with Matilda. But Victoria had sworn off ever being a mother. How fair would it be to expect that of her? Even if that was what she thought she wanted. Had she thought about it from that angle? Instant motherhood? Again?

Vic could feel him watching them. 'What type of boy do you think your dad is?' She noticed Lawson frowning in her peripheral vision and ignored it.

Matilda swallowed a mouthful of ice cream. 'The first kind.'

Vic smiled at her. 'And wouldn't you prefer to have a boyfriend who was like your dad? Someone who knew how to treat a girl properly.' Even though he didn't have a clue how to treat her properly. The way she wanted to be treated.

Matilda looked at her father. 'I want to marry someone just like Daddy.'

Vic felt her heart squeeze painfully in her chest. She knew exactly how Matilda felt. Lawson smiled at his daughter and the pain intensified. They were such a duo, a team. 'Probably best to stay clear of boys like Hamish, then. Don't you think?'

Matilda smiled at Vic. 'Definitely.' She spooned another mouthful of ice cream in and swallowed. 'So I shouldn't let a boy kiss me until we're married?'

Lawson, who was in the process of taking a sip of his hot chocolate, coughed and nearly choked on it. 'That's right,' he managed to gasp.

Vic glared at him. 'No, it's not. Your dad's just being a dad. He's supposed to say that. Kissing is fun. But it is part of being grown up. At your age it's okay to have boys who are friends. But it's probably better to leave the kissing for high school. Okay?'

Matilda thought for a moment. 'Okay.'

'High school?' Lawson demanded as they pulled out of his driveway fifteen minutes later to respond to a thirty-eight-year-old female with abdominal pain. 'How about uni? How about when she turns thirty?'

Vic laughed. His outrage had eroded the barriers he'd put in place and it was the most natural she'd seen him since they'd done the wild thing and she'd gone and ruined it by telling him she was staying on Brindabella with him. 'Oh, hey, how about never? How about she joins a convent?'

Lawson nodded. 'Brilliant idea. I don't think I've ever heard a more sensible suggestion.'

'Lawson, she's going to have boyfriends whether you like it or not. You can forbid her and watch her rebel or you can give her some leeway and keep your fingers crossed.'

He snorted. 'Easy to say when she's not your child.'

Vic felt as if he'd slammed a sledgehammer into her chest. 'You could change that. Just say the word.'

'I thought you didn't want to be a mother? Never ever, you said.'

'Yes, I did say that, but I know you come as a package deal. And I love Matilda and have known her for ever. We get on. I think it would work. I could certainly handle the girl-talk situations way better than you.'

How acutely had she felt the loss of her mother when she'd been going through what Matilda had gone through? How desperately had she longed for her mother's advice, for her words of wisdom? She wanted to be there for Matilda. She wanted to be her mother.

Lawson looked at her incredulously. 'And how would you ever get overseas then, Victoria? What about what you want? How long would it take you to resent me being tied here with Matilda?'

'The last time I looked they actually did allow minors to travel on planes, Lawson.'

He shook his head. 'She has her school and all her friends here. I know firsthand what it's like to be dragged from pillar to post, to live in constant upheaval. I'm not going to do that to her. I can't just pick her up and move her to the other side of the world.'

'I'm not talking about moving. I'm talking about holidays. Yes, my plan was to live in London, work there. But do you really think I care how I see it? Not when I can have you, too. I understand your responsibilities. Love that you put Matilda's needs first.' She saw him flinch at the L word and felt a jab in the vicinity of her heart. He was obviously still not ready to hear it. 'It's one of the many things I like about you.'

Lawson couldn't believe what he was hearing. She was willing to sacrifice what she wanted for him? He didn't want that responsibility. He didn't want to be the one she hated in years to come because she hadn't followed her plan. 'So you're giving up on your dreams?'

Vic shook her head. 'I'm compromising, Lawson. That's what you do when you find someone worthy. Are you willing to meet me halfway?'

Lawson felt as if there were a rusty knife in his chest and she were twisting the handle. And deep down the well of feeling he'd felt blossom earlier pushed against the bounds he'd placed around it. He knew what was best for her. He was older. Had seen more. Lived more. He knew she'd regret it if she didn't follow her dreams.

He looked away from her and pushed the side button on his radio. 'Coms, this is nine six zero. ETA two minutes.'

Vic shook her head. Apparently the conversation was over.

'Victoria. Wait.'

Vic kept walking. It was the end of the shift. They'd worked through their break and done two hours' overtime. Without speaking to each other. She was beat. Physically and emotionally. And after their earlier conversation she didn't want to talk to Lawson. Hell, right at this moment, she'd be happy never to see him again.

Lawson followed. He didn't want to leave it like this. 'Victoria.'

She pushed the unlock button on her key ring and reached for the car door. Lawson's big hand appeared in front of her, pushing against the frame as she tried to pull it open.

'Wait.' He had things he wanted to say. He just didn't know what. Or how.

His voice was rough, full of pleading, and his breath was warm on her neck. She didn't turn to face him. She didn't speak, just dragged in deep breaths, her senses filling with him.

Lawson could feel the warmth radiating from her body and his hand moved to her hip of its own volition. 'I do have…feelings for you,' he murmured, his lips close to her neck. 'But every time I go to examine them a part of me says they're wrong.'

Vic's heart banged in her ribcage. Was he about to be honest with her? With himself. She turned slowly. He didn't make any move to step back and she felt a wild trill of anticipation trip through her veins.

'You're…special to me. And I know it's not just because I've known you for ever or you're my partner. I know it's more than that.'

She could see he was trying hard to find the right words and she was grateful. But why was it so hard to say what was in his heart? 'Well. Looks like we're finally getting somewhere.'

He gave her a grim smile. 'I haven't been able to stop thinking about how you were with Matilda today. You're right. You're good with her. You're good for her. She needs a strong woman in her life.'

Vic stiffened. This was about Matilda? What about

what he wanted in his life? She straightened and pushed away from the car, forcing him to step back.

'I don't want you to want me because I'm good with Matilda or because I love her and she patently adores me. She has plenty of strong women in her life. She has Dorothy and her aunt and she has me anyway whether I'm with you or not. I want you to want me because you can't live another day without me.'

Lawson swallowed. After twenty years of his thinking of her in a totally platonic way, she was asking a lot.

Vic shook her head, a surge of anger rising in her throat at his hesitancy. What had she expected from a man who never verbalised his feelings?

'You know what—screw you. I thought if I hung in there I could wear you down. But I don't think you're ever going to change, are you?' He stood there passively looking at her and she wanted to scream. 'Why should I have to erode your exterior until you finally give in? I want you to look inside and break through all the outer bullshit by yourself.'

She yanked her door open. 'Don't talk to me until you're ready to face your real feelings. Not about Matilda or what you think is best for me or what you know my father wants. Your real feelings. The ones you're too afraid to examine.'

Then she slipped into her car and slammed the door shut. As an afterthought, rage still bubbling in her veins, she wound the car window down. 'I think you were right a few weeks ago. Maybe we should change partners.' And she gunned the engine and took off in a hail of gravel.

* * *

The next morning Lawson sat in the staffroom and watched as Carl and Victoria left on a job together. Carl had his arm around her shoulder as they joked about something. Her laughter tinkled towards him and Lawson wanted to break Carl's arm into little pieces.

A red-hot ball of burning bile rose in his chest and that was when it hit him. He loved her. He'd been hiding from it, fighting it since she'd confessed to deeper feelings for him, but it would no longer be denied.

It hadn't seemed right to admit it before now as he'd struggled with the confines of their old relationship. As he'd grappled with the way he'd always seen her— Bob's daughter, his partner—to the way she wanted him to see her.

But watching her with someone else, their old dynamic blown to pieces, he knew it deep down in his bones.

Loving her suddenly seemed like the most natural thing in the world. She was his. She belonged to him. In an ambulance next to him. In his bed every night. In his life. He couldn't live another day without her.

He quickly formulated a plan to woo her, to win her back. He just hoped it wasn't too late. He hoped his indecision hadn't lost her for good.

Vic went to retrieve her backpack from her locker at the end of her shift and found a note doubled over and taped to the front. She pulled it off the metal and unfolded it, her heart thundering in her chest as she recognised Lawson's slashing scrawl.

*We need to talk. Meet me at the beach tonight
after work. Our special place.*
Lawson

She read the note over and over, her hands trembling.
She'd told him she didn't want to talk until he was ready
to face his feelings. Was that what this was? Or was it
just another excuse to talk her into leaving? Wouldn't
he have signed it *love Lawson* if it were about them? But
then why would he? Overt signs of emotion weren't his
style. She knew that. She'd always known that.

After her tenth read-through she screwed it up and
threw it in the nearby bin. She should leave him hanging. Make him come get her if he was serious about it.
But she knew she wasn't strong enough to resist the lure
of the note. The possibility in his words.

Our special place. She didn't have to ask him to
know where he was talking about. Was that how he
saw it? Their special place? And if so what did that
mean exactly?

Half an hour later, after a quick trip home for a shower
and change, she was walking down the beach, her pulse
pounding as loudly as the surf far down the beach.
Butterflies fluttered in her stomach like grains of sand
swirling in the current.

It was darker tonight, the moon a thin sliver in the
sky. The rocks loomed ahead of her in the night and in
her hand she clutched a torch so she didn't break her
neck scrambling over them in the scant light.

But she needn't have bothered. A warm orange glow

illuminated the rocks and lit a path to the secluded cove. When it came into sight she could hear the crackle of a fire and see Lawson, his hands burrowed into his pockets, staring into the flickering flames.

'Hi.'

Lawson looked up. She was standing on the rocks looking down at him, the glow from the fire caressing her cheekbones and glistening in her lip gloss. 'You came.'

She nodded. 'Of course.'

He moved, covering the distance from the fire to the rocks in three easy strides. He reached up for her and she leaned down, placing her hands on his shoulder as his hands encircled her waist. He lowered her down, her body sliding along every inch of his.

Until today he would have ignored the way his body responded, but right now he revelled in his arousal. She stood in his arms for several seconds, looking up into his face, and he ducked his head to claim her lips.

When she turned her face to the side and moved out of his arms he let her go even though his body urged him to pull her closer. He had some ground to make up tonight and he was not going to blow it this time.

Vic moved towards the fire. She noticed a picnic blanket and a basket set up under the overhang. Her pulse throbbed in her temple as hope surged through her system. It was very romantic and she had to stop herself from turning around and running into his arms.

Lawson brushed past her. He dropped to his knees under the overhang and opened the basket. 'Do you prefer pink marshmallows or white?'

Vic gave a half-smile. 'They all look the same colour after they've been on fire.'

'Ah.' He chuckled. 'You're a burner, not a toaster.'

His laugh brought goose bumps to her skin. It was so good to hear. She wanted to spend the rest of her life listening to it.

He turned and sat on the rug holding out a long thin stick and patted the space beside him. 'Care to join me?'

Vic took a few seconds. It looked so inviting. A bonfire in her favourite spot with the man she loved. Surely he wouldn't bring her here, take the time to set it all up if he were going to give her a 'let's-just-stay-friends' speech.

She crossed her fingers behind her back and walked to where he sat. She took the proffered stick but kept a little distance between them when she chose her spot on the rug.

For the next ten minutes they compared techniques and generally avoided any personal conversation. Lawson liked to gently brown all over, turning the stick repeatedly above the flame as it slowly toasted. Vic preferred to plunge the stick into the guts of the fire and wait for it to catch light.

He watched her tip her head back and drop another unrecognisable sticky, charred lump into her mouth. She sighed and smiled at him as she savoured it in her mouth. 'That's disgusting,' he murmured, totally distracted by the way the light from the flame licked orange tentacles along the ridge of her throat.

Vic laughed, impaling a soft pink marshmallow. 'Nuh-uh. You have to try it first,' she said, stabbing the stick into the heart of the fire again. 'There's all this wonderful crunch and then gooey sweet liquid explodes in your mouth.' She watched as the marshmallow finally flamed and pulled it out. It looked like a beacon in the dark and she gave it a second or two before she blew on it, extinguishing the flame.

'Here,' she said, removing the marshmallow and bringing it close to his lips. There was a second when they looked at each other and the blaze in their eyes had nothing to do with the fire. 'I dare you,' she said, nudging his lips.

Lawson held her gaze as he opened his mouth and sucked the gooey treat inside. He captured her fingers too, sucking the sticky residue from them as he stared into her fiery whiskey eyes.

Vic felt desire burst inside her like liquid marshmallow and she withdrew her fingers only to replace them with her lips. She heard his indrawn breath as he opened his mouth to her, cradling her jaw, pushing his fingers into her hair.

'Lawson,' she whimpered, gasping for breath herself. She felt as if the fire had broken the ring of stones that encircled it and set up camp in her belly.

Lawson groaned, pulling back slightly only to home in for more, bending her back, pushing her down onto the rug, stroking his fingers down her face, her throat as she locked her arms around his neck.

He pulled his lips away slightly, dropping kisses all over her face. 'I love you,' he murmured. 'I love you so much.'

Vic stilled, the words she'd been longing to hear stroking seductively against her skin. She pushed against him, raising herself on her elbows. 'Are you sure? You know, I hear sometimes it's easy to get sex confused with other feelings.'

Lawson rested his head on her shoulder, trying to catch his breath. *He guessed he deserved that*. He pushed himself into a sitting position, struggling to get his mind back on what he needed to say.

'I've been so blind,' he said, staring into the flame. 'Can you forgive me?'

Vic sat too. She reached out and placed her hand on his shoulder. 'Of course I can. I know this hasn't been easy for you.'

'Yesterday…what I said, about Matilda. It came out all wrong. I was trying to tell you I knew I had feelings for you and then I mentioned Matilda and it got all screwed up.'

Vic gave him a rueful smile. 'I may have overreacted.'

Lawson looked at her. 'No. No, you didn't. I was still fighting it. What I knew deep down inside but had been too afraid to admit because somehow I thought people would think less of me, would judge all my actions with you up to this point as if I had some ulterior motive all along.'

Vic gasped. 'Oh, no, Lawson. No one's going to think that. That's just hideous.'

He gave her a sad smile. 'Some people will, Victoria. They will. But I can't be responsible for other people's thoughts. And you were right. You do deserve to have someone who wants you for you. Not for any mothering abilities or girl-talk skills. And I lay in bed last night and I missed you so much. I can't get your smell off my sheets or the memory of what we did in my bed out of my head. But I still didn't let myself think about what that really meant.

'And then I arranged for you to go out with Carl today knowing it was all for the best and he put his arm around you and I wanted to tear him apart.' He turned to gaze at the fire. 'Pretty Neanderthal, huh?'

Vic shook her head. 'No. Pretty damn sweet, actually.'

'It hit me then. I didn't want to share you with anyone. I didn't want you to be someone else's partner. It was suddenly so clear. I loved you. And I didn't care who knew it or what they thought. I love you. And I know you should go overseas and do what you need to do but I'll be miserable if you do. I can't live another day without you. I don't want to.'

Vic felt a rush of emotion flower in her chest and a solitary tear trekked down her face.

Finally.

Finally she'd heard the words she'd been waiting to hear.

The silence grew with just the crackle and pop of flame on wood and Lawson turned to look at her. She wouldn't reject him now, would she? He noticed the tear. Had she changed her mind? Had she decided to go overseas after all? He reached for her, pulling her into his arms. 'Don't cry,' he murmured, kissing her forehead. 'Please don't cry.'

Vic choked on a sob. 'Oh, Lawson. I love you too. I've always loved you.' She raised her face to his and pulled his neck down to claim a kiss. 'I can't believe you're saying this. I'd just about given up.'

He shook his head, his heart filling with joy. *She*

loved him too. Somehow, though, he wasn't surprised. Somewhere deep inside he knew they'd been destined for each other. He kissed her eyes and her nose. 'Believe it.' He dropped a kiss on her mouth. 'But I'm asking a lot of you, Victoria. I'm asking you to be a mother as well. Something you've been for the last eighteen years. Something you've told me repeatedly you never ever want to be. Can you handle that? I don't want you to regret this choice years down the track.'

Vic smiled. She lifted a hand and stroked his face, running a finger down his scar. 'Of course I won't. Lawson, even if you and I never came to be, I know I belong here. I know now I could never leave. This is my home. It holds my heart. There's a world out there, I know that and I do want to see it, but it's nothing compared to what I have here. All I need now, all I'm ever going to need, is you. If I have that then the rest doesn't matter.'

Lawson smiled. He felt warm all over and it had nothing to do with the fire. 'It's still a big ask. Instant mother. I'm scared stiff that one day you'll start yearning for far horizons again and turn around and walk away. Like Matilda's mother did.'

She ran a finger over his lips. 'I'm not Deb, Lawson. I'm not someone you barely know. I certainly couldn't walk away from you or Matilda. When you love someone that means you love all of them. And you and Tilly are a package deal. She's the sweetest thing. She's part of you—why wouldn't I want her? I would be honoured to be her mother.'

Lawson swooped down and took her mouth in a kiss

that he felt all the way to his groin. She clung to his shoulders and her moan empowered him to go deeper. Linger a while. He pulled away minutes later, with difficulty. 'We're getting married. As soon as your father's well and we can arrange it.'

Vic smiled, her heart full of the most incredible sweet ache. 'Here on this beach. Matilda can be flower girl.'

'And then we're going on a honeymoon. For six weeks. We're going to London. And Italy.'

Vic felt her heart flutter in her chest. 'And we'll take Tilly.'

Lawson's heart filled so much he thought it was going to burst out of his chest. 'But in the meantime, you're coming to live with me. With us.'

She grinned. 'Yes. Sir.' And she pulled him down with her into the sand, eager to comply with his commands.

And all that could be heard for the next little while was the crackle of the fire and the pounding of the surf as their bodies promised each other a life full of happily ever afters.

THE BOSS AND
NURSE ALBRIGHT

BY
LYNNE MARSHALL

All the characters in this book have no existence outside the imagination of the author, and have no relation whatsoever to anyone bearing the same name or names. They are not even distantly inspired by any individual known or unknown to the author, and all the incidents are pure invention.

First published in Great Britain 2010
Harlequin Mills & Boon Limited,
Eton House, 18-24 Paradise Road, Richmond, Surrey TW9 1SR

© Janet Maarschalk 2010

ISBN: 978 0 263 87683 3

Harlequin Mills & Boon policy is to use papers that are natural, renewable and recyclable products and made from wood grown in sustainable forests. The logging and manufacturing process conform to the legal environmental regulations of the country of origin.

Printed and bound in Spain
by Litografia Rosés, S.A., Barcelona

Lynne Marshall has been a Registered Nurse in a large California hospital for twenty-five years. She has now taken the leap to writing full-time, but still volunteers at her local community hospital. After writing the book of her heart in 2000, she discovered the wonderful world of Mills & Boon® Medical™ Romance, where she feels the freedom to write the stories she loves. She is happily married, has two fantastic grown children, and a socially challenged rescued dog. Besides her passion for writing Medical™ Romance, she loves to travel and read. Thanks to the family dog, she takes long walks every day! To find out more about Lynne, please visit her website: www.lynnemarshallweb.com

Praise for
TEMPORARY DOCTOR, SURPRISE FATHER
by Lynne Marshall:

'A touching, tender and engrossing Medical™ Romance, TEMPORARY DOCTOR, SURPRISE FATHER is a wonderful story which I devoured in a single sitting! Don't miss this talented storyteller's enchanting tale of second chances, devastating secrets and the redeeming power of love!'

—*Cataromance*

'Lynne Marshall's excellent writing skills lend excitement and credibility to this story… The tension between Jan and Beck is realistic, and keeps you reading to the very end.'

—*The Pink Heart Society Reviews*

This book is dedicated to the smartest woman I know,
my wonderful daughter and future Nurse Practitioner,
Emily. Your beauty shines through your eyes
and brightens every room you enter.

CHAPTER ONE

JASON looked up from his desk to find big blue eyes staring at him. He'd been sailing all weekend and by Sunday, with nothing else to do for the afternoon, he'd come into the clinic to catch up on patient labs and charts rather than face being alone at home. The pint-sized human stood in his office doorway, watching him, unblinking.

"Man," she said. She wore a jacket which had slipped from her shoulders, held in place solely by her arms through the sleeves as she pointed at him. A simple pull-on shirt that didn't quite cover her pudgy tummy, and patterned pants in varying shades matched the bright green jacket. Corkscrew light brown curls surrounded her chubby face.

"And who might you be?" he asked, fighting off a sinking feeling as the memory of his daughter flashed in his mind.

Long slender arms swooped in and scooped up the child, who looked to be no more than two or three. Hanna had been four.

"OK, pipsqueak, I told you to stay by Momma." She

didn't talk to the child like some parents did with high whining sounds, as if they were the favorite family pet. Her voice had a mellow, husky tone, like an actress from a classic movie. "Oh! I didn't know anyone else was here," she said.

He shouldn't be here, but the ocean had turned from glassy smooth to choppy and restless, and though the sun always soothed his emptiness by heating the cold blood pulsing through his veins, nothing seemed to help today. So he'd decided to work.

"Thought I'd come in to play catch up before another crazy week of overbooking." He stood and held out his hand. "I'm Jason Rogers, the family practice GP of this group."

The young woman accepted his greeting. Her hand was cool and slender like the rest of her. He liked how her height almost brought her eye-to-eye with him, and how she looked at him as steadily as her daughter had.

"And I'm Claire Albright, the new Nurse Practitioner," she said with her child slung easily across her hip. "I think I'm supposed to remedy some, if not most, of that over-booking." She smiled just enough to show bright straight teeth. "You weren't at the meeting when they hired me."

"No." He dropped her hand and scratched the back of his neck. "I leave all that business up to the others." Phil, Jon and René had kept him emotionally afloat the last four years. In return his ample wealth had supported the clinic through its growing pains. He didn't know where or what he'd be without his medical partners.

The woman had ash-colored blond hair with streaks, like streams of light weaved through it. She had a high forehead and soft brown brows that showcased her hazel eyes. There was strength to her nose and chin, which he liked. He looked away.

Though definitely attractive, her appearance didn't matter. Beyond his medical practice and patients, nothing much mattered. At all.

"I'm moving in down the hall." She seemed at a loss for what else to say. He wasn't helping a bit by standing like an idiot with his usual blank stare. "I love this building," she said. Her eyes shone as she mentioned the three-story cream-colored Victorian house turned medical clinic. "I used to drive by, read the MidCoast Medical Group sign, and say, 'one day I'm going to work there', and now I do."

Her enthusiasm pained him. It smacked of idealism and hope—things he couldn't remember. Jason couldn't think of an appropriate response, and stared blankly.

He'd purchased the mansion several years back for his partners' business venture with his wife's encouragement. She'd loved the building, too. Back then, the optimism now glimmering in Ms. Albright's eyes had resided in his heart.

"And this is Gina." With a mild blush across her peach and olive-tinged skin, her smile widened, pressing dimples into her cheeks, and it almost felt contagious. But he'd given up smiling a long time ago.

The little one ducked her head into her mother's shoulder, no longer bold. She'd no doubt realized Jason was not someone she could trust with her clear eyes and easy smiles.

"Hello, Gina. And Ms. Albright, you should be a

good fit for our practice." He recited the hollow words to keep up the façade of being human—at least half human—for the child's sake.

Having completed his duty with a begrudging greeting, Jason sat down, sending a direct message that their introductory chat had ended. There was nothing more he could say. Not looking the least bit flustered by his blunt move, Claire nodded. The child on her hip squirmed to get down. She obliged, but held the girl by her shoulders and marched her down the hall without another word.

So the medical group had finally hired a fifth practitioner. They didn't want to bring in another full-time doctor, but had decided an RNP would be a big help. Besides seeing the routine overflow patients, she'd be counseling the diabetics and high cholesterol clients on diet and exercise. Or so René had promised. She could also perform physicals on both adults and children, and routine PAP smears on the female clients. The others would think of more to keep her busy as time went on.

René had mentioned something about the new employee taking a more holistic approach to patient care, whatever that meant. As long as her medical advice didn't get too out there, what did it matter to him?

Jason did have one concern about adding a fifth group member, though—what was he supposed to do with his freed up time? The clinic was as much of an escape from life as it was a means to practice his profession. If he ever caught up with his backlog, he'd be faced with dealing with the world outside. He couldn't afford to let that happen.

* * *

"Not exactly the friendliest guy on the planet," Claire mumbled to Gina, closing the door to her new office two doors down from Dr. Rogers. Her daughter scampered across the room, not interested.

Though overall he was good-looking, with straight brown windswept hair and strong masculine features, there was a deadness in his steel-gray eyes as if he'd had the life sucked out of him. It unsettled her. His empty gaze had sent a chill down her spine.

Jason Rogers struck Claire as a wounded soul. A fit and sexy man wearing a drab gray polo shirt and wind-breaker who looked very much alive, but in his core he seemed damaged and unable to connect.

"It takes one to know one, Dr. Rogers," she whispered. The thought of reading his obviously broken aura both intrigued and frightened her.

Her snap assessment of her new employer didn't matter. She'd joined this medical group for the opportunity to practice a more inclusive style of medicine, not to make friends. And after the doozy of a job her ex-husband had done on her, her lagging self-esteem needed a positive boost.

They'd married young, with plans to travel the world. Shortly after their first anniversary, she'd started experiencing strange symptoms, which interfered with their plans. He'd been unforgiving, and chastised her over the next couple of years for not being strong enough when she couldn't finish a hike or a long bike ride. When she'd taken to bed with unexplained aches and pains, he'd accused her of faking it, as if she were nothing but a hypochondriac. A year later she'd become pregnant and things between them seemed to look up, but everything changed for the worse when she was finally diagnosed.

That was all water under the bridge, as the saying went. She'd learned so much in her quest to make her life better. She credited alternative medicine for giving her life back to her, and she wanted to extend her knowledge to her future patients here at MidCoast Medical.

She'd vowed that the new job was about what was best for the patient. The total patient. For all she cared, if Dr. Rogers wanted to weave a standoffish cocoon or hang upside down in his office and spit at people, it didn't matter. She wouldn't give him the power to matter to her—as long as he left her alone to do her job.

Gina ran to the window and pointed to the sparkling Pacific Ocean off in the distance. "Pwetty."

"Yes, it is." Claire studied the resplendent view as a warm rush of excitement rippled through her. The clinic was situated in the heart of downtown Santa Barbara, a few streets over from State Street, the main boulevard. She stepped closer to the window and saw the pier through the palm trees. She'd definitely moved up in the world since, as a Nurse Practitioner, she'd also completed a degree in holistic medicine.

This was her chance to prove that medicine was evolving away from the old cut and dried methods to a more symbiotic approach connecting traditional medicine with holistic and alternative care. She treated the whole person, not just the physical aspect, but also the emotional, social and spiritual being. She'd already gained the other doctors' trust, when she'd introduced them to the world of homeopathy during her interview. They thought she'd be a good fit for their practice.

Claire was living proof that alternative *and* traditional methods worked best for chronic illness. She couldn't remember the last time she'd had a relapse from her Lupus, and she'd managed to keep her daily aches and pains to a minimum. As long as she kept everything in balance. She glanced in the direction of her new colleague's office; something about Jason Rogers knocked her off kilter.

Gina tugged on her pant leg. "Hungwee."

Claire scanned the several boxes yet to be unpacked. She grinned at the greatest gift she'd ever known. "OK. Give me a second." Her daughter smiled up with innocent, trusting eyes. It was almost two o'clock, long past lunch time. They needed to eat. Maybe after, Gina would take a nap while Claire finished setting up her new office and attached exam room.

The Victorian mansion, complete with wraparound porch, gorgeous bay window and princess tower was big enough to house a spacious waiting room in what used to be the sitting room, while the receptionist's office would have been the dining room, and there was still room enough for three doctors' offices plus exam rooms on the first floor. The kitchen, pantry and laundry rooms had been turned into the doctor and nurse lounge, and the nurses' downstairs supply and procedure room.

The second floor, where Claire's office was, had been left to Jason and his family practice until she'd barged in. One of the bedrooms had been turned into a small waiting room for his patients, and another had become the nurses' upstairs station plus another procedure room. The high ceilings with crown molding throughout gave a spacious feel, and the wainscoting made each room special. The third floor had been left for storage, or so René Munroe had said when taking Claire on her initial tour a week and a half ago. Jason's door had been closed that day, and René hadn't made an effort to tap on it or to say hello.

Claire needed to pinch herself to believe she'd been hired into such a prestigious and beautifully housed medical practice. But what would it be like working down the hall from the standoffish Jason Rogers?

"Hungwee!"

If only everyone on earth could communicate as directly as a two-and-a-half year old, life would be so much easier. "OK, pipsqueak, let's go."

Claire thought about Dr. Rogers, alone in his office, and how René hadn't included him in the clinic tour. She wanted to make a good first impression, and decided to give him another chance. She popped her head around the corner of his door. "We're going to the health food store up the street for some sandwiches. Can I bring you one?"

He barely glanced up. "Oh, I'm about done here. I'll grab something on my way home. Thanks, anyway."

OK, she got the point. Rogers wanted to be left alone, which was exactly what she'd do from here on out.

Monday morning was a blur. Claire had to get up extra early to get Gina to childcare in order to make it to the welcome breakfast René Munroe had planned at the clinic. Her muscles ached from all of the lifting, packing and unpacking she'd done yesterday, and she needed to add extra wild yam to her daily herbal cocktail to help ease the pain. So far, so good.

She rushed up the front steps of the clinic on stiff legs, across the potted plant-covered porch, through the entryway, past the reception office and into the kitchen at 7:45 a.m. Philip Hanson, the pulmonary doctor of the group, greeted her with a glass of fresh squeezed orange juice and a bowl of granola with blueberries on top.

"Since you're our homeopathy guru," he said, "I didn't want to get off on the wrong foot with sticky buns or anything overindulgent." Though in his mid-thirties, he'd retained a youthful quality, and his broad, accepting smile helped ease her first day jitters.

Jon Becker, the cardiologist, called out a greeting from a table set with china, flatware and a peach-colored cover. "Join us," he said, as if she'd been working with them for years.

She sat next to him and reached for the cinnamon, and sprinkled some over her bowl of granola. Besides stimulating her immune system, cinnamon helped maintain a healthy cholesterol level; she never went a day without some.

Dr Becker's salt and pepper, close-cropped hair gave him a scholarly air. On the initial tour of the clinic, René had mentioned that Dr. Becker was a long distance runner, and his wiry build and angular features proved her point.

"Good morning, Claire. You'll have to excuse me if I'm not exactly perky today," said René Munroe, the OB/GYN element of the practice. She was already seated across the table from Claire, with a mug of coffee in her hands. "I delivered twins last night."

"Oh, how wonderful. Everything go OK?" Claire asked, spooning her first bite.

"The mother had planned on a natural birth, but after the first baby was born, the twin slipped into breech and I didn't want to risk it." She swept a thick lock of auburn hair behind her ear. "She had to go through eight hours of labor and childbirth with the first baby, only to wind up having a C-section after all that."

"Oh, the poor thing!" Claire assumed the babies were at the local hospital, since it was the only one in town.

Though she'd known they'd planned this first day meal together, she couldn't take her a.m. meds at home on an empty stomach, so she ate her second breakfast, not wanting to insult her new partners. They all seemed so welcoming and friendly, and she had a great feeling she'd love working here.

Philip handed her a bran muffin, still warm from the oven. "I baked them myself," he said with a proud smile. She noticed a deep and attractive cleft in his chin. René had also informed Claire that Phil had been an award-winning surfer in his youth, and his dark tan and blond-tipped hair suggested he still enjoyed the sport.

She broke apart the muffin and let the steam rise. It smelled like pure comfort, and her mouth watered in anticipation of the first bite. If she read her tea leaves, she suspected she'd see weight gain in her future.

After taking a bite and savoring the fresh-baked flavor, she brushed some crumbs from her skirt. Today she'd worn power purple. A simple patterned wraparound dress with matching necklace and shoes to make a good first impression. She'd also worn her hair down, had even curled it for the big day. She'd been caught by Jason Rogers in crop length workout pants and matching jacket yesterday, with her hair pulled back into a low ponytail, and she'd been a bit embarrassed about her decision not to wear a stitch of make-up, when, by chance, she'd run into him. Today she'd outlined her eyes in liner and had even worn mascara and a touch of plum-colored eye-shadow.

She glanced around the room. The circa 1900-styled kitchen hadn't changed much at all except for an updated stainless steel refrigerator, and microwave with stove combo. She smiled, thinking how the newer appliances matched the original tin ceiling. As evidenced by the dish drainer on the counter, they hadn't installed an automatic dishwasher. She liked how they'd used a tablecloth and someone had put a small vase of fresh flowers at the center. Everything felt homey at the clinic and it seemed filled with goodwill.

Two of the nurses strolled in, followed by the receptionist, and Claire got introduced. She liked how there didn't seem to be an invisible barrier between the doctors and nurses. They all seemed to greet each other and interact casually as they filled their coffee cups and nibbled on muffins, as though one big happy work family.

Claire was thrilled to be a part of it.

One person was conspicuously missing, though. Jason Rogers was nowhere in sight, and no one but her seemed to make note of it.

After breakfast, Claire went upstairs to prepare for

her first patients. Gaby, the receptionist, had booked all the last minute add-ons who were willing to see the newest addition to the clinic, with her. Rather than make the patients wait for an appointment with their assigned doctor on another day, as they used to, this default system gave the clientele a sense of easy access to medical care. Down the hall, she noticed Jason's door ajar, but didn't dare walk over to say hi. He'd made it clear he wasn't the sociable type, and being a quick study, Claire knew she wouldn't be able to change him.

She sat behind her sturdy oak desk, adjusted her hips into the comfy leather-bound chair, and marveled at how her life had changed. A year ago her husband, Charles, had divorced her, and immediately had taken up with another woman who'd wanted little to do with children. Charles couldn't accept that he'd married a woman with a chronic illness and after her diagnosis, as the months clicked by, he'd grown more and more distant. Other than occasional weekend visits, poor Gina had been left on the sidelines of her father's new marriage.

Charles had let Claire know, in no uncertain terms, that he couldn't put up with her having Lupus. She'd been the same woman he'd met, fell in love with, and married, with the addition of a new diagnosis, but he couldn't understand that. She'd become imperfect to him, and he couldn't accept it. He'd made her feel guilty for getting sick, and ugly, when he'd look at her with disdain when her Lupus rash flared.

He was a successful businessman who insisted on a healthy partner to join him on adventures and extensive travel, and the once-loving man had shut down and turned away. Just like that. As if it was all her fault.

The pre-nuptial agreement left Claire with nothing beyond modest alimony and monthly child support payments. She knew Charles would come through in an emergency, but refused to depend on him for anything else. His not accepting her chronic illness had shattered her trust in both love and men, and she'd vowed to move on with her life—alone.

She'd recently had a stretch of good health and, with the new job, good fortune. As far as she was concerned, her past was just that. Over. And, with time, she hoped to get over the emotional damage, too.

Claire stood and moved to the window. She lifted the sash to allow fresh air inside and, gazing across rooftops, trees, and eventually toward the huge blue sea, she couldn't help thinking that her luck had finally turned.

By early afternoon, Claire had seen a dozen patients and was getting into the routine of the clinic's patient flow. Twenty-minute appointments were generous compared with the hospital where she used to be affiliated, which allowed only half that.

She read her next patient's records on her computer, and heard footsteps down the hall, then a looming shadow covered her desk and Jason appeared. His mouth was in a straight line, and his eyes squinted tensely. He looked perturbed, to put it mildly.

"A back rub? That's what you recommended to Ruth Crandall to add to her medical regimen?" he asked.

Claire had seen so many patients already, she had to

stop and think who he'd referred to. *The woman battling depression.*

"Well, I noticed she'd had her antidepressant increased at her last visit and her general complaints were unchanged. I thought we'd try something different."

"A massage?" He lifted a brow and handed the phone message toward her.

Claire read. Mrs. Crandall had called to tell him, after her visit that morning, what a great idea it had been to add daily massages to her routine, and how much she'd enjoyed meeting the new Nurse Practitioner. Under usual circumstances, a message such as this would be considered high praise, worthy of a pat on the back or handshake for a job well done. Evidently Jason Rogers didn't see it that way. His irritated attitude put her on defensive.

"Daily massages are invaluable for depression," she said. "They help relieve the aches and pains, and increase the release of endorphins for a sense of heightened well-being. There is healing power with touch."

"Is that so?"

Claire stood. "It's a perfectly good alternative to increased drug therapy. Wouldn't you agree that it isn't all about 'find and fix' anymore in medicine?" She waited for a response, but he just stood there with a steely glare. "Sometimes medical professionals need to integrate all avenues of health care for best results."

"You may have a point, but I've never once considered a massage as health care." He paced toward her framed credentials hanging on the wall. "Next you'll be prescribing aromatherapy, I presume."

She made a sly smile, and he caught her. "Maybe I will." Their eyes met for the briefest of moments, and paused. He'd obviously come to reprimand her, but nothing in this lingering gaze could prove it. He investigated her face and she felt suddenly self-conscious. She fought off the urge to pat her hair, wondered if her lipstick had smeared. "I've studied alternative medicine, and I believe there is much to be said for balancing the systems. After interviewing Mrs. Crandall, I identified her as a specific constitutional type who would benefit from massage." *And, speaking of constitutional types, you'd be classified as uptight!*

"She lost her husband last year," he said. "She's grieving and depressed. My job is to get her through this rough patch with the medicine available and a grief support group, not to send her to a spa to waste her money for a superficial beauty treatment." He leaned his knuckles on her desk and stared deeper into her eyes.

Claire refused to back away. "The power of touch is hugely beneficial for depression," she said, staring back. "Have you ever tried it?" His left eye twitched. "I didn't tell Mrs. Crandall to stop the medications you've prescribed."

Jason eased back, no longer on the attack. "This isn't how we practice medicine here, Ms. Albright."

"You told her to get exercise. What's the difference if I suggest massage? And the only complaint I see in this phone message—" she waved the message in the air "—is your interpretation of it. I'd say she was thoroughly happy about her visit today."

"That's not the point," he said.

He seemed a bit unsure and she couldn't help playing with him. "So one of our goals *isn't* to make our patients happier?"

He tossed her an exasperated glance. "Just do me a favor and consult me first, Ms. Albright."

She had the urge to say *Aye-aye, Cap'n* but noticed his glare had softened, and the tension around his eyes had disappeared. He really wasn't comfortable interacting with people. Or was it just with her? Wanting desperately to make amends for any hard feelings, Claire smiled. "OK. But would you do me a favor and call me Claire?"

He glanced at her one last time, nodded in a stiff business fashion, and left the room.

Claire sat down and tossed her pen on the desk. She hadn't given the woman a list of herbs to run out and buy, or asked her to ignore her medicine. She'd merely suggested that daily massage might help her through her depression. And the patient had been very receptive to the idea, enough to send a complimentary message about her add-on appointment to her regular doctor.

Why did Jason Rogers have to be such a wet rag about it?

She ran her hands through her hair and thought about the man who'd left her completely confused. She didn't know his history, but would bet her first pay check that something awful had happened to him. Maybe he was one of those people who felt entitled to happiness and things hadn't panned out, so he'd turned bitter. Whatever the reason, on a whim, she decided to go out of her way to be nice to him. Just to bug him.

* * *

When her first day at the clinic was over, Claire gathered her belongings, and prepared to leave. In the future, she'd be careful when counseling Dr. Rogers's patients. One nasty run-in with him was enough.

Her eyes got big with the thought. She hoped Jenny Whatley, the university student, didn't tell Dr. Rogers about what she'd suggested for her daily eyestrain headaches.

Not one second later, as she shut down her computer, Jason came barreling into her office.

Claire set her jaw and straightened her spine.

"What the hell is natrum muriaticum, and why did you suggest it to my patient?"

"You've been reading my patient progress notes, I see." She tamped down her brewing anger over the fact he'd been checking up on her, and walked around her desk. She dared to look into his eyes and received a cold dull stare as her reward. This was nothing like the more reasonable man from earlier today. "It is commonly known as table salt and salt tablets are best used for chronic ailments."

"Such as…"

"Such as daily headaches from eyestrain and tension. Jenny Whatley has been complaining to you about her headaches for over a year. She has all the classic traits of someone out of balance. Her complexion is pale and waxy. She looks emaciated and has cracks at the corners of her mouth. She's anxious, irritable and stressed out. And she gets throbbing headaches everyday at the exact same time."

"For which I have checked every possible condition and come up without a reason," he said.

Oh, the old take two aspirin and call me in the morning approach, I see. She couldn't help the snide thought. Jason Rogers seemed to draw the worst out of her. "But you haven't solved her problem."

"She has tension headaches. What does table salt have to do with any of that?" he said.

"It can regulate and balance the body fluids."

He gave her an incredulous look.

In defense, she glared back. "I made sure she doesn't have any counter indications for taking these tablets. Her labs checked out and so did the physical exam. We agreed she'd try them for a month. And she'll call immediately if there are any adverse reactions, which I went over thoroughly with her, and *which* I predict won't happen."

"You don't belong in this clinic. We are a reputable medical clinic, not some hocus-pocus guesswork group. If you want to prescribe table salt to patients, then set up a stand at your local health food store."

Stung by his insult, she crossed her arms. "I beg your pardon?"

"You heard me."

René appeared at the doorway. "Is there a problem?"

"She's a quack," he said.

"And he's a closed-minded medical robot!"

CHAPTER TWO

"HOLD on. Hold on." René stepped between Jason and Claire in the cramped office.

Claire couldn't believe her loss of control. His insult felt like a slap in the face and she'd retaliated without thinking. How had he gotten under her skin so easily?

"I don't think she's a good fit for our practice," Jason said.

Claire's heart sunk to her knees. She needed this job. Her ex-husband's nominal child support payments barely covered the cost of pre-school and child care. As it was, she could only afford to rent the maid's quarters in a seen-better-days mansion in Montecito. She needed to provide a life for the two of them. She had to make this job work.

"If I've stepped over the bounds, then I'm sorry," Claire said, scrambling to make things right.

Jason's glare softened. Had he heard the desperation in her voice?

"I'm sure we can work something out here," René said.

"I thought we hired a Nurse Practitioner. Now I've come to find out we've got our very own faith healer."

"I will not stand here and allow you to insult me like that!" Heat burned on her cheeks. She'd meant to keep quiet, but his words cut to her insecure core, and she needed to stick up for herself. No one would be allowed to walk all over her ever again.

"Then I suggest you leave," he said with a glacier-cold stare.

Don't back down. Even though my livelihood is at stake, he cannot be allowed to talk to me as if I don't matter!

"I deserve just as much respect as you do, Dr. Rogers."

"Hold on, you guys," René interjected, her gaze jumping wildly from Jason and back to Claire. "We can work this out civilly."

Jason shoved his hands in his doctor's coat and punched his tongue into the side of his cheek. He glanced at her desk, and the framed picture of Gina. "Only because she has a daughter to support am I willing to let her stay."

Who the heck did this guy think he was? The Emperor? *Well, how kind of you, sir, and I shall be forever grateful. Not!* "There are three other doctors in this practice who agreed to hire me. If you want to kick me out, I suggest you take a vote." With fear quivering her insides, Claire worried she'd pushed things too far. She fought to cover up her apprehension by widening her stance and leaning slightly forward.

Jason also leaned closer, and his glare delved into her eyes.

Why did she feel transported back to grammar school and smack in the middle of a sand box dispute? Back when boys and girls didn't know how to show they liked someone so they pretended to hate them. And why, upon looking closer into his eyes, did Jason Rogers appear to be enjoying himself?

"Hold on!" René said. "We don't need to take a vote. We can work this out like adults."

Claire wasn't sure what had clicked in Jason's mind, but his puffed up chest deflated infinitesimally and he stepped back.

"Look," he said. "I know with the economy the way it is, no one wants to lose a job." He ran his hand through his hair. "I'd appreciate it if you'd leave my patients alone. That's all. You can pick up the overflow for René, Philip and Jon. If you agree to that, I'll call a truce."

Claire glanced at René, who wore an earnest expression, as if encouraging her to take the deal. Accepting his offer for a truce seemed like the sane thing to do. Anything seemed better than standing around arguing with the obstinate and unlikable Jason Rogers. On her first day at work, no less!

If he wanted her to leave his patients alone, she'd be glad to comply. And once she was given the chance to get solid results with the other doctors' clients, maybe he'd come around to trusting her with his patients. And, if he asked nicely, she'd reconsider screening them for him.

She offered her hand, and he took it. The angry electricity that had jumped between them only moments before was still there. His palm was hot. And calloused, which surprised her. He stared intently into her eyes, and she almost needed to take a step back…but refused. There was something in his gaze that she hadn't detected before and, coupled with holding his hand, it knocked her a bit off balance.

"Truce," she said.

He nodded, dropped her hand and stepped away. After a brief glance in René's direction, he said, "Sorry to drag you into this." Then he went back to his office.

René stepped inside Claire's office and closed the door. "He's never offensive like that," she whispered. "He's sullen and moody, but never like that. I swear."

Claire studied her open-toed shoes, trying her best to figure out what had just happened. "I'm sorry. I am so sorry. I'm never like this, either. Please don't hold this against me."

"Not at all." René cupped Claire's arms. "We want you here. We're glad to have you. You've got to understand that Jason, well…" She hesitated, as if she didn't know how much to disclose about the man.

Who knew what his problem was? Perhaps he'd been through a rotten divorce like she had, and he held a grudge toward women the same way she did toward men. Maybe they had more in common than either would like to admit.

"Jason," René continued, brushing her hair behind her shoulder, "how should I put it…he leads a lonely life, and sometimes he forgets how to treat people. His patients love him, though, and he's an incredibly good doctor. Just give him time."

"It's apparent that he cares about his patients, I just wish he'd be a bit nicer to me. Hey, I'm a tough girl. I'll live with this set-up. You know how much I want this to work out."

"Good, because he essentially owns the building and practice."

Claire's throat dried up. Of all the people to pick a fight with. She needed to sit down. "I promise this will never happen again."

René nodded and offered a reassuring smile. "Now, did I hear right—this was about table salt?"

Jason paced his office, exhilarated. A sensation he hadn't experienced in a while. All because of an argument with Claire Albright? Albright—hah! She couldn't have a more appropriate surname. Whenever she entered a room it brightened. She didn't need to wear that becoming purple dress to make a lasting impression. All she had to do was smile. He remembered how taken aback he'd been when she'd smiled and introduced herself to him yesterday. He'd thought about her smile once or twice last night when he'd dined alone in his big and empty condo.

So why did he feel compelled to chew off her head? Because she dared to approach his only remaining thread to life, his sacred craft of medicine, differently. Table salt and massages—what a bunch of bunk. Just the thought of it rankled him all over again.

But there was something more to his reaction. She made him "feel" things. He'd stared into her eyes and felt his heartbeat pound in his neck when he'd argued with her. He'd been hot-tempered about what he'd said because it related to his patients and medical practice, the only thing left he cared about, and she'd thrown the passion right back in his face.

And she smelled like cinnamon, which did crazy things to his line of thinking. He dug his fingers into his hair.

Damn. The strangest notion overtook him. It made him pace.

After four years in limbo, he almost felt alive.

He came to a dead stop.

He'd soon put an end to that "feeling" business, by avoiding her at every turn.

The next morning, Claire entered her office before Jason had arrived. She needed to work up the courage to consult him about a plan to help the waiting room patients relax. They'd gotten off on the wrong foot, and here she was with another plan, but she couldn't back down. It had come to her in the middle of the night; something he'd said in a snide way about "next you'll start aromatherapy" must have planted the idea in her subconscious. He'd absolutely hate it, but if her trial run worked out in the upstairs waiting room, she planned to suggest they try aromatherapy in the larger downstairs waiting room, too.

If Jason owned the building, and he didn't like her or her ideas, he could get rid of her without consulting the other partners. Though she hoped and prayed he wasn't anywhere near as big an ogre as she'd imagined.

Mid-morning Claire saw Jason escort an older woman past her office door. His arm was on her shoulder, and he wore a concerned expression. "Mrs. Lewis, I'm sending you to the best surgeon in Santa Barbara. We caught the lump early…"

This from the grumpiest guy she'd ever met? Maybe

he wasn't so bad after all, and perhaps now was the perfect time to approach him.

She stood at her desk and waited for him to return. Her aromatherapy blend of lavender and ylang-ylang had been on the warmer all morning.

She used her hands to push the scent out her door, then rolled her eyes. This really was nuts—the markings of a desperate woman. The two things she needed to do to make him happy were to stay out of his way, and take care of every patient to the best of her abilities. But helping his outlook along with a little relaxing aromatherapy couldn't hurt, could it? Without his knowing, she might successfully change his sour mood and lift his spirits under the guise of helping their patients. And if it didn't work, no harm would be done.

She heard footsteps coming up the stairs and scrambled to her desk.

Jason slowed and hesitated outside her door. He turned his head and mumbled, "Morning."

Better late than never. Her mouth almost dropped open. Was he trying to be friendly?

"Good morning!" she said.

"What's that smell?" he asked.

Here was her chance. She popped up from her desk chair. "I was going to wait for you to get settled in and then tell…I mean ask you about this idea I got after we had our…uh…discussion yesterday. I mean last night. It came to me last night. The idea…I mean…"

"You're babbling, Claire. Get on with it."

OK, so he wasn't trying to be friendly, and she *was* babbling. At least he'd called her Claire.

"You've heard of white coat syndrome, right?"

"Of course." In his favor, he didn't look impatient.

"I was thinking about helping our patients relax while they're in the waiting room before their appointments by using a couple of essential oils that are known to calm people down. Would that be OK with you?"

He gave her the most curious look, as if she might be from an alien planet, but to her surprise he nodded his approval, then walked to his door and shut it soundly. She could have sworn she heard him mumble, "Whatever."

Claire ran behind on her morning appointments, and finished entering her last progress notes into the computer at quarter to one. She hustled down the stairs and into the kitchen to find it empty, except for Jason Rogers heating something in the microwave. She almost turned around and headed out the door, but he lifted his head, glanced at her and nodded.

Jason used a tissue to wipe his nose while he waited for his lunch to warm. "I needed to get out of my office. My eyes have been bothering me all morning, and now my nose is stuffed up."

The lavender and ylang-ylang? Claire widened her eyes, but caught herself from reacting too obviously. "Spring is just around the corner. Are you allergic to pollens?"

"Not that I know of." The microwave dinged and he reached for his lunch.

OK, so they proved they could have a semi-civil conversation.

Great idea, Albright. Instead of making him relax

with aromatherapy, you gave him a headache and a stuffed-up nose. Maybe she should add some rosemary drops to the mix to help with decongestion.

She left the kitchen and ran up the stairs to turn off the aromatherapy diffuser in the waiting room. Maybe she'd overdone it, but none of her patients had complained. In fact, a couple of them had lower than usual blood pressures during their appointments that morning. She'd definitely add the rosemary drops tomorrow. Maybe his reaction had nothing to do with the aromatherapy.

She returned to the kitchen just as Jason was exiting. He glanced briefly at her when he passed, but didn't say another word. Could he have thought she was avoiding him when she'd run out of the room so quickly? And, just when they'd made a mini step toward progress, too. She wanted to throw up her hands. Instead of easing the tension between them, she'd succeeded in irritating his nose and giving him the impression she couldn't stand being in the same room with him.

Things were not going well.

Two of the nurses had arrived back from picking up takeout food, and sat chatting happily at the table. She nodded to them and pointed to the back door.

"It's so lovely out today. I think I'll eat in the garden."

One of the nice extras about having a Victorian mansion as a medical building was the well kept back yard and garden, complete with arbor, gazing globe, and fairy statues. English and painted daisies, camellias, bleeding hearts and crocus in pinks, whites and purples, and many other perennial spring flowers she didn't have a clue about, were so pleasing to her eyes in the garden, she couldn't resist eating outdoors. And though it was sunny and warm today, and she needed to avoid the sun because of her Lupus, the yard provided a huge ash tree for shade and a convenient bench beneath it.

She sat and inhaled to help her relax. Maybe she should have set up the ylang-ylang and lavender for herself. She rolled her shoulders and watched a couple of robins hopping around the verdant grass in search of food as she unwound. High in the tree, other birds called their greetings to one another and rustled the leaves as they flapped away into the sky.

This was the place she needed to be at this exact moment in her life. In this garden. At this medical clinic. She'd do anything she could to keep her job, even if it meant putting up with Jason Rogers. She took a bite of her grilled veggies and hummus sandwich and chewed contentedly…until…she noticed the bee.

Back in his office, Jason needed to consult his drug formulary and went to his bookcase to retrieve it. From his upstairs window he noticed Claire on the bench in the garden eating her lunch.

She'd worn a sunflower-yellow dress today, and had taken off her lab coat before she'd taken her lunch break. And she'd worn her hair down again. He liked how it settled on her shoulders in waves. For someone who took herself so seriously, she certainly dressed in fanciful colors. Purple yesterday, bright yellow today. It said something about her, he didn't have a clue what, yet he found it curiously appealing and he felt drawn to her lively spirit. That disturbed him, made the hair on his neck stand on end.

He glanced at the picture of Jessica and Hanna on his bookcase that he kept out of view of others. Mother and child posed perfectly for the camera on one of their many vacations…so many years ago. God, he missed them. Was he being unfaithful to Jessica's memory by feeling a distant attraction to this new woman?

It wasn't purely about Claire being a good-looking woman, or the fact that it had been ages since he'd been intimate with anyone. No. And he definitely wasn't looking for anyone to become involved with. But Claire had guts and had stood up to him when he'd used his bully pulpit yesterday to call her out for trying new treatments. He respected her for standing up for what she believed in, no matter how off the mark she'd been. Table salt. Hah.

But really, what harm could a massage do to a depressed person? Had it been necessary for him to take such offense? First and foremost in the Hippocratic Oath he'd taken when he'd become a doctor was—Do No Harm. And Mrs. Crandall had sounded so hopeful in her message.

What did he know about hope anymore?

He shook his head, replaced the photograph on the shelf, and watched Claire as she bit into her sandwich.

Suddenly, she sprung up and her sandwich went flying as she jogged around in a circle flailing her arms. She flung her head around and frantically used her hands to brush her hair away. Over and over. With a contorted face, she danced in spasms and bent over, shaking her head, and swiped through her hair as if it were on fire. Again and again.

At first he was alarmed that something was terribly wrong. He started for the door, hesitated, then glanced back out the window. She wasn't calling for help. As she continued to gyrate and swat at the air, her fitful dance became…entertaining. Had something flown into her hair? If she gave one sign of being injured, he'd be down the stairs quicker than a three-star alarm. Until then, he'd watch from his prime position.

She stopped just as suddenly as she'd started. She smoothed the skirt of her dress and patted down her hair, then glanced around, as if to check if anyone had seen her.

A smile stretched across Jason's face as he observed a new side of Claire. A humbled, slightly embarrassed side.

Next he heard an unfamiliar noise. The sound of laughter. *His* laughter rumbling all the way up from his gut. It sounded like a foreign language, and he almost looked over his shoulder to see if someone else was making it.

After he turned his back, as he replayed in his mind Claire freaking out and jumping around swatting at her hair, he continued to laugh, a solid belly laugh. Why had the incident struck him so funny? Because it was so out of character for the woman. He really shouldn't be laughing at someone getting caught in a compromising situation. That was unkind, he thought as he wiped away tears from laughing so hard. She could have gotten stung by a bee and that would have hurt like hell. Though she'd shown no evidence of that. No, he shouldn't laugh.

Definitely no laughing.

He turned around again. She sat back down on the bench and ate the other half of her sandwich, after she'd retrieved the first half and tossed it in the trash. She glanced around a second time, no doubt hoping no one had seen her antics. She was obviously unharmed, except for maybe her pride.

And the replay of her dance in his mind made him laugh again. "Your secret's safe with me."

A few minutes later, he sat back at his desk, still grinning.

How odd it felt.

The next morning, Jason stopped at Claire's office door with an impish look on his face. It made her pause. He cleared his throat.

"I brought you something," he said. He reached into the sack he carried and withdrew a safari hat complete with a veil made of netting and handed it to her.

"What's this?" She stared at the object she'd only ever seen in the movies before.

"In case you decide to eat outside today," he said, one side of his mouth ticking into a smile.

The blush started at her neck and promptly rose up her cheeks. "You saw me?"

He nodded and grinned, a bright flash in his eyes.

"The whole thing?"

"As a physician, I needed to make sure you weren't injured or anything."

She covered her eyes and grimaced. "I'm so embarrassed."

"Don't be." He looked uncomfortable, his teasing stance having vanished as quickly as it had appeared. "Please." They shared a gaze, and she instinctively knew he'd meant no harm. "I've botched things up, I see." He scratched the side of his mouth. "I guess I'm out of practice."

"No," she said, lifting the hat even as her cheeks heated to what she assumed to be bright red. "This is very funny. Really."

On an awkward note, he tipped his head and went to his office.

Claire had to give him credit for trying to act like a regular person instead of a recluse. In fact it touched her. She collapsed into her chair and continued blushing for a few more moments, but decided her embarrassment was worth it to see Jason Rogers's gorgeous smile.

And, to remind her he had a sense of humor, she hung the beekeeper's hat on the antique coat rack in the corner of her office.

The next day, to her surprise, Jason personally escorted one of his patients to her New Diabetic Class.

"This is Leona Willis," he said, assisting the middle-aged lady to sit. "I think she can use a refresher course on diabetic care."

This was a change. Jason had specifically told Claire to keep away from his patients, and here he was delivering one to her. She smiled at the new student, and then at Jason, and felt a mild blush dance across her cheeks, which seemed far too much like it was becoming a routine. He seemed to hesitate before walking backwards to the door with an odd expression in his eyes. It made her pause to remember what she'd been talking about. "Where were we?" she asked the class.

"The importance of eating several small meals a day," one craggy old gent replied.

Claire nodded and, instead of concentrating on the subject, took one brief moment to ponder the fact that Jason seemed to be reaching out to her as one professional to another. The thought buoyed her spirit and set the tone for the rest of her day.

One week of truce with Jason had made working at the MidCoast Medical Center so much more bearable for Claire, yet she was still antsy about her first administrative board meeting. Jason couldn't have chosen a worse night. Monday was the one night this week her childcare provider couldn't keep Gina past six p.m. And the meeting was scheduled for six-thirty.

René had arranged for dinner to be delivered, but Claire brought a special kiddie meal for Gina at the local organic market. She tried to set it up as a "treat", telling her how she'd get to have her very own picnic while the grown-ups had their meeting. Gina didn't seem too impressed. Running a bit late, Claire gritted her teeth and pushed through the clinic's kitchen door with her daughter toddling beside her.

The others, Phil, Jon, René and Jason, were already seated and passing around their individual reports.

"I'm so sorry to have to bring Gina tonight." She glanced around the room for sympathy and understanding and found it with everyone except Jason, who'd made a merely tolerable glance her way. "Babysitter problems," she said.

Claire situated Gina in the corner with a few books and small toys, then opened and served her dinner after washing the child's hands with disposable wipes. "Be a good girl for Mommy, OK?" She tried not to plead but, depending on Gina's mood, her personality could range from introspective to gregarious, and there was usually no warning which way the wind would blow.

As the meeting went on, Claire got a glimpse at how the clinic ran through spending reports from Jason, trends in ailments from Jon, recommendations on being more efficient from René, and meeting the Occupational Health and Safety standards for clinic care from Phil. Just as Claire prepared to give her report, Gina decided she'd had enough self-entertainment.

She brought her favorite book and plopped it on the table next to Claire. "Read me," she said.

"Mommy can't right now. I have to work."

Instead of fretting, Gina picked up the book and went back to her assigned corner.

Claire took a deep breath and prayed she'd stay there.

"OK," Claire said. "René asked me to talk a bit about CAM—complementary/alternative medicine—and its prevalence of use amongst our client population. My statistics show that thirty to forty percent of the general population is using or has used some form of herbal compound in the past year."

Gina stood and opened her book. "Thnow White and the theven dorfs," she recited aloud to the wall.

René and Phil tried not to snicker.

Claire swallowed and continued. "I feel it is very important to identify which of our patients are using these herbal medications. Many patients think of them as dietary supplements or natural health products, not medicine."

"Onth upon a time," Gina recited as she paced back and

forth in a similar fashion as her mother, pretending to read from the page. "A printhess had to run away from her meanie tep-mommy." She turned the page with great flair.

"Gina, honey, can you wait until later to read your book out loud?"

"Can she read already?" Jon asked.

Not wanting to pop Gina's bubble, Claire shook her head surreptitiously and mouthed no. "She's working on it," she said, with sing-song optimism for Gina to hear. "Wait until later, OK, honey?"

The child turned to the wall and continued to "read" the story in a whisper.

Phil grinned, and René mouthed "aw". Claire nervously glanced at Jason and, instead of finding a scowl, she noticed one corner of his mouth edged up into an almost-grin.

"I'm so sorry," she repeated to everyone.

"Not a problem," Jon said. "Continue with your report."

She raised her voice and rushed through her carefully planned presentation, hoping her daughter wouldn't make any more disruptions. Claire had run down the list of herbal compounds most frequently used, and had offered her theory why patients failed to report the medication to their care providers, when Gina grew louder.

"Who is the faw-wist of them all!"

Even Jason snorted a laugh this time. He stood, and Claire figured she'd never get her chance to propose her clinic-wide survey. But, instead of suggesting the meeting be adjourned, he walked over to Gina and crouched beside her. Claire blinked, thinking she was imagining things.

"Hey, squirt, I'll make you a deal," he said. "I'll read that book to you if you'll sit quietly for just a few more minutes. What do you say?"

Amazingly, Gina didn't cower or get embarrassed, as she so easily did with her father when he reprimanded her. "'Kay."

Jason nodded, stood and went back to his seat. Gina followed him, something he obviously hadn't planned on. Surprise widened his eyes when she brought the book to the table and crawled up into his lap. Without saying a word, he helped her get settled and, when Gina was sufficiently at ease, he nodded to Claire to continue as if a minor miracle hadn't just occurred.

Claire cleared her throat and said, "I would like to conduct a clinic-wide survey of our patients to find out who is taking which herbs. If you'll look at the handout, you'll see I've named the ten most widely used herbal supplements and identified the potential drug interactions, some of which can be life-threatening. I believe it is imperative that we know *every* pill our patients are taking."

The group of doctors seemed impressed with Claire's suggestions, and began a lively discussion of how to go about surveying their entire patient population. Claire noticed that Jason lightly stroked Gina's curls as he read each handout.

The man had never looked more natural. Or relaxed.

His unconscious gesture did wonders for Gina, too. The child had fallen asleep.

Fifteen minutes later, the meeting came to an end. After gathering all the reports and putting them into her briefcase, Claire glanced at Jason. She caught him studying Gina's slack mouth with a melancholy gaze. It made her chest squeeze.

He was a father. She knew it. But where was his family?

She leaned over to retrieve her daughter. "Thank you," she mouthed.

"No problem," he said with a muted voice. But the torn look on his face contradicted his words. Somehow she knew holding her daughter hadn't been easy for him, and she instinctively knew she owed him a huge favor.

When Claire picked up Gina, she automatically woke up. "Man read," she said, rubbing her eyes and kicking her feet. *Oh, not now. Please don't throw a fit, child.*

Claire glanced at Jason, who had a soft but distant look in his eyes.

"I did make her a promise," he said, lifting the storybook.

Relieved, Claire delivered Gina back to his lap and the child settled in immediately, ready for her story. As though he'd read a million children's books, Jason began. "Once upon a time…"

As Jason read to Gina, Claire helped René gather up the take-out cartons and wash the flatware. She caught René's marveling glance, then nodded in agreement when she mouthed "wow". She kept busy, collected Gina's toys and books and carried everything to her car. She was on her way back into the clinic when Jason met her halfway down the walk. He carried Gina down the steps and hoisted her into her car seat expertly.

"Thank you so much, Dr. Rogers," Claire said.

"Call me Jason, will you?"

A look passed between them that said so much more

than "truce". For the first time since she'd been working in the new job, Claire felt she belonged. And Jason had shown the first signs of crawling out of his cave.

Jason watched Claire and Gina drive off. The wrenching pain in his chest made it hard to breathe. He'd paid a price for holding that child. Memories of cuddling Hanna had been dredged up from their carefully fortified cave: the softness of her hair, the perfection of her complexion.

He couldn't go on like this.

He clenched his jaw and watched the taillights turn the corner. He wanted to hit something. To take a sledgehammer and bash to smithereens the tomb that kept his daughter and wife from him.

That woman and her child had gotten under his skin, had forced him to feel things—things he never wanted to experience again. Feelings he couldn't bear.

The damp night air enveloped him as he bit his lip and paced against the torment.

CHAPTER THREE

TUESDAY morning, Claire passed the mock-up version of the patient herbal survey to Phil Hanson as he sat in his office. She'd stayed up past midnight putting it together. Aside from his medical school and specialty certificates framed on the walls, there were several surfing trophies and photographs of him with his board. His laid back attitude often carried over into his clothes, and today he wore a Hawaiian patterned tie with a pale blue denim shirt.

"Looks good," he said. His thick wavy hair appeared to only have been finger combed, yet he still managed to pull off a charming air. She wondered why he wasn't married, then remembered René had commented he was a happy and confirmed bachelor.

"What looks good?" Jason's deep voice came from over her shoulder.

It almost made her jump. She turned and found she was the closest she'd ever been to him, but the door-frame kept her from stepping back. His face was freshly shaven and he smelled of sandalwood and citrus, which tickled her senses. Though his hair was neatly trimmed, the longer top part had fallen across his forehead. She fought the urge to sweep it aside. Up close, his gray eyes had tiny flecks of blue in them, and they looked kinder than she'd thought. Or maybe that was because she'd seen him in a new light last night. After he'd read to Gina, her daughter had talked about him the entire ride home, until she'd fallen asleep.

"Well?" Jason said.

"Oh. The herbal survey. Here's a copy for your approval," she said, handing the pages to him.

He avoided her gaze, studying the paper instead. In contrast to Phil, his stiff collared white shirt hugged his tanned neck, and he'd made a perfect knot with his drab tie. Someone needed to brighten this guy's wardrobe up, but it wouldn't be her.

After her disastrous marriage, she wanted nothing to do with men. In her time of greatest need, she'd been kicked to the curb by her husband. Hadn't the wedding vows said "In sickness and in health"?

"Looks good to me, too." Jason handed the survey back and continued down the hall and up the stairs. His dark gray, perfectly tailored silk suit molded well to his broad shoulders and narrow waist.

Phil cleared his throat. Claire snapped back to the task at hand, and retrieved the survey from the doctor. He had a funny look in his eyes, as if he'd caught Claire ogling Dr. Rogers, which may have been the case but she hadn't meant to be so obvious. Her cheeks heated up and she made a quick getaway.

In a room of men, most women would notice Phil Hanson first, with his striking good looks and surfer boy features. But Dr. Rogers had a subtle solid handsomeness that caused her eyes to linger. After swearing off the entire gender, she wondered why she was suddenly comparing the men she worked with.

Claire shook her head, and strode to the receptionist's desk for the list of patient addresses.

"We'll need eight thousand surveys to go out," Gaby, the receptionist, said.

"Wow, this is a bigger practice than I thought." Drs. Munroe and Becker had already approved the survey. Now she had Phil and Jason's blessing, too, so it was just a matter of mailing it.

"That's the number of families, not the entire patient population. Some will need multiple surveys in one envelope."

"Oh, and do we have a budget to include a stamped return envelope?"

"I'll have to run that by Dr. Rogers," Gaby said.

Claire wanted this survey to be a success and knew that including the return postage made for a higher return rate, but she didn't want to break her employer's budget in the process. She mentally kicked herself for not getting the budget approved at the meeting last night.

"No problem. Dr. Rogers is a kitten. He'll do whatever I ask," Gaby, the plump, nearly fifty matron said, revealing yet another side of Jason Claire hadn't counted on.

She thanked Gaby, and felt relieved she wouldn't have to confront Jason a second time that morning, since he seemed to be pushing buttons she'd forgotten she had over the last year.

The concept of finding Jason Rogers attractive seemed ridiculous!

So why was she still thinking about him in his classy tailored suit?

Three days later, the first of the patient surveys were ready to get mailed. Claire sat with a stack on her desk, double checking to make sure no one had been overlooked. She glanced up to find Jason, looking tall and dashing, in her doorway.

History had proven that it was never good when Jason stood at her door. Her throat went dry before she could utter a sound.

He scratched the back of his neck. "I have a question for you," he said.

On a rush of relief, she smiled.

He entered and sat in the chair across from her desk and leaned forward, elbows resting on his knees. "First off, I wanted to let you know that Jenny Whatley has told me she no longer has daily headaches."

"That's wonderful." She'd already heard from Jenny but, being a lady, she hadn't rubbed his nose in it.

With a conciliatory gaze, he continued. "I guess I owe you an apology."

"Not necessary," she said, though shocked that he'd mentioned her success.

He nodded, looking relieved. "So now she says she needs something for her anxiety, but doesn't want to take any of the mild sedatives I've offered." He stared into her eyes, and she found it hard to think of one single thing. He looked earnest and she realized he was having a difficult time saying what he'd come to her office for.

"Are you asking me to recommend an alternative medicine for one of your patients?" This time, she couldn't stop herself from rubbing it in, just a teeny bit.

He grimaced. "Actually, *she* asked me to ask you."

She grinned. "Ah. OK, well, I'd recommend valerian. As long as she's not on any other sedatives."

"No. None at all."

She told him the dose and what to watch out for, went to her bookcase and retrieved her favorite herbal medicine book. "Here. You might like to read up on it."

He nodded. "Thank you." And he looked sincere, which touched her in a gratifying way.

It was Claire's turn to hesitate. As if he could read her body language, he lingered in her office. She scratched her cheek. "You made quite an impression on my daughter the other night."

He gave a self-deprecating laugh. "She's too young and innocent to know the real me, I guess."

Claire reached into her desk and pulled out a crayon stick figure picture. "She asked me to give this to 'Man' this morning."

Surprise colored Jason's usual pewter eyes to a softer gray tone. "She still remembers me?"

"Talks about you every day. I tried to teach her your name, but…"

He glanced at the mostly-scribbled picture. "This is sweet. She's adorable, by the way."

"Thanks. I think so, too." And, since he seemed receptive to the latest drawing, she reached back into the same drawer and pulled out several more pictures. "She's asked me to give you a picture every single day since you read her that bedtime story Monday night." She handed them to him.

"You've been holding out on me?" His attempt at humor was gratefully accepted.

He glanced into her eyes and she could see pain written in his gaze. With anyone else, she wouldn't have thought twice about bestowing them with her daughter's latest artwork. But with Jason she wondered if she was being kind by sharing them, or causing him trauma.

He nodded, almost smiled, took the pile of papers and, without another word, left her office.

Over the next few days Jason enjoyed the respectful routine he and Claire had slipped into. If she arrived in her office first, he'd pause by her door on his way down the hall. He'd nod and say "Morning."

And she'd beam back in whatever brightly colored blouse or dress she'd chosen for the day. Dangly earrings waving, hair up or down, eyes flashing with life. No matter what the weather, her office seemed filled with light. And it always smelled good, too.

Cinnamon came to mind.

And if he'd beaten her in to work, she'd take the extra few steps to his door to say hi and wish him a good day. The added effort validated him as part of the human race, something he'd forgotten he belonged to.

He wouldn't admit to anyone, almost couldn't admit it to himself, but he looked forward to his daily greeting from Claire. The seeds of life seemed firmly planted in her being and, even though he'd grown used to hiding in the shadows rather than attempting to live like everyone else, he felt drawn to her brand of energy. Wanted to feed from it. And some days, since she'd come to the practice, he even felt like smiling.

Later that morning when Jimmy Dixon cried when Jason entered the examination room, and wailed after he'd made several attempts to look down the boy's throat, he decided to get backup.

"Excuse me a minute," he said to the distressed mother, then padded down the hall to Claire's office. She wasn't there.

He walked to her exam room and tapped on the door. She opened it just wide enough to peek out. She was gowned and gloved, and most likely in the middle of a pelvic examination.

"Sorry. When you're done could you help me out in exam room one?"

Her naturally arched brows lifted in surprise. "Sure. I'll be there in a couple of minutes."

Five minutes later she joined him in his office. Feeling a bit chagrined, he explained his predicament.

"I'm usually really good with kids, but Jimmy hates me, has since the first vaccination. His mother thinks he has strep throat, and I can't get him to let me touch him, let alone get a throat swab."

Claire smiled at his request, and he could have sworn the room got brighter.

"Sounds like me trying to get Gina to take liquid antibiotics," she said. "I'll give it my best shot."

"I'd better wait here." He sat in his office and

thumbed through a pile of reports that needed his attention, but thought about the newest employee instead.
Aside from her crazy attitude about alternative medicine
being the answer to everything, she was undoubtedly
pleasant to work with. He sniffed the air for the telltale
sign of her fruity floral scent and enjoyed the added
touch of cinnamon he'd always noticed around her. The
woman smelled good, and he liked it.

Without warning, the image of his wife came to
mind, and how she'd always smelled sweet like
vanilla. He tortured himself with memories of how
he'd loved to kiss her neck and inhale her scent. How
she'd always caressed him back. He'd loved her so
much, but feared her image was growing harder and
harder to capture. He closed his eyes tighter to bring
her back into focus, and massaged the sharp pain in
his neck as the ethereal vision of his wife dissolved
into nothingness.

"All done."

His eyes popped open. Claire stood in the doorway
with the throat culture in hand. He didn't remember
hearing so much as a peep from the examination room.

"How d'you do it?" he asked, still rubbing his neck.

"I have my ways," she said with a teasing glimmer
in her eyes.

How could he be thinking of his deceased wife one
second, and then be taken aback by the simplest gaze
from Claire the next?

"Thank you," he said. His nurse walked by and took
the culture from Claire on her way to the exam room.

"Anytime," Claire said, with the same glint in her

eyes. What had gotten into her? "Maybe you should have that looked at," she said.

He screwed up his face, then realized she'd referred to his hand kneading his tight neck and shoulder. "Oh, it's nothing."

"If you change your mind, I'm also trained in acupressure." She wiggled her fingers in the air. "I could work that knot out in no time."

The thought of Claire touching him set his nerves on end. He covered by acting gruff. "I'll keep that in mind, Albright. Now, don't you have a patient waiting?"

She nodded, then mocked him with a salute. "Yes, sir."

He felt unnerved by the reaction she'd caused. He suddenly recalled the long-lost game of flirting with the opposite sex, and went completely still. A wave of unfaithfulness stopped him in his tracks, and the pile of lab reports received his undivided attention. Claire disappeared from his door without another word.

The next morning, Jason tapped on Claire's door wearing a perplexed expression.

"What's up?" she asked, noticing he was wearing a pale blue shirt under his doctor's coat that brightened his eyes.

"I have a patient who has red welts all over her back. She's trying to explain something to me, but I can't understand her."

This piqued Claire's interest. She rose from her chair and followed Jason down the hall. As they walked, he explained that the patient was a newly immigrated Chinese woman who usually brought her daughter along to interpret.

When they entered the room, Claire noted that the patient had a temperature, and she seemed congested and coughed into her hand from time to time. Claire introduced herself, but didn't offer her hand until she'd donned a glove.

"I was about to listen to Mrs. Ching's lungs when I noticed the welts," he said.

"I'm going to have a look at your back," Claire said to the patient, noticing puffiness around her eyes before stepping behind the exam table and opening the patient gown. When she saw the uniformly placed, fifty-cent sized welts across her entire back, she knew the answer. She closed the gown, removed her gloves, and motioned for Jason to follow her outside.

"She's been treated by a Chinese traditionalist and had a cupping."

Jason screwed up his face. "A what?"

"You've heard of Ying and Yang."

He nodded, his expression unchanged, which almost made her laugh.

"Her Yang is working overtime, and by cupping they tried to put her back in balance. The heat from the cups is supposed to suck out the toxins and restore her health."

"Well, it obviously hasn't worked this time around," he said. "She's feverish and congested and probably needs an antibiotic."

Claire nodded. "So her daughter made the appointment with you."

"I wonder if Mrs. Ching's daughter even knows she's been treated with Chinese traditional medicine?" he said.

"Good question. Why don't you give her a call?"

As Claire prepared to leave, Jason stopped her by reaching for her arm. The contact startled her, but she held her reaction close. "I would have put this poor woman through a full panel of blood tests to try and figure out what had caused those welts, if you hadn't been so astute. Your quirky background is proving to be very helpful."

A smile tickled across her lips, and Jason telling her that he appreciated her alternative medical expertise kept the smile spreading wider and wider.

"Cost-effective, even," he added, with a look of chagrin.

She opened her eyes with a mocking "no kidding" stare.

He shook his head and forced a partial smile. "And yes, that was hard for me to say."

She liked how his stately features seemed to pool into a puddle of warmth when he smiled. How his eyes relaxed and creases bracketed his mouth. Satisfaction trickled across her skin. "Then your compliment means all the more," she said.

He clicked back into his tough guy act. "Don't let it go to your head, Albright." She knew it was all show.

She gave him one last grin. "I wouldn't dream of it," she said, and turned to leave.

The third week after Claire Albright's arrival, Mrs. Crandall had responded beautifully to daily massage to the point of having her antidepressant decreased. Jenny Whatley continued to sing the praises of table salt, the waiting room patients commented how much they enjoyed the pleasant aroma while they waited for their appointments—the very same aromatherapy which no longer sent him searching for a tissue. Jason had changed his mind about Claire's alternative voodoo practices.

After reading her *Herbal Medicine* book from cover to cover, he decided to test her out and refer one of his patients to her.

"Forty-nine-year-old Hispanic female with chief complaint of ongoing hot flashes. Hormone replacement is not an option. See patient history. Seeks alternative phytotherapeutics."

Proud that he'd even used her terminology, he signed his name and marched down the hall to hand deliver the request for consultation. He wanted to see her reaction. Wanted to see her brighten and smile the way he'd come to enjoy. And he was fully prepared to receive an I-told-you-so smile—and even looked forward to it!

Claire's door was closed. He tapped, but no one answered.

He thoroughly trusted his office staff, and assumed she'd requested a day off that he didn't know about. Why should he? Her personal life was none of his business.

Jason walked back to his office and checked the schedule. Claire was supposed to be at work today.

Before he saw his next patient, he trotted down the stairs and asked Gaby where Ms. Albright was.

"She called in sick, Dr. Rogers."

He tilted his head and went back to work but, before he reached his office, he slid his consult request into her in-box.

The next day, her door was still closed and the

consult was exactly where he'd left it. And on the fourth day, Thursday, he marched into René's office.

"Jason, this is a surprise."

"I was wondering where Claire has been, and if she's all right."

René's greeting smile faded. "She's had a setback."

He sat. "What do you mean?"

"I think she has some sort of chronic ailment, and she got a virus which has knocked her for a loop."

"Has anyone checked on her? Is she all right? What about the child?"

"I'll call her later, if you'd like."

Thinking he'd like to be the one to call her, he deferred to René's offer. He had no business checking up on Claire. She was merely a business associate. Would he run out and call Jon if he was home sick? Why treat Claire any differently?

On Friday, René came to Jason's office. "I wanted to let you know that I've spoken to Claire. She is still quite miserable, poor thing. But she's hanging in. Maybe she'll get her strength back over the weekend."

"Yes. Well, I guess flu can really take its toll." He didn't want to let on to René how worried he was about Claire and her daughter. He had no right to be.

Then he remembered that Claire hadn't signed up for automatic deposit and today was a pay day. The other day, when she'd wiggled her fingers in the air at his office door, he'd noticed she didn't wear a wedding band. And by the way little Gina ate up his attention when he'd read to her, he suspected there was no man in her life. Someone needed to make sure she got paid.

Gaby had left for the day. They closed the clinic down two hours early every other week on Friday afternoons.

As soon as René left, he looked up Claire's home address and made plans to deliver her check. He could postpone his planned weekend sailing trip until Saturday morning.

Jason chastised himself for allowing "feelings" to inch back into his life. He had no business getting "involved" with anyone. He was emotionally DOA—what could he possibly offer another living soul? He pictured Claire's natural beauty and her disturbingly alluring personality, and shook his head.

She'd been off sick all week, she needed to get paid, and…maybe she needed a doctor?

The Italianate-styled house in Montecito suffered from years of neglect. Thick ivy vines covered the entire façade with cutouts for windows and the huge front door. The mansion sat in the middle of a cul-de-sac in a secluded neighborhood on a hill.

Jason parked his car and got out with the warm package he'd brought. He inhaled a faint hint of smoke. The last wildfires had come dangerously close to this area, and evidence of charred trees and hillside were in abundance in the near distance.

He strode under the portico to the door, and used the heavy brass knocker several times. After what seemed like close to a minute, a faint voice on the other side asked, "What do you want?"

It wasn't Claire. In fact the voice seemed ancient and quivery.

"I'm here to see Claire Albright. She works at my clinic."

The door squeaked open, and a frightfully thin woman with opaque skin marked with a map of blue and pink veins looked curiously into his face. She was dressed neatly, in clothes like his grandmother had used to wear. A wool skirt, with a sweater set and supportive black oxfords. Her mostly-white hair was pulled back into a thin knot.

"I have her home address as yours. I wanted to deliver her pay check. I'm sorry if I've made a mistake."

He could see the woman weighing the circumstances in her mind. He was a stranger. Claire was a single mom. Yet he knew he looked official.

Jason reached in his suit pocket and held the pay check in a neatly addressed envelope for the woman to examine. If she didn't trust him, she could deliver it to her tenant, though admittedly he'd be disappointed. He flashed a smile. The kind he used to gain the confidence of his patients.

"No mistake. Claire and Gina live in what used to be the maid's chambers. And, since she works with you, I guess it would be all right. There's a separate entrance at the back of the house." She stepped outside, and pointed him around the corner of the gravel-filled driveway toward the back yard.

The first signs of twilight were bearing down on the day. The path looked dreary and cold, but at the end a tiny bungalow had a large planter bearing a burst of color beside the entrance. He'd never imagined Claire living in such a place. Her rent payments most likely helped the landlady pay her property taxes in the upscale county.

His soles crunched on the gravel as a rush of misgivings slowed his step. What the hell was he doing here? He hugged the warm container. Right. Delivering money and holistic penicillin.

He reached the stoop, took the stairs two at a time, and tapped on the door.

After he knocked again, Claire's weak voice almost matched Mrs. Densmore's in tone.

"It's Jason. I've brought your pay check and, since I heard you've been sick, chicken soup to cure whatever ails you." He tried to sound light and jovial, nothing like himself.

She opened the door. "Jason?"

He raised his brows. "In the flesh. You gonna invite me in, or are you quarantined?" He worked to disguise the shock he felt at her pallor, her frailty, her droopy hair. Every last sparkle had left her eyes.

"I look a mess," she said.

"Hey, I'm a doctor. I deal with sick people every day."

She wore an azure-blue spa-styled robe, which seemed to gobble her up due to obvious weight loss. Her shoulders slumped and the furry slippers she wore made a shuffling sound across the entryway as she walked him inside.

A small, untidy living room revealed she'd been lying on the sofa, with a dented pillow on one end and a crumpled blanket cast over the back. The bright peach living room walls contrasted with the dreary hostess, and a fireplace served to keep her warm.

"So here's your pay check. Figured you might need it."

"How thoughtful of you."

"If you need me to deposit it for you, I can do that, too."

"That's very kind."

"You lie down," he said. "Point me to the kitchen and I'll heat this up." He held up the bag with the soup in it.

She gestured toward the hall. "I don't have much of an appetite."

"You need to eat. Now sit."

A few minutes later, after scavenging for a bowl to microwave the soup he'd bought from the best deli in Santa Barbara, he served her supper, and brought a bowl for himself.

She seemed grateful, but somehow humbled.

"This is so embarrassing. I hate for you to see me like this."

He slurped a taste of broth. "Don't give it another thought. Just eat."

She took a dainty sip and nodded her approval. As she continued to eat, he surreptitiously studied her face. For the first time he noticed a faint butterfly rash across the bridge of her nose and cheeks. Perhaps she was still feverish.

When she'd eaten half the bowl, she cast it aside on the coffee table. "It's very good, but I've eaten so little all week, I've lost my appetite."

"Then I'll be back tomorrow morning with fresh rolls and fluffy eggs."

"I can't let you do that."

"Of course you can. I'm a doctor. Let me help you get better. Now, tell me your symptoms and I'll try to figure out if you need antibiotics or something. I've got my bag in the car; I can give you a check-up if you'd like. And, while I'm out there, I'll bring in more wood for your fire and start this one up again."

"It's Lupus," she broke in.

He stopped his rambling.

"I have Systemic Lupus Erythematosus. I caught an everyday virus, something Gina brought home from pre-school, and now I'm having a flare-up."

That explained the rash on her face. "How long have you had SLE?"

"I developed it after Gina was born. I'd had lots of weird symptoms for years, but I think the post partum hormonal imbalance finally knocked me over the line."

"I had no idea," he said, feeling an overwhelming desire to somehow make her life better. Easier. She'd given no clue that she lived with a chronic autoimmune disease. Especially one that could be as debilitating as Lupus. "You're under a doctor's care?"

She nodded. "I see a Lupus specialist. And I add some complementary herbs to my regimen, too." She offered a wan smile. "Sometimes the cure seems worse than the disease."

No wonder she was such an alternative medicine advocate. Now it all made sense.

Satisfied she was doing the right thing, he relaxed. "Let me make you some tea." He jumped up, wanting nothing more than to wait on her.

He realized, by her obvious hesitation, she probably didn't want any tea, but even when sick, she was gracious.

"There's some chamomile leaves in the cupboard next to the refrigerator," she said in an anemic voice.

Or maybe she was just too weak to protest.

As he went about boiling water he called out, "Where's Gina?"

"With her father."

A pang of guilt made him realize he was relieved he wouldn't see "squirt" on this visit.

"He picked her up this afternoon. The poor thing has been so good about my being sick all week. And my childcare lady has been picking her up every day. She even took her to pre-school. Mrs. Densmore has been watching her for a couple of hours in the evenings. I don't know what I would have done otherwise."

The predicament of being a single mother was daunting enough, Jason imagined, but having a chronic illness on top of it seemed unfathomable. Again, he marveled at how he'd never had a clue about Claire's personal plight; how upbeat and cheerful she always seemed. Now that he knew, he'd find a way to help relieve her burden.

They sipped their tea, as Claire stretched out her legs and covered up with the blanket. He resisted tucking in her feet, using the poker to move a log around in the fireplace instead.

"Sometimes it's too much to lift my head off the pillow. Charles couldn't take the thought of living with an invalid, even though I rarely have flare-ups."

"You mean to tell me he divorced you because of your Lupus?"

She nodded, a look of resignation dulling her features. "That and a perky waitress at his favorite harbor bar."

Jason shook his head. As he drank his tea in silence,

he thought of his deceased wife and what he'd give to have her back. Then he thought how stupid Claire's husband was for turning his back on her. The Claire he knew at the clinic was vital and witty, feisty and bright, and...*quit denying it*...sexy.

Perky waitress or not, the man obviously didn't know how lucky he'd been being married to a woman like Claire. But Jason didn't know the whole story, so he reserved his full judgment.

Jason hoped Charles was at least good to Gina. If he did anything to hurt her... His blood pressure rose just thinking about the potential. Had he inadvertently transferred his feelings for Hanna to Gina? He hardly knew the child, yet he'd already seemed to form a bond. Didn't he have an art gallery's worth of drawings to prove they were special to each other? He couldn't let that go any further.

A rueful smile creased his lips. Jessica and Hanna would never be a part of his life again, and their loss stained every breath he took with guilt and anguish. A kid like Gina and a woman like Claire only complicated things.

"Are you OK?" Claire asked.

"What?" For crying out loud, he'd come over here to help her feel better, and now she was the one worrying about him. "Oh, I'm fine. I was just thinking of the irony of it all. You're a living breathing woman with a lot to offer, and I think your husband is a fool for leaving you."

She made a weak attempt at a smile. "Thanks. It's been hard, but things are looking up with the new job and all."

"I'll make sure you get paid sick leave," he said,

though usually any new employee needed to work three months before sick leave pay kicked in.

Her feeble smile grew stronger. "For such a grouch, you're a prince. Thanks," she said. He thought he saw a quick glint of life in her eyes, and he was willing to take the cheap shot as a sacrifice.

"*Moi?* A grouch? Are you sure you're not feverish?" He knew damned well he wasn't an easy man to work for, but he was surprised she'd been so candid. That was something else he liked about her. She was honest with him. Hell, hadn't she called him a closed-minded medical robot on her first day at work? That took guts.

He clapped his hands together. "So what time do you prefer breakfast?"

"Honestly, Jason, you don't have to do that."

Their eyes came together. He held her gaze long and sternly. "Don't be a martyr." Wasn't that a bit like the pot calling the kettle black? But he'd made his stand and he wasn't backing down now. "I want to help you, and I make a mean omelet."

She laughed. It sounded more like surrender than joy. "Then I'll have Cheddar cheese with fresh avocado slices on top."

Ha! He might have to get up early to drive to the farmers' market to find a ripe avocado, but he wasn't about to let her know that. "As you wish, my lady." Only because she'd called him a prince did the "my lady" tag occur to him. It sounded completely unnatural, something he'd never say, and he wanted to cringe the moment he'd said it. It felt too intimate and foreign when it slipped out of his mouth, but he'd said it and couldn't take it back. He glanced at Claire, reclining on the sofa looking pale and angelic. Really? Had it felt that foreign to call her "my lady"?

"And sourdough toast," she added, bringing him out of his convoluted, awkward and uneasy thoughts.

"Strawberry preserves?" he said.

"Marmalade, please."

"Hmm. I hadn't pegged you as a marmalade kind of girl."

She forced a smile through her compromised state, and he recognized a trace of the vital woman he'd come to know at the clinic. He stood, crossed the room and straightened the blanket over her feet.

"I'll be here at nine. I'll bring the food. You bring your appetite."

She gazed gratefully into his eyes. "I'll do my best, boss."

"See to it." He stopped himself from patting her shoulder. "I'll let myself out. You get a good night's sleep. That's an order."

As he reached the door he heard a faint, "Thank you."

And, just before he closed the door, he turned. He could go sailing any weekend with the mild local climate, and he would gladly cancel the weekend plans in favor of helping out a sick employee. A new friend? "You're entirely welcome," he said.

A slender arm with graceful hand and fingers waved above the back of the sofa, and a strange feeling came over him.

Was getting more involved with Claire Albright a good idea or a recipe for disaster?

CHAPTER FOUR

CLAIRE didn't want to be a medical burden to anyone but herself. Being sick had ended her marriage, but she also knew if she'd married the right guy he would have stuck it out with her. When Charles had proposed, she'd been positive he was the one for her. He might have been if she hadn't gotten sick. When her illness had developed the real Charles had emerged and, because her heart had been nearsighted, nothing had prepared her for his rejection.

Since then, she'd made a vow to deal with her illness alone.

So why had she allowed Jason to bring breakfast today? Because he seemed to be on her side, and she could use a friend. At least that was how it had felt last night when he'd shown up at her door with her pay check and chicken soup. He'd made an extra effort to stop by and, since she'd been feeling very alone lately, it had touched her.

After taking a shower and forcing herself to get dressed for the first time all week, she felt a lot better. Almost human again. And she wasn't sure if she'd washed and combed her hair for herself or partially for Jason. The notion disturbed her but was a revelation she'd have to deal with when she wasn't sick. She simply didn't have enough energy left now.

She'd decided to wait to take her morning cocktail of medicine until she'd eaten breakfast. And she'd take Jason up on his offer to deposit her check in the bank for her. The thought of running errands seemed overwhelming. Last night, he'd brought the paperwork for her to sign up for automatic deposit, and that thoughtful gesture almost made her cry. How long had it been since someone had looked out for her?

She shook her head. The Lupus flare-up had weakened her resolve. She'd never depend on anyone but herself again.

Now that she was clean and dressed, she felt as though she needed to take a nap, and it was only a quarter to nine. She plopped onto the couch and stared at the ceiling.

Jason had been a prince to stop by last night. She had barely believed her eyes when she'd opened the door. And he'd appeared genuinely concerned for her. Though she'd been caught looking her worst, she'd been too sick to feel embarrassed about it. Now he knew about her condition. After he fulfilled his obligation to feed her breakfast, she could expect him to back off. No one wanted to be strapped to a chronically sick person. Wasn't that what Charles had finally admitted when she'd had her third relapse in one year?

"Look at you," he'd said. "You're nothing like the woman I married."

Claire remembered examining herself in the mirror

thinking she looked the same, but she knew he referred to her fluctuating pain and energy level. He'd made her feel ugly and unwanted, and it had broken her heart.

She shook her head. The steroids always messed with her mind. She definitely hadn't been thinking straight by allowing new feelings to sneak into her life since meeting Jason Rogers. Today, she'd put an end to that.

The knock on her door startled her. She stood and felt light-headed, leaned on the back of the couch and, when he knocked a second time, she straightened and headed on unsteady legs toward the door.

Jason's broad smile surprised her, since he shared it so infrequently. "Welcome back to the living," he said, giving her a once-over. "You look…nice."

"Nice" was a bland description, but it was better than *like a zombie*, and he seemed to need time to think what he wanted to say. He was definitely being polite.

The Saturday morning sunlight made her squint. A rich blue sky with cotton ball clouds had her wishing she could go out to play. He entered the house looking downright debonair in a nautical shirt, khaki Dockers and deck shoes without socks. And the way his hair always fell across his forehead… Well, what could she say, but she liked it. She liked the whole package.

He'd probably deliver the food and run. Saturday was his day off and, from the looks of him, he had a date with his sailboat. She'd seen the picture of the sleek white craft named *Hanna's Haven* on his office wall. And his constant light tan indicated he spent a lot of time outdoors.

Jason barreled through the entryway and headed straight for the kitchen with grocery bags in hand. She followed him. He removed a Thermos, and his eyes brightened.

"I've brought my special breakfast coffee blend. Sit down and relax." He pulled out a chair, and when she sat he scooted a second chair toward her. "Put your feet up." He scanned the cupboards and she pointed to the one that held the mugs. He seemed excited and happy to be here, which took Claire by surprise. Wasn't she merely an obligation he'd inadvertently tied himself to?

Fifteen minutes later, as Claire sipped the richest coffee she'd ever tasted, breakfast was ready. Her eyes widened when he placed a perfect omelet in front of her.

"Are you a chef in your spare time?"

"I've been known to tinker around in the galley, though I haven't done much of that for a while." His bright eyes dimmed and his demeanor changed. He became quiet and joined her at the table.

They ate in silence, Claire forcing herself to clean the plate. How could she not when he'd found a perfectly ripened avocado to top off the light and fluffy egg and cheese dish? With the added calories, Claire felt more energetic. "I'm a pretty good cook, too," she said. "I'll have to pay you back when I get better."

He looked tenderly at her. "I'll hold you to that," he said, as they shared a smile.

Maybe he was just humoring her, but the glint in his eyes told her otherwise. Claire did feel as if she'd rounded the bend on this flare up, and, if things continued in this forward movement, she could hope to be at work on Monday.

"Some of the surveys have already been returned," he said, mid-bite.

"Great, I can't wait to put the data together."

"I took the liberty to start a spreadsheet of the findings," he said.

"That's wonderful. That will help me a lot."

"I'll give you all the help you need."

She saw sincerity in his blue-flecked eyes. Ever since she'd noticed the distinction, his gray eyes would never be the same to her. That was the steroids thinking. They made her emotional. Logically, she knew theirs was purely a business relationship, but having him here in her kitchen, casually eating and talking around the table, she became aware of a longing she'd pushed away—a longing to connect with another human being.

She had her daughter and her job, she thought as she took the last bite of omelet, and that would have to be enough.

Monday morning Jason was glad to see Claire at his office door. The second floor had seemed dull and quiet without her, and he'd even admitted to missing the aromatherapy, but not enough to learn how to turn on the diffuser.

Her being here meant she was back on the mend— the most important reason he was glad to see her.

"Good morning," she said, looking a bit pale, but far better than she had the last time he'd seen her.

"How are you feeling?" He jumped up from his chair and joined her at the door.

"Almost a hundred percent. I wanted to thank you again for helping me out."

Jason cupped her arm. "I was glad to do it."

He studied her warm hazel eyes and wondered what

thoughts might be tumbling through her mind. Aware of the point of connection and how natural it felt to touch her, he removed his hand. Fortunately she'd worn a blouse with sleeves, though he did wonder how her skin might feel. A flash memory of his wife caused him to retreat to his desk.

If Claire thought his action abrupt or odd, she gave no hint of it. A smile spread across her face, and she held up a paper. "I got your consult request."

"Maybe you can straighten Ms. Garcia out. I give up."

She laughed, and the sound made him think of a babbling brook. It became impossible to stay aloof.

"It's all about keeping a positive attitude, Jason," she said as she wandered back to her office in a flowing gypsy skirt. She'd worn her hair up today and he liked the view of her slender neck above the white lab coat.

His attitude toward Claire had changed over the last few weeks from annoying employee, to useful addition to the practice, to potential friend, and possible… The next thought made the hair on his arms stand on end.

Then he remembered what tomorrow was. He didn't need to look at the calendar to know that it was his daughter's birthday.

His nurse appeared in the doorway with a patient chart and, with the threat of purgatory bearing down on him tomorrow, he was grateful for the distraction of his job.

Tuesday morning Claire arrived at work to find Jason's office door closed. She knew he was there because she'd seen his Mercedes in the parking lot. Something told her not to bother him, and an hour later when they both exited exam rooms at the same time, one look at him and she knew she'd made the right decision.

Jason looked as if he hadn't slept all night. A shadow of his usual self, he hadn't even bothered to shave and his appearance stopped just short of disheveled.

His gaze fused with hers and she saw pain cutting through his stare. On reflex she wanted to reach out to him, to comfort him in some small way from the torment so apparent in his eyes, but the invisible barrier he wore was solid and impenetrable, and she instinctively knew to leave him alone.

She nodded a respectful greeting, wishing she could do much more for him.

He acknowledged her and retreated to his office.

The next day, Claire was elbow-deep in patient surveys—each day brought in another fifty to a hundred of them—and she had high hopes of completing her first report in time for next week's staff meeting. Every flat surface in her office was piled high with the envelopes.

One of the surveys concerned her, and she needed to speak to Jason about his patient. When he walked right by her door and straight to his office without saying hello that morning, she hesitated. Looking over Mrs. Ching's herbal supplements, she couldn't let Jason's somber and standoffish mood hold her back.

She gathered the list and took a deep breath, then headed down the hall.

Claire peeked around the door and tapped on the frame. "May I talk to you?"

Jason had managed to shave today, but the dark circles remained under his eyes. He glanced up and gave a solemn nod.

She swallowed, her throat suddenly dry. How did he manage to make her this nervous without so much as a spoken word?

"I was looking at Mrs. Ching's survey and discovered she takes several herbs used in Chinese traditional medicine."

He gave her a blank, uninterested stare as if to say *more holistobabble?*

"The thing is," she said, "I remember her face being puffy that day when you asked me to look at her back. Especially around the eyes. And I noticed in her chart that her last labs were several months ago."

"The results were normal."

"Yes, which makes sense why you haven't repeated them," she said, plowing on. "But I'm concerned about some of the supplements she's taking. I'd like to call her daughter and find out all of the ingredients."

"You have my permission." Could he be more aloof?

"And I'd like to order more labs."

He nodded, concentrating on whatever lay on his desk, as if she were nothing more than a small distraction.

Claire thought they'd taken three steps forward over the weekend, but it was only Wednesday and they'd fallen ten steps back, like when she'd first arrived at the medical clinic. It was clear Jason was unreachable today, so she'd remain professional, do her job, and leave the man alone.

* * *

Jason had made it through his daughter's birthday for another year. She'd have been eight. Would the pain ever go away? He'd spent last night drinking, combing through her belongings he couldn't bear to part with, and biting back the tears. He'd cursed the world and ranted about the injustice of it all, as he did every year. She should be losing teeth and studying multiplication tables. She should be arguing with her best friend one day and making up the next. She should be his date at the father-daughter school dance. She should be sitting on his lap, letting him spoil her.

She should be alive.

He swiped his jaw. He was at work, and the dreaded day was over. He needed to get a handle on his emotions, but the room went blurry again.

Damn it!

He stepped outside his office to see his next patient and caught the rustle of Claire's turquoise-blue dress as she entered her exam room. He glanced toward her office, which seemed to glow, then back to his dreary room. Hell, he hadn't even bothered to turn on the lights today.

In the waiting room, the gentle scent of lavender and whatever the hell the other essential oil Claire had told him it was, smelled good. He took a long inhalation, and squared his shoulders. He'd survived the hell of Hanna's birthday again, which always led to reliving her last day. He had three months to go before his wife's birthday, where he'd descend back into hell for another day, and then the fourth anniversary of the accident a month after that. God, would it ever get any easier?

He glanced toward Claire's office again. She had her

share of obstacles to overcome, yet she always seemed optimistic. There was a quiet strength in her that he respected. Her life hadn't turned out the way she'd expected, the way she'd deserved, yet she kept moving forward and didn't gripe about it.

Existing in limbo was hell. And exhausting. And tedious. Maybe he'd try to join the living and look on the brighter side of life for a change.

Jason packed up his briefcase Friday night. He'd played catch up on labs, special tests and consult reports after the clinic closed rather than go home to an empty house. He planned to pick up some take-out food on the way, then he'd leave before dawn Saturday for an all-day sail.

He missed the soothing sea, the one place where life seemed to make sense to him. The silence and magnitude of the ocean brought him peace of mind: The luffing of the sails before they filled, the creaking and stretching of the rigging, and the water lapping against the topsides. He'd made it through another week at the clinic, and through his daughter's birthday, and he'd reward himself with a day on the water.

Claire appeared in his doorway. "Jason? Mrs. Ching may have Chinese herb nephropathy."

"What?"

She rushed into his office and leaned over his desk. "Her labs show evidence of renal ischemia. She may be toxic. I spoke to her daughter, who said she was taking these herbs for joint aches and pain relief for the last month. One of the ingredients may contain aristolochic acid."

"And I should know this?"

"No," she said, cheeks pink and eyes shining. "I should because I've studied it, but it isn't commonly known. There could have been an inadvertent mix-up in one of the ingredients with this herbal mixture. What should be *A. Fangji*, a harmless herb, could actually be *A. Fangchi* a herb that contains aristolochic acid, which can cause renal failure. Something like this happened a few years back. I remember reading the article."

"What do we do now?"

"I called Mrs. Ching's daughter and told her to stop the herbs immediately—that they could be life-threatening—and I've left a message for her herbalist to call me."

Claire took her job seriously, and had managed to identify a potentially fatal herb interaction for one of his patients.

"Good idea." He smiled at the vibrant woman in front of him.

She blushed and he definitely liked it whenever she did. "So, assuming the worst and you're right and Mrs. Ching can potentially go into renal failure, what do we do next? Are renoprotective agents enough to turn her around?"

"I think we should admit her," she said.

"Treat her like any other nephropathy patient?"

She nodded. "Hopefully, the damage is reversible. In extreme cases, the kidneys and ureters are so damaged, they have to be surgically removed. There's no telling what's going on with her at this point."

He got on the phone and started barking out instructions. "I'm heading over to the Hospital to prepare for Mrs. Ching's admit. You call her and tell her daughter to bring her and meet me there. If she gives you any trouble, I'll personally go to her house and drag her there myself," he said.

"I'd like to come, too," she said.

"Sure."

"Oh, but wait. Gina." Claire tapped her finger on her mouth. "I know! I'll call my landlady and ask if she can watch her. She loves Gina."

Claire grabbed her cellphone and made the calls while following Jason out to the car.

"Mrs. Ching's on her way and Gina gets to have delivery pizza for dinner tonight with Mrs. Densmore. Lucky girl."

They spent the next two hours at the local E.R. having Mrs. Ching admitted, while Jason wrote out a plethora of kidney specific tests to be performed. When he was satisfied he'd covered everything from basic kidney function labs to ultrasound, MRI, IVP, cytoscopy and renal biopsy, he glanced up to find Claire looking over his shoulder. She'd been sick in bed all last week, and here she was one week later, like a trouper sticking by his side while he took care of one of his patients. If it hadn't been for her astute find, Mrs. Ching could have been on the fast track to dialysis or, worse yet, a nephrectomy.

Claire looked a little drawn and her stomach made a gurgling plea about the missed dinner hour.

"Excuse me," she said as she grabbed her waist, color rising on her cheeks.

"Let's get some dinner," he said.

She opened her mouth, but he didn't give her the chance to protest.

"I owe you," he said. "It's the least I can do."

"Well, since you put it that way…let me call my landlady and ask if it's OK with her."

Claire snapped her cellphone closed with a smile on her face. "Now they're watching a Disney video, and Gina's already in her pajamas. She'll be happy to tuck her in bed for me."

"That's great."

A half hour later they were being seated at Aldo's, his favorite Italian restaurant on State Street. He ordered a bottle of Chianti and, while they waited for their pasta dinner for two, they drank wine and relaxed.

Without her lab jacket on, her peach-colored crinkly top brought out all of the finest aspects of her complexion. Her eyes looked more green than hazel tonight, and she gave him an inquisitive glance as he watched her sip her drink. He'd noticed her mouth on several occasions, but hadn't allowed himself to study the fullness of her lips. They looked smooth and soft and he wondered what it would be like to kiss them.

The wine had obviously gone right to his head, and when the waiter brought out the fresh baked bread he slathered a piece with butter and took a large bite. Anything to get his mind off her mouth.

"You like to sail?" she asked.

"It's my passion. Nothing like it in the world. You?"

"I've never had the opportunity to try it."

He told her about the summer he hired on as a deck hand on a schooner and sailed all the way to Hawaii, and how he'd owned his first sloop by the age of twenty-one. It had been a birthday gift from his parents for finishing his pre-med courses a year early. His current schooner, *Hanna's Haven*, had been a gift to himself when he'd passed the family practice boards.

He'd wanted to spend his honeymoon sailing around the Caribbean but Jessica hadn't been a natural born sailor, and they'd flown there instead. He didn't tell Claire *that* part of the story and, while he ate more pasta, he pondered how all the roads in his life seemed to lead back to Jessica.

In turn, Claire told him about her upbringing in Los Angeles, how she'd wanted to be a gymnast when she was little, but had grown too tall and had turned out to be a bit clumsy, and since she couldn't cut it as a gymnast had decided she'd become a nurse. She finished by telling him how she'd gone to Santa Barbara University and could never get herself to move back home after that.

And after a satisfying dinner following a strained and uncomfortable week, they looked at each other in a different light, more on the lines of the prior weekend when they'd forged new ground, established respect for each other, and become unlikely friends.

"You seemed to have a rough week," Claire said, running her finger around the edge of her almost-empty wine glass.

"I've had worse. I'm OK now."

"If you ever want to talk about it," she said, "I'd be glad to listen."

He nodded, feeling the Chianti warm his chest. With his hunger satisfied, and no desire to open up about himself, Jason suggested they walk up the street for ice cream. That way he wouldn't have to keep gazing into her empathetic, appealing eyes.

"I think after tonight I'll have made up for all the weight I lost when I was sick," she said as they strolled.

He glanced from her head to her open-toed shoes. She always painted her toenails, and he liked that. She wore beige slacks instead of her usual skirt or dress and, though a little thin, for the first time he noticed how nicely shaped she was. "That's not a bad thing, is it?"

Jason knew that figuring out the female psyche and ideal weight was beyond his capabilities, so he trod lightly.

She laughed, and there was that babbling brook image again. He smiled at her, grateful she hadn't taken offense on any level, and they continued to walk up State Street on the brisk but clear evening.

Maybe tonight, for just one night, he could forget…

Claire glanced at Jason as they ambled up the red-brick walk toward the ice cream store. She'd learned more about him tonight, yet still felt he was mostly a stranger. He never seemed to completely open up, and it made her think he was an emotionally unavailable man. That was the last thing she was looking for. She'd been married to one, and look how horribly that had turned out. She'd never repeat the same mistake.

This was just dinner with a business associate. They'd admitted their patient and had been hungry. It only made sense he'd ask her to eat with him. So why was she making more out of it than it was?

Because the restaurant had been cozy and romantic, with white tablecloths and dim candlelight.

Because the conversation had come easy and she'd kept getting lost in his ocean-at-dusk-colored eyes. Because she couldn't deny it any longer—she was attracted to Jason. He was a skilled and dedicated doctor who loved his patients. Unbeknownst to her, he'd been the force behind the medical group that she'd discovered in the renovated Victorian house, the place where she'd yearned to work. He was kind to her daughter. And he'd proved to be a concerned business partner when he'd gone the extra mile last Friday night to bring her pay check, and he'd surprised her even more with a gourmet breakfast Saturday morning.

Chianti or no Chianti, she found him extremely attractive, even liked the way he talked, with his deeper than average voice. He had a wide smile when he cared to share one with her, and masculine lips, the kind that had made her mind wander to kissing when he'd told her about sailing. She found it fascinating how his beard had darkened as the day progressed into the evening, was glad she'd been around to notice, and surprised to realize she wanted to touch the stubble.

He glanced at her and tilted his head with an inquisitive expression when he realized she'd been studying him. Again.

Thankfully, they'd reached the ice cream store because her line of thinking needed to stop.

"How should we work this?" Jason asked later, after scooping up the last of his ice cream from the small foam cup. "Should I drive you back to the clinic to get your car, or should we buy Gina a mini ice cream and take it right to her?"

"That's sweet of you, but no. It would just get her all wired. You can take me back to my car. What she doesn't know won't hurt her feelings. But thanks for thinking about her." His small, yet considerate gestures kept adding up, and it made him hard to resist.

Fifteen minutes later he'd parked in the medical clinic lot and something told Claire to be still. Jason didn't make a move to get out of the car; he stared straight ahead for a few moments, and she could hear each breath he took. Then he turned toward her. "I can't remember the last time I asked a woman out to dinner."

She wanted to brush off his statement. To say *oh, I'm just a business associate, we were working late and got hungry*, but she didn't want to believe that. And he'd hinted that he'd made a point of asking her to dinner. He didn't have to. It complicated things, and she opted to keep the mood light by mocking herself.

"I'm glad you did," she said, "even if I had to go to great lengths to figure out a way to get a patient to take toxic herbs, and get hospitalized, in order to get you to ask me." She grinned.

He grinned back. "So this was all your devious plan," he deadpanned.

"Oh, yes. I thought of everything."

His smile slipped away as his steady gaze melded with hers. "Then I'm glad, too."

She couldn't fight the growing attraction, even though it was the last thing in the world she needed right now. She also considered herself good at reading people—a natural ability that she'd enhanced with her homeopathy studies—and, by the look on Jason's face, he seemed deeply interested in her, too.

He leaned toward her. With the smoky tinge to his eyes, she knew what he planned.

Before she had a chance to think one extra thought, his mouth covered hers. The lips she'd wondered about were warm and smooth, and they fit perfectly over hers. She relaxed and let him take the lead, enjoying the feel of him. Though waning, the sandalwood scent of his aftershave still invited her closer. He slowly pulled back, but she wanted more. She followed his mouth and pressed her moistened lips to his and, to keep him from retreating more, her hand caressed his jaw and neck. His ear was warm and she finally got to test the stubble on his cheek. She didn't detect any resistance from him when she kissed him again.

She loved the sounds they made when their lips parted to kiss again and again. He kissed her lower lip, and tugged on it, and sleepy sensations tugged in other areas of her body. His hand found her back and he drew her closer. They breathed over each other; she sighed, and kissed him harder. He deepened the kiss, making it moist and silky. Their tongues met and a tiny sound escaped her throat. He must have liked it. His hand kneaded her back as their tongues continued to test and explore. Her fingers splayed into his hair. It was thick and newly trimmed across his neck. She wanted more kisses and planted several of her own as a sensual awareness started to throb deep within her.

And then he ended it. He abruptly dropped his hand and backed away from her mouth. A complicated expression shadowed his face. Was he appalled by what they'd done, or just not into her?

All she knew was that she missed his warmth. She missed how his barriers had tumbled down as they'd kissed, and how he'd pulled her tight, inviting her to know him a little deeper with each kiss.

But it was over now. He was back to staring out the car windshield, and she felt obligated to say something. She didn't want to make a single comment about the kisses, preferring to hoard them rather than allow him to steal them back with an apology or an excuse. They were real and they'd felt wonderful. One second he'd been warm and inviting, the next his lips had turned to marble and he'd disappeared.

The kiss probably didn't mean a thing to him. It was just a bit of extra-curricular activity on his part, and she'd taken it too seriously. It served her right for breaking her own rule about getting involved with a man again. How easily Jason had persuaded her to reconsider that vow.

Claire reached for the door handle and opened the door. "Thank you for dinner, Jason. I really enjoyed myself." Even after scolding herself, she still hoped he'd hear the double message. How messed up was that?

He turned slowly to face her. Night shadows slanted across his jaw, making it hard for her to read his expression. "You're welcome," was all he said, with a distant stare.

* * *

Jason watched Claire get into her car; his hands gripped the steering wheel in a lifesaving strangle. What the hell had he done?

He'd come out of hibernation; let his guard down enough to enjoy Claire's company. He'd noticed her sensual mouth, enjoyed every second of their shared kisses, discovered he wanted to ravage her, then the dark thoughts had returned. How could he be unfaithful to Jessica? To this day, her memory wouldn't let go of him. And his guilt would never let him forget.

Claire had managed to find the dwindling spring of life at the bottom of his well. He'd been bone-dry until then, and she'd tapped into what was left of him. Made him feel almost human again. He'd wanted more; had that been so awful?

He was supposed to have been with Jessica and Hanna the day of the accident, but the new medical clinic had delayed him. *Go ahead,* he'd said over the cellphone. *I'll drive up later and meet you there.* They'd planned a weekend in Pismo Beach.

He didn't deserve to be alive, or to feel, or to enjoy anything.

He wouldn't slip up again.

CHAPTER FIVE

MONDAY morning, Claire and René had the medical clinic kitchen to themselves.

René poured herself a large cup of coffee; her full-bodied auburn hair was styled in layers and rested on the white of her doctor's coat, and Claire admired how she always looked perfectly put together. She'd alluded to Jason's troubled past in prior conversations, and after Claire had fruitlessly racked her brain all weekend over the cause of Jason's odd behavior, she needed some answers.

Her divorce had left her wary of men, and maybe the same had happened to Jason, though he never made reference to his ex-wife, as most divorced men did.

They'd had a great dinner together, she'd realized how much she liked him, and he'd kissed her. Then he'd stopped. From one moment to the next, things had changed. Was she a bad kisser? Or had Jason had a sudden change of heart about her?

Something had kept Claire from writing Jason off as another of life's disappointments wrapped in a male package. She needed to know the whole story before she did that. She sat beside René and dipped her tea ball in the steaming mug of water.

"You have a minute?" she asked.

"Of course. What's up?" René's amber-brown eyes reminded her of a cat's.

"I can't figure Jason out. He's a grouch one minute, kind the next. Did you know that he brought me soup and my pay check when I was sick?"

René's perfectly made-up eyes widened and her brows rose halfway up her forehead. "Jason brought you soup?"

Claire nodded, with a wan smile at the memory. The man thoroughly confused her.

"He did seem to ask a lot of questions about where you were and what was wrong when you were out sick."

The notion of Jason worrying about her caused a warm sensation in her chest.

René tilted her head in thought. After several moments and a sip of coffee, she looked Claire in the eyes. "Jason used to be the life of the party. He had more charm than the President," she said. "His family is filthy rich, in case you didn't know, and he never wanted for anything. He was a devoted family man. Completely content. And a great doctor. Still is a great doctor, just a little less accessible on the personal level." René glanced at Claire with a rueful expression.

"Did he get divorced?"

René shook her head. "These days, he's just doing the best he can." She looked as if she wanted to say more, but before she could her nurse stuck her head around the door.

"Dr. Munroe? Mrs. Callahan is on the phone. She thinks she's in labor."

René popped up from her chair. "Looks like my day has officially begun. We'll talk more later."

Claire shook her head. If he wasn't divorced, then what was he?

She'd give Jason some space for now but, having recently been introduced to his passion for the sea, she couldn't let him continue to sail at half mast. He needed a friend. And if they were going to be friends, he needed to talk. She shook her head, knowing there was no way she could force him to open up and talk. The man was so closed off; he'd probably never bring the subject up. But he'd shown early signs of life at dinner the other night, and there had been passion in his kiss. And she did owe him a dinner.

A relationship was probably the last thing he needed. Or wanted. Come to think of it, it was the last thing she needed, too. They could be friends, and together, as *friends*, they might find a place for him to begin to live again.

And if she were lucky, through that friendship, maybe she could learn to trust again, too.

After a few more moments lost in thought, Claire scrubbed her face with her palms, finished her tea, and set off for her first physical exam of the day.

Breaking through to Jason and becoming his friend seemed too much to ask for, but she'd never shied away from challenges in her life. Why start now?

As the morning wore on Claire's insecurity got the best of her. How was she supposed to go about this? *Hi, I'm Claire. Can I be your friend because I think you need one, and I have the audacity to think I can help you?* Ridiculous. She couldn't even help herself get over her lack of trust. What made her think she could offer Jason anything?

She wound up being a coward and avoided him the rest of the morning.

He'd made it easy by staying in his office with his door closed in between patients. She kicked herself for not having any guts, but just before the end of the morning clinic, she had a perfect excuse to tap on his door.

But Jason's door was open, and she needed to borrow his more up-to-date drug formulary, so she went inside. She glanced around the bookcase to locate the bright orange 2010 handbook, when her gaze settled on a small picture. A lovely dark-haired woman and a little girl with impish eyes smiled out at her from the delicate frame. They had to be the family René had referred to.

What had happened?

Jason barreled into the room and tossed some paperwork on his desk. Startled, Claire almost dropped the picture.

"Oh," she said. "I was just looking for your drug formulary."

"And you decided to snoop while you were in the neighborhood?" He pinned her with an accusatory glare.

"I'm sorry, Jason. I just happened to notice this lovely picture and…"

He walked to another bookcase across from his desk and flipped out the item in question. "Is this what you're looking for?"

At a total loss for what else to say, she nodded. "Yes.

Thank you." She took the book and retreated to her office, feeling humiliated and angry, and avoided Jason the rest of the afternoon. The man's barriers were thicker than steel trapdoors.

Frustrated by an afternoon that had seemed to yawn on, Claire arrived home with a bag of groceries and Gina in tow to find a message on her answering machine from her landlady, Mrs. Densmore.

"Claire, I'm not doing well. Can you check in on me?"

A chill cut through Claire. Mrs. Densmore never complained about anything. Though frail, she was still one of those robust North-eastern transplants who laughed at the spoiled mild climate residents of California, and who could be seen gardening in the foulest coastal weather. Her violet-colored hydrangeas, lipstick-red hibiscus, and cross-bred multi-colored roses were proof positive of her green thumb. She walked daily with a fancy carved walking stick, and scoffed at people who rushed to the doctor for little problems. Only something major would cause her to ask for help.

Claire put the groceries that needed refrigeration away, and left the rest. She gave Gina some wheat crackers and string cheese, took her by the hand and rushed to Mrs. Densmore's door. It seemed like ages before the woman answered.

On the surface Mrs. Densmore looked her usual self, except she hadn't bothered to pull her shock of white hair back in a bun. It hung thin and limply on her hunched up shoulders. Her face seemed stiff, dried drool clung to the corners of her mouth, where a peculiar grin contradicted her plea for help. No, this wasn't at all like the normal Mrs. Densmore.

"I'm sick," she said. "I thought it was flu. It's something else."

"Do you want me to take you to the urgent care or E.R.?" Claire asked, trying to hide her alarm.

"I don't want to go there. Can you examine me?"

Now was not the time to argue with someone about their being stubborn. Her landlady needed her help.

Gina wanted to hug Mrs. Densmore the way she always did. Claire bent down to make eye-to-eye contact with her. "Mrs. Densmore is sick, Gina. I need you to be good."

Gina's wide blue eyes stared at the older lady. "She thick? I be good." With that, she walked across the room, patted Mrs. Densmore's hand, then crawled up on her favorite antique rocking chair and started it in motion. "Where you hurt?"

Mrs. Densmore didn't respond to Gina, a child she normally showered with attention, and Claire knew the woman needed medical attention.

She cleared her head and opened her nursing bag. Normally, she didn't do home visits, especially when casual acquaintances were trying to tap her for an easy diagnosis. The liability issue was an entirely different matter. But her landlady wasn't like that.

She listened to Mrs. Densmore's list of complaints: back pain, generalized stiffness, and jaw pain for the last week, which had been getting progressively worse. Heart attacks presented with non-traditional symptoms in women. She needed to rule that out. Or a stroke.

"Have you lost consciousness at any time?" Claire asked, and noted the woman's head shake. "Are you sure?"

Mrs. Densmore gave a sharp stare in answer.

"Give me your hands. Squeeze mine." Mrs. Densmore's grip was equal on both sides. Normally she'd ask a patient to smile to help check for stroke, but the odd grin was already in place. And she'd had a steady even gait.

Claire did a head to toe assessment. Mrs. Densmore's heart rate and rhythm were normal, and so was her blood pressure. Her lungs sounded clear, though it seemed hard for her to take in a deep breath. When Claire got to the woman's hands, she saw several scratches and one angry, swollen cut on her middle finger.

"Gardening," Mrs. Densmore said. "Those stubborn roses." It seemed difficult for her to talk and swallow.

Gardening. Cuts. Generalized stiffness. Facial spasm. A stubborn woman who avoided the doctor. Mrs. Densmore had recently cleared out a new area in the overgrown back yard. The soil hadn't been disturbed in decades. A dismal thought unnerved Claire. Anaerobic spores in old soil.

"When was the last time you had a tetanus shot?"

The woman made a *pfft* sound, as if to say *Those silly little things?*

Claire didn't want to make a snap decision, but she had a horrendous feeling that her landlady might be in the early stages of tetanus. But who in the world got tetanus these days? Claire had read a recent article in a geriatric journal about an increased incidence of tetanus in elderly gardeners and, if her memory served her right, the older the patient the higher the fatality rate.

"I'm taking you to the E.R.," Claire said.

"No. I won't go."

"You may have had a heart attack or maybe it's tetanus!"

"You don't know that for sure. You're not a doctor."

Mrs. Densmore's traditional and outdated views surprised Claire, but she wasn't about to argue with the woman in her time of need.

"Then I'll get one." And though she'd been a coward all day and had avoided Jason at work, she was worried enough on Mrs. Densmore's behalf to dig into her purse, fish out her cellphone, locate his number and speed dial it.

"Jason? I need your help. My landlady wants a doctor's input before she'll let me take her to the E.R." Claire gave a frustrated glare at her stubborn landlady. "Where she belongs."

When Jason offered to come right over instead of brushing her off, Claire was both surprised and relieved. He may have clicked into concerned doctor mode, but it hadn't made her any less upset with him for being such a jerk earlier.

"How long ago did you get those scratches?" she asked, focusing back on her patient.

"A week or so, but I get scratched up all the time." The woman looked at her wounded hands, then at Claire. Fear sparked in her eyes. "I started having trouble swallowing today," she said in a confessional voice. "That's why I called you."

Claire rushed to her side and put an arm around her. "If Dr. Rogers says you need to go to the hospital, please don't fight him. OK?"

A tinge of regret crossed over Mrs. Densmore's face. "I know you know what you're doing. It's just that I'm afraid to go to the doctor. When Gerald went, he never came home."

Claire found and handed her a tissue to wipe the brimming tears.

"Medicare can only pay for so much, then you're on your own," Mrs. Densmore said. "They wanted to take our house. It's all I have left." The Densmores had never had children. The woman didn't have a family support system that Claire knew of.

"I'll pay for whatever your insurance doesn't. Don't sweat it." A sharp pang of empathy had Claire making a promise she wasn't sure she could keep. Hell, she could hardly handle her own finances. If she had to, she'd moonlight somewhere in order to help Mrs. Densmore.

Jason must have flown instead of driven because it seemed that only ten minutes later he banged on the mansion door.

Gina ran across the tiled foyer. "Man," she said with a squeal, pointing to Jason when Claire opened the door.

He crouched beside her. "Hey, squirt. What's new?"

Gina jumped up and down. "I drawed you pictures."

"And they were pretty," he said.

"Pwetty." Gina ran around in circles to show her delight. "Pwetty!"

Though distracted at first, Claire and Jason greeted

each other cautiously. She thought she'd noticed a hint of contrition in his expression, but he didn't apologize. Claire was grateful to see him and, since they were both focused on a medical condition, none of the awkward fallout she'd imagined there'd be after their first kiss and his subsequent jerk attack at work existed.

Less than fifteen minutes later, he'd convinced Mrs. Densmore where she needed to be. They got the woman into his car and decided that Claire would stay home with Gina.

Jason backed the silver Mercedes sedan out of the circular driveway. "I'll talk to you later," he said.

By eight o'clock, Claire had fed and bathed Gina, read her a goodnight story, and put her to bed. She'd changed into more comfortable clothing—navy-blue velvet warm ups—and fed Mrs. Densmore's litter of cats, then tried to catch up on her *Holistic Health* journal reading, though she had trouble concentrating. By quarter to ten she thought about calling Jason, but didn't want to interfere if he was still at the E.R.

At 10:00 p.m. she heard tapping at her door and reacted with static electricity on her arms and up her neck.

There he stood, hair across his brow, looking depleted but with enough energy to engage her with a single earnest glance. "You were right," he said with half a smile. He followed her into the living room, took off his jacket and laid it over the back of couch, then sat. She joined him on the opposite end, aware of his after-shave and evening stubble.

"So what do they do now?" she asked.

"They've already started her on tetanus immuno-globulin and transferred her to the ICU."

Claire flopped against the cushions. "Can you believe it? Tetanus in this day and age?"

"You've done another terrific job of diagnosing," he said with admiration in his eyes.

It made her want to smile, but she curled her toes instead. "You look tired. Would you like some chamomile tea?"

"Sounds good," he said, "but first I owe you an apology."

"I wasn't snooping, Jason."

"I know that. I'm sorry I snapped at you."

She stared at him for a long moment, and sensed his sincerity. "Apology accepted." She stopped herself from saying—*tell me about that picture. Where are they? What happened to them?* "Why don't you make yourself comfortable while I get that tea."

He kicked off his shoes and put his feet up on her coffee table, and it surprised her. Maybe he'd relax and finally open up.

On the way to the kitchen, she felt jittery and ex-citable, as if she'd injected a pot of coffee into her veins. Jason had done that to her. She fished around for some cookies to serve with the tea. Why had he chosen to come in person instead of call?

She wouldn't waste the chance to talk to him. Who knew if she'd ever have another opportunity?

Jason had put his hands behind his head and closed his eyes when she returned. They opened shortly after she entered the room.

"It's been a long day," she said.

He responded with a sleepy smile and, fighting off a yawn, he reached for a chocolate chip cookie. "My favorite," he said. "How d'you know?" His eyes teased her as he crunched.

She curled into the corner of the couch and faced him, teacup in hand. Now that Mrs. Densmore was under the appropriate care, she wondered how to broach the other subject foremost on her mind: her new quest for friendship with Jason.

"While I'm apologizing for things, I guess I owe you an explanation for the other night, too," he said.

She almost spilled her tea, but quickly gathered her thoughts and decided to take a huge risk. "And I'd like to know about your family."

He scrubbed his face, and stared hard across the room, as though at nothingness, for several long moments.

"Ten years ago I married my wife, Jessica." His voice sounded monotone and guarded. "Two years later we had Hanna. You found their picture today. They were the light of my life, as the cliché goes. We talked about having more children, but it never happened. Thought maybe the summer would be a good time to try again." He paused and took a deep breath. "When the clinic opened Phil, Jon, René and I vowed to give it our undivided attention. We worked hard and long at seeing extra patients, hoping word would get out and we'd pick up more clientele. So Jessica and I decided we needed a weekend away. We wanted to do something Hanna would enjoy. She was four, so we made plans to take the train up the coast. But I got held up at work."

He squinted hard at the fire, as if visualizing something horrible.

"I told them to go ahead. That I'd meet them up there." He stopped, his brows twisted, and he pinched his lips together as if fighting off a wave of emotion.

Claire's line of thinking jumped ahead. She remembered a horrendous train crash four or five years ago. She remembered seeing the human carnage amidst twisted metal and derailed train cars on the local TV news. Fifty people had died that day. Her heart squeezed, trying to fathom Jason's pain. She wanted to lunge for him, to throw her arms around his neck and cry with him, but he wasn't shedding a tear. He sat as if numbed by the memories. As if oddly removed from the story that had once been a dark and tragic reality.

He glanced toward her with haunted, weary eyes. "I was supposed to be with them."

Claire's throat tightened, making it difficult to swallow her tea. She couldn't believe what she'd heard. In one instant his family had been wiped out. How could anyone deal with such loss? He seemed to stare right through her. She didn't know what to do. Her hand shot for his. "Jason, I'm so sorry."

A lump clogged Claire's chest. She found it hard to breathe. She thought about the precious gift of her child, and wondered what she would do. She couldn't survive if Gina died.

And Jason had lost both his wife and child.

He moved his hand. "Don't."

She thought of how he'd gazed gently at Gina when she'd fallen asleep in his lap that time, and she wanted to cry. What must he have been thinking? Without knowing it, she'd probably caused him more grief.

He put his shoes back on, grabbed his coat and headed for the door.

She rushed to beat him there and, not giving a damn about what his rules were, hugged him, long and tight. She buried her head under his chin and snuggled against his chest, wanting only to show him he wasn't alone in this world. He may have lost the most precious part of his life, but he wasn't alone.

Instead of being embarrassed about it, she was glad she'd kissed him with her soul Friday night. He deserved no less. And he'd taken a risk with her by reaching out. It touched her. Made her wish things could be different.

He felt rigid and unreceptive, like a man too proud to let anyone help. What a pair they made. She who'd never allow herself to trust a man again, and he who'd never let another woman into his heart.

She gradually disengaged from the one-sided hug.

"I won't tolerate your pity, Claire," he said, then left.

His warning took her by surprise, as if he'd pushed her against a wall. She stared at him as he walked away, and heat rose up her cheeks.

"No more than I'd accept yours!" she called out before he got into his car. A ball of anger and confusion twined around her as she slammed the door with shaky hands.

Tuesday morning, Claire went into work early to make calls to patients who were taking herbs that interacted negatively with their current prescribed medications. She'd chosen to call patients she knew worked and were up early. This way she'd have time in the evening to visit Mrs. Densmore. She heard Jason's footsteps up the stairs and her heart stumbled over the next beat. He stopped outside her door. Turned his head and nodded a greeting.

"Hello, Jason," she said, as casually as her thrumming pulse would allow.

"What are you doing here so early?"

She explained why she'd come in and he stepped inside her office. "Give me some of those," he said, reaching for her pile of surveys.

"You don't have to help."

He tossed her an impatient glance and grabbed half the stack on his way out the door.

As she shook her head at the empty doorway, she heard him step into the waiting room and fiddle with something. Was he turning on the diffuser for the aromatherapy?

A few minutes later when the scent of lavender, ylang-ylang and rosemary wafted up her nose, she smiled in disbelief while she made her next phone call.

Throughout the day, in between her patient appointments, she cogitated over how to reach out to Jason, how to be his friend. He wasn't looking for a replacement for his wife, and she didn't want to ever depend on a man again—theirs seemed like an ideal friendship. Except her body always reacted in unexpected ways whenever he was near, and she was confused about desiring him as a man while settling for a tame friendship. It seemed such a shame to let a good man like Jason live life as a zombie. But if he continued to shut her out of his personal life, all she would have was their business relationship.

She wanted more. The thought sent her sitting back in her chair. She was kidding herself about only wanting friendship with Jason. If she analyzed further, this desire to be friends with Jason was her way of working up the confidence to trust a man again. She shook her head. Of all the men in the entire world to get involved with, Jason seemed the least likely candidate.

That evening at the hospital ICU, Claire was surprised to see that her landlady had been intubated. Claire reached for her hand and squeezed when she arrived. Mrs. Densmore's anxious flitting eyes found Claire and blinked with questions.

Her nurse explained that reflex muscle spasms were causing respiratory compromise, and they planned to perform a tracheotomy the next day. She said they intended to use neuromuscular blocking medications and Mrs. Densmore needed to be mechanically ventilated.

The thought of Gerald Densmore going to the hospital and never coming home had been enough to make her delay seeking medical advice. She could only imagine what was going through her landlady's mind now.

Claire got close to her face. "You are going to pull through this. I know you will." She held both of her hands and squeezed. "I'm taking care of the cats, so don't worry." The irony of a woman who'd avoided the doctor all her life, only to wind up in the ICU in such distress, didn't go unnoticed by Claire, and she suspected it was all that Mrs. Densmore thought about while lying in the bed staring at the ceiling.

Wednesday Claire worked like a fiend to complete her initial herbal supplement survey, and gave the "What to Expect When Nursing" class for René's pregnant clients in the morning. After, she called the hospital and found out Mrs. Densmore's procedure had gone well, and she was stable.

In the afternoon, she facilitated the "Stop Smoking Now" class for Phil's pulmonary patients. When the memo came across her desk about the staff meeting on Thursday night, Claire worked even faster to finish the survey. Unfortunately for the other doctors, Gina would again be taking the meeting along with them.

Gina brought her brand-new board book, *Find the Puppy*, along when Claire picked her up from the sitter's Thursday evening before the staff meeting. She'd also drawn another picture for Jason. They'd spent no less than five minutes rehearsing how to say his name.

This time, they arrived early enough for Claire to feed Gina some finger sandwiches and apple slices before the meeting began.

Jon was the first to arrive, looking as though he'd just completed a mini marathon in a damp T-shirt, warm-up pants and running shoes with huge soles. He'd been known to hit the beachside trail during his lunch hour for a quick run, but today he must have gone after the clinic had closed. It was no secret he was training for the May marathon in Los Angeles and, for a man his age, he looked in tip-top condition.

Phil swaggered in next, looking ready for a hot date in dark slacks and a thin baby-blue, long-sleeved v-neck cashmere sweater that brought out his dreamy eyes. In comparison to Jon, he smelled great!

René and Jason arrived together. They spoke casually and laughed like old friends. Claire was surprised by the spike of jealousy that came over her.

Everyone greeted each other, and Jason's eyes met Claire's for a brief moment before he called the meeting to order, causing a quick release of butterflies in her stomach.

As with the last meeting, each member had their specific area of clinic business to report on. When it was Claire's turn she was prepared with her spreadsheet and several surprising revelations about their clientele and herb-drug interactions.

"Though drug-to-drug interactions are usually more serious, many herbs can interfere with or create potential hazards for our patients," she said. "For example, we know that grapefruit juice can cause abnormally high concentrations of certain drugs in the blood because it inhibits a specific liver enzyme. And did you know that some patients take grapefruit concentrate pills from the health store?"

She looked around the table and noticed a few raised eyebrows.

"We know to warn our patients on those specific medications to avoid grapefruit and grapefruit juice, but can we trust they'll put two and two together about the Pill? And if we don't know that our patient is taking, let's say Goldenseal, when we prescribe them erythromycin for an infection, they may experience toxicity." She glanced around the room, and found everyone, including Jason, to be listening intently. Fortunately, Gina was just as intent drawing yet another picture for her new favorite person—Jason. "And it's also important to be aware some herbs can greatly reduce the effectiveness of our prescribed medications."

To conclude her report, she passed around her list of common herbs and potential drug interactions. "I'd like to make sure that every patient receives this flyer at each medical appointment to remind them to check with their doctor before starting a new herb. And I'd also like to say a word on behalf of the benefits of supplementing medical care with herbs. It has helped tremendously with my battle with Lupus. So herbs aren't by any means all bad. We just have to stay on top of things where our clinic patients are concerned."

"Thanks for this," Jason said, speaking for the group. "How is the survey coming along?"

"We've got a few stragglers who have yet to send back their information. I'd like permission to work a few extra hours Saturday morning to call each of them and encourage them to fill them out and send them in."

All the doctors nodded their approval.

At some point, during her presentation, Gina had wandered over to Jason and crawled into his lap again. He didn't seem to mind. When Gina heard the trigger word, Saturday, she parroted Claire's promise made earlier that evening.

"We go to park on Saturday."

She'd forgotten! Now she'd promised to work Saturday, and Gina would be very disappointed.

All the other doctors had left, and Claire smiled ruefully at Jason.

"I totally forgot about taking Gina to play at the

park Saturday." Before Claire could say another word, Gina broke in.

She jumped up and down. "Da park! Thwings." She clapped her chubby hands.

"Maybe we can go on Sunday, honey," Claire said, using her calming mother voice to help ward off the inevitable Hurricane Gina.

The child screwed up her face in preparation for crocodile tears. "Thwings," she cried.

Jason tossed Claire an exasperated glance, then got down to Gina's level and cupped her arms. He gazed into her big blue eyes. Without meaning to, Claire had put him on the spot. "I'll take you to the park on Saturday so Mommy can work. OK?"

"Oh, Jason, you don't have to do that."

"You said so yourself, this survey is very important to the clinic, and the sooner we complete it the better," he said.

"But what about your weekend off?"

"I've got to see my hospitalized patients in the morning, but I'm free in the afternoon, if squirt here can hold her horses."

Gina looked to Claire to help her figure out what that meant. "Dr. Rogers will take you to the park after you eat lunch," she said.

"Better yet," Jason said, "I'll take you to lunch, too."

Gina looked at Claire again, excitement brewing in her eyes. "Yay! Da park."

"Yay, the park," Claire said, as she clapped her hands along with Gina. Now all she had to do was figure out a way to get him to stay for dinner.

CHAPTER SIX

CLAIRE brushed her hair and put the finishing touches to her make-up on Saturday afternoon. Though she'd worn her new aqua-blue blouse, she threw on her favorite threadbare jeans to give the impression she hadn't planned everything, down to the slivered almonds on fresh steamed green beans.

Not only had Jason agreed to take Gina to the park, but to the zoo, too. The Santa Barbara Zoo was a small and perfect place for a pint-sized person to visit.

Claire knew the last thing Jason wanted was to be pitied, and she didn't pity him. She hurt for him; she'd seen the fallout from his misfortune and wanted to offer her friendship. He deserved to salvage his life from the tragedy that had annihilated his family.

The fact that his mere presence gave her crazy thoughts about kissing and touching was something she'd have to deal with another time. Her emotionally unavailable ex-husband had cured her of ever wanting to get involved with a man who'd withhold his heart, for whatever reason, noble or not. And when a man did that, wasn't that the first step toward making it easier to walk away when things got tough? No matter how much her body reacted to Jason, she would guard her heart from any more pain.

The man deserved a friend. And he'd done a very big favor for her today.

The dinner was a chance to get to know Jason better and to ease him back into the world of the living, hopefully without him even realizing it. She had a big job on her hands, but her famous beef stroganoff and made-from-scratch apple pie should do wonders to break through some of his barriers.

The way to a man's heart, as the old saying goes...

No! Not his heart. She brushed the thought from her mind.

The doorbell alerted Claire that, even though she didn't feel quite ready for them, Gina and Jason had arrived home. She took a deep breath, hoping she could pull off her well-planned faux spur-of-the-moment dinner.

"Dock-to Wah-durs took me to the zooooo!" Gina hugged Claire's knees and squealed. "I saw Gemina! Her neck is hurt." She went into a play-by-play description of the giraffe with the crooked neck who was twenty-one-years old, then talked about all the animals she'd seen and imitated the sounds they made. Jason stood quietly as he closed the door, watching Gina's delight with a serious expression.

Claire met his gaze and she could see a hint of sadness. "The zoo was one of Hanna's favorite places," he said in a guarded tone.

Claire's shoulders slumped and she fought the urge to hug him.

"Something smells fantastic," he said, in an obvious attempt to change the subject.

"Oh, it's just one of those candles that smell like homemade apple pie," she said, picking up Gina and delivering a huge kiss to her cheek. "And the other candle just happens to smell like beef stroganoff."

He sniffed the air. "Amazing. And you've got a fresh baked rolls candle, too?"

She blurted a laugh, then grew serious. "Actually, I was hoping I could repay you with a home-cooked meal for bringing me food and fixing me breakfast when I was sick, and especially for helping me out today."

"I'd have to be nuts not to take you up on that," he said, his mouth creasing into a pleased smile.

She mentally blew out a breath, since it was highly likely that Jason could have been insulted about being bamboozled into dinner. Or he could have made plans for his Saturday night, and all of her cooking efforts would have been for naught. Even hermits had *some* friends.

Claire poured and handed Jason a glass of merlot while she put the finishing touches on the meal. After setting up Gina at the table in her booster seat, they all sat in the small dining room adjacent to the living room. She could count on one hand the number of times she'd used this dining set. She'd bought it when married to Charles, but since the divorce and moving into the bungalow, she'd hardly ever had guests.

Jason ate with gusto and paid numerous compliments about her cooking skills. It made her want to snap her fingers and dance in her chair. He also had a second glass of wine, and this time she joined him with her first.

Surprisingly, he offered to do the dishes while she bathed Gina. All set for bed in her blanket sleeper, Gina hugged her new best friend goodnight. Though he'd been attentive enough to Gina during dinner, Claire saw Jason stiffen with the hug. And when Gina kissed his cheek, he flinched ever so slightly. Claire read Gina's favorite story in the bedroom to give Jason some time to himself, and the child fell immediately to sleep.

Claire stopped off in the bathroom to fluff her hair and put a bit more lip gloss on. Jason was a colleague. A friend, she reminded herself, but she thought about the goodlooking, suntanned man sitting in her living room and a shiver ran through her. Who was she kidding?

"I hope you don't mind, but I started a fire," he said, putting a second log in the fireplace when she returned.

Claire had only lived here for six months, and had rarely used the rugged rock fireplace. The golden glow and crackling fire made her already-small living room feel even cozier. He sat on the couch, and it occurred to her that it would be odd to sit in the chair all the way across the room, so she sat next to him. Then jumped back up.

"Oh, I should put on some decaf or tea to have with our pie."

He clasped her wrist and tugged her back down. "I need more time to digest that fantastic dinner first."

She landed a bit closer to him than she'd intended, but didn't move. The fire made her want to snuggle with someone. With Jason. Crazy thoughts. She'd blame the merlot.

Claire suspected Jason's gesture with the fire was a signal. Maybe he was reaching out to her. She protected herself with professionalism and went off on a safe and chatty tangent about all of the lame excuses their clinic patients had come up with for not returning their surveys. And if laughing proved he enjoyed listening to her, he must have. Good. They'd slipped back into a familiar level of comfort.

Jason told her about all of Gina's reactions to the animals at the zoo, though she sensed it was out of obligation. And he mentioned how she'd kept wishing her mommy were there. Claire had the urge to wake her daughter up and kiss her back to sleep. Jason must have noticed the depth of her love for her daughter, because when she ventured to look into his eyes they were steady and full of kindness, and they set off a warm implosion in her chest. She wasn't prepared for the reaction and pulled inward.

She noticed something else, too. His gaze had clouded over with nostalgia, and it occurred to Claire how hard it must have been for him today, and she quickly regretted putting him through it.

"I think some coffee and pie are in order," Jason said, obviously sensing her shift in mood.

Hair had slipped across his forehead again, and the fire had warmed up the room enough for him to take off his sport jacket. She'd remembered his well-developed arms from the first day she'd met him, but tonight they looked particularly strong, and her resistance was suddenly weak. He followed her into the kitchen.

She'd made a huge mistake forcing him to spend the evening with her. He'd relaxed and she'd coiled tighter than a tangled Slinky. Her fumbling fingers proved he'd taken her out of her comfort zone. He seemed to watch her every move, and her cheeks heated up at the thought. Could she be anymore clumsy?

"I make a galley-chowder that will knock your socks off," he said with a broad smile. "That is if you like clams."

Grateful he'd tried to lighten the mood, she nodded. "Love chowder," she said, slicing the pie while the coffee-maker trickled steaming brown liquid into the glass pot.

"I'll have to invite you aboard sometime."

She almost cut a jagged line. Could she consider the invitation a date? Nah. Friends hung out on boats together. She handed him both pieces of pie, and followed behind with the mugs of coffee. They settled in front of the fireplace and sipped and ate and Jason made appreciative noises over the deliciousness of the apple pie. All of her efforts had paid off.

"This is the best crust I've ever had," he said. When he noticed she'd left a portion of hers on the plate he lifted his brows and reached for it. "You mind?" Without waiting for her answer, he popped it into his mouth.

It occurred to Claire that she'd never seen Jason act more naturally. He'd spent an afternoon with her daughter and survived. Now he seemed playful and content, probably from the carbohydrate overload, but still, it was progress.

She fell back into the cushions and put her feet up on the coffee table. "I'm so full I could pop." He watched her with amusement.

"I like that blouse," he said, totally taking her by surprise. "It suits you."

With cheeks on fire, as if she was a schoolgirl, she glanced at him, then at her hands. "Thanks."

Perhaps it was her sudden discomfort, but Jason touched her hand and stood. "I should probably be going," he said.

Her uneasiness had rubbed off on him. She regretted it. "Pipsqueak wore you out, eh?" she said, wanting to keep things light, and wishing she could rewind the moments that had changed his mood.

"Gina's a pistol. I get a real kick out of her," he said. "I'm kind of glad things worked out the way they did." He stopped mid-stride and looked deeply into her eyes. "There's something special about seeing the world through a kid's eyes. I've missed that."

Jason's nearness confused her. She hadn't expected to turn into a shrinking violet under his scrutiny. Empathy had driven her to ask him to dinner. She'd accomplished her goal on that count, and he'd come out of his cave a little more tonight—an added benefit. She could pat herself on the back for making progress with him. But his penetrating gray eyes sent her straight back to last Friday night in his car. How many times had she relived those kisses this week?

Swept up by the moment, she reacted on impulse and kissed him goodnight. It was only a light peck on the lips, but more than a *friend* would give.

Jason seemed surprised at first, but he kissed her back, even put his hands on her waist to pull her closer. He tasted like nutmeg and sweetened apples. She wrapped her arms around his neck and soon they picked up where they'd left off before. There was no telling with Jason how long before he'd come to his senses and back out. So far so good. He'd found her tongue again and this time the sound effects were coming from *his* throat. She had to be delusional if she really thought she could keep theirs a friendship.

His hand discovered the skin beneath her blouse, and his warm touch sent tingles up her back. She kissed him frantically, afraid he'd change his mind again, and greed to touch him made her squeeze the muscles across his shoulders and arms. She traced light breathy kisses along her jaw and his grip tightened on her hip, the other hand edging closer to her bra.

He walked her backwards, and they managed to find the couch without breaking another of his deep kisses. He eased her against the sofa cushions with feathery lips down her neck. Her pulse flittered in her throat.

Jason pulled back to look at her, and she worried he would stop like he had before, but she saw the fire in his eyes. She hadn't imagined their *mutual* attraction after all. They'd been tugging and pulling on each other's libido since their first meeting, the day they'd yelled at each other. Maybe they could make this work. He was turned on and gorgeous and she made a snap decision to make love with him if he wanted her. From the hungry look in his eyes, he definitely wanted her. Now.

The fire crackled in the background and cast a bedroom glow over his face. His long fingers worked quickly to unbutton her blouse. He stopped briefly to look with obvious admiration at her lacy bra. Before she realized it, he'd undone the front clasp and released her. His hands caressed her breasts with near worshipful tenderness. His eyes briefly closed as his thumbs lightly swept across her nipples, and he swallowed before kissing the pebbled tips of first one and then the other. He wouldn't dare turn back now.

Claire savored the exquisite feel of his mouth on her breast. She couldn't believe how quickly she felt ready for him. She wanted to feel every part of him, and unbuttoned his shirt. They kissed again, ravenous kisses. She slid her hands under his shirt to pull it off, and was surprised to find smooth skin with little chest hair. She couldn't wait to see the rest of him.

Hot as the fire flaming across the room, she lifted his shirt above his head, and he eased her blouse and bra off her shoulders. Though nervous about what might happen, she gave herself to the moment and smiled, and he drew her flush to his chest. It felt like heaven to brush his skin with her breasts, to breathe his heated scent. He kissed her shoulder and toward the back of her neck, sending chills fanning across her skin. Every touch made her long for another. She tasted his faintly salty neck, slid her tongue along its surface, heard a sound deep in his throat and watched gooseflesh rise on his skin. She had him now, and savored every sensation awakening inside her. Tightening, heating, melting, pooling. She hadn't wanted to be with a man since her divorce. With only a few kisses, Jason had chased away every precaution.

She kissed his muscled chest, then lifted her chin to find his mouth again, but something had changed. The magnetic heat and longing she'd felt in the last moment had been tempered in the next. *Not again.* His tight embrace loosened, then went limp.

She wanted to scream, *no!* but kept kissing him, though he'd quit kissing back. Just like the other night. His warm lips had turned to rubber bands. She couldn't go through another rejection from him. Either he wanted her or he didn't.

He disengaged from her, rested his head on the couch and stared at the ceiling.

She'd sent mixed messages all night. She'd convinced herself she'd only wanted to share a friendly dinner with him, but whenever they got together things seemed to happen. He was obviously as confused as she was.

"Jason, we've got to talk about this."

He took a deep breath and shook his head. "I'm sorry."

"Is it me?"

"No," he answered in a flash. "It's me. It's them."

She knew he referred to his wife and daughter. "You can't go on punishing yourself for something you couldn't control."

"You're a beautiful woman, Claire." He made a half-hearted reach for her fingers. "I'm just too messed up. Why screw you up, too?"

"Life doesn't come with a pain-free guarantee."

He glanced at her face, her breasts. "I still feel married. I'm sorry."

"It's been four years," she whispered.

As if paralyzed in the past, he didn't respond.

She buried her face in her hands. How could she argue with Jason's sense of faithfulness to his deceased wife? Wasn't that what every woman hoped for? For a man to be so devoted to her that he'd love her long after she'd died?

It occurred to Claire that it was a cruel wish for the loved one left behind. And, being on the other side of the scenario, she couldn't believe how wrong it felt. He'd punished himself, held back from living, and was willing to live half a life rather than risk being unfaithful to a memory. Or to feel again. Not that what they felt was love, but surely, with physical attraction such as theirs, the possibility of love could happen.

"I'll try to understand, but right now I feel as if you're afraid to live," she said, "and you're using your deceased wife as an excuse."

His jaw tightened. He put his shirt back on. She remained topless on purpose. One of them needed to take a risk, and it was clear it wouldn't be Jason. His gaze drifted to her breasts again. She saw his hunger for her, but he wouldn't budge from his misguided martyr pedestal.

"I guess I'm just not ready to move on yet," he said, reaching for his jacket and heading toward the door. "I'm sorry."

Devastated, Claire chose not to show him out.

Sunday morning Jason took his smaller sailboat, the sloop he'd had since college, out to sea. He hadn't slept all night. He needed to get away. To go fast. He hoisted the mainsail and secured the halyard, then repeated the procedure with the jib. The wind was strong. He set up tight.

The sea would take his mind away from the vision of Claire, half nude and beautiful. At least that was his plan. So far the shifting of the azure waters had only reminded him more of her…in her gauzy blue blouse… and how he'd undressed her.

He scrubbed his face and reached for the tiller. There was no pretending. No going back. He and Claire had crossed a line. And he'd stumbled and fallen on his face.

He prepared to jibe and ducked as the sail swung from one side of the boat to the other. He'd thought he was the luckiest man alive to meet and fall in love with Jessica, but he'd lost her. Too soon. In the four years since she'd died, he'd had sexual urges but had never acted on them. They were the biological needs he'd endured as a widower, and had never been the result of an actual living breathing woman.

Until Claire.

Once he'd taken off her blouse he'd wanted nothing more than to be inside her. To know all of her. The thought made him reel. He couldn't forget Jessica. He was supposed to be with her.

Till death do us part...

Death had parted them. He'd lost his wife and daughter in the damn train wreck. Why couldn't he have died with them? The tears came, as they always did, and he bit back the salty taste. How was he supposed to move on?

The sun glared at him. He shut his eyes tight. Jessica's face materialized and drifted farther and farther away. He tried to will her back, but her image faded, and along with the next wave she disappeared as if sea mist. Then Claire's beaming face appeared and breezed over him like the wind.

After his crazy behavior with Claire he'd blown any chance of being with her. What woman would put up with his unpredictability?

The sloop had hit a dead sector and he trimmed the

sails in tight, braced his feet on the deck and leaned out over the edge of the boat. He needed to change tack, head up toward the wind.

If only life was as easy as sailing.

Claire had survived a divorce. She would prevail over Jason's rejection, too. The man wasn't ready, and that was all there was to it. What made her think she was any more ready than him to get involved in a relationship? Hadn't her plan been to be his *friend*, not to jump all over his bones just because he was a good kisser and looked so damn sexy?

The man needed someone in his corner, not in his bed.

Time was the answer. The fact that they worked together would make things awkward for a while, but she was determined to keep her job and be whatever level of friend Jason would allow her to be. Her newly awakened fantasies of being with him sexually would just have to be put on hold.

Only one last question niggled in the back of her mind. Could she wait indefinitely?

Sunday afternoon she took Gina to visit Mrs. Densmore in the hospital. She still had some lingering muscle spasms and sympathetic nerve hyperactivity, and was being fed high caloric nutrition through a tube in her stomach, since she had a tracheotomy in her throat. Her rigid grin had disappeared, and it gave Claire hope all of her other symptoms would recede too.

Gina cried and didn't understand why Mrs. Densmore couldn't come home with them. And later, when she asked if she could see *Dock-to Wah-durs* and

Claire said no, Gina got fussy and threw her cookie on the ground.

Monday morning in her office, Claire lost herself in paperwork and barely noticed Jason's footfalls in the hall. He paused at her door, freshly tanned, dressed to perfection in another perfectly tailored suit with a green shirt and complementary tie. At least his choice in clothes had brightened up.

The sight of him raised her nipples. So much for friendship.

"Good morning, Claire," he said in a deep and apologetic tone. At least he hadn't ignored her.

So he'd decided to take the safe route and pretend nothing passionate had happened between them, that they were business associates, nothing more. Be careful what you wish for. Hadn't she wanted to be his friend? If he needed a bland work existence, he could have it.

She glanced up from her desk. "Morning," she said, then went quickly went back to shuffling papers, determined not to look again until he'd left, though a trail of lost hope seemed to follow him down the hall. She wished things could be different, and gave a wry laugh, realizing that if wishes *could* make things different, Jason would still have a wife and child.

Where did that leave her?

By Thursday the civility was killing her, and she left her office door closed until after he'd arrived. She studied her scheduled appointments and noticed a patient she'd seen last week for stomach upset had been added on again today, and her symptoms had progressed to nausea, vomiting and problems with her vision. The new symptoms concerned Claire.

Instead of waiting until the afternoon to see the patient, Claire asked Gaby to have her come in this morning. She'd squeeze her in early between the other patients. By 10:00 a.m. Mrs. MacAfee had arrived. Claire had Gaby send the patient directly to their downstairs lab for stat blood tests.

She juggled two scheduled patients by sending one for X-rays and the other to Dr. Hanson's nurse for a blood gas test, then rushed Mrs. MacAfee into the newly vacated exam room.

One look at the poor woman and Claire knew she'd made the right decision.

Claire had discovered in her survey that this patient had been taking ginseng along with digoxin and due to the risk of toxicity had asked her to stop taking it immediately. She'd followed up with blood work, and fortunately the digoxin levels, though edging up to the high end, were within normal limits. Most importantly, her electrolytes had been in balance. With the new symptoms of nausea and vomiting, those lab findings could change today.

What concerned Claire the most was the patient's newest complaint of dimming vision.

"Tell me everything that has happened since last week," Claire said.

The woman recited a litany of problems, and Claire listened carefully for any clues.

"…and on top of that, I've been having such stomach problems, I think I may have ulcers," Mrs. MacAfee said.

"I can order a special upper endoscopy test for that, if you'd like."

The woman nodded enthusiastically. Claire made a note to write the referral to gastroenterology.

"You stopped the ginseng like we discussed, right?"

The woman nodded again, and Claire believed her. When she did her physical assessment, her blood pressure was within normal limits, though her pulse felt thready and fast.

"May I use the bathroom?" the woman asked, looking pale as if in need to vomit.

"Let me give you an emesis basin," Claire said.

"That's not what I need to do," the woman said.

Claire escorted her out the door and down the hall, just beyond Jason's office. Unfortunately, he was inside and seeing him after avoiding him all week made her stomach jump.

"When you're done go back to my exam room so my nurse can do an EKG."

Claire distracted herself by going over the patient's results, which had just been called up from the lab. Her eyes almost bugged out when she heard the digoxin level.

She rushed down the hall and tapped on the bathroom door. "Are you sure you stopped the ginseng, Mrs. MacAfee?" Nothing. Not a sound. "Mrs. MacAfee?" Claire jiggled the door handle and called her name out several more times.

Her nurse rushed over. "The skeleton key is on the door ledge," she said.

Claire felt around and found it, and opened the door to find Mrs. MacAfee passed out on the bathroom floor.

"Call a code assist," Claire said, checking the patient's carotid pulse. The woman was breathing and her pulse was present, though still thready. "I think she's dehydrated. Let's start an IV. But first let's get her on the gurney."

Jason appeared in the hall, pushing the emergency gurney toward them. "Let me help," he said.

"She's *dig* toxic and now she's passed out," Claire said, taking the woman's feet while Jason lifted under the patient's arms and hoisted her onto the gurney.

The next several minutes were a blur as they worked to start an IV and set up the EKG monitor. Mrs. MacAfee was slipping in and out of ventricular tachycardia. She needed to be in the E.R. stat.

"Call for an ambulance," Claire said to the nurse. Mrs. MacAfee's eyes fluttered; she fought to keep them open.

"Let's get some lidocaine on board," Jason said immediately after Claire placed the intravenous line.

As Claire opened the emergency cart, she added everything up in her head. The patient had all of the cardinal signs of digoxin toxicity: nausea, vomiting, anorexia, amblyopia. She'd need to be admitted to a monitored unit and receive antidigoxin antibody fragments, and to get her electrolytes back in balance. Claire shuddered, thinking about what might have happened if she hadn't brought the patient in this morning instead of waiting to see her in the afternoon.

But if Mrs. MacAfee had stopped the ginseng, what had made her digoxin levels continue to rise?

Jason stayed by Claire and the patient as the lidocaine drip helped stabilize the intermittent ventricular tachycardia on the monitor screen, and Mrs. MacAfee drifted in and out of consciousness. His presence brought her an added degree of confidence.

Once the ambulance arrived and the patient was safely on her way to the hospital, Claire took a deep breath and noticed Jason had put his hand on her shoulder. Instead of bringing comfort, the gesture made her tense up even more. She needed to get away from him, and made the excuse of calling the woman's husband.

An hour and a half later, eye to eye with Mr. MacAfee in the E.R. waiting room, Claire was grateful to deliver good news. His wife was responding to the treatment, and would be admitted to a monitor bed in the ICU. Once she'd calmed him down, she asked several of the questions floating through her mind.

"How long has she been complaining about stomach pain?"

"Two or three weeks," he said. "She'd started taking this special tea to help."

"Special tea?"

"A long time ago, a lady at the health food store told her that licorice tea was supposed to be good for stomach problems."

Off the top of her head, Claire had a vague memory about licorice being very helpful with soothing stomach pain and even treating ulcers, but why would the woman keep drinking it when she was getting progressively sicker? Buried in the myriad herbal treatments in her mind, a side-effect jumped out at Claire. Patients who used licorice and who were on digoxin were at risk for toxicity. No sooner had she weaned Mrs. MacAfee off one potentially dangerous drug/herb interaction with digoxin and ginseng, than the woman had replaced it with another—licorice.

After she informed the attending doctor at the hospital about the tea, and knowing Mrs. MacAfee was in good hands, she went back to the clinic. Bedraggled and stressed out, she nibbled at lunch at her desk, and took some extra red yam powder along with some anti-inflammatories to offset the ache she felt growing between her shoulders.

She heard a tapping at her door. It was Jason. Too tired to fight her feelings for him, she picked at her food and told him about discovering the licorice tea their patient had been taking unbeknownst to them.

"You can't know everything, Claire. You'll drive yourself nuts if you try," he said.

"Mrs. MacAfee jumped right out of the frying pan and straight into the fire, and all she wanted to do was help herself feel better." Claire dug fingers into her hair and stared at her desk. "I don't think the survey was extensive enough. How do we get through to these people to check with us before adding any new herb to their regimen?"

"You said it was tea," he said, sounding far too level-headed. "How many people are going to think of tea as medicine? People on high blood pressure meds take over the counter cold medicine all the time, then they wonder why their blood pressure is sky-high afterwards. It's just human nature to try to take things into our own hands and fix it without bothering anyone else."

He looked far too sympathetic with his soft gray eyes as he walked around her desk, and sat on the edge. She tensed and sat back farther in her chair. If he touched her again, she might not have the strength to fend him off. And if he wasn't capable of reaching out emotionally, then she didn't want to start something that was bound to end badly. She'd be his friend and associate. That was her mantra and she was sticking to it.

"You can't catch everything, and you'll never be able to stop people from hurting themselves," he said softly.

How ironic the statement coming from Jason's beautifully formed lips, and she was on the verge of calling him out on it.

Someone tapped on the door. "Claire?" Her nurse. "Our first afternoon patient is here."

CHAPTER SEVEN

JASON unlocked his condo door. After the accident, he'd moved here from the luxurious family home set high on the hillside above Santa Barbara. He couldn't bear to live in the place filled with memories in every room. He'd been in shock at the time and could hardly function. Jon, Phil, and René had arranged everything: Found the condo; listed his house for sale; packed and moved him. In a daze, he'd followed along.

Even the spacious two-bedroom ocean-view condo felt too big for him to rattle around in. He'd lived here, if you could call it that, for the last three and a half years.

He tossed his jacket over the back of a chair, eased off his loafers, and padded across the hacienda-styled tiles to the kitchen. He poured some of the coffee left from the morning and warmed it in the microwave. As a bachelor, he could do that, not giving a damn how bitter it tasted. Heading straight to the terrace, he opened the French windows and sat at the glass and wrought iron table to sort through the mail he'd brought in.

His eyes were drawn to the coast and out to sea, the

only constant thing in his life. How many times had he considered sailing off and never coming back?

Lately, the thought had less appeal. Since meeting Claire.

As it often did, his mind drifted to Claire. She'd been willing to give herself to him. The thought of her, topless and vulnerable, waiting for his touch, made him crinkle then wad up an advertising flyer.

I'm not ready to move on, he remembered telling her. And if by chance he were ready to get involved with her, was he ready to take the risk? Rationally, he knew Lupus wasn't deadly, that people lived with the autoimmune disease for years and years. But it affected the quality of life and, if not controlled, it could shorten hers. If he allowed himself to care for her, could he survive losing her? If a flare-up attacked an organ like her kidneys, she'd have to go to extreme treatment like chemotherapy to ward it off—a risky process. Was he ready for any possibility if he allowed himself to become involved with her?

Instead of only thinking of himself, he should consider her feelings. Was he a better man than her ex-husband?

He palmed his eye sockets and rubbed vigorously.

Would he look back at fifty and wonder why he'd squandered a chance at something real with a living breathing woman, when all he had left of Jessica was faded memories?

Opening up to Claire would be hard enough, but being around Gina made him ache so much for Hanna he could barely keep from tearing up at times. He remembered the wondrous look in his daughter's eyes whenever he'd taken her to the zoo, and he'd seen the exact same look on Gina's face the other day. His heart had twisted and cramped the entire afternoon Saturday.

It all felt too familiar. Claire and Gina. Jessica and Hanna. Maybe if Claire wasn't a parent. Maybe then easing back into a relationship wouldn't feel so daunting.

Right. And blink three times to make everything different and achieve world peace.

The child was just another excuse to stay living the life of a monk who preferred the sea to human beings.

After he'd finished his coffee he went back inside and, halfway down the hall, he stopped outside the guestroom door. He hadn't planned on coming here; he'd been heading for his bedroom. Yet here he was. All Jessica and Hanna's belongings that he couldn't bring himself to part with were stored inside. He thought of it as his torture room, the place he went to grieve and rent the air with painful moans and curses. Every leftover trace of their existence had been stored in this room. Things. Objects. Doodads. Jewelry. It was the room he entered when in a masochistic state, to sniff the few favorite dresses he'd kept of his wife's and mourn for their lost life and love. Again and again.

As if he thrived on punishment, a too-familiar routine, he turned the handle and went inside. The room was dim with drawn shades, and smelled stuffy. There was a stack of empty boxes Jon and René had left for him, and he'd kept promising to fill and give them away. He'd put it off for over three years.

He opened the closet door, where several dresses hung neatly in storage covers. He unzipped one and fingered the fabric, smooth and silky, tried to remember his wife wearing it, but couldn't. He sniffed the sleeve, but her scent had long vanished from the material.

A shelf of stuffed animals, everything from monkeys to cats to teddy bears, stared out at him from brightly colored faces and button eyes. He reached for a giraffe, one of Hanna's favorites. Its long neck had bent with time, and he thought how Gina might like it because of the giraffe they'd seen at the zoo, and set it aside.

He remembered how much he'd wanted to put his arms around Claire today when she'd been hurting, to offer her some support, but the threads from this tomb had held him back. He tilted his head at the notion that he'd never thought about anyone else before when he'd been in this shrine to his lost life. Yet Claire and her shining work ethic and heartfelt concern for one of the clinic patients had just woven its way into his thoughts.

He couldn't live out in the world if his heart was locked in here. The room closed tightly around him. The stale air made it difficult to breathe.

He'd begun to think about a better life. The kind of life he'd once shared with his wife and daughter, filled with laughter and love. And brightness. He glanced around the ever darkening room at the slowly disintegrating objects, and switched on the light. Jessica and Hanna were no more in this room than was Gemina the giraffe from the zoo.

Did he really want his memories to depend on disintegrating material and dust-covered toys?

No.

Jessica and Hanna would remain forever in his heart, but not here.

The irony hadn't gone unnoticed. He'd mentally chastised Claire's husband for walking away from a living, breathing, wonderful woman, and here he was doing the exact same thing by shutting up his heart in this stagnant room and keeping her at a distance.

Jason looked over his shoulder at the boxes and back at the objects that could never bring his wife and daughter back, and scooped up most of the toys, then deposited them into the nearest box. Next he gathered Jessica's shoes, her clothes and almost all of her jewelry. An hour later, feeling an odd burden lift from his shoulders, he placed a call to the local rescue mission to arrange for them to pick up everything but one small box.

Thursday evening, after making a brief hospital visit to Mrs. Densmore, who remained stable, Claire rushed to the babysitter's to pick up Gina. Her daughter's bright eyes and beaming smile made up for all the frustration and self-doubt she'd harbored from the day. They hugged and giggled and Gina told her all about her adventures with her new "bestest" friend, Emily.

Their daily routine of dinner, bath, reading a book, sometimes a second book, and bedtime, helped distract her thoughts from Jason. He'd been on her mind a lot all week. It was just her luck to accidentally find an intelligent, appealing and sexy man, only to discover he was incapable of having a relationship.

OK, she got the point. She'd finally learned her lesson about closed off men. They couldn't be changed and they only brought heartache. She wasn't going to beat her head against any walls on Jason's behalf. She'd done her share of wishing things could be different with her ex-husband, and it had only proved one thing. Things didn't change. People didn't change.

The next time she let herself get involved with a man, it would be with a guy who was crazy about her, an open and caring guy whose only desire was to make her happy.

Didn't she deserve it? And, more importantly, did that guy exist?

Friday morning, Claire saw a routine ear infection on the verge of perforating in a six-year-old boy, and prescribed the pink bubblegum-flavored medicine to ensure he'd take all of it as indicated. By late that afternoon she got word that the child was in the E.R. with anaphylaxis. She wanted to cry. The mother had assured her the child didn't have any allergies to medicine, yet he'd had a life-threatening reaction to what should have been a harmless and helpful antibiotic.

What else could go wrong?

She threw a book across the room in frustration, then flinched when it inadvertently shattered a vase. She grimaced, and rushed over to pick up the glass.

"Damn, damn, damn," she grumbled.

"What's going on?" Jason had caught her at her worst. Again.

"I seem to have a knack for almost killing our patients!" The events and surprising outcomes of the last couple of days had made her lose confidence. A sudden whirlwind of emotions ranging from anger to fear took hold and made her eyes sting, and soon she couldn't control the release of tears. Why did Jason have to see her crumbling in defeat like this?

He rushed toward her, concern furrowing his brows. "Don't touch the glass, you'll cut yourself."

"It would serve me right," she said, sounding petulant.

"I'll call the janitor to clean this up, but first you have to tell me what's wrong," he said, and placed his hands on her shoulders to steer her back to her desk chair. There it was, the little surface explosion on her skin whenever he touched her, even now.

"I ordered antibiotics for a peds patient who turned out to be allergic."

"It happens. We can't predict how our patients are going to react."

He handed her a tissue, called Gaby to alert Mr. Hovanissian about the problem, then placed his hands back on her neck and started a gentle rolling massage. Unlike her patient, she *could* predict how she was going to react.

"Please don't touch me," she whispered.

He immediately backed off. "I didn't mean to upset you, Claire. I'm not an acupressure expert, but I thought a neck massage might help you relax."

She wanted to be snide and say, *and just when I start to like it you'll stop,* but swallowed instead.

"You're as tightly strung as one of the jam cleats on my boat."

"I don't have a clue what that is," she said.

"Sounds like reason enough to bring you out on the boat sometime. Trust me, it's tight. Tight enough to snap. I'd be remiss if I let that happen to you."

Claire heard both concern and sincerity in his tone.

"Look, you've had a tough week, and I hate to see

you like this," he said as he rubbed his hands together. "They're nice and warm. Why don't you give it a try?" His silver eyes almost twinkled with goodwill.

She remembered his warm hands on her body and how incredibly good they'd felt.

Whether poor judgment or unadulterated weakness, she swiveled in her chair so he could rub her neck. At first she tensed more, but realizing how she'd let her job affect her body, which could set off her Lupus, she allowed Jason to continue. He had magic fingers, and she let him knead and stroke her aching neck and shoulder muscles. The raised hairs on her skin, and the accompanying goose bumps, would have to be dismissed as a side-effect of stress relief, nothing more. She hoped he'd buy that lame excuse.

Claire was grateful when the janitor appeared and Jason removed his soothing hands. He might not want to have a relationship with her, and she'd vowed for sanity's sake to be nothing more than a friend, but his mere touch had made her damp and wishing she had a pullout bed in her office. So much for her resolve.

One more thought occurred to her as Mr. Hovanissian swept up the shards of glass. Now that she'd given up on Jason Rogers, he seemed to be the one person at her side at the first sign of a crisis.

That evening at home, Claire had changed into her sweats to do laundry when she heard a tapping on her door.

It was Jason, with a sheepish look on his face. He nodded, rather than say hello.

Unsure of what else to do, Claire invited him in.

From behind his back he pulled a huge-eyed, gangling giraffe with a bent neck.

"What's this?"

"I thought Gina might like to have it."

"That's very sweet, but she's already asleep. I think you should wait and give it to her yourself. She'd really like that."

"Is that an invitation to stay the night?"

Claire went still.

"That was a joke, Claire." He nodded again, and seemed to hesitate about leaving. "I've been doing some house cleaning," he said. "That belonged to my daughter."

The fact he'd been clearing out his daughter's belongings sent a clear message: he was trying and, as a friend, she needed to be supportive of his efforts. Trying? Hell, his efforts were monumental.

Her thoughts felt so clinical, yet she had to protect herself. A knot bunched in her chest. The gesture of giving Gina one of Hanna's stuffed toys was beyond kind. It made her want to cry. The man had a good heart. A wounded and healing heart. He just wasn't sure how to use it anymore.

And he had a body which would waste away without benefit of touch or love because he couldn't let go of his lost family. She gazed at him standing there looking gorgeous as always. He'd even attempted a dorky joke about staying the night. That was definitely progress on the Jason Rogers front.

"Come in and sit for a while," she said. "Tell me about this." She held up the giraffe and he followed her to the living room, though neither of them sat.

"Last night, I cleared out an entire room of 'things' that belonged to Jessica and Hanna. I'd been hoarding them, as if I could scrape off their DNA and make them come back to life." She could see the familiar pain in his eyes, but he communicated something else, too. Something had definitely changed. Maybe he'd had some kind of breakthrough. Her whirling thoughts kept her from uttering a sound.

"Someone at the rescue mission is going to get a whole new wardrobe," he said, making a rueful smile. "Even if some of the clothes are out of date."

Claire had been wallowing in guilt and self-doubt over Mrs. MacAfee's problem, and for sending a child into anaphylaxis. She'd been self-centered. This beat-up giraffe quickly reminded her again of the oppressive grief Jason must have had to endure every day of his life for the past four years. It made her problems seem infinitesimal. Being reminded again of his devastating loss made her want to weep.

It made her want to love him.

She broke free from the self-imposed caution and took two long strides to meet him. Her hands cupped his face, forced him to look into her eyes. She prided herself on reading people, and it was pain and hope she saw in his gaze. Overwhelmed by the sacredness of his admission, and the dusty and goofy-looking stuffed toy he offered, she longed to ease his pain. An optimistic rise in her heart caused her to throw away all caution and concern, and she covered his face with kisses. Instead of worrying about herself, she'd think only of him.

And, without hesitation, he kissed her back.

Jason caught her lips with his own and feathered kisses at each corner. Happy kisses. Smiling kisses. Laughter bubbled up between them, then disappeared as her hands wrapped around his neck and his arms stretched around her back.

They kissed, as they always had, with passion and lust, and when the heat had turned up to the point of no return, and Jason gave no sign of quitting before the fun began, she walked him down the hall to her bedroom.

Jason found Claire's bedroom to be reflective of her: uncluttered, bright and colorful. Daffodil-yellow walls, a large dark wood bed frame with a padded leather headboard. Extra pillows encased in patterned and solid-colored shams to complement the muted green duvet. One lone dresser across the room matched the bed, and a full length oval-shaped mirror on a stand took up residence in the other corner.

He glanced at Claire; color was rising to her cheeks. He'd done that to her—his kisses, his craving to be inside her; his single-minded desire to finally break out of his self-imposed celibacy.

He wanted nothing more than to express with his body how he felt about Claire. Words couldn't do justice to the cresting, powerful feelings rolling through him. He pulled her sweatshirt over her head, happy to find she wore nothing beneath it.

His hands roamed across the soft tissue of her warm breasts, and quickly found the silken rosy skin around her nipples. They tightened from his touch, and teased him to take them into his mouth. When he did, her encouraging murmurs and invitations made him rock-hard.

She stripped off his shirt, and soon they were both naked, his sailor's tan a contrast to her creamy tones. She smiled at him with blazing eyes, and he took her mouth with his, holding her flush to his body. Her long and slender legs allowed their stomachs to touch, sending a shockwave of tingles across his skin, and his erection grew firmer.

He smoothed his hands across her back and along the curve of her hips, then pulled her closer. She felt like heaven and smelled like a tropical garden. They stood undulating body to body through several more penetrating kisses, until he couldn't take another second standing up.

He lifted Claire, placed her on the bed and lay down beside her. Her arms quickly wrapped him close, and their kissing started all over again. His hand traced along her flat stomach and found the light patch of hair he'd only glimpsed before. He kissed her mouth, searched for and found the dampened smooth skin between her legs, and the area that made her moan when his finger slid over it. He lingered there and, with their lips and tongues penetrating each other's mouths, his fingers mimicked the motion below.

She rocked against him, quickening his touch, and wrapped her leg around his hip, pressing the tip of his erection to her thigh, sending a shock wave through his groin. While his excitement flourished, he brought her to quick release.

He watched her; his own nerve endings vibrated and tingled as he strained with longing. Sensations from every part of his body converged in a powerful force until he had to be inside her. It had been four years since he'd made love; he couldn't wait one more second. He rolled her to her back and parted her legs, pressing hard and long at her entrance.

Claire's hands held tight on his hips, urging him inside. The inviting expression on her face from earlier had changed to one of pure need.

Crazy with desire, he looked into her fiery eyes. Her surprisingly strong hands urged him deeper, and he didn't put up a fight. His response was no longer under his control. He slipped inside her luscious warmth and thought only of Claire as they rocked together toward satisfaction. Forgotten sensations and her exquisite body lured him deeper, straining for relief.

She rolled on top and held his shoulders as their hips lifted and rolled like the sea. The vision of her straddling him nearly sent him over the edge much sooner than he wanted. But she was all powerful, and her controlled rhythm pushed his desire to the brink. He flipped her onto her back and drove deeper inside, again and again, and she rose and spasmed around him, driving out the last of his resistance.

Thinking only of Claire, the here and now, he thrust against her perfect fit, until he caught up with her and they came together. His release was the most intense since he'd been a randy teenager. It racked throughout his body and seemed to last forever. He caught his breath and watched while her eyes fluttered and her face strained against the same consuming sensations he felt rolling through his body.

After years of deep-seated pain, he'd finally plunged into new territory and had rediscovered long forgotten feelings. She'd given him profound pleasure and, from the look of Claire's euphoric smile, he'd done the same for her.

Before he could think another thought, Claire pulled him toward her soft and inviting body, and they lay entwined in a state of bliss in the kind and welcoming light of her bedroom.

CHAPTER EIGHT

"DOCK-TO WAH-DURS!"

The next morning, Claire's eyes popped open to find Gina jumping on the bed in her powder-puff-pink sleeper. She'd meant to wake Jason up early before Gina got up, and to have it appear as if he'd shown up for breakfast, but they'd made love throughout the night and finally, just before dawn, collapsed in deep sleep.

Their hunger for each other had been equal and nearly insatiable. She'd never been pushed to such limits with her husband. Jason had spent four years living as if a monk, and when he'd finally broken through his un-natural vigil, his basic need had been astounding.

Not having ever been in this situation since her divorce, Claire scrambled to think of something to say to Gina.

Jason rose up on his elbows, dark brown hair draped across his forehead. "Hey, squirt, who told you to wake us up?"

"Why you here?" Gina asked.

He glanced at Claire, who wanted to hide under the sheets. "Um, he brought you a present." *He had a mind-blowing surprise for Mommy, too!*

"Where is it?" Gina, who had stopped long enough to ask her question, jumped up and down again. Fortunately, her curiosity about her mother's bed partner had been overshadowed by the present, though in the future she vowed to be much more discreet.

Claire sent Gina off to the living room to retrieve the giraffe from the couch, then glanced at Jason. "What should we do?"

He pecked her on the lips, threw back the covers and slid into his jeans before Gina could find him in all his gorgeous male glory. "I'll make breakfast. That's what we'll do."

Gina came galloping down the hall. "It's Gemina! It's Gemina!"

"That's right, squirt, it's Gemina," he said.

After a surprisingly relaxed morning together, Jason left to make his hospital rounds with a promise to call Claire later. Somewhere after the coffee and before the French toast, she felt a subtle shift in his demeanor, but couldn't quite pinpoint what had occurred. She hoped he didn't regret what they'd done. He kissed her goodbye, but Gina giggled and commented, "You kissing, Mommy," and Jason cut the cool kiss short.

Claire went about her usual Saturday chores, though nothing was remotely the same from the last time she'd cleaned her house. Last weekend she'd been confused and frustrated by Jason's unpredictable behavior, and this weekend he'd left her both aroused and sated, happy and concerned. Why did life have to be so confusing?

Her body hadn't hummed this much since puberty,

and she'd risked total openness with Jason last night. If he rejected her now, it might tear her to the core, but she'd survive. Because she'd held something back.

Her heart.

She had to.

Claire was in charge of her feelings and she'd guard them, because of Gina. Her baby had already gotten attached to "Dock-to Wah-durs" and Claire couldn't bear the thought of Gina getting her heart broken.

Driving home to change his clothes before checking in on his list of hospitalized patients, Jason got hit by a tailwind. He'd broken through a huge barrier with Claire, and the results had been amazing. Claire was everything in a lover he'd missed. The long legs, high small breasts, and curves in all the right places were definitely a plus, but something else made the difference when they'd made love. She was open, responsive, and assertive. Just thinking about her made his body react.

He felt alive today. He'd come out of his coma. The sensations that had rippled through him last night had cleared his head. Rippled? More like white water rafting, he thought with another grin erupting.

The beach looked whiter, the water clearer, and the sky endlessly blue. And, for someone who'd never given a damn about palm trees, today, their existence added the perfect touch to his picturesque city. Was this what he'd been missing out on? He continued to grin and thought about Claire in several appealing positions, and almost turned his car around.

Yet something else held him back, and it came in a

tiny pink package. The breakfast scene in the kitchen had felt too much like old times with his family. He'd managed to separate Claire from Jessica—they were very different in stature, appearance, personality, demeanor, well, just about everything. But each glance at Gina reminded him of Hanna and the injustice of her life being stolen. Gina's big blue eyes, and the innocence they reflected, tore at his heart and kept the old wounds raw and jagged. She was easy enough to be around, with a good disposition in general, but he had found himself recoiling from her as the morning had gone on. He couldn't help it.

As he drove past the harbor, Jason spotted his boat down the dock. "I can't quit thinking about Hanna when I'm around Gina," he muttered as he pushed the gas for a green light.

He needed to think of a way for him and Claire to be together all by themselves. And that realization made him aware of an old and constant companion—guilt.

That evening, Jason showed up at Claire's house with Chinese takeout, and a kids' DVD for Gina. After eating dinner, Claire and Jason snuggled and kissed while Gina sat rapt, watching *Pinocchio*.

As the hour drew on, Claire expected Jason to stay and make love to her again. Instead, he got up to leave. "I've got an early day sailing tomorrow. Hey, would you like to come out with me?"

She knew his passion for sailing. She also knew the sun was deadly for her Lupus. And what about Gina? "Too much sun can set off a flare."

He anchored his hand under her chin and drew her close enough to kiss. After a slow, warm and teasing taste of what he could do to her, he broke it off. "That's why they make broad-brimmed hats and thirty block sunscreen."

She fought off her schoolgirlish reaction to him. They'd explored every part of each other last night; what was there to feel shy about? "You've got a point, but maybe another time? I don't have anyone to watch Gina tomorrow." She didn't want to hit him over the head with it, but she definitely wanted to give him a hint about including her daughter, who'd never been sailing, either.

"Next weekend. Just you and me." He reached for her hands. "Come away with me." He lifted a brow and the tempting glint in his eyes seemed irresistible.

She brushed away the hair from across his brow and the plethora of thoughts and questions racing through her mind: Do I dare let go and run with this man? Is it a mistake to get involved with my boss? Has he really had a breakthrough? Will he pull back again? What about Gina? "OK."

He kissed her again, slower this time. They folded into each other and shared lingering, inviting kisses. He breathed deep and glanced toward her bedroom. She smiled and rested her forehead to his, clearly on the same wavelength.

"I'd better go," he whispered.

Surprised by the contradiction, she took a chance. "You can stay if you want to."

"You know I do, but…" he said, avoiding her eyes.

She could feel him retreating. She tried to put herself

in his position. It had been four years since he'd lost everything. He was finally venturing back into life. Another night of passionate lovemaking might be too overwhelming. She'd let him define his own re-entry.

"I've got a lot of stuff to do tomorrow," he said.

"I understand," she said, her emotions contradicting her words. The best she could do was *try* to understand.

One step forward, two steps back, Jason thought as he drove up the coast past the small college and toward home. He could have been making love to Claire right this minute, but he'd taken the coward's route and left. He didn't want her to think he was using her, and he'd been out of the loop for so long, he hadn't a clue what a guy did in a situation like this. If he went with his feelings he'd be making love to Claire right now, but he'd put on the brakes. Something told him to slow down.

With Claire, he wouldn't just be dating her, he'd be involved with Gina, too. He'd made it over one hurdle, only to stumble on the next. Claire was a package deal, and though her daughter was as cute as a button, the double whammy of moving beyond being a devout widower into a relationship, *and* having to be a father of sorts, too…well, it boggled his mind and messed with his mojo.

He'd been in a pleasant light state of sleep that morning, slowly feeling his body come alive—in one part in particular—when the earthquake named Gina had rocked and rolled into the bedroom. He'd been thinking about making love to Claire again, but Gina had changed his plans. Fortunately, they'd made love a couple of times last night. He may have been out of practice but, with Claire's amazing help, he'd quickly gotten into the swing of things. And they'd been damn good together. A satisfied smile stretched across his face, then quickly faded.

Gina popped into his thoughts again. The little one had a father. He wouldn't be stepping into anyone's shoes. It was Hanna, his precious girl, who tugged at his memory and gazed at him with her huge brown eyes. He'd finally made peace with Jessica and his desire for Claire, but who would have guessed that losing his child would be the hardest thing to let go of?

Don't forget me, Daddy.

He'd never forget her.

Never.

Monday at work, Claire worried she and Jason were a bit obvious when they grinned at each other like fools, and when she turned four shades of red, while he went directly into bedroom eyes mode right in front of Gaby. But it was the first time they'd seen each other since Saturday, and they'd happened to meet up at the receptionist's desk. How could one day away from each other seem like a week?

He'd called her Sunday night when he'd arrived home from sailing. After they'd chatted for a while, something that seemed effortless and as if he'd been gone for weeks with so much to catch up on, they'd made plans to eat lunch together. And, if it was another beautiful spring day, they'd eat under the ash tree. She'd fixed her special chicken salad with sliced grapes, celery, walnuts and cinnamon, and had brought chocolate chip cookies because she'd remembered they were his favorite.

Later that day all the nurses, even René, made a double take out the kitchen window as she and Jason sat on the bench under the tree, laughing and eating together.

The late spring weather was inviting and warm enough for Claire to leave her lab coat in her office. She wore a fuchsia-colored top and, around her neck, several strings of tiny beads in various shades of purple. She'd applied vanilla and spice body lotion, and had used the curling iron on her hair. He'd made her feel pretty again, not like the unattractive, chronically ill woman her husband had seen. She wanted to impress Jason, to keep him looking at her as if she were the prettiest girl in the room and, judging by Jason's continuous enamored gaze as they ate, she'd achieved her goal.

Nibbling on a walnut, she smiled a Mona Lisa smile and thought about her new guy and her great job, and how life was definitely looking up.

"Do you remember the first week you started here?" he asked.

Quickly swimming out of her thoughts, she nodded. "Of course."

"The day you ate your lunch out here and thought a bee had flown into your hair?"

She stopped mid-chew. He'd given her a beekeeper's hat after that day. It was the first sign she'd had that the guy had a sense of humor, but his gesture had rankled her and made her feel embarrassed.

There was an impish glint in his gaze. "I saw the whole thing," he said, a smile tickling at one edge of his mouth, soon spreading to the other side.

She cuffed him on the arm as her face grew hot. "How embarrassing. Why do you have to bring it up again?"

"I thought it was cute. Enchanting. I knew you'd be someone special to me right then, because you could make me laugh, make me feel things, but I kept myself in denial for as long as I could."

Were these wonderful confessions coming from the closed off man she knew Jason Rogers to be? Touched by his openness, she squeezed his arm. She wanted to blurt out her "special" feelings for him, too, but being at work and realizing people might be watching, and so early in the relationship, she opted to keep it light.

And to add a little spice. "You weren't exactly the easiest man to work with, you know," she said.

"And you came off a little ditzy." He grinned and popped a whole cookie into his mouth.

Claire tried to be insulted, but Jason's cockeyed and charming expression defused her reaction. She liked the new swagger to his style. It turned her on.

After he'd swallowed, he glanced over his shoulder toward the kitchen window, where Gaby and the nurses had huddled around the sink as if washing dishes, a poor excuse to spy on them. He turned back to Claire and leaned forward. "Why don't we really give them something to talk about?"

He took her by the hand and led her around the other side of the enormous tree trunk and, once safely out of their view, he did what she'd been hoping he'd do ever since she'd seen him that morning. He kissed her.

* * *

The week at the clinic sped by with manageable patients, no medical surprises, and a kindling heat in Claire's belly to make love with Jason again. He'd apparently wanted to make sure she'd go sailing with him by holding off on getting skin to skin until the weekend. With her awakened physical desire for Jason, against her better judgment, she agreed to try the wide-brimmed hat, long sleeves and sunscreen method for dealing with the sun on his sailboat. She also hoped for an overcast sky.

Thursday afternoon, Claire got word that Mrs. Densmore was being discharged from the hospital. She'd have a home health aid around the clock the first few days, and nurses visiting a couple of times a week, but Claire felt compelled to accompany her home and make sure everything was in proper order.

When she arrived at the hospital ward, she came prepared to be sent to the business office and, with her credit card in hand, hoping she'd have enough to pay the balance for whatever had accrued, she marched down the hall.

"She's all set to go," the nurse in charge of Mrs Densmore said.

"Don't I need to sign my life away?" Claire asked.

The seasoned nurse studied the discharge papers and raised a graying brow. "Everything's been taken care of by Dr. Rogers."

Claire paused. As she accompanied the nurses' aide rolling her landlady out to the car, she thought about Jason and how he'd paid the medical bills. The thought edged her one step closer to falling in love with him.

* * *

Charles had agreed to take Gina for the weekend, and, after dropping her daughter off Friday evening, Claire nervously finished packing her bags as Jason knocked at her door.

"We'll eat and sleep on board tonight," he said, "then tomorrow after dawn we'll set sail." He brushed her lips in greeting. "You taste great." He kissed her again, and every spark imaginable jumped between them. "And you feel even better."

Relieved that he hadn't forgotten how great they were together, a laugh tumbled from her chest. "This has been the second longest week of my life."

"And what would be the first?"

"My first week at the clinic, having to face the world's biggest grump everyday." She smiled playfully.

"Don't have a clue who you're talking about," he said, and made a sweeping glance from her head to toes, as though conjuring up a great idea.

Before she knew it, they'd forgotten all about dinner and had landed back in her bed for a send-off session of lovemaking.

Could life get any sweeter?

Hours later, in the cabin below deck, Jason wrapped his arm around Claire as they snuggled together in the cozy bunk bed. The undulations of the harbor water gently rocked them toward sleep. Claire was the only other woman he'd ever brought here. He glanced out the cabin porthole and into the clear night sky to catch a glimpse of the waxing gibbous moon. It glistened on the water, and Jason knew in his gut he'd done the right thing by asking her to come with him.

"I've missed this." He hadn't meant to say it aloud, but the words had popped out regardless.

Claire furrowed her brow, as if the phrase wasn't what she'd hoped to hear.

Earlier he'd given her a tour of the narrow chambers he called home while at sea. He'd replaced the cabin sole with teak wood for added warmth the summer before the train wreck. The mahogany cabinets and brass fixtures were original and gave the cabin its authentic nautical feel. The galley, complete with stainless steel sinks and stove, was well planned without an inch of wasted space. Every item was secured in place. The leather upholstered booth with thickly varnished wood table could easily seat four for meals. He proudly kept his boat in shipshape by spending most weekends either cleaning or sailing, as an excuse to avoid the rest of his life.

It had made him smile when he saw the genuine awe and excitement on Claire's face as she'd explored the smaller cabin and head. He'd always prided himself on being completely contained on *Hanna's Haven*, even after his world had come to an end.

And yes, he'd missed sharing it with someone. He was glad it was Claire.

Jason studied her face by the moonlight. She had slipped off to sleep. Her lashes were long, and the tiny tension lines between her brows that always seemed to be there at work, had disappeared. He dipped his head and gently kissed her forehead, then held her a little closer.

The next morning he gave Claire a short lesson on what she could do to help him and, being a quick study, she caught right on. They set sail on a glassy-smooth sea. She gave no sign of being seasick after sleeping on the boat, but he still suggested she take a pill to fight off any potential nausea from rough patches at sea.

The success of their trip would depend on an invisible and ever varying force—the wind. And the success of their relationship would depend on another invisible force—his desire to finally break free and move on in his life. Was he there yet? He had a feeling this weekend would give him the answer.

Claire wore loose white pants and a bright yellow zip-neck, long-sleeved crew shirt with one of his old sailing jackets as she re-emerged from the galley Saturday morning. She brought two seaworthy mugs of coffee with her. The crisp morning air bit through his windbreaker and had quickly woken him up. But not until Claire had delivered his coffee and slipped under his free arm, as he manned the tiller, did he feel alive. He smiled as her hair flapped beneath her baseball cap with the extra-wide brim. It hid her eyes, and he wanted to take it off so he could see them, but knew it protected her from the sun's harmful rays.

She was beautiful, and tightened the sinews of his chest just by gazing into his eyes and dropping sweet, reassuring kisses on his lips. Each one made him eager for another. The day was bright and the sea ebbed and flowed beneath the boat. It was a fine day for sailing.

"Do you have your sunscreen on?"

"Aye, aye, Captain," she said.

Just before noon he navigated through an amazing section of ocean, the dolphin feeding grounds. Hundreds of the mammals leapt and frolicked around their boat. Pods had joined together in aggregates to fish and play, and several of them seemed to chase the sailboat. Their powerful flukes propelled them through the teal-blue water in a most entertaining way. Claire laughed and gasped at their antics, and exclaimed she'd never seen anything like it in her life, and Jason played along, challenging the dolphins to try to catch him. They shared a smile followed by a kiss, and Jason thought the day was close to perfect.

By early afternoon they'd reached Anacappa Island off the Ventura coast, and found a quiet cove in which to anchor. Claire quickly disappeared into the galley to make lunch while Jason tended the sails. When he'd just about finished, Claire called out his name.

"Jason? Lunch is ready!"

A minute later, he hustled downstairs to find her resplendent and waiting for him…wearing nothing but a huge grin.

"Coffee, tea or me?" she said.

Amazed by her radical surprise, he couldn't get undressed fast enough.

Claire didn't know where this crazy idea had come from. It seemed completely out of character for her, but with Jason it felt astoundingly right. Maybe it was the constant roll of the ocean, or Jason looking super-masculine manning the schooner. Or the fact that she wanted to do something to blow his mind, so he'd never forget the day he'd taken Claire Albright to sea. Whatever the reason, she'd taken a deep breath and stripped down and had been rewarded by an ultra-appreciative stare when he'd entered the galley.

Jason disrobed fast as a squall, rushed to her and dove into her neck with kisses as one hand weaved into her hair and the other located her breast. They kissed eagerly and wantonly, and her hands roamed over every bit of his flesh she could find. She'd been ready for him before he'd even found her naked, and with little effort he'd already grown hard.

Before she realized it, he'd lifted her hips and sat her on a counter, the perfect height for him to press into her, which he did quickly and with vigor. The rush of hot sensations made her cry out.

"Did I hurt you?" He stopped abruptly.

"No," she said breathlessly. She kissed him firmly as she wrapped her legs around his waist so he could deepen the penetration and soothe her edging desire.

He used the counter as leverage and dove into her time and time again. "I think I'm falling for you," he whispered over her ear, taking her totally by surprise.

She wanted to say something back to him, searched for the words, but he'd taken control of her body and she couldn't form a single thought, let alone a sentence. Both heat and chills fanned across her skin. Every hair seemed to stand on end. His unyielding thrusts found their mark, teasing and tightening her insides into frenzy as her mind whirled with his confession. He was falling for her.

Her nipples ached with pleasure that coiled through her belly. She came quickly with a consuming shudder and wave after wave of tingles under her skin.

She'd barely recovered when he thickened and pulsed inside her with several more lunges. The building wave started again, and she felt as if she were spiraling through the air until she came undone a second time, matching his powerful release.

They held on to each other as if they'd disappear once they let go. He may have stunned her silent with both his actions and words, but in her heart she'd already fallen for him. Could love be next?

After Jason made a makeshift canopy on deck for Claire, she snuggled beneath and watched him do a little fishing. If he got lucky, he might catch their main course for dinner. Or so he'd promised. The seasick pill she'd taken earlier in the day had made her drowsy, and she floated off to sleep without a care in the world.

Later, heat and a trickle of sweat woke her up. She checked her watch. It was four o'clock, the sun had shifted and was still bright and shining off the water, right into her eyes. She searched for Jason on deck, but he was nowhere around.

She shook her head to help wake up, and scooted out of the sun's direct path.

Jason appeared with a large iced tea, and she greedily reached for it as the combination of sun and medicine had made her thirsty.

"On the other side of Santa Cruz Island—" he pointed to another island out further "—there's a place called Potato Bay. It's well protected from the sea, and I thought we'd sail over there and anchor for the night. In the morning we can do some hiking before we head home."

"That sounds wonderful. Count me in, Captain."

He kissed her, then put her to work on the jib while

he lifted anchor and manned the mainsail. He sailed into the constant wind and made good time. They found the bright blue horseshoe-shaped bay surrounded by high jagged cliffs, and she saw hikers along the edges waving down at them and she waved back. Two other boats had moored across the way. Jason anchored the boat and prepared dinner before sunset.

Opting to eat outside, they sat on the smooth varnished wood of the deck and had a picnic. Jason poured a rich burgundy wine and, because he hadn't been successful fishing, they broke off pieces of baguette and ate assorted cold cuts and cheeses along with grapes, nuts and orange wedges.

With a light breeze lifting her hair, Claire couldn't remember when she'd felt more alive. Jason had shown her a whole new world at sea and she liked it, thought she could grow to love it. And him. She knew about his haunting battle with his lost family, and the thought of being treated differently because of it, or forever held at a distance, worried her. Would she have enough patience to give him time to heal? It had already been four years.

Earlier Jason had said, "I think I'm falling for you." The kind of phrase a woman longed to hear from the right guy. A stepping stone toward the promise of love. Yet his comment felt more like a general statement that had slipped out of his mouth in the heat of passion, and she'd just happened to be in on it. He'd taken her by total surprise.

He'd invited her into his world, but he'd never discussed anything personal with her, other than telling her about the train wreck. And he'd never mentioned it since.

She had no idea how he felt about getting involved with a woman with a chronic illness. Would he get bored with her need to rest more than the average woman, as Charles had? Could he understand that relapses would happen, no matter how diligent she was with her medicine and holistic remedies? Charles never had. Would he hold her responsible for any setbacks, as her ex-husband had?

Each step closer to Jason forced so many more questions.

Claire came out of her thoughts and scratched her neck in answer to a blossoming itch. It dawned on her that her face felt warm and tight. She'd slipped up by falling asleep and getting exposed to the sun; now she feared she'd set off a Lupus rash.

"What's the matter?" Jason asked.

She touched her face. His eyes widened. He put down his wine and came close enough to examine her.

"You're pink, looks like sunburn across your nose and cheeks."

"I'd better double up on my NSAIDS. I don't want to wind up on steroids unless I have to."

Jason jumped up. "I've got some ibuprofen in the cabin. Let me get them for you."

"Could you bring up my purse? I've got some wild yam and licorice extract I should probably take, too."

Despite doing her best to avoid the sun on the sailboat, she'd still gotten a sun rash. Would she have to paint her face in zinc oxide and look like a ghost in order to sail with him? Sailing was Jason's true passion in life, and she'd already flunked the test at being a part of it. What did that say for the odds of them being together?

He brought her some water and a couple of anti-inflammatories and she hoped to keep at bay any further reaction. He gazed cautiously at her, and she used her best fake smile to reassure him that she was fine. She'd rehearsed and used that smile plenty of times for Charles, especially when he'd grown impatient with her illness if it interfered with his plans.

"Have you ever used anti-malarial drugs in place of cortico steroids?"

"I've tried every combination of treatment except chemotherapy."

Worry etched two lines between Jason's brows, and in order to distract him she offered him a cluster of grapes, while she ate more cheese and bread, then took the extra pills. He sat next to her and patted her knee, nibbling on the grapes. At least he hadn't moved as far away as he could and acted as if she was a burden and spoiler of all things fun, as Charles often had.

"We'll take care of this," he said.

His earnest reassurance gave her hope he was a better man than her ex-husband.

As the clear sky darkened and the moon rose high and round above, Claire noticed mild aching in her muscles and joints, and hung her head in defeat. She feared this flare was beyond adding herbal remedies to her usual medicine, but she refused to give up and took more wild yam.

Jason watched her when she changed into her nightgown, and couldn't disguise his surprise at how quickly the rash had spread across her body, turning her bright pink.

"Oh, honey, what can I do for you?"

"I'll be OK, Jason. I'm just going to go to bed now and rest." It was only eight o'clock. She coughed as she turned back the covers.

"Let me listen to your lungs. Sometimes Lupus affects them."

She shook her head. "Not mine. Not so far, thanks to this special herb cocktail I take."

He reached for his doctor's bag in the storage bay on the opposite wall. "Indulge me. I'm worried about you."

She sat still while he placed the bell of his super-sized stethoscope on her back. He'd warmed it on his hand, yet still it felt cold against the heat of her rash and she straightened her spine. Her lungs were clear, as she knew they would be, but when Jason moved to her chest he listened intently.

"You have a murmur. Did you know that?"

"Mitral valve prolapse is a common problem with SLE. I've never had symptoms from it, though."

"No skipped beats or rapid pulse?"

"I only get that when I'm on heavy doses of steroids. Or being ravished by you." That drew a smile from him.

"Let me put on some sunburn balm, at least." He put his stethoscope away and found some cool aloe gel. His hands were gentle and there was a caring look in his eyes as he applied it.

"I'm sorry to ruin your day," she said.

He stopped and shook his head. His ocean-gray eyes were clear with sincerity when he gazed into her face.

"Other than your breaking out into a rash, this was the most perfect day I've had in years."

She brushed his lips with hers. "Thank you," she said, over his mouth.

They kissed again, and it was clear Jason wasn't sure how much pressure was OK to apply on her skin, or whether to touch her at all. After his hands grazed her arms but never settled, he solved his problem by digging his fingers into her sea-tossed hair and kissed her soundly.

He looked hungrily into her eyes. "I wish you were feeling better," he said.

"Me, too," she whispered.

With that, he tucked her into the bunk. "You warm that up for me later, OK?"

She smiled and nodded as she snuggled down into the pillow, hoping a good night's rest would solve her physical problems. As for her confusion over her growing feelings for Jason, that would take days to figure out.

"I'll be on the deck if you need anything," he said, shutting off the cabin light.

Claire closed her eyes and listened to his retreating footsteps. He'd called her "honey" and had said he thought he was falling for her, and it gave her hope that they could find a special meeting place. One that wasn't haunted by the past.

She'd wanted to make a good impression on the man she'd quickly come to care about. She hadn't set out to fall in love with Jason Rogers, but it seemed to be happening anyway. Why else would she strip buck naked and serve herself for lunch?

She covered her eyes and fought off a cringe, but soon remembered what had followed and decided she'd definitely done the right thing.

For the first time since her divorce, she wanted to be in a relationship again. If only her Lupus would cooperate.

Jason didn't deserve the burden of a chronically sick girlfriend. Not after all he'd been through. The thought made her queasy, though it could be the extra ibuprofen. Fighting off sleep, she lay and waited for him.

He couldn't bring himself to go to her. Sitting on the deck, listening to the waves lap his boat, Jason stared into the dark. A scattering of stars had already appeared, but the distant shore lights made them weak and dim. He'd slipped up earlier and said something that had shocked him. He wasn't ready to tell Claire how he really felt.

He thought about her below deck, stricken with a rash and Lupus flare, just because she'd spent the day on his sailboat. The last thing he wanted to do was cause her pain. One nagging morbid thought repeated itself. What if her disease progressed and one day he'd lose her? Could he allow himself to fall in love with another woman he might lose?

And, if that weren't enough to keep him awake all night, he still needed to work out his resistance to the little one. It wouldn't be fair to love Claire and not Gina, too. The child deserved nothing less.

But not from him. He wasn't her father.

"Hanna. Baby girl. I'd give anything to change places with you," he whispered into the dark.

He'd said it with conviction on so many occasions

over the past four years that it took him awhile to rec-
ognize how hollow the words sounded this time. Had
he said it out of habit, or did he still really want to die?
He thought about Claire below in his bunk and longed
to go to her but, burdened by a million thoughts,
couldn't bring himself to move.

He was a doctor; he knew how to deal with illness,
but…

Two children stood between them. One living. One
dead.

Jason cupped his hands behind his head and stared
intently into the blackening sky.

The next morning, though Claire's body aches and rash
showed strong signs of improvement, they opted not to
hike, and to sail home early.

By mid-morning, they approached the palm tree
lined shore of Santa Barbara harbor, where Jason found
his berth and docked.

"Before we pick up Gina," he said, "I'd like to drop
off some of this gear."

Claire had never been to his house, and was interested in seeing where Jason lived. Twenty minutes later,
just beyond the community college with the seaside
track where a huge track and field meet was going on,
they entered his Spanish-styled condo with arched
entryway, red tiles and dark wood posts. The layout
was open and inviting with the living room and dining
room flowing into the surprisingly large kitchen
complete with cooking island, and a terrace with an
ocean view opening out from the dining area.

The first thing that hit her between the eyes was a large family portrait oil painting hanging on the living room wall. Seeing Jessica and Hanna made her stop in her tracks. Jessica had large attractive eyes and full lips, and dark brown hair. She perched on the arm of the high-backed chair that Jason sat on with Hanna on his lap. A traditional pose. The little girl had thick, wavy hair down her shoulders, and bright inquisitive eyes. She was skinny and looked consumed by her father's large hands. The complete happiness evidenced in Jason's face was something she had yet to witness.

Her heart ached as she studied the portrait, and wondered if she could ever replace that joy. The thought made her shoulders slump.

Jason had bustled ahead down the hall to unload his gear. Rather than gawk at the portrait, and indulge her worst fears, Claire glanced around the room. The long tastefully upholstered couch had most likely been chosen by Jessica. The lamps looked like Tiffany heirlooms. On a nearby table was a box of shoes by a brand Claire particularly liked but could never afford. She lifted the lid, expecting to find a pair of stylish stiletto pumps, perhaps Jessica's, but found a pair of bronzed booties with Hanna's birth date inscribed in the stand; a well chewed combination teething ring and baby rattle made out of silver; a slab of clay, brightly painted and glazed, with Hanna's hand print on it; a homemade Father's Day card from the year of the accident; a mother's locket with Hanna's picture inside; a multi-jeweled necklace and matching earrings fit for a rich doctor's wife; a half empty bottle of perfume, a brand far too expensive for Claire to ever consider buying; a Valentine's card for Jason from Jessica, which Claire did not open; and a mangled wedding ring. A platinum cushion-cut diamond rock that had lost several of the smaller stones outlining the warped band.

Claire's pulse sped up when she realized the ring would have had to be removed from Jessica's hand after the accident. Her heart ached for Jason. Tears welled up in her eyes as she realized the significance of this box, and she bit her lip to keep from crying.

Jason found her there, holding the ring.

"I'm sorry," she said, swiping at her lashes. "I didn't mean to snoop. I expected to find a pair of shoes, not this."

Jason picked up the box and reached for the ring. "That's how we finally identified her." He studied the misshapen object. "They had to use metal cutters to get it off her finger." With a distant look in his eyes, he put it back in the box and closed the lid.

At least now, Claire knew where he kept his heart.

CHAPTER NINE

"CAN we talk about this?" Claire asked, gesturing toward the box.

Last night on the deck, Jason had thought long and hard about their situation. His family. Claire's Lupus. Her daughter. His daughter. The time they shared with each other, and his losses, which could never be recovered. He wanted Claire, though he didn't know where a relationship with her might lead since he still didn't know if he could separate Hanna from Gina.

He needed to delay what he suspected Claire wanted to discuss. He glanced toward the kitchen. "I'll make some lunch," he said.

"I don't think I could eat," Claire replied, an earnest appeal in her eyes.

She'd found the shoe box. Clearly, she wanted to talk about his family and letting go. The last thing he felt ready for. His stomach clenched as he led her out to the terrace and gestured for her to sit in the shaded area. "At least let me get you some water or soda."

"Let's just talk," she said, patting the chair next to her.

He sat, but couldn't get comfortable, leaned forward, edgy, and tried not to jiggle his foot.

"Now that I've gotten to know the other side of you, Jason, I'd like to have a relationship with you. It's scary for me to admit, because my ex-husband made me feel like I'm not much of a catch."

"He's an ass," he said. Anything to avoid what he feared would come next. "No disrespect to Gina's daddy, but the guy did a terrible thing to you."

"I'm glad you feel that way." She sighed. "You know me. I like to lay my cards on the table." She glanced at him with a nervous flutter of lashes. "Jason, you've come so far, you've opened up and shown me another side of you I never dreamed existed. You're a decent and honorable man, and I love that about you. You've shared your passion for sailing—" she blushed and her voice lowered "—and for making love with me."

He liked that even after they'd been together several times, and she'd stripped buck naked for him, she could still turn pink and look uneasy discussing their sex life. But he'd as near as told her he loved her, and she hadn't come close to repeating the sentiments. The topic was a touchy one, to say the least, and his silence wasn't making it any easier for her. Every muscle in his body tensed rather than blurt out the truth. He loved her, but didn't think he'd ever make it over the hurdle where Gina was concerned.

"I…uh…heard what you said yesterday in the galley," she said. "I wanted to say something back, but…uh…you made me very distracted." She forced a nervous smile, making her lip twitch at the corner. "But it's been four years, and a huge part of your life is still in that box."

Rather than look at him, she gazed off in the distance at the ocean. He wondered if it was because she was afraid what she'd see in his eyes, or what he'd see in hers. He wanted to grab her hands and tell her not to worry. To give him more time. He felt confident he could work through this if she'd just give him a little more time.

But the best he could promise was maybe. Would that be enough for her?

"I don't expect you to ever forget Jessica or Hanna. Please don't get me wrong, I don't want to replace anything. I just want a shot at getting all of you, not the leftovers." Her gaze settled on him, and he sat perfectly still, knowing how hard it must be for her to tell him this. "I guess what I'm doing is laying myself on the line."

He understood what she was getting at, but felt pushed in a direction he wasn't completely ready to go. "You mean like giving me an ultimatum? Move on or else?" The spoken words sounded harsher than when he'd thought them.

She looked quickly at him, as if startled by his blunt assessment.

"Look, I know I've been holding out on you, Claire. I'm trying to change. I thought we had a pretty damn great weekend."

Her smile was weak. "We did."

"It's just that I've been in this holding pattern so long, I'm stuck." He leaned forward, resting his elbows on his knees, earnestly searching her eyes. "I want a relationship with you, too." He reached for her hand. "I have feelings for you, please know that."

She squeezed his knuckles. "And I have feelings for you, too, but I don't know how we can explore them if…" She glanced at the shoe box.

If I don't let go of my dead family? "I know what you're saying. And I'm not going to revert to my mantra about how you can't possibly understand how hard it is to lose what I've lost."

"No one could ever know that, and I'm not trying to make less of it. My heart aches for you and your losses. I can only imagine the pain you've gone through, and it makes sense to want to protect yourself from more pain. But Jason, it's time to make a decision whether you want to continue living half a life alone in a carefully protected world, or risk living a full life with someone else but with the possibility of more pain."

The ongoing doubt forced a new wave of frustration through his chest. He dug his fingers in his hair and exhaled. "Don't you think I know that? I've thought about it every single day since I met you."

She nodded. "There's no way we can know the future. We may wind up just having an affair and hating each other." With a half-hearted smile she swung her arm dramatically, as if trying to lighten the mood. "Who knows?"

"I can't believe that." He smiled and patted her knee. "It's more than just sex with us."

A quiet laugh escaped her lips. "I don't know, the sex is pretty good." She shook her head and quickly grew serious again.

"Since we've gotten to know each other I've been

beating myself up over my stubborn ways. It's just that I've been living like this for so long, I…"

"Maybe your stubborn attitude is telling you something. Maybe it's my Lupus?"

"No! I know we can deal with that. I want to keep you healthy and, between your medical knowledge and mine, there's no reason we can't do that." He'd be damned if he'd brand her as damaged and unworthy of love like her ex-husband had.

"I can't even go sailing with you without breaking into a rash," she said.

He lifted a skeptical brow. That was the least of his worries about pursuing a relationship with Claire. "Haven't you ever heard of sunset cruising? And besides, if I'd been more attentive and kept you out of the sun, this may never have happened."

The corners of her mouth twisted up into a cautious smile, but it didn't reach her eyes. She laced her fingers together and stared at her hands. "Then maybe it's Gina?"

Oh, damn, he didn't want to talk about this. What kind of jerk had second thoughts about a woman's child? He glanced towards the shoe box, thinking of Hanna's tiny handprint.

Claire saw a telling glint in Jason's eyes. He'd hesitated when she'd asked the most pressing question written in her heart, and he seemed incapable of giving her a straight answer. She'd been afraid to ask it, but after he hadn't slept with her last night, she knew something was wrong and needed to know the answer, no matter how painful it might be. He'd said it wasn't her Lupus and, barring any other unforeseen problems, that left her daughter.

She swallowed her disappointment, and took his hands in hers. "All we can do is see where things go. I'm not asking you to forget your family. I'm just asking you to quit living in that box." She needed to be more direct, to let him know things couldn't go on if he had any doubt about accepting her daughter. "And one more thing, Jason. I'm a package deal. If you can't…"

Her cellphone rang. Their eyes met for a moment-of-truth stare. She saw a flicker of fear before he blinked.

After a brief conversation with her ex-husband, filled with excuses and a change of plans, she hung up. Charles had been the biggest disappointment in her life, but Jason was on the verge of breaking her heart. She swallowed back the bitter taste of defeat, and decided to revert to business as usual.

"That was Charles. Good thing we got home early today, because he wants to drop off Gina already." The irony curved her mouth into a sarcastic smile. "He's probably tired of entertaining her. He doesn't under-stand that kids are perfectly capable of keeping them-selves busy. All she wants is to know someone who loves her is around."

Jason rose, not uttering a sound. He headed to the door to give Claire a ride home. As they walked to the car, he thought about Gina, and Claire's comment about how all Gina wanted was to know someone who loved her was around. He had that in common with the little one. On impulse, he hooked his arm through Claire's, swung her around and kissed her. "Don't give up on me."

She didn't answer, and he couldn't discern what was written in her eyes.

Half an hour later, after a long and silent drive, they arrived at Claire's home. A tall thin man with pale, deep-set eyes and longish brown hair paced back and forth. Gina swung happily on the makeshift rope and wood contraption Mrs. Densmore had managed to hang from the ancient oak tree on the property when they'd first moved in. She wore purple denim overalls, with a big pocket on her chest.

"Puth me, Daddy! Wee, look at meeeee. Mommy!"

Gina almost jumped from the swing when she saw them, and Claire sprinted to her side before she could fall on her hands and knees in the gravel or, worse yet, her face. She exhaled an exasperated sigh and flashed an irritated glance toward Charles, who hadn't been nearly close enough to protect Gina.

"Listen, I've got to go. Willow has tickets to the Starlight bowl tonight, and she wants to meet up with some friends for dinner first," Charles said.

"Thanks for watching her."

"No problem," he said, brushing a kiss across Gina's cheek. "Bye, tweety-bird"

"You tweety-burd," Gina said with a giggle, swatting at his face.

When Charles drove off, big drops of tears fell from Gina's eyes, and Claire scooped her into her arms and hugged her tight. "I missed you so much," she said.

Gina rested her head on Claire's shoulder. "Mommy," she sighed, as if she were finally home.

Jason glimpsed a moment that perfectly explained how he'd felt about Claire since last weekend. Not that she was a mommy figure, but that she felt like home. A new and exciting place he'd forgotten existed. She was steadfast and understanding, and she'd never let anyone down if she could help it, especially someone she loved. And she'd made her point perfectly clear. *Take both of us or nothing at all.*

He wanted a new start. With her.

He loved her. He did. He loved her.

After the dizzying revelation, instead of running off, he wanted nothing more than to stay with her. "Mind if I come in for a while?"

"I'd like that," Claire said.

With her father gone, Gina discovered Jason's presence, and squealed, "Dock-to Wah-durs!"

"Hey, squirt, you glad to see me?"

Claire let her down and she ran toward Jason. She took his hand and started chatting away while leading him into the house. "I had wunch at MicDonauds…"

Jason had hoped to pick up the conversation with Claire where they'd left off, to bargain for more time in her good graces, but Gina had other plans. She walked him down the hall to her room and grabbed her favorite book.

"Read me."

He started the story about a corduroy bear, and glanced down at her curls. They looked soft, and a tender feeling whispered through him. He read to distract himself from the feelings.

Claire took her overnight case to her room, and when she'd unpacked she stopped by long enough to say she was going to check up on Mrs. Densmore.

After fifteen more minutes of Gina handing him book

after book, Claire reappeared at the door. "Gina, honey, I need to talk to Dr. Rogers."

"He read me." He'd just finished reading a book about a princess marrying a prince, and she handed him yet another one, after she picked up a doll half as big as her.

"Maybe later," Claire said.

"Read." Gina ignored her mother and opened the book for Jason, then pointed to the page where she wanted him to start.

Claire crossed the room, removed the book from Jason's hands and gave the girl a stern stare. "No. That's enough for now."

Gina screwed up her face and threw her dolly down. She opened her mouth without making a peep while tears pooled in her eyes. After what seemed like several seconds, a long wrenching wail finally escaped her mouth.

Claire dropped to her knees and cupped the little girl's arms. "Calm down, Gina. Get a hold of yourself."

Uncharacteristically, Gina swung at her mother and stomped her foot. "No!" she said. "No!"

"Sometimes she gets like this after being with her father," Claire said over her shoulder, a pleading look in her eye. "I'm not sure if it's because he spoils her, or if it's just too hard for her to say goodbye." Claire held her daughter close, though she squirmed and flung her head around. "What's wrong, Gina? Use your words."

"No!"

"If you can't calm down, I'm going to put you on time out to help you."

"No!"

Remaining calm, Claire stood up and took Gina by the

hand, picked up one of her kiddy-sized chairs and led her to the end of the hall. "Sit," she said, matter of factly.

To Jason's amazement, Gina sat facing the wall, fussing and sobbing. The kid knew the routine.

"Two minutes," Claire said, without a hint of emotion in her voice.

Gina grumbled and kicked the wall she faced.

"I'm not setting the clock until you quiet down."

More grumbling. Jason tried not to crack a smile.

Claire sighed and rolled her eyes as she tiptoed down the hall, bringing Jason along with her to the kitchen, where she set an egg timer. "Sorry about that."

"Hey, I've seen this behavior plenty of times. It's got to be hard on her, going back and forth between two parents."

Claire nodded. "In a perfect world, right?"

He knew exactly what she was talking about.

"Can I make you some coffee?"

Happy to be invited to stick around, he nodded. "Sounds good." He listened for a moment. "Hey, the squirt has quieted down."

"Works every time. Thank God for time outs." Claire flashed a brilliant smile, and Jason couldn't stop himself from kissing her. Just when their lips were getting warmed up, the egg timer went off.

Claire broke away. "Time's up, Gina," she called out. She strode toward the kitchen door, peeked outside, then sprinted down the hall.

A scream rent the air and Jason rushed to find Claire holding a limp Gina in her arms.

"What's wrong?" he said.

"I don't know if she's having an allergic reaction to something or choking."

Gina's face was blotchy and pink, her eyes dilated wide. She didn't appear to be breathing. "Gina said they'd eaten at McDonald's. Is she allergic to any food?"

"Nothing that I know of."

Jason grabbed Gina from Claire as an epiphany hit him between the eyes. He couldn't save his own daughter, but by God he wouldn't allow this child to die!

"Call 911," he said as he rushed her down the hall to the better lighting in the living room. Gina wasn't breathing. He opened her mouth to try to see if there was anything blocking her windpipe. He thought he glimpsed something, but knew he could make things worse by trying to pull it out.

As Claire paced and talked on the phone, giving all the specific information, Jason turned Gina over his arm and gave her five strong strikes between her shoulders, then flipped her over to check her mouth again. He thought the object was a little more evident, but Gina still was unable to breathe. Her lips were turning blue and her little fingers had gone limp. Her eyes were fluttering open and closed. He laid her head-down on his thigh and used the cuff of his hand to push upward five times on her sternum. There was no response, so he repeated the procedure of slapping her back and pushing on her diaphragm several more times. He'd lost count, but knew he was working against the clock. Gina hadn't gotten oxygen for at least two minutes. He worried what the consequences would be.

With the cuff of his hand pushing upward above her

stomach, he heard something pop. He looked inside the mouth of the lifeless child and found a tiny plastic figure.

"Your fingers are smaller than mine," he said to Claire. "Can you dislodge that?"

Claire was on the job in a heartbeat and pulled out a tiny toy from her daughter's throat. Then discovered a couple more inside her bib pocket. Had they come from the lunchbox toy?

Gina had been unconscious long enough to not automatically start breathing on her own. Jason knew choking was the number one cause of cardiac arrest in children. He felt for a brachial pulse, and thankfully found one, then he gave two quick puffs of air into her mouth.

Gina coughed and spluttered, and soon the sweetest sound emitted from her lungs—she cried. Loudly. Music to his ears.

He glanced at Claire, holding Gina as the firemen and emergency techs stormed the house. Claire explained everything that had happened, all the way back to where Gina had had lunch.

"That's exactly why the packages say ages three and up," one of the firemen said.

"He saved her life." She pointed at Jason and smiled with tears shimmering in her eyes. He saw love and admiration there. When he glanced at Gina, as the emergency personnel worked on her, he took a deep breath and suddenly knew everything would be all right.

In the height of the emergency one clear thought had come to him—he loved Gina just as much as he loved Claire. He loved them both. They were the most important people in his life. And life could be taken away in an instant. If he waited for the assurance that he'd never lose a loved one again, he'd die a lonely man.

If it came down to protecting himself and being alone, or letting his heart continue to come alive, even if it meant feeling the dagger of loss, he was finally willing to take the risk.

He rushed to Claire and took her into his arms as they rolled Gina out the door.

"The mother can come along," one of the men said.

Claire grabbed her purse and ran alongside the gurney.

"I'll meet you there," Jason called out.

"I'm counting on it," she said with a wave just before climbing into the back of the ambulance.

He'd finally let himself be counted on again, and that sealed the last gap in his heart.

CHAPTER TEN

THREE hours later, Gina had been admitted to the hospital for overnight observation. The ordeal had worn her out. She napped peacefully in the crib-sized bed in the Peds unit, and Claire couldn't take her eyes off her. Soft brown curls haloed her head, thick dark lashes kissed her cheeks, and her Cupid's bow lips puckered and twitched from time to time.

Jason sat quietly across the room in one of the two chairs. He'd been by her side through every horrific moment of the choking ordeal.

"In one instant I felt the magnitude of your losses, Jason." Claire looked at him with the recollection of every ounce of pain she had felt so heavily in her heart. "I'm amazed you were ever able to function at all."

He laughed ruefully. "I think you figured out soon enough I wasn't."

Claire was torn between running to Jason and hugging him and leaving her baby's bedside. She wasn't ready to let go of Gina's dimpled fingers. The child slept quietly, eyes moving behind her lids. What dreams she must be having, Claire thought. She'd been fighting off a headache since finding Gina unconscious. The memory made her heart speed up again.

Jason appeared beside her, as if reading her body language, and put his hand on her shoulder. "It took almost losing our Gina to get me to see the light," he said.

Our Gina. Claire liked the sound of that phrase. She sighed and rested her head on his shoulder. "And what light was that?"

"Life is too short to drag my feet. I'm not going to waste another moment of it." He turned Claire to face him and studied her eyes. "I was lying when I said I was falling for you."

She tensed and mini-fireworks shot off in her chest. Did he actually want to back-pedal with her at Gina's bedside? Had she completely misread the whole weekend and their earlier conversation?

"I'd already fallen in love. I started feeling it the day I saw you dancing with that bee, and I've continued to feel it grow, step by step, each day you've graced my life."

After her heart did a quick spin, she broke into a smile and threw her arms around his neck in relief. He caressed her, but continued talking.

"What I'm trying to say is I want the three of us to be a family. I love you, and I want to marry you. I've waited long enough to breathe again."

Thoughts spun through Claire's head. She'd been coming to a similar conclusion about Jason. Day by day he'd passed her office door and, against his will, he'd turned and wished her a good morning. He'd begrudgingly followed his innate will to live and had gotten involved with her. And it had taken another near tragedy to bring him to his senses.

"I've never jumped into anything so fast in my life," he said. "But I've lost a hell of a lot of time and I don't want to waste another moment."

He covered her mouth with warm lips and reminded her of the special chemistry they shared. How often in life did a person get such an opportunity to be with someone so perfect for them?

The strangest thing was, now that he'd laid it on the line for her, as she'd done at his house earlier that afternoon, she was the one with reservation in her heart. Could she trust him?

They kissed again.

He was the most trustworthy man she'd ever met.

His fingers splayed at the back of her head and moved her closer to deepen the bedside kiss.

Would he stick by her side when she had relapses? He'd told her as much earlier. He'd already nursed her back to health a couple of times, and who better to care for her Lupus than a man who understood the disease? He was a doctor, and he'd be entering the marriage with his eyes wide open.

His tongue traced the lining of her mouth.

She'd worried that he couldn't accept Gina, but hadn't he fought for her life like a true hero? The way a father would fight for his child? She'd be forever grateful to him for saving her. She didn't need him to prove himself, but seeing him desperately working to keep her daughter alive had completed her love for him.

Claire pressed her tongue to his and gave him one last

kiss. She pulled back so she could look into his eyes. Jason was a man who had never wanted to love again, yet he was also a man who had proved himself to her in a thousand little ways over the last couple of months.

She glanced at her daughter, who still seemed to be sleeping.

If Jason could make this huge leap of faith in love, why couldn't she?

"I see a million thoughts swimming behind those eyes, Claire. We can have as long an engagement as you want; if that will help you make up your mind."

"Oh, Jason, this is all so sudden."

"I just want to know one thing. Whether it's today or next week or next year, do you love me?"

"I do, Jason. I love you with all my heart."

"Then will you marry me?"

"Marry you? Oh, Jason, this is the craziest day of my life."

A creaking on the crib springs drew their attention to Gina, who'd sat up.

"Thay yeth, Mommy."

Claire and Jason laughed together when they found Gina's precocious blue eyes wide and alert, and a smile tickled across her mouth. "Thay yeth."

And suddenly Claire thought with all of her heart that it was a great idea.

One month later

Claire left René Munroe's exam room a bit in a daze. She fidgeted with her engagement ring as she took the stairs toward her office. She'd been mildly queasy over the weekend when they'd taken the sailboat out, but had blamed it on the choppy sea.

The first clue had been yesterday when, for the first time in her life, she'd become a sympathy puker. One of her patients had come in complaining of a gall bladder attack, and when the cholecystitis had caused the patient to use an emesis basin, Claire had needed one too.

This morning when she'd woken up with a familiar feeling, and opted for saltine crackers for breakfast instead of her usual oatmeal, she'd asked René to examine her.

She approached Jason's office full of jitters.

"Hi, honey. What's up?" he said.

She loved how his eyes always brightened when he saw her, and how, since they'd been engaged, she'd never once doubted his true feelings for her.

"You know how you left it up to me to put the time limit on our engagement?" she said.

"Yep."

"I'm calling it in."

He cocked his head and narrowed one eye. "Why the sudden change?"

"I'm pregnant."

He hopped from behind his desk to hug her. "This is great news!"

She told him the due date René had just given her and, instead of being worried, she laughed. She was engaged to a wonderful guy and she wouldn't trade one day of their romance…except maybe for that first day at MidCoast Medical clinic. Nah. Not even that!

Just that morning they'd had a minor clash over what

he still referred to as her *woo woo* alternative medicine. He wasn't sure about her suggestion of acupuncture for one of the patients who'd had little success with traditional smoking cessation techniques. But he'd come around and had agreed to give it a try.

And as Charles had seemed to fade into the background where Gina was concerned, Jason had gladly stepped forward. And Gina had rewarded him with a new name—Daddy Wah-durs.

Little did she know…

Jason kissed Claire and together they did the math right back to the first night when they'd been together. His gaze fused with hers and a tender smile lifted one corner of his mouth. "I guess some things are just meant to be."

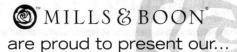

MEDICAL™ 2-in-1

MEDICAL™

Single titles coming next month

A BABY FOR THE FLYING DOCTOR
by Lucy Clark

Doctor Phemie Grainger prides herself on her cool resolve –
until a chance encounter with her professional idol,
Gil Fitzwilliam, throws her into turmoil! As she starts to fall
for the English doctor's charm, Phemie can't help
wondering if, with Gil at her side, her dreams of holding
her very own baby might one day come true…

NURSE, NANNY…BRIDE!
by Alison Roberts

Nurse Alice Palmer's world is turned upside down
when the new A&E consultant is none other than her
teenage crush, Andrew Barrett! The attraction she feels
to him is hard to deny, so when Alice becomes part-time
nanny to his beautiful little girl, it's as if fate has dealt
her the most remarkable hand of all…

On sale 2ⁿᵈ April 2010
Available at WHSmith, Tesco, ASDA, Eason and all good bookshops.
For full Mills & Boon range including eBooks visit
www.millsandboon.co.uk

MILLS & BOON® ROMANCE

is proud to present

Jewels of the Desert

Deserts, diamonds and destiny!

The Kingdom of Quishari: two rulers, with hearts as
hard as the rugged landscape they reign over,
are in need of Desert Queens…

When they offer convenient proposals, will they
discover doing your duty doesn't have to
mean ignoring your heart?

Sheikh Rashid and his twin brother Sheikh Khalid
are looking for brides in…

ACCIDENTALLY THE SHEIKH'S WIFE

And

MARRYING THE SCARRED SHEIKH

by Barbara McMahon

in April 2010

millsandboon.co.uk Community

Join Us!

The Community is the perfect place to meet and chat to kindred spirits who love books and reading as much as you do, but it's also the place to:

- Get the inside scoop from authors about their latest books
- Learn how to write a romance book with advice from our editors
- Help us to continue publishing the best in women's fiction
- Share your thoughts on the books we publish
- Befriend other users

Forums: Interact with each other as well as authors, editors and a whole host of other users worldwide.

Blogs: Every registered community member has their own blog to tell the world what they're up to and what's on their mind.

Book Challenge: We're aiming to read 5,000 books and have joined forces with The Reading Agency in our inaugural Book Challenge.

Profile Page: Showcase yourself and keep a record of your recent community activity.

Social Networking: We've added buttons at the end of every post to share via digg, Facebook, Google, Yahoo, technorati and de.licio.us.

www.millsandboon.co.uk

2 FREE BOOKS
AND A SURPRISE GIFT

We would like to take this opportunity to thank you for reading this Mills & Boon® book by offering you the chance to take TWO more specially selected books from the Medical™ series absolutely FREE! We're also making this offer to introduce you to the benefits of the Mills & Boon® Book Club™—

- **FREE home delivery**
- **FREE gifts and competitions**
- **FREE monthly Newsletter**
- **Exclusive Mills & Boon Book Club offers**
- **Books available before they're in the shops**

Accepting these FREE books and gift places you under no obligation to buy, you may cancel at any time, even after receiving your free books. Simply complete your details below and return the entire page to the address below. You don't even need a stamp!

YES Please send me 2 free Medical books and a surprise gift. I understand that unless you hear from me, I will receive 5 superb new stories every month including two 2-in-1 books priced at £4.99 each and a single book priced at £3.19, postage and packing free. I am under no obligation to purchase any books and may cancel my subscription at any time. The free books and gift will be mine to keep in any case.

Ms/Mrs/Miss/Mr _____ Initials _____

Surname _____

Address _____

_____ Postcode _____

Send this whole page to: Mills & Boon Book Club, Free Book Offer, FREEPOST NAT 10298, Richmond, TW9 1BR